What readers of *Ghost Hampton* are saying...

To say Ken McGorry's *Ghost Hampton* is an entertaining read is a massive understatement. Through his skillful development of the downtrodden main character, Lyle, and the perfectly crafted temptress, Silk, the author somehow manages to get us all hoping for an unexpected happy ending to this fast-paced novel. – Kevin McCormick

Ken McGorry is an inveterate purveyor of wry humor and, with his latest effort, *Ghost Hampton*, he has expanded his sophisticated vision into, appropriately enough, the netherworld of the chic Hamptons. This is a horror story you will read with a smile. It is full of memorable characters, is suspenseful, with enjoyable sub-plots, and is funny, clever, sometimes poignant, and always intelligent. – Corey Dwyer

I always have great respect for an author who can get me to care about his protagonist and make to feel part of their journey. Through various sub-plots, a generous helping of subtle (perhaps sardonic) humor, "Lyle" and I embarked on a mission that at times evoked empathy, anger, frustration and fear (both for personal safety and that of a loved one). *Ghost Hampton* really paddles to the middle of the lake in terms of asking the reader to abandon disbelief and buy in. Chaos and terror ensue but ultimately we reach the shore with a resolution that left me exhausted but satisfied. – Edward Ahern

I don't usually read ghost stories, but I loved this book! I was completely wrapped up in the story and all the characters. Ken McGorry is so descriptive with the people involved and what they are thinking, feeling and seeing that it's like I am actually seeing what I'm reading. I can't wait to read Ken's next book. I may as well just plan on reading right through the night! It happened with *Smashed* and now again with *Ghost Hampton*. – Suzanne Ball

If someone explained the premise of *Ghost Hampton* to me, I probably would have found it hard to believe. But somehow Ken pulled it off and made the implausible possible. "Lyle" was very real and the context was so familiar. I became immersed in the characters (both living and dead) and the story. The frenetic pace of the journey deserved an ending which went to another level and *Ghost Hampton* did not disappoint. I thoroughly enjoyed it! – Rebecca Foley

GHOST HAMPTON

Ken McGorry

to Friends of HVS

[signature]

GHOST HAMPTON
Copyright © 2016 by Ken McGorry
All rights reserved.

Permanent Record Books
565 Plandome Road #164
Manhasset, NY 11030

www.ghosthampton.com
www.facebook.com/ghosthampton

ISBN 978-1-5305-7723-1

Revised edition.

Cover design: Price Digital
Cover photograph: Andrea Hill/Getty Images
Author Photograph: Dawn McCormick

For Mary Liz

The devil's agents may be of flesh and blood...
– A. Conan Doyle

PART ONE

CONDEMNED

1. Rush Hour

It was the roadwork on Montauk Highway that made Lyle Hall get the electric chair.

Since last winter, he'd made do with the self-propelled kind—his daughter Georgie called it the "Mr. Potter model." To Lyle, it said *temporary*. A new electric wheelchair with high-end options would say *permanent*.

At 55, Lyle was not ready to say that. He'd made good progress over the spring and summer, strength-training his upper body. A perky female physical therapist came to his house in Bridgehampton twice a week; a tattooed trainer guy beat him up on Fridays. Lyle had the stretchy resistance bands and a rack of light dumbbells in embarrassing lavender in the living room. Dangling in the dining room doorway was the "Torquemada"—a sling-like contraption he used to hoist himself up and perform certain torturous routines.

Any strain or discomfort he felt was north of his L4 vertebra. Lyle had no feeling from the lower back down, since killing Elsie Cronk with his stupid Hummer last October. Almost a year now.

Each week he journeyed to Southampton to the spinal-injury clinic where they worked miracles. Lyle fully expected them to make him their next miracle and the team there was so positive and effusive that they kept the dream alive. As professionals, they didn't hold Elsie Cronk against him, but they knew. Everybody knew. Even though Lyle and Elsie and an old duffer walking his dog were the only witnesses, they knew.

With his SUV piled up on the War Memorial at Bridgehampton's main intersection, windshield spider-webbed and red, the first-responders, busy trying to free the elderly lady from her big old Ford, initially pronounced him dead. Lyle had a bona fide near-death experience and was comatose for two weeks. But few really cared. Elsie was the tragedy. Elsie had been on her way to her son's 50th birthday party. Lyle Hall lived.

Lyle's weekly visits to Southampton included sessions with Dr. Susan Wayne, a therapist specializing in post-traumatic stress disorder. Her job was to stave off depression, incrementally step down his benzodiazepine dosage, and provide mechanisms to mitigate survivor guilt. Which Lyle had, though he didn't admit to it.

It wasn't his fault that Elsie blundered into his path, 85 years of age and blinded by the setting sun, cautiously making her overly wide right turn onto Montauk Highway— *who can't execute a simple right-on-red?*—in her late husband's aircraft-carrier-size Ford Futura. And everyone guns it a little, not just Lyle, when Bridgehampton's last traffic light turns yellow. Another damning detail was his destination—a bar in Montauk. Practically everyone believed Lyle was drunk when he collided with Elsie. Incredible how easy it is to believe the worst about somebody. Yeah, he drank. But he wasn't drunk when he hit the sweet old lady with the fresh-baked birthday cake on the seat beside her. He was on his way *to get* drunk. Huge difference.

Since last year, Lyle's had scant contact with people other than medical professionals and service providers. He spends the most quality time with Fred, the MediCab driver who's been getting him to his appointments since March.

Georgie's also a professional. Just 30, she's a newly promoted Southampton police detective. What she'd always wanted. Trouble is, now that she's thrown herself into her new job, she has this albatross of a dad distracting her. He bluffs that he can do for himself, but that makes things worse. Her solution is surgical strikes—like dropping off prepared meals that Lyle can microwave. And she makes sure to nag him over the phone. Take your meds. Keep up your hygiene. Drink plenty of water. Do your exercises. Shave off that unbecoming beard. Get a damn electric wheelchair, for God's sake.

Lyle has no one else. Certainly not Dar, his Floridian ex. Her role—play trophy wife to Lyle and wicked stepmother to

Georgie during the crucial teenage years following her mom's death—ended acrimoniously years ago.

So Lyle is Georgie's cross to bear. And it was Lyle, before the accident, back when he was an important lawyer, who twisted a powerful arm to get her promoted to detective. She is abundantly qualified—a master's in forensic psychology and all—but she was still considered a girl entering a man's world. Now she's in a position where the man who made her challenging job possible is also a big, daily pain in the ass.

Georgie's nagging inspired Lyle's spiteful solo excursion. To prove his mettle that day of the roadwork, he took the Long Island Railroad from Bridgehampton to Southampton. Fred merely dropped him at the station. Later, when Lyle returned on the "rush hour" train, one of a half dozen travelers disembarking at Bridgehampton, he was visibly exhausted from the day's effort. Fred saw Lyle wheel out of the train car and quickly joined him on the platform to help negotiate the handicap-ramp switchbacks leading to the parking area.

The whole point had been to show Georgie that he could "do stuff" on his own, like propelling himself to his appointments in Southampton. The challenge proved otherwise, but Lyle would craftily use his physical meltdown as a cover for making his sudden about-face on the electric chair question. He could withhold the true reason for the new chair.

He'd be unable to withhold what was to follow. The detour took traffic slowly past the abandoned house.

~~~~~~

2. The Whisperers

He heard her here. She was one of the whisperers. It seemed weirdly flattering at first.

Ensconced in the back of the MediCab that exhausted evening of the detour, Lyle had the windows down, allowing in fresh air and the angling rays of the setting sun. Commuter traffic from the train station had been annoyingly redirected onto Poplar Street. Fred crept forward, foot on the brake, eight more cars ahead of him. Wrung out after his wrongheaded foray to Southampton, Lyle's arms and shoulders ached; muscles, joints, his hands too. And he felt the onset of what Dr. Susan Wayne called "free-floating anxiety." In Lyle's case, a blob of uneasiness that could intensify into inchoate dread.

He was slumped in his Mr. Potter when the imposing shambles of a house came into view on his right. Everybody called it Old Vic. Sporting dumb old "No Trespassing" signs as long as anyone could remember, it was commonly held that Old Vic was once a brothel. Long ago, when Bridgehampton was part of the East End's whaling industry, before it grew into a high-end summer getaway, real-estate bonanza and snob haven.

Then there's the suburban legend that Old Vic was haunted. Who says? No one and everyone, whether they believe it or not.

The MediCab was crawling by Old Vic when Lyle first heard the whispers. He rose on his elbows, his chair secured to the van's floor, and listened. Cats in heat. No, wait. This was more subtle, conversational. A furtive murmur that piqued his curiosity. He needed to listen again.

"Hey Fred, make a right at the corner, please?"

"Course correction, Mr. Hall?"

"I want to circle back for another look at the old house. And Fred, call me Lyle, okay? Lyle is fine." It had been six months with the same driver.

Fred made the turn. Any such whim of Lyle Hall's, he knew, was good for a crisp off-the-books twenty. It was even worth a twenty to stop at the ATM—Lyle would entrust Fred with his debit card and pass code to avoid the hassle. He also let Fred smoke.

Fred drove around the block clockwise. From each side street Lyle got a view of Old Vic's battered cupola poking above the trees and roof lines of summer homes. It was unsettling—the cupola, a little booth standing atop the third story, was Old Vic's most exposed and weather-beaten feature. Any paint was scabby and vestigial. The cupola's large oval oculus suggested a blinded Cyclops, its leaded glass shattered by determined boys with BB guns long before Lyle was born.

They turned onto Poplar again, and approached the house.

"Slow down, please, Fred? Actually, could you park?"

Fred did so. Odd request, but Mr. Hall is, or was, a real estate tycoon.

"And roll down the windows, please? And mind turning off the radio? ...Thanks. Cut the engine too, please, Fred? ...Thank you."

If Mr. Hall wants to smell Old Vic, Fred figured, this could be worth more than one folded twenty. He glanced at Lyle through his mirror, lit a butt, and texted his wife.

To the west, clouds glowing orange and pink were eclipsed by the hulking old house. It grew darker. The last of the traffic was now gone. Lyle strained to hear. He tried to listen *harder,* if that's possible.

Quiet. Listen.

He was right. Whispers, very hushed. They seemed to leach through the cracks in the Victorian's boarded windows. Random, silken sighs. Like a swirl of fallen leaves. The whispers sent a sharp chill through his chest. It didn't sound like English. Italian, maybe. But he picked up the expression of human suffering and sorrow. Worse still, a profound loss of hope. And something more—dread. The voices were female. He imagined them mourning something. Maybe a daughter. Or a baby. He imagined

5

them conferring in secret. As if choosing one from among them, a brave one, to come forward.

Lyle shut his eyes and let the whispers penetrate him. That's when he saw it. Lids tight, he saw Belinda's tombstone. His first wife. The sweet-hearted one. But a new name was inscribed under *BELINDA*. His heart pounded to a stop. He could only make out that it began with a *G*.

Stunned and shaky now, he clearly heard a solo voice. It was delicate. A girl's.

Eye you touchy.

It wasn't a question. *Eye you touchy.* It wasn't English. It was terrifying.

As if discovered, the young voice, the headstone, the whisperers, all abruptly vanished. Lyle opened his eyes wide.

Fred at the wheel. A decrepit old house. Sundown. A chilling breeze.

Fred admitted to hearing nothing unusual. The whole village would be chattering about disembodied voices if anyone else had heard the whisperers. Especially now, mid-October, when Bridgehampton turns quiet and there's little to bullshit about.

Fred started up the van and shifted into drive. Lyle took a last look at the brooding Victorian. The blush of sunset created a phantom red glow up in the cupola. He snapped a photo of it with his phone. But he didn't want to make a big deal of this. Cats in heat. Fred agreed. Cats can even sound like a crying baby. There was a sudden skitter as they pulled away. A black thing swooped out from the porch and darted into the dusk.

But this whispering was a big deal. A name added to Belinda's gravestone. An unearthly voice. Strange words. Waves of sadness. Lyle's mind, slowed to a crawl for months by his accident, now percolated with fragmented thoughts. Only a family member could be added to Belinda's grave. *G* could only stand for *Georgia*. At that realization, his heart skipped one icy beat. The whisperers wanted Lyle to see a vision of that tomb.

6

Maybe all this was nothing—a simple symptom of exhaustion. But Lyle didn't want another symptom. He'd like to be singled out. Flattered. Maybe this meant that, a year after his deadly car crash in the middle of town, Lyle Hall was somehow special.

Or had finally lost his mind.

Either way, the old wheelchair had to be replaced. The medical supply company was still answering the phone when he rang them. And they deliver.

~~~~~~~

3. Under Surveillance

"Dad, what are you doing?"

Georgie's standard cell-phone greeting. It's Tuesday morning and her tone—*keep this brief and to-the-point*—conveys how busy she is these days. How she has no time for her father's eccentricities. Lyle knows this, but last night has changed everything.

"Surfing. Why."

"I know you're in town. I can hear angry townspeople. Going for coffee?"

Georgie's voice grips his heart after last night's strange vision. Her attempts at repartee feel precious now, it's like he must memorize her words, or lose them.

"You must have eyes everywhere."

"You know coffee's not allowed, Dad. Caffeine. Heart trouble. Et cetera."

"You would deprive me of my one guilty pleasure. Gertie's coffee doesn't have much coffee in it, by the way."

After a groan, Georgie says, "So you finally got a motorized wheelchair."

"I'm impressed—your master's in forensic psychology paying off."

"Don't do anything forensic and you'll be fine. Listen, if you're venturing out on your own in an electric chair, you have to have an orange pennant."

"So I can look like the village idiot?"

"Your words, not mine. This is about not getting crumpled by a semi while crossing Montauk Highway. Which I know you just did."

"Oh, Big Brother meets Big Daughter!"

"*Dad*," Georgie is impatient now. She needs to get into a meeting with Aiden Queeley, Chief of Southampton Police. "We live by rules. That's a new one as of today. I'm getting you a pennant for that chair. You're going to use it. Okay? Gotta run."

"Fine, fine, fine," Lyle says, feeling her withdraw. The line goes dead.

Parked outside the Southampton Police Department staff entrance in her unmarked Crown Victoria, Georgie sighs at her phone. There's a bicycle shop nearby she can call. They sell pennants. Later for Citarella. Tired from her overnight schedule, the back of her head meets the headrest and she closes her eyes a moment. Dad. Lyle Hall, Esquire. Her responsibility. He was once hell on wheels. Like flash cards, her mind flips through images of life with Father. His absenteeism, his drinking and his known eye for the ladies. That came into focus most disturbingly back when Mom was in the final throes of her battle with breast cancer, and Georgie was only 15. His fixation on Dar. Her elevation to difficult wife and stepmother. Yet Lyle was generous with his money, an abrupt way to express his feelings, such as they were. Georgie eventually cut that cord, informing him she would pay for college herself with a school loan. And then another loan for grad school at John Jay. But when Lyle insisted on pulling strings to get Georgie her shot at a detective's badge, she had to accept. Then, after his horrific car crash, she had to make an effort. Drop off his meals and, now that he's out and about, monitor his movements. However, spending real face time with Lyle, even now in his damaged iteration, was still tense—so much old baggage. These days there were moments she thought she might lose it and just scream at him over the dumbest thing, like his forgetfulness. Other times she thought she'd burst into tears in front of him, confined to his chair. She was glad she could truthfully say she was busy, had to run, had a meeting. He had, after all, gotten her this job. So here she was at 30, Lyle's enabler and scold. She takes a deep breath and swings open her heavy car door. Oddly enough, they gave her a white car, but she tells herself *choose your battles*. Next up, Chief Queeley.

Rolling on the sidewalk toward Gertie's luncheonette, the beauty of the October morning strikes him. The cool crispness of the air seems to promise something to come. Lyle passes a parked police cruiser. The big cop at the wheel, Sergeant Frank Barsotti, nods to him.

~~~~~

4. Upstanding Man

Heading out alone now for the first time since his accident—Lyle had let go his hired "man handler" earlier—he encountered challenges right away. Just getting down the ramp from his porch is tricky. Then there's the cemetery. It's right across the street from his house. It's very old. And Belinda's there. Lyle's been more conscious of that since his return home. And during his sleepless night a burning urge developed to just drive his chair over to her grave and look at the headstone. Did it have a new name? No way it could. And there was no way he was going into that cemetery alone. Instead, Lyle had formulated a shaky plan. Coffee's a big part of it. As is his new chair.

Before hitting the coffee shop, he needs to stop by Fraser Newton's office. Lyle's first visit to see his ex-partner in a year. The quaint bungalow office stands just off Montauk Highway, behind a five-foot privet hedge. It has a handicap ramp Lyle never noticed before. The new chair handles the incline nicely as he rolls up to the door. It feels awkward. But the office is open. Fraser starts early.

Lyle had typically worked from his home office but he'd stopped by Fraser's routinely. Entering now, he's struck by its familiarity. The reception area's leather chairs, working fireplace, framed whaling prints, hurricane lamps, scrimshaw and seafaring artifacts all mean to convey a sense of history and Protestant work ethic. And there sits Josie, Fraser's longtime assistant, at her desk, smiling at him. Josie is self-assured and smart, attractive at 40 with her blond-streaked hair and firm figure. They exchange pleasantries; it's been a while. But something vaguely uncomfortable hangs in the air between them.

Josie takes in the new Lyle. His beard, she knows, covers scars. Then there's the weight loss, gray temples, exhausted eyes.

And, of course, the wheelchair. Not the Lyle of old—tall, impetuous and able-bodied—but interesting.

Fast talking can be heard from the adjoining office.

"Is he on the phone?"

"He's awake," Josie deadpans.

Lyle rolls to Fraser's door and nudges it open to make his presence known. Fraser Newton, super-WASP: handsome, thick dark hair, mid-forties, married, two kids, made a boatload of money with Lyle in their lawyer/mortgage-broker partnership, is indeed on the phone.

"No. That's right. No can do. Trust me. My way is for the best. You'll see. Gotta run. You too. Later." He hangs up and meets Lyle's gaze.

"Fraser." Lyle rolls into the office. Fraser wears a navy blazer and gingham shirt.

"*Ebenezer*. Are you still paralyzed or something?"

"No, I just really love my new chair."

"It is nifty. I got your surprise text—what was it you wanted?"

"To thank you personally for your support during my long, difficult recovery."

Lyle studies Fraser's expression for any sign of human commiseration.

"Hey, Newton Properties' slogan is 'We Care.' Oh, Josie?"

"What," comes Josie's voice from the outer office.

"Didn't we send something to Lyle in the hospital? Last year?"

"The complete get-well helium balloon collection. Two dozen. With unicorns."

"There you go. And considerately hypo-allergenic."

"I still have them at home." Lyle rolls closer to Fraser's desk. "I've got two things I want to discuss." Fraser glances at his desk clock. It's brass and nautical. "But first, who were you just screwing over on the phone? Anyone I'd know?"

"The deli. Ordering breakfast. So who do *you* want to screw over today?"

"Fraser, I want to *unscrew* something." A wave of residual exhaustion hits him.

"Unscrewing, huh? Is that like the opposite of sex?"

"Possibly. Listen—first, I want to take care of Dar."

"Take care of your second ex-wife? In a *Sopranos* kind of way?"

"I'm serious. I want to set things right. Ameliorate the bad blood. I want to purchase the Florida condo for her. Buy it outright and let her have it."

"Let her have it, huh..." Fraser considers this. "You are a changed man. What if Dar remarries? Brassy blonde. Sunburned cleavage. Still in her forties. Some coot down there could be falling in love right now and getting himself a prescription."

"Spare me your image of my ex. I just want her to be secure in her home." Lyle leans toward Fraser. "Look. Last year I threatened to put her in a much cheaper place— *inland*—once the Bonita Shores lease was up. The end of this year."

"So she expects the worst. During the holidays, no less. That's so Lyle."

"That's what I want to change. Buy her the condo. They're selling, right?"

"Florida? There may be a unit or two. What kind of mortgage you want?"

"Fraser, I want a cash purchase. And I'll pay the maintenance."

"I'm a mortgage broker and you don't want a mortgage? Have I shown you the door?" He gestures behind Lyle.

"C'mon, Fraser. Make it happen. I'm just not into mortgages at this point in life."

Fraser sighs as he swivels to face a cabinet full of hard-copy files.

"Hmmm...Hall...Hall... Cash purchase...not into mortgages..."

Lyle takes in the sixty-inch oil painting over Fraser's fireplace: sailors killing a big whale at sea. "The other thing is the old Victorian house on Poplar," he says offhandedly.

"What about it?" says Fraser, his back to Lyle.

"I want to buy that, too."

Silence. Fraser extracts a file and rotates back to his desk and Lyle Hall.

"Here's the Bonita Shores file. Note how I'm ignoring your last statement and continuing as though you are not out of your fucking mind."

"One-eleven Poplar."

Fraser tries to read Lyle. "Ah yes," he says with mock seriousness. "You speak of the, how shall I say, *haunted whorehouse?* You want to rescue a derelict property Southampton took over under eminent domain. A site whose condemned structures the township will demolish shortly, in order to build a park for preschoolers."

Oh, shit. The old place is finally coming down. Soon. Why now? Lyle punts.

"Yeah. Fraser, I want to restore it," he bullshits.

Fraser winces. "No you don't, old boy. That place could collapse on its own this afternoon. It's an eyesore, a public hazard. Shelter for vermin and who knows what."

Lyle looks down. He actually does know what. And a terror is building in his heart that, if this demolition proceeds and he never hears that girl's voice again, he'll never decipher last

night's premonition——young Georgie's name being added to her mother's headstone. And he'll never hear his own girl's voice again.

Fraser cannot see Lyle's hands, how his fingernails dig into his palms. He narrows his eyes at the man in the wheelchair. "What have you done with the real Lyle Hall? The wise-ass. The man who'd pick up a truck if he thought there was a nickel under it…"

"Fraser." Lyle looks up. He sounds uncharacteristically earnest. "I just really want that place to remain standing and be renovated."

"For *what*? You're into historical preservation now? Isn't Dar pro bono enough? How often do we restore our old whorehouses anyway? Seriously, Lyle, I'm concerned about you." Fraser peers intently at his old partner. "Really. You don't look so good. And another thing, where you gonna get the whores?"

Lyle grimaces as he meets Fraser's eyes. Decades of their business deals and close friendship swirl through him in an instant. He snorts. Suddenly both men burst out laughing.

"That's another reason I came to you," Lyle says through laughter. He takes a tissue from Fraser's desk and dabs his eyes. "I'll need your help with staffing."

"Gentlemen," says Josie from her desk, "I can hear you."

"Ah, I miss our old times," Fraser smiles. "Listen, I have a conference call in a minute. How about we circle back tomorrow? Maybe you'll be of sound mind by then."

"Maybe. So Fraser, as far as Bonita Shores. I need you to call Dar. I can't do it."

Fraser frowns. "That's a deal breaker. I am not calling Dar Hall."

"This is me begging. It'll be a good call. I just can't."

"Tweet her, Lyle. I ain't callin' that gal for no amount o' money. Oh, and the way you want to structure it, this actually is for no amount o' money!"

Fraser is already on the phone as Lyle rolls back out to reception. Josie is up and leaning against her desk, her palms on the desk edge and her ankles crossed, barring his path. Lyle sees she's wearing a fitted shift dress hemmed above the knee. It's an autumnal bronze that sets off her gypsy-princess pearl necklace. Her legs, still tan, taper down to black heels. Josie pouts quizzically.

"You're not upstanding today?"

That means something, but Lyle can't place it. There are lots of things he can't place these days. Is she trying to bust his balls? They already are busted.

"No, but I do see a spinal-injury specialist in Southampton once a week."

Josie smiles and stands. She leans toward Lyle. Her necklace dangles down as her fingers find the collar of his polo shirt. Lyle's neck tingles, he absorbs her warmth and her fragrance. Familiar. Josie flips up Lyle's collar so it's standing, framing his head like a modern day Elizabethan. And something very strange ripples through his heart.

She stands back, hands on hips. "There. Upstanding, right?"

"Oh. Yeah." He's a little embarrassed. He actually used to pop up his polo collar when not wearing his usual expensive suit and tie. So obnoxious. Josie called the look "upstanding." The thought gives him a twinge of regret. Why?

Josie now pauses outside Fraser's office. He can be heard on the phone.

"I recall that rakish old Lyle of yore," she smiles.

Rolling to the front door, Lyle grins. "Well, old Lyle rides again."

Resisting an impulse to help him out the door, Josie watches him maneuver onto the ramp and roll down. The new Lyle certainly has issues. Even his issues have issues. Still, the man is…interesting.

Out on the sidewalk Lyle halts his chair. *Shit!* What an *idiotic* retort! His uneasiness returns. Then a flicker of memory comes. Then a flood.

Josie, younger. Lyle, healthy, clean-shaven. Josie would occasionally drop off papers at Lyle's home office on Ocean Road. He might be there, dressed casually. Josie might playfully check the collar of his polo shirt and, if it wasn't "upstanding," she'd make it so, her forearms resting on his shoulders. One time, following golf and the inevitable cocktails, Lyle called Josie, asking her to bring over a client's contract while he showered and dressed to meet the client for dinner. He now recalled how Josie arrived at his office, and there he was in a terry robe. How something else was upstanding. How pretty her panties were.

Ten minutes later, Josie was back in her top-down Fiat and Lyle was in his shower. Dar could have returned from shopping or tanning at any time, which intensified the secret dalliance. Lyle made subsequent phone contact with Josie at the office. He recalls referring to Dar as his "future ex-wife" and saying he needed to see another contract. How she could let herself in.

16

How she wedged the contract inside his screen door, rang the doorbell and drove off.

Josie got Lyle, all right. He hides an unexpected wave of emotion behind his sunglasses, suddenly feeling how Josie must feel. A good girl. Who he let go. Or drove away.

He gets his chair in gear and gets on his phone. He needs to connect with local historian and prig Noah Craig.

Coffee first.

~~~~~~~

5. Luncheonette

Wheeling up the sidewalk to Gertie's, he files away his flashback of Josie and shifts his thoughts to how dramatically life has changed.

Something else arose from Lyle's collision with Elsie Cronk's old Ford. Something weird. Emerging from coma, he noticed he was increasingly aware of people's feelings. Particularly alien to the old Lyle, he'd grown sensitive to people's pain. Lying in traction in his hospital room last winter, drugged, bored, he tried developing this extra sense as if it were a skill. Then one day he "read" a nurse who popped in. It came as a shock—he could tell she actually believed Lyle was drunk when he caused old Elsie's death; and that he was undeserving of good treatment. The old bag.

Lyle eventually mentioned this new sensitivity to Dr. Susan Wayne in a session. She allowed how empathy could be an outcome of his ordeal. But not mind-reading.

These days he was getting more used to his extra sense. Except just now when he felt an extraordinary rush of feelings about Josie. Or *for* Josie.

This was Lyle's first solo outing into town. The medical-supply delivery guy came last night and showed him how to use the chair and, importantly, how to recharge its batteries. It was very cool. For the past few weeks, Lyle had been trying to work his way back, just a little, into circulation. A hired helper had been pushing his Mr. Potter chair down Main Street/Montauk Highway so he could run his own errands. But Eli, a big, good-humored man who wore a service-provider V-neck scrub top, made Lyle feel like Stephen Hawking's dumber brother to onlookers, many of whom were well aware of his past. Earlier this morning, Eli went home happy, with full pay and a pocketful of twenties.

18

Lyle had also ditched his white socks and Crocs for his old Topsiders. And leaving his water bottle with sipping straw home created space for a large coffee. He needed a change and the freedom his motorized chair afforded was exciting. So was his plan for late tonight, when it's quiet. The chair will easily cover the eight blocks from his house to Old Vic.

It's going on 9:00 a.m. and sunny as he approaches the coffee shop where Gertie the counter woman works the express window. Lyle likes the no-name, wheelchair-inaccessible greasy spoon. Open all year, it's a pre-war Andy Hardy-style eatery with creaky stools, worn Formica counter and an old grump in the galley unapologetically grilling up savory heart-stoppers that send a bold message to anyone with a functioning nose: *bacon.* Also, too many people at the Starbucks know Lyle.

Stopping at Gertie's walkup window, Lyle remembers Susan Wayne saying how a near-death experience—an NDE—may provide opportunities to improve relationships. "Not just with your daughter," she emphasized. "Everyone you meet presents an opportunity for your growth as a human being." Right.

"Mornin' Gertie," he says from the sidewalk. Gertie narrows her eyes down at Lyle, then fetches his usual: black coffee and a *New York Post.* He can hear the hot stuff splash into a large Styrofoam cup. She works in silence; the chatter from the patrons at the counter quiets, too. But Lyle can see the No. 2 pencil poking from Gertie's hair bun. He inhales a waft of bacon and attempts to converse.

"How you like them Yankees?" he says to the window.

Gertie rarely opines, but today, without glancing out at Lyle, she blurts, "I hate the Yankees. Hope they lose." His coffee and paper appear in the window. Lyle hands her four singles from the old-man fanny pack Georgie got him.

Speaking pleasantly to the empty luncheonette window Lyle says, "Well that puts you squarely in the majority!" Almost instantly, three quarters plunk down on the sill. She doesn't accept his tips.

Lyle collects his purchase and his change. The *Post*, folded, slides into his canvas saddlebag. He pries off the lid and inhales. Not bad. He takes a sip. Hot. Black. Shit! *Very* hot! Especially following long months of tepid hospital decaf and other watery fluids at home, where Georgie banished all coffee and alcohol months ago. Lyle tries a bigger slug, and gags. It's superheated and burns his tongue. She microwaved it.

Lyle pours off an inch into the soil at the base of a scrawny sidewalk tree. Securing the container in his cup holder, he rolls past the luncheonette's open door and pretends not to notice how every head at the counter is turned his way. The new Lyle holds his burnt tongue. The patrons resume their chatter.

Leaves crinkling under his wheels, Lyle negotiates between some eye-averting pedestrians and feeble sidewalk trees displaying their sparse autumnal foliage. He wonders what's eating Gertie. She didn't hold his gaze—that may have prevented him from reading her. If he is empathic, why can he only read certain people, and not everyone? Just as well. Imagine being subjected to the woes of the mailman, every truck driver, every passing train loaded with people... No thanks.

Protected from any October chill by his so-out-of-style Members Only jacket, his polo collar standing tall, Lyle navigates to the Hampton Library, Bridgehampton's seat of learning. Somewhere in its bowels lurks his childhood friend and eventual legal adversary, Professor Noah Craig, retired history lecturer at Southampton College. Lyle craves more information about Old Vic before he attempts his planned maneuver in court. And before tonight's return visit. Maybe there are records of its former occupants. Records might shed some light on the whisperers and the girl's voice. But Lyle has no taste for researching old documents and musty books. The logical move is to go directly to someone who does. As many locals know, Noah Craig is hard at work on a boring history of the East End.

There is one obstacle. During Lyle's years of defeating Noah and his fellow historic-building preservationists in court, their friendship, which dated back to grammar school, had calcified and been replaced by animosity. Asking anything of Noah Craig today could be delicate. But Lyle feels compelled to understand the mournful voices emanating from Old Vic. He needs to return there equipped with some answers.

Right now Lyle has to circumnavigate something else—granite. Dr. Susan Wayne has advised him to avoid the site of his accident, the Bridgehampton traffic triangle with the big stone war memorial and towering flagpole. Too much pain. Especially if he is a bit empathic. So he cuts left and heads north, up a retail alley. Most of its shops are closed for the season.

Approaching the library from this direction, he'll pass Dunbar Automotive. Augie Dunbar's place is not a NAPA franchise; it's a survivor—a classic shade-tree-mechanic garage. There's even a giant oak standing next to the garage and a working vintage gas pump. Augie did some work last year on Lyle's short-lived, middle-age-crazy Hummer. Over the years Augie developed a good business in classic-car restoration, attracting summer people with showy old cars. The annual growth of the Bridgehampton Road Rally, held each October for classic-car aficionados, helped boost Augie's business. This year's rally had just concluded on Sunday.

As Lyle rolls by this morning, a startling vision of perfection stands outside Augie's garage bay. A mint Stutz Bearcat convertible, brilliant in the morning sun. Two-tone burgundy and black—the gleaming paint job alone could make you cry. Spare tire recessed in the driver's side running board. Polished chrome grille and horns. Two plush leather seats. White walls—white on the reverse sides, too. The morning sun's rays make the wire wheels sparkle. Original hood ornament. Another original is at work under the open hood. Lyle hasn't seen Augie in a year, but hears him tightening something.

"Mornin' Augie."

Augie Dunbar pokes his bald, 61-year-old head out from the hood and regards Lyle Hall. He reminds Lyle of the geezer in the painting *American Gothic*.

"Mornin'."

"Beautiful day." Lyle feels a chill come his way. A dog growls nearby.

"I suppose."

"And that's a beautiful automobile."

"Suppose." Augie turns back to the engine.

"That was quite a road rally over the weekend. Biggest yet, huh?" There's a grunt from behind the hood. It's accompanied by a deep, bestial growl. But Lyle presses on. "You know, when I was a boy, I built a model of a Stutz Bearcat like this from a kit. Never forgot it."

The growling grows more committed. Lyle pushes a bit further.

"What year is it?"

Augie's head reappears from behind the hood. His expression is that of a man detained from important work.

"Two-thousand-ten."

That said, Augie sets back to work. Lyle sighs, gets his chair in gear and rolls forward. Then he sees the muscular black mutt the locals call Augie's Doggie. It eyes Lyle in ominous silence from behind a rickety gate Augie keeps across his open office door. Then it explodes with canine fury, up on its hind legs, testing the gate. Lyle speeds up.

Rolling on, it occurs to Lyle that Dunbar's was where kindly old Elsie Cronk's battered car was towed last year after the accident. Augie may have cleaned out the birthday cake himself. And Augie has breakfast early each morning at Gertie's counter.

~~~~~~

6. Professor Craig

Noah Craig, retired professor, underemployed local historian, preservationist, and perennial Bridgehampton Village Board guy, is already at work this morning. As usual, he's set up at a table in the library's basement—the stacks—surrounded by old books and archival documents. These days he gets by on his pension and a stipend from the local historical society. His current mission: a coffee-table book on the East End's whaling heritage.

Like most local residents, Noah can do without Lyle Hall. Unlike most, he and Lyle were best friends as kids. In adult life, Noah brought a personal understanding of Lyle Hall, Esq., to the various court cases in which he spoke for preservation and against relentless land-development efforts. Over the years, Noah's insights proved less effective, as Lyle and his mortgage-broker partner Fraser Newton became an implacable force for real-estate sales. Their style was either steamroll the opposition or pay off weak-kneed complainants to "avoid a long and costly court battle." Noah knows too well how local farms and vineyards were increasingly replaced by undifferentiated fields of McMansions, even in areas where salt air and the seaside were only a rumor.

Last year, before Lyle's accident, the Shinnecock Indian Nation had been preparing a court battle to turn a large tract of former Southampton College acreage into a casino. Had that case gone to court, Noah Craig, Southampton College world history professor emeritus, would have faced Lyle Hall. He was about to face Lyle again.

Entering the library now, the place is quiet and cool. Librarian Sheila Dowd averts her eyes as Lyle approaches her big desk and her brass nameplate, but he picks up a cloud of unresolved conflict around her.

"Missus Dowd? Is Noah Craig here?"

"Downstairs." Chilly. Curt.

Lyle looks around. "Where is the elevator?"

"Downstairs." Sheila stamps some Dewey Decimal date-due book cards. Hard.

Makes sense. If Noah took the elevator downstairs, that's where it is. Lyle spots the elevator bank and calls up the car.

Noah, scribbling into a yellow legal pad, paid no attention to the elevator's trip upstairs.

But when it returns, its door opens and a strange vision in a wheelchair rolls out and heads directly to his table. It's Lyle Hall...in a Members Only jacket.

Lyle picks up Noah's surprise. But nothing's changed about Professor Craig—the salt-and-pepper hair, granny glasses, waistcoat, elbow-patch tweed sport coat slung over a chair. Not in shape, but not yet gone to seed, Noah gives the impression of a divorced academic who has not been sexually active for a long time. Which is correct.

Noah squints at Lyle over his glasses. He's barely recognizable. The wheelchair cuts his height in half. He's thinner, has gray temples, and his head of hair, still mostly brown, is uncharacteristically mussy. The beard is new. It looks like a baked Alaska. And there's this haunted look in his eyes. Like he's endured pain. A lot of it.

Lyle rolls up to the table. There are fresh legal pads and a laptop. Lyle is hit with a flood of Noah's weird emotions, defensiveness and animosity, but must ignore it.

"Noah. I need to talk to you."

"Apparently." Noah dispenses with the whole *so how have you been* thing.

Lyle leans forward on his arm rests. "So how have you been?"

"I'm fine. It's my sister and her husband and son I'm worried about."

"Oh?" Here it comes.

"You know Janice and Randall. You bought their potato farm and then flipped it to that winery company that went out of business before they got to plant any vines."

"Oh. Yeah. A few years back. Jan and Ran."

"Janice and Randall didn't come away with much in that transaction after they paid their creditors. At least when they had a farm they could grow potatoes, you know?"

"I'm familiar with the concept."

"I doubt that."

"Look, Noah, no one coerced them to sell." Lyle feels his blood pressure rise. "It was a business transaction. Many people are quite happy to sell their potato farm."

"After the sale, they couldn't afford college for their son, my nephew. He's the local kid who was arrested over the summer for selling meth."

Shit, Lyle thinks, *conflation*. It is not easy being new Lyle. But he doubts that potato farm could put a kid through college, even a cheap one.

"They couldn't swing a college loan? No Southampton College?" he ventures.

"Southampton was expensive, Lyle. And it's closed now, by the way."

"Oh. Right. Noah, look, I didn't...I never..."

"So now you know how I am." Noah switches gears. "Your coming to see me is highly unusual. Why are you here?"

"Uh, I need to do some research."

"Oh? Seeking people who haven't sold their farm yet?"

"Actually, they already bought the farm."

"Deceased."

"Sort of. Noah, are you still on the Bridgehampton Historical Society...uh..."

"The advisory board, yes. Why?"

"Well this might be up your alley. What do you know about One-eleven Poplar Street? Anything?"

Lyle starts to describe the creepy old place and Noah cuts him off.

"One-eleven Poplar. Commonly known as 'Old Vic.' It's a teardown. Only value might be the copper pipes, if any. The even older barn behind it may be pre-Revolutionary War, but it's ready to collapse. The name of the original owner has been lost or, because of the whorehouse rumors, buried. Nobody today knows who owned the property. If anybody did know, I'd know." Noah peers at Lyle. "You want that site? It'll be a playground soon."

A *playground* soon. Shit. Fraser was right. Lyle suddenly feels queasy.

"Yes...well, I'm working pro bono on behalf of someone who wants the house to remain standing." Out loud Lyle's impromptu response sounds very wobbly.

"Some kind of a nut, you mean? Not even the Historical Society wants to preserve that wreck. I've seen it—it's not viable. You'd have to raise a fortune in donations just to keep it standing. The roof for instance, you can punch your fist through it. It's a dangerous eyesore that drags down property values..."

"Noah, I live near it..."

"...And it has a bad mojo."

There it is. A weird, left-field remark that reminds Lyle of attending a Dr. John concert with Noah when they were teenagers. Researchers must be oddballs.

"Bad mojo, huh?"

"So some say. Now what would you expect to do with it? What's your client's trajectory? Scary bed-and-breakfast?"

"We don't want the place torn down."

"You already said that. This is quite a reversal for you, professionally.

"I'm into reversals these days."

"But why, Lyle?"

"She, my client, used to live there." The old, well prepared Lyle is now a new, unprepared Lyle, unaccustomed to being cross-examined.

"Used to live there? Not in our lifetime. Your client is zooming you—have you become gullible? And how *old is she?*"

"That's part of the problem, Noah..." Mentioning a phantom *she* was a mistake.

Now there's a sudden *bump* from one of the aisles of old books. Noah ignores it, but Lyle starts. He thought the stacks were deserted. He gazes into Noah's eyes. A torrent of sensations spanning decades hits Lyle full on—years of court cases, old school days, rock concerts, even a flashback to Noah and him as kids, throwing rocks at Old Vic's broken windows.

Lyle blurts it out. "Noah. She's dead." He feels like an idiot.

Silence. The historian's eyebrows rise. He searches Lyle's eyes. Yeah, Lyle survived his accident, but he woke up crazy.

Another sudden noise, closer this time, really startles Lyle. Shuffling movements behind a bookshelf. Someone is there—has been there, all along. Lyle feels increasing nausea. How fucked up is this?

A head of flaxen blond hair appears. It's a shock at first—a college-age young woman in fitted jeans and a gray sweatshirt that says, for some reason, PINK. She's cute. Barely noting Lyle's presence, she dumps an armload of old books in front of Noah.

"This is everything from that year, Noah." She takes a step back, as if awaiting further orders, glancing only briefly at the old guy in the wheelchair.

Noah takes a book off the top. "Thanks, Ginny." He flips open the cover. Finally he looks back at Lyle, giving him a *You're still here?* feeling.

"Lyle, we've got a ton of work in front of us. I hope your own research goes well...and your recovery. A good day to you."

Ginny the intern leans over the book Noah has open and points to something. Her healthy hair spills forward past her shoulders.

Lyle gets it. End of conversation. He blew it. He withdraws to the elevator bank.

Noah peeks up from his book as the poor guy maneuvers into the elevator car.

~~~~~~

7. Plan of Action

The sun high now, Montauk Highway is busy with traffic. Except for the couture shops, most stores are open and more people are out and about in town. Lyle knows he needs a plan of action and knows he's totally alone in this. He can't go to Georgie. To tell her what? She'd have him committed. Noah is a dead end. He'll need to set up a one-man command center in his office. To do that, he'll need supplies.

Grind, the specialty coffee store, is open. Lyle deposits Gertie's styro of bad coffee in a sidewalk wastebasket and rolls in. His new modus operandi is to ignore stares and glances—his sunglasses help—and go about his business. There are a few patrons mulling over packaged coffee choices. They glance, but don't bother staring. Grind sells "K-cups" for individual-cup coffeemakers, and Lyle grabs two boxes of Dark Sumatra. Georgie may have rid his house of coffee, but the machine still stands in the kitchen. The perky young staffers, in their uniform black polo shirts, work as a team at the checkout counter.

Back on the street, he pauses. He's broken the coffee barrier. Georgie also cleaned out his wet bar. He'll need something to offset the caffeine and the liquor store is nearby and open. There are no cop cars on the street presently. The store has automatic doors and he rolls inside with ease. He's the only customer.

Lyle grabs a fifth of his old standby, Dewar's blended scotch whiskey. He rolls up to the register and plunks it down in front of a bored looking college-age young woman who is apparently not in college. Liquor-store cashiers are trained not to comment on purchases, and she conducts the transaction in awkward silence. His basket loaded up, the automatic door shushes behind him and he heads for home, south of the highway. Poplar Street and Old Vic are a few blocks north. Later for that.

Lyle's nicely paneled home office is comforting and familiar. He feels empowered as his computer boots up and his chair recharges. He's got a fresh cup of Sumatra, black. He's back at work. He researches the legal paths to blocking the demolition of condemned buildings in Suffolk County. A lot of recent activity he can see online involves Save-a-Barn and Becky Tuttle. Noah Craig is even mentioned in a piece from a few years back on 27East.com. There are more reports in the *Southampton Press* online. Lyle makes sure to skip over any mention of himself. Particularly stories filed by that annoying fat guy who covered the Justice Court.

After noon, Lyle orders lunch from Fraser's deli. His old standby—roast beef on rye, lettuce, tomato and mayo. They deliver, no problem, and he keeps at his work. Now Lyle is on the Southampton Justice Court's site looking for forms relating to his planned motion in court. Old Vic is a historic building. To raze it would be a crime.

Lyle has a fourth coffee, way more than he's had all year, with his roast beef sandwich. Roast beef, hard to digest, is also on his verboten list. But it's great. The new Lyle is testing the boundaries of old Lyle. Except for the scotch—that's still in its plastic bag on the bar. Waiting.

That afternoon, something strange happened. Despite all the coffee, Lyle fell into a deep sleep, as his printer chugged out legal forms. His system was working hard to deal with the beef, gluten and mayo. And strange dreams came. Old Vic. The cupola and its red glow. A girl's hushed voice. And Belinda's headstone. Lyle saw it clearly as it really is:

BELINDA HALL
Beloved Mother
1955-1995

~~~

He sees for the first time that he left out *Wife and!* Big mistake. Beneath it was something new. Something very bad.

GEORGIA HALL
Beloved Daughter

Lyle screamed the kind of scream no one can hear when you're asleep. When you're that alone. He opened his eyes to utter darkness.

~~~~~~

8. Kohl Dark

It's almost midnight. *Shit, what happened?* Lyle flicks on some lights and cleans up the deli sandwich debris. Then the shower routine the physical therapy girl taught him—into the plastic shower chair, deal with his "ostomy" bags. He promises himself he'll no longer need them one day soon—his mantra. Drying off and dressing in fresh clothes—khakis, white button-down, navy sweater—is a chore, but he gets it done. Finally Lyle grabs his dumb old Members Only jacket. His expensive leather jacket is still in storage. He's going out.

It was easy getting across Montauk Highway at nearly two in the morning. Not so during the summer—he'd be a hood ornament by now, even at this hour. But this is a cool, quiet October night. Faint silvery light filters through the remaining leaves overhead and he rolls, chair fully charged, right up the middle of Poplar Street. Why not—most homes in town sit deserted until spring. Old Vic is two blocks ahead. It's not deserted.

One-eleven Poplar stands under a sickle moon. It seems even older as shadows creep across its jagged shingles in dim moonlight. There are new official signs posted. *This Property Condemned by the Town of Southampton. KEEP OUT. No Trespassing.*

Noah was right. Fraser was right.

Lyle appraises Old Vic with a real-estate lawyer's eye. The half-acre it stands on has been subdivided over the years from a much larger property. The shambling three-story Victorian, a high-style Second Empire beauty in the 1880s, was left to ruin maybe a century ago. Dormer windows project from its imposing Mansard roof. One dormer is raked by the bough of a towering white pine that stands in the front yard. Atop it all sits the cupola, hollow and moaning as the wind catches its shattered oculus. Old

Vic's first-floor windows were boarded with ancient planks. Its upper-floor windows were smashed long ago. Why not—could some old ghost ever catch hooting boys on bikes?

Two a.m. All is quiet as a sharp wave of sadness floods over him. Some tragic loss. Good. Lyle strains to hear what he came for—the whisperers.

The pine rustles high above. A gust makes the cupola groan. His eyes are drawn to the inky cracks between the boards covering the porch windows. He listens intently but hears only his own heart. Then something makes the hair on his neck stand.

A shadow flits across a crack. Something inside. It can't be alive. It's too silent.

Lyle's senses crank way up; he feels a strange thrill. And his heart rate increases—very quickly, its fluttering feels much too intense. Is it dangerous? He's had supraventricular tachycardia since the accident and doesn't want more heart trouble. But maybe it's a signal from the whisperers. Gotta tough it out.

The old porch doors are slightly ajar. Suddenly the air turns sharply colder.

Look there...

Oh, God. Just a glimmer; so fragile, floating onto the porch. Maybe a dozen feet away, glowing faintly.

Lyle's heart starts to really pound. His upper body pulsates, his ears ring. It's a challenge; embrace it. Focus. It's an *apparition*. He wants to see more of it.

And then he does.

Good God…a girl materializes on Old Vic's porch. A beautiful, young, dead girl.

He gasps, trying to control himself in mid-freak out. He wants to commit this vision to memory, but he's getting mixed signals. He's drawn to her eyes, so hollow and kohl-dark. She's so pale. Her beauty seems Mediterranean. Her white-lace dress is Victorian. Her rich dark hair, gathered up in a pompadour, falls behind her head in braids. Her imploring mouth. Back to those eyes. Heartbroken. Incredible. But Lyle senses courage, too. And the way she holds her chin up, maybe pride.

Damn. His heart is definitely working too hard, but he's desperate to see this through. The whisperers chose a *girl* to come forward. Can't be more than 12. He must learn what she wants. And her name.

"Hello!" he croaks through frosty breath. It's so cold now. "What is your name? My name is Lyle. Please, tell me your name?"

Nothing. Just this resolute gaze, afloat on a tide of unknown past. Her head at a slight angle, thin girlish arms seem to float toward him, palms open.

"Please, your name! Won't you tell me? What do you want from me? *Please!*"

He gulps air, hoping to calm his heart, and stares back at her, aching to hear something. Moments pass slowly. Then, like a breeze, a cautious whisper floats his way.

Eye you touchy.

The strange phrase shatters through him. It's a quiet plea.

"I don't understand!" His heart pounds harder. "Please, what does that mean?"

Then, hushed and secretive...

Tee eye you toe.

Uncomprehending, Lyle gasps, "Oh, God!" then asks, "Can you tell me your name? Your *name?*"

A new whisper:

Jewel.

"Jewel? Your name is Jewel?"

Cold sweat trickles down his temple. He needs air or he'll black out, but he must not—this is an incredible breakthrough. God, she's so young. Adolescent. Twelve?

That's when the tremors start undulating through his paralyzed legs. Like the electro-stim they give at the spine clinic.

33

He looks down in shock, grabs his dead legs and rubs his quadriceps. Could they be coming back? They actually ache. Is this good? Can they move?

The pale girl draws closer and Lyle senses apprehension building within her. Of what? She wants Lyle to close his eyes. He forgets his legs and closes his eyes.

Now he sees fleeting, gruesome visions. A man's big hand grips an old kitchen knife. It's all bloody. A newborn swaddled in coarse fabric. Blood flows. Lots of it. Why is he seeing these things?

Then he's shown a scene he recognizes—the local cemetery. Why? Some headstones bear familiar names. Then there's the headstone he knows best…

BELINDA HALL
Beloved Mother
1955-1995

And then that nightmare inscription appears again below Belinda's. Just like it was in Lyle's dream.

GEORGIA HALL
Beloved Daughter

Seeing Georgie's name this second time makes the threat much more credible. And it gets worse. He sees a date carved by an invisible hand. Georgie's date of birth. It's correct. Then another date takes shape. It seems to cut into Lyle as it cuts into granite. Georgie's death. His heart beats harder still. It's October 16. *This Saturday*. No. No! That cannot be!

A helpless rage erupts in Lyle. *Says who?* His stomach churns with revulsion. No parent can bear the sight of his own child's headstone. His heart seems to be weakening. His leg muscles jitter. His eyes sting with tears as Jewel silently reappears.

"What does this *mean?* My daughter's *alive!* What do you want from me?"

But now the girl's lovely face shudders and darkens ominously; deep cracks extend across her features. She withdraws as a strange chorus wells up—miserable wailing voices. Who? Lyle's leg tremors intensify to painful spasms. But then his legs abruptly revert to lifeless slabs. What follows is a surreal revival of the injuries from his accident. The pains are agonizingly familiar: broken ribs, broken jaw, concussion, punctured lung and kidney, emergency surgery—all that and more return with searing accuracy.

He reaches out to Jewel but her image disintegrates to dust, just as a violent shockwave stabs his heart, thrusting him back in his chair. Is this the end?

"Wait!" He clutches his pounding chest. "Answer me, for God's sake!" he gasps.

Somewhere, collective voices moan. Smoky wisps, the remains of Jewel's apparition, linger in the chill air, then swirl back behind the front doors. Lyle forces out a last plea. "Jewel! What does this mean? What do you *want??*"

Disembodied moans stir in the air and he doubles over, fighting back bitter vomit.

One syllable cuts through like a knife. It's horrid, guttural.

YOU.

The moans morph into a swirl of derisive laughter. Then all goes quiet.

Sitting up, rubbing his eyes, all he can see at first is a gaping black chasm.

It's filling with a dark, rising tide of fear.

~~~~~~

9. Beloved Daughter

Lyle Hall slept one sporadic hour at home—catnaps, slumped in his chair, stricken with guilt and dark, fearful visions. What was to become of his only child? How could a prediction of her death possibly be real? Can a ghost *lie?* And what was that "You" shit? *Who said that?* How can he possibly watch over Georgie and protect her? She's the one taking care of *him.*

Rain fell during the early morning hours as Lyle, agitated and excited, replayed his unnerving encounter with the apparition in his mind, trying to draw out its meaning. Her riveting, sad beauty and the sharp impact of her strange plea were etched in his consciousness. He could not dispel the sense that this young girl, *Jewel*, was chosen by the whisperers to represent them. But why?

And they chose him, damaged goods, to hear her. Why?

His difficulty breathing and stabbing heart pains might be chalked up to the thrill of the moment. But his leg muscles, no, that was something else entirely. Could it be an offer of reciprocation? A wish fulfillment? Do dead girls typically correct spinal injuries? Until the sun finally rose, Lyle kept bumping into dead ends: He's a real-estate man. Old Vic is real estate. His daughter's a cop. Could Saturday be her last day? Repeat.

Sunrise broke through the clouds, and Lyle was happy to have coffee for his coffeemaker. Daylight intensified his need to solve problems on two fronts. Protect his headstrong daughter from some unknown threat without letting her know she's in danger. And save a haunted whorehouse because a dead girl wants him to, with the possibility of a weird quid pro quo. It's already Wednesday. Best to get a grip on his salad spinner of problems by learning some real-world facts about Old Vic. Which means prostrating himself before that difficult know-it-all Noah Craig again, damn it.

Lyle downs two Sumatras while scanning the Internet for old news about Old Vic. Nothing. He also gets his court documents in order. Caffeine gets his thoughts churning. Jewel's haunting face. Georgie has a police sketch-artist friend. Maybe she'll give him his cell number. But how can he persuade Noah to come on board? He sticks a go-cup of Sumatra in his cup holder and dons his Members Only.

As Lyle rolls across a quiet Montauk Highway, visions of the ghost girl nag him to peek at Old Vic in daylight. Now. Lyle pauses at the handicap curb-cut the village has provided at the corner of Poplar, and gazes up the street. The beech trees form an autumnal canopy over the road, morning sunlight dappling the pavement with a cozy "Bedford Falls" feel. The morning air is crisp and tart. Two blocks up, the effect is disrupted by the decrepit Victorian eyesore and its scraggly pine tree.

Shit. Men in DayGlo vests are positioning a front-loader tractor in Old Vic's weedy side yard. *Fuck.* No time to lose. Lyle gets in gear and heads for the library. He reminds himself that convincing people of things was once his specialty. He needs Noah badly and he needs to be persuasive again.

Now Georgie is calling his cell. An unspeakable dread for his daughter turns to acid in his stomach. He fends off flashbacks from their long years of discord—basically the last 15 years, since her mother died—and answers.

"Dad, what are you doing?"

The edge to Georgie's voice gives Lyle a bittersweet pang this morning. She sounds so full of life he can feel it over the phone. He instinctively tries to mask his exhaustion and his dread for her. Maybe he can fix the whole headstone problem. Maybe it's totally unreal. Georgie would never believe him anyway.

"Just hitched onto the back of a truck headed for Montauk."

"*Dad...*" Georgie can hear a truck rumble by over the phone.

"If you know what I'm doing, why ask? Trying to entrap me?"

"Don't give me any ideas. So what is it with you and the library?"

"Visiting my old friend Noah."

"Noah isn't your friend, Dad. You're not the library type. Hence my question."

"Ask your observers. That the only reason for this morning's call, Sunshine?"

"I'm dropping off lasagnas from Citarella later. You'll be home?"

"Outside. Shivering. My ramp has wet leaves. Barely made it down."

"Get a neighbor to come with a rake."

"What neighbor? Mister Rosewater hasn't ventured outside this century." Lyle overhears Georgie say something to a coworker. Then he asks, "Georgie, your sketch artist friend...what's-his-name. Can he draw me a something?"

"*Linder?* He can if you're reporting a crime. See? This is why I worry."

Georgie speaks to another cop again, then says hurriedly into her phone, "I'll be by later. And I have the orange pennant for you. Gotta run..."

"Oh, so I can look like the village idiot?"

She's gone. Suddenly a new fear grips Lyle's gut. How does he know if it's the last time he hears his daughter's voice? Lyle shakes that off and texts her.

Linder's cell? Please?

~~~~~~

10. Noah Redux

The library elevator opens and Lyle Hall rolls directly toward Noah's table. Ginny the research assistant is seated next to Noah. The two look up at a distraught, exhausted man.

"Déjà vu," says Noah.

"Did you get my text?"

"Cell phones are not allowed here."

"Well, I need to talk to you."

"So I gather."

Lyle looks at Ginny. She is cute in her stylish eyeglasses. The pink tops of her ears poke through her silky blond hair, like a studious elf. Lyle regards Noah.

Silence.

Lyle takes a swig of his coffee. Finally the historian blinks.

"Ginny, was there more for you to do at the Whaling Museum?"

Taking in Lyle's worn visage, Ginny responds, "The collections manager will be in today, but he wants to see you, Noah. Not me."

"He wants to see you, too. He can see me later. Why don't you take a ride over to Sag Harbor and make nice. There's a lot there for us."

For Ginny, unsupervised unspecific research is a good thing. And lunch is paid for. She slings her backpack over her shoulder and grabs a notepad. Lyle watches her enter the elevator and thinks *Youth.*

The basement room goes quiet.

"Thank you."

Noah sighs. "Lyle, this is beyond weird. *What*, may I ask, do you want from me?"

Lyle takes a deep breath. Tries to dredge up some energy. Out with it.

"Okay. I won't mince words. Noah, that house—is *fucking haunted.*"

Noah searches Lyle's eyes. He's not kidding. He's crazy. Or worse.

"By...?"

"A girl. Maybe twelve years old. Victorian dress..."

"Uh-huh...*and?*"

"She spoke to me. Late last night. A few words. And told me her name."

"*Really.*" Noah sips his water. "What'd she say, 'Get off my lawn'?"

"What she said sounded like a foreign language."

"Oh?" Noah places his bottle down. "Lyle, you're not well."

"I am not shitting you."

Noah straightens some papers, then checks his watch. He looks up at Lyle.

"So you don't know what language she spoke. What's her name?"

"Jewel. I swear, Noah, I'm not shitting you."

"Uh-huh. She told you her name in a foreign language?"

"Jewel. That's what I heard." Then a phrase comes back to him. "And she said something very strange like *are you touchy* or maybe *eye you touchy.* Accent on the *you.*"

Noah removes his glasses and squeezes the bridge of his nose.

"Lyle, *sei pazzo.*"

"Say 'pot so'? Why?"

Noah sees Lyle doesn't know Italian. But is he telling the truth?

"Lyle. *Aiutaci?*"

"Yeah. Like that. Only she sounded way younger."

Noah replaces his glasses and closes the record book before him.

"Lyle. That's Italian. It means 'Help us.'"

Lyle exhales deeply and stares back at Noah. *Help us* makes simple sense.

"Listen, Lyle, I drive an SUV. Your chair folds up?"

~~~~~~

Noah pulls his aging Ford Explorer to a halt in front of 111 Poplar with Lyle awkwardly seated next to him. On the way, Lyle had given Noah more detail on last night's paranormal experience. He included his cardiac event, the muscle tremors, the harsh voice that seemed to drive Jewel away, and the shocking return of his car-crash injuries. He stopped short of describing Georgie's name appearing on Belinda's headstone. Remaining in the SUV the two men stare up at Old Vic. The workers have gone. In daylight the place looks even more like the teardown Noah described—a derelict eyesore way beyond renovation. The one remaining second-floor shutter hangs akimbo. The Mansard roof is ready to cave in. The old back barn is a rickety horror you can see through. It's barely standing. The CONDEMNED signs posted everywhere and the big front-loader standing nearby send a blunt message.

Lyle stares at the rotted front doors—they're now boarded shut *and* cordoned with yellow police tape. He selfishly does not want Jewel to appear. He wants Noah's help, but wants to keep Jewel for himself. And he wants her suffering to end. His, too.

"Lyle," Noah begins, all business, "as you can see, this place is hopeless. And as far as your uh, extrasensory experiences, who knows? All that could have been a hallucination that won't return—and I'm being kind. Your muscle spasms could be psychosomatic, a form of hysteria or phantom-limb syndrome."

"Hysteria, huh? Listen, Noah, since my uh, accident, I feel…different. Real different." Lyle decides to share something. "I can feel people's suffering."

"*Really*. Feeling rather than causing must be something new for you."

"It's true. My therapist says I may be empathic—feeling the pain of others. Especially when I come near a place where there was suffering. Like this house. I get this sense of long-ago misery, deep sadness. Loss."

"Oh? Do you feel any of that now?"

"No. Last night, yes. Noah, something terrible happened in this house. I need to research it. You're the man to do it. I'll double your rate. Triple it. Your intern too."

Noah positions his chin on the steering wheel. His gaze is drawn up to Old Vic's cupola. He drums his fingers on the dash and exhales a quiet whistle. "Three times nothing, huh? I don't get paid for being a preservationist, though the village does provide a stipend for my research on a new coffee-table book. Ginny works for college credit." He glances at Lyle. "But I can probably fold a little Old Vic work into my routine."

"There's not much time, Noah. And exactly how much is a 'stipend'?"

"You don't want to know, Lyle. Suffice to say, no money need change hands."

"You'll have the appreciation of a grateful community."

"The community will *not* appreciate digging up dirt on Old Vic. And no non-profit, not even Save-a-Barn, would be dumb enough to get involved." Noah pauses. He takes in all the broken windows. "You know, you and I would come here as schoolboys and throw rocks through the windows."

"That's why there are no rocks left on the property."

"That was over forty years ago," Noah muses. "Your ghost girl would have been dead for sixty years by then."

"We could have been throwing rocks at Jewel."

"Lyle, I don't know from empathic and supernatural, but I do know that a cardiac event like you described, if real, can be fatal."

"I didn't know you cared." Lyle senses a breakthrough. "What's your point?"

"My point is, don't ride back here alone at night like some kind of disabled paranormal cowboy." Noah looks Lyle in the eye. "Bring *me*."

Lyle returns his gaze. "Speaking of which...could you bring me to Southampton Justice Court?"

~~~~~~~

11. Justice Court

Noah Craig grips the wheel tightly as he drives Lyle to Southampton.

"You know this is an hour out of my way? I'm expected in Sag Harbor."

Lyle makes a nonverbal noise as he pores over his court documents.

"And then there's gas." Noah notes how his old frenemy has tuned him out. "Still as opportunistic as always."

Lyle makes phone calls as Noah drives. One is to his usual driver. Noah is thankful to hear Lyle succeed in cajoling Fred, who had other plans, into collecting him at the courthouse later. Then there's an odd call about meeting some guy who is apparently an artist. Noah also hears Lyle's side of an awkward conversation with, of all people, a Catholic priest in Southampton.

"Lyle," Noah inquires, "you have a friend who's a priest? You have changed."

"An old client." Lyle stares out the windshield. "Any port in a storm, you know?"

Arriving at Justice Court, Noah performs the chore of setting up Lyle's chair as Lyle gives directions. He finally swings himself down into his seat and smiles up at Noah.

"Thank you, old friend. Sorry about being opportunistic. I owe you."

"You owe me a trip to Old Vic, Lyle. To meet that girl. If there is one." Noah gets behind the wheel. "Oh, and a suggestion? Mention 'whaling heritage' whenever you can. And 'ship's captain.' It works."

With that he pulls away from the courthouse. Watching Noah maneuver into traffic, Lyle wonders if he really can dig up any useful facts while Old Vic is still standing. And Noah wonders

43

something, too: Could there be a book deal, a real one, to come out of Lyle Hall's *pazzo* story?

Lyle looks up at the courthouse. He's struck by how imposing the place feels, viewed from a wheelchair. The courthouse itself is a brick Georgian with four three-story white pillars and the requisite handicap ramp. Exhaustion, dread and even a little excitement mingle inside him as he takes a last sip of his coffee, now cold.

Inside, though nothing's changed, it feels weird. Lyle steers around people in groups—fast-talking trial lawyers huddling with clients. He notes the bored court reporter for the *Southampton Press* lurking at the periphery of one group. Rotund. Smudgy glasses. Bad comb-over. Old suit. Scribbling in a reporter's pad. What was his name…Moses something. He used to fire a few questions at Lyle after a particularly intense day in court, then file some bullshit in his weekly column. Lyle never read it, but Fraser would quote from it sarcastically. Not being noticed is a good thing.

What has changed here is Lyle Hall, Esq. People don't recognize him, down at chair-level, bearded, thin, older-looking. Wearing the old Members Only jacket he found in his closet instead of his customary tailored Ralph Lauren suit.

The shield of the Town of Southampton looms from high on a wall. The big circular plaque features a cartoonish depiction of a Pilgrim and claims that Southampton is the "first English settlement in New York State." *Those Brits*, Lyle ruminates, *are planning more?* The Pilgrim guy looks especially dumb today. Lyle rolls onward.

The lady at the clerk's window does not recognize Lyle. Today, Alpharetta, a big-boned black woman of indeterminate age, has her hair in tight braids with little beads. *Nice work,* Lyle thinks. *Somebody has to do that for you on a vacation island.* His paperwork is ready. He retrieves it from his canvas side bag and hands it to her. Lyle wrote his complaint—that 111 Poplar Street in Bridgehampton should be designated a historic site—around six a.m. The exact opposite of everything he ever stood for.

Court is busy today, Lyle thinks, as she peruses his forms. Then there's a gasp.

"*Lyle Hall??*"

Alpharetta can seem intimidating if you're seated. But Lyle recalls they had a kind of fun kinship. She was one of the very few who'd poke fun at his success. She'd refer to herself facetiously as "just one of the little people" toiling away in a legal system whose function was to enrich Lyle Hall.

"*Lyle Hall!!*" She looks at a form he signed and then at him.

"Hi, Alpharetta."

"You're back working?"

"No, not really. Just a...a pro bono motion I'm filing."

"Lyle Hall? Pro bono? I need to go on my break!" She smiles broadly.

"This must be difficult for you."

"You kidding? My life's been easy since you...you, ah..."

"I'm glad my absence has brought some cheer to otherwise dreary lives."

Alpharetta laughs out loud at that. Too loud. Then she reverts to professional mode and shuffles Lyle's papers. "I see the demolition of this property is imminent."

"Yes. Demolition equipment is actually on site now."

Head down, braids jiggling, Alpharetta stamps the top sheet and says, more to herself, "I'll get this in front of Judge Sloane right away."

Lyle thanks Alpharetta and rotates his chair to face a man standing before him. A pudgy, rumpled man with a reporter's notebook.

~~~~~~

12. Meet the Press

"Lyle Hall? Mose Allen, *Southampton Press*. Remember me?"

"Of course, Mister Allen. How are you?"

Right. Mose Allen the reporter. Fraser called his column "Court Weakly." Lyle is able to read the man instantly. The lonely boy. The excited and hopeful cub reporter with dreams of becoming a new Hemingway. The years of court reporting giving way to giving up on making a good impression. No longer bothering to brush off the dandruff, press the suit, clean the eyeglass lenses. The years of honing his craft so that people in the legal profession must read him, like him or not. Years of zeroing in on the right person to interview, including Lyle. Today, Lyle senses, Allen's under some pressure. He's right, Allen now works for a much younger editor who expects his staff to prove every day that they are solid contributors. Especially as they transition to online distribution. And Lyle picks up on something else, deeper down, an emotion. Envy.

"Did I overhear you filing a pro bono motion? I thought you were no longer, uh, practicing after, uh..."

"Correct. I'm simply filing a cease-and-desist as a concerned citizen. The town wants to demolish a local historic building." Lyle deeply hopes this bland explanation is enough, but he's already getting a sinking feeling.

"Really. An about-face for you. I thought next time I saw you would be to contest the uh, wrongful-death civil suit..."

Lyle flashes on emerging from his coma to face the Cronk family's lawyer. Lyle told him there was some old guy who "saw the whole thing" while walking his dog.

"In *that* case, Mister Allen, the wheels of justice, as you know, grind slowly."

Allen is scribbling rapidly in his pad. Lyle notes how he can ask questions and write at the same time.

"Or perhaps we'd see you here to fight your disbarment."

"No, sir." Lyle pauses. "In fact I'm considering letting them disbar me. At this point, I might like to fade away into the sunset."

"To mix metaphors. So you're now with a pro bono organization of concerned citizens? Like Save-a-Barn? Which property are you trying to save?"

"It's an old house near my neighborhood. I...we strongly believe it has historical significance. Also it's beautifully designed and constructed—Second Empire Victorian—the detailing alone is incredible." Lyle feels how easy it is to get up his old head of steam. Coffee works. Allen scribbles on. "You know, Mister Allen, so much of our local history is tied to whaling. This house may have been owned by a prominent ship captain. We are working to unearth the documentation that will show how this home is a little gem of Long Island history. We just need more time."

Allen looks up from his pad and down at Lyle. "A 'little gem'? You're talking about the haunted whorehouse, aren't you."

"Well that's a matter of conjecture and hearsay, Mister Allen."

"Mose. It's Mose, Lyle. It was Mose before your, uh, accident. Let me offer something. The whaling-sea-captain thing won't fly because Second Empire home design came in after whaling was over. The eighteen-eighties. You have an org ready to raise funds and renovate? To get a favorable decision you have to prove you're ready to make the place safe and habitable. In a timely manner—but you know that. I've seen that house, by the way, and it's about to fall down. And any 'fine detailing' you're talking about rotted away long ago. Then there's the background problem—the house-of-ill-repute rumor. Proven or otherwise, the township will look bad if it allows a brothel to be preserved. What next, people will ask, preserve a crack house to recognize the drug dealer's place in our history? So whose money is actually behind this? Yours?"

When they have you, don't flinch, smile. Lyle smiles. "Mine."

"Why? That's what you'll be asked. You might as well start with me."

"It's still a beautiful old place that should be saved. We don't need another McMansion."

"The question is *why*, Lyle. Haunted whorehouse. We've ruled out whorehouse and historical sea captain and beautiful craftsmanship."

As they've been chatting, the crowd has made its way into the courtroom, leaving the main hall echo-y. Mose Allen looks to the courtroom doors. A policeman is closing them, making eye contact with Allen's glasses. He has to go cover the case; the reason his editor sent him here.

"Lyle. That leaves *haunted*."

Lyle looks up at this guy. He is annoying.

"What if it does?"

Allen reacts. "What if it does, indeed? You think that old wreck is actually haunted? You live nearby. Have you noticed, uh, supernatural goings-on?" The policeman sticks his head out from between the doors and Allen nods to him. "I gotta run. Lyle, do you believe that place to be haunted?"

Lyle peers into Allen's lenses. If he answers poorly his battle could be over before it's begun. "Mose, our region has a rich history and enjoys a unique position in the..."

"Is it *haunted*, Lyle?"

The policeman gives a low whistle. From inside the bailiff intones, "All rise." The reporter gets visibly edgy.

"Okay, Mose. I believe there could be a spirit of some kind on the premises."

How can an expert lawyer cave in to the questioning of a two-bit local reporter? Times have changed.

The cop is staring at Allen as he scribbles furiously.

"You're serious, aren't you. One or more? Male or female?"

"One. Female."

"How do you know?"

"I saw her face."

"Approximate age?"

"Maybe twelve. Mose, when did you become a paranormal enthusiast?"

"I didn't. Thank you. Here's my card." He hurries toward the big doors the cop has disappeared behind.

"Mose, are you going to write something next week?"

Allen looks back at Lyle. "That's up to my editor. But we file every day now. We're online."

~~~~~~

13. Facial Recognition

The riskiest encounter so far this week, Lyle fears, was with Mose Allen. Fraser Newton used to say there's no such thing as bad ink. Not bad for Fraser, that is. Maybe there'll be a little helpful publicity. But it's unnerving, giving up so much information—and disinformation—to a reporter who has clearly never been in his corner. Writing a snippet regarding Lyle's civil complaint might be a pleasant diversion for a dullard like Mose. And that may have been a good idea about allying with Save-a-Barn. But how could Lyle Hall let Mose peel him apart in two minutes and then make his escape? Maybe it doesn't matter. Since his accident the new Lyle is a good man. Not a conniver. Upstanding.

Out in the parking lot the old Sabrett guy doesn't know the new Lyle. Lyle scarfs down his dirty-water dog and swigs his Diet Snapple as he scans the lot for a red Jeep Wrangler. Ray Linder, Southampton Police sketch artist extraordinaire, drives one.

"Mister Hall?"

It's a young guy with a laptop case. "I'm Ray Linder?" He extends his hand. "So I thought we could do a session in my Jeep? But..." he takes in Lyle's whole wheelchair thing. Lyle takes in Ray's thing: jacket, slacks, no tie. Young, in good physical shape, sports a blond crew cut that shows signs of incipient male pattern baldness.

"Yeah...well."

Linder's style swings between businesslike and boyish-techie. It seems every phrase starts with 'so" and ends in a question mark. He explains, "So, doing outside work might possibly compromise my position vis a vis the police force?"

They agree on a bench situated on the far side of the parking lot. Linder seats himself and Lyle pulls up his chair. Linder opens his laptop to a facial-recognition program he uses at work.

"So how do you know this individual?"

"Relative of a client. Did Georgie—Detective Hall—tell you anything about the case?" Lyle begins to realize that just saying Georgie's name now gives him a stab in the gut. Guilt, doubt, fear—what can he actually do about her premonition?

Linder shakes his head. "Is it a police matter, Mister Hall?"

"No, a legal matter. I'm doing some research and I need a visual of this girl. Twelve years old. And please call me Lyle."

"Okay..." Linder positions his laptop so both can see. "So, what face type?"

"I don't know what that means."

"So, there are different face shapes? Round faces? Oval? Heart-shaped?"

"Let's go with heart-shaped."

Lyle describes Jewel to Linder in detail. They give a lot of attention to the eyes. Bigger, darker.

"Ray, can you make her eyes more, uh, soulful?"

"Soulful? I'll try? I'm just on my lunch break?"

Finding and applying the Victorian hairdo is fairly straightforward. The sketch artist does not question the girl's Victorian time frame. Linder works on her mouth while Lyle rolls back to the Sabrett guy to buy him a dog, a Diet Coke and a big pretzel. Linder's focused intently on the illustration when Lyle returns with his lunch. The artist takes a bite of the giant pretzel without taking his eyes off the screen.

"So, you said it was a white lace dress?" he says, chewing. "Circa turn-of-the-century? So, these are the choices I have..."

Lyle views a series of old-fashioned lace dresses on the screen. He points to one.

"It's like that."

Linder looks at Lyle. "You said she's twelve?"

"Thereabout. Why?"

"So, look what happens when I add the dress you chose?"

He clicks and there she is. Jewel. Not exactly perfect but gorgeous nonetheless. The dress is right. Linder clicks between headshot and full-body images. Staring at Jewel on the laptop, Lyle thinks he's starting to feel a slight sensation in his legs—he tries to will the feeling to come on.

"Ray, that is damn good!"

"So, I have doubts?" Linder swigs his Diet Coke and chomps on the dog.

"Why?"

"Twelve years old is adolescent? This is a grown woman?"

Lyle looks again. Of course, Linder's right. Between the dark eyes, the full lips, which Linder colored red, and the mature figure, you get Penelope Cruz.

"So, look here," Linder says. He flicks between two dresses onscreen. "See? This is what you say she wore? But this is what a twelve-year-old girl would wear? More modest? No bust? See, the lace collar comes up under the chin?"

The young girl's dress looks all wrong on Jewel. But Lyle knows—he's unsure how—that the girl is, or was, only 12.

"Can you...flatten her chest but keep the mature dress?"

"Photoshop can."

Linder does so quickly. Lyle looks. "Yeah, that's closer. Can she be shorter?"

"So, height has no meaning without reference points?"

"Oh. Anything else you can do to make her look young?"

Linder fiddles with the head-to-body ratio. A small head, a large head. He explains that children have proportionally larger heads so increasing the subject's head size can signal youthfulness. Linder also downplays the lipstick. Suddenly, Lyle realizes, making the head just a bit larger is just right—a mix of innocence and experience.

"That's got it, Ray! Right there! Whatever you just did, that's damn near perfect! I can't believe it!" My God, Lyle thinks, I could make copies of this and show it to Jewel.

"Glad you're happy?" Linder admires his own work. "I like it too? So, I'll tweak it and then email you the file—then it's all yours?"

"Sounds fine. I know you have to get back to work." Lyle counts out 13 twenties, $60 more than agreed, from his old-man fanny pack.

Linder thanks him, places his laptop back in its bag and stands.

"Ray, give my regards to Detective Hall, if you see her."

Linder nods and starts for his Jeep, then pauses. "So, I hope you find this...girl?"

"Thank you," Lyle says. "So do I."

Lyle rolls back to the front of the courthouse. No Mose Allen; that's good. Wheelchair battery running low; that's bad. He spots Fred's MediCab approaching. It has an electrical outlet. Lyle is unused to this much trucking but, if this keeps up, he'll need a lot more twenties for Fred.

Fred pulls up and Lyle suddenly realizes he was wrong. Mose Allen is standing under the courthouse portico with a camera. He raises it and points it at Lyle. Lyle experiences a rush of bitter feelings and weird premonitions. All bad. This guy Allen is a rat planning to prey on Lyle and his situation for personal gain. How does he know? He just knows.

He acts on impulse. As the MediCab's lift settles on the sidewalk, Lyle grins sardonically at Mose and raises his fist, middle finger extended skyward.

~~~~~~

14. Our Lady of Poland

"A *ghost*."

"Yes, Monsignor. In a house. I wanted your advice about...that."

Lyle watches Msg. Eamon Hannan seat himself behind his desk in the warmly paneled rectory office at Our Lady of Poland in Southampton. Fred is parked at the curb. This stop was not on his itinerary but he's got a fresh twenty in his shirt pocket.

Lyle receives conflicting emanations from the old priest. Hannan is a short Irishman with a bowling-ball belly restrained by a black cassock. He sports a red nose and a shock of yellowing white hair. The old parish has a bona fide Polish-immigrant background and Polish-American clergy have served families here for generations, but Hannan serves mostly as an administrator. While the congregation has divided in recent years to include more Hispanic families and non-Polish retirees, the pastor, Rev. Vitalis Wozniak, still offers a daily Mass in Polish.

Lyle knew both Hannan and Wozniak from a successful real estate deal he undertook on their behalf a few years ago. He called the monsignor today because they had worked closely together on that deal. And this was a touchy subject. Now, Hannan shifts uncomfortably in his seat.

"Mister Hall..." The man in the wheelchair is not the rich lawyer he knew.

"Lyle is fine, Monsignor."

"Lyle, we know each other professionally, rather than spiritually, and this is a highly unusual request. I take it you are not a Catholic?"

"Correct, but I was raised a Christian. Presbyterian." Lyle swallows.

"Lyle, Catholics are taught the common idea of 'ghosts' is wrong, superstitious. Angels and demons, yes. Saints, yes. Souls in heaven and purgatory. Damnation. But *ghosts* as some reflection of 'lost souls'—no. God doesn't work that way."

Shit, Lyle thinks. Catholics don't do ghosts. And the monsignor is the closest thing Lyle has to a priestly friend. Now he's sorry Hannan took his call. Embarrassed, Lyle grabs at a straw.

"What if the house is possessed? Can I get an exorcist?"

Hannan stares at Lyle. "I don't think you know what you're talking about."

"Neither do I."

Hannan bites back a grin. "Okay, give me some idea what's going on with you."

Lyle eyes an electrical outlet behind the Monsignor's chair. He unspools some of his power cord. "Monsignor, may I plug in?"

Hannan plugs Lyle in and he delves into his story, omitting the terrible premonition of Georgie's death.

Hannan takes it all in, his rheumy eyes fixed on his guest. Lyle meets Hannan's gaze but finds him difficult to read. Can he not read strong-willed people? Or is his empathy a passing phase? That would be a relief. As Lyle sums up, his iPhone thrums and he notes that a compressed file has arrived from one RLINDER.

Elbows on his desk, Hannan makes a steeple with pudgy fingers. "Let me see if I have this. You believe there is a spirit of some kind occupying an old house near your home. The house is to be torn down soon. You feel you're in communication with this entity and it wants the house to remain standing. So you want the Town to spare the house. In addition, you think the entity can perform miracles and cure your injured spine. So you want the entity to remain available in its accustomed…lifestyle."

"Well, something like that, Monsignor. Though it's not exactly a lifestyle."

"Lyle, the story doesn't hold together for me. You seem pleased to have an opportunity to champion a cause…but your experience is very likely a psychosomatic hallucination. And your motivation to help is linked to a belief it can make you...*walk?*"

Lyle leans toward Hannan. "This is confidential, right?" The priest nods solemnly and Lyle continues. "Seeing her makes you care. And I felt what I felt in my legs. And it's definitely a girl."

"It wants you to think it's a girl."

"It's doing a good job of that." Lyle opens Ray Linder's sketch of Jewel on his iPhone. His heart jumps; the finished rendering is stunning. He shows it to Hannan.

Taking in the iPhone display, the priest is surprised by an eerie chill. He looks up at Lyle. "You had this drawn from memory?"

"Yes, by an artist my daughter knows."

Hannan tries to hide his wonder. "I see. Well that's quite...quite a drawing."

"It's quite accurate. This is who I saw in the doorway."

Hannan looks at his appointment calendar. "Well I'm surprised this is what you wanted to discuss today, Lyle, but I don't know what I can do about it."

"Monsignor, I'm just very concerned for this...*girl* if her house comes down." He pauses. "Since seeing her, I've had nightmares that something bad happened there."

"Really. Demolition sounds pretty good to me, Lyle."

Lyle offers a deeper reason for coming to Hannan. "Okay. Well, once I experienced the leg spasms last night, I became worried that maybe she wanted to enter my body. So she'd have a place to stay."

Hannan winces. "Now you're way off, Lyle. You're saying this dead girl read the Town of Southampton's condemned sign and decided to possess your soul?"

Lyle hunches in a touché. "Monsignor, I've thought about this a lot, and I believe that, whatever she is, she exists. She needs some kind of help and the Town of Southampton will only hurt her. I've filed a motion to postpone the demolition but I don't know what else to do. I understand that, as a rule, you do not believe in what they call ghosts...but I don't know who to turn to now."

Pretty good rebuttal. Thirty years of practice paying off.

Hannan silently searches Lyle's tired eyes. Finally he says, "Lyle, you've been through some life-altering trials over the past year. And I hope you achieve some kind of spiritual growth and find peace." He blinks. "You know, we have a priest visiting here from Malta. Father Xerri." To Lyle the name sounds like *Sherry*. Hannan continues, "Matteo Xerri. He was here for the summer and is returning home soon." He looks at Lyle again. "He's a very spiritual man and he has some experience in...these matters."

Hannan makes a call and reaches the rectory cleaning lady. "There's someone here I'd like Father to meet." He hangs up and stares at Lyle for a moment, chewing his cud. Hannan's red nose moves slightly as he works his jaw.

"Lyle, you did a great service for this parish."

"It was my pleasure to help." It was also Lyle's pleasure to earn a healthy fee.

"We were able to completely redo the church. Otherwise, the place would still be sadly in need of renovation—the leaky roof, lack of bathrooms. This is Southampton but our congregation is not..."

"Understood."

Lyle had worked with Fraser Newton to sell a parcel of parish property, refinance the parish's debt and create a fund to rebuild Our Lady of Poland's dilapidated church. It's completely updated today; the clergy and the parishioners are proud of it.

"Lyle, I think Father Xerri may shed some light on your, uh, questions."

"What kind of 'experience in these matters' has he had? Is he an exorcist?"

Hannan furrows his brow. "We'll let Father Xerri address that personally."

There's a knock on Hannan's door and it opens. Slanting sunlight hits Lyle's eyes. A tall man in black hesitates in the doorway.

~~~~~~~

15. The Maltese Exorcist

"Father Xerri, come in and meet Lyle Hall. He's been very good to our parish."

Xerri steps toward Lyle and extends his hand. "Of course-eh. Lyle Hall-eh."

They shake, and Xerri seats himself as Hannan outlines his take on Lyle's experiences. Xerri listens with a studied expression as Lyle appraises this thin, dark-haired, surprisingly young priest. Lyle cannot read Xerri either—only a jumble of conflicts—so Lyle studies his olive facial features trying to place the ethnicity. Maltese is what—Italian? Sicilian? Egyptian? Greek? All of the above? Xerri's richly accented English presents a similar puzzle.

"So," Hannan wraps up, "Mister Hall feels strongly that there's something, uh, supernatural going on at this abandoned house. It's probably nothing." He unplugs Lyle's power cord. "Usually is nothing. But I thought you two could have a talk. Maybe go for coffee." Hannan shuffles some papers on his desk. "I have to get back to this."

Outside, Fred sees the two men approaching his MediCab and lowers the lift for Lyle.

"This is how you get around-eh?" Xerri asks.

"As long as I keep peeling off Jacksons," Lyle says. The lift raises him into the van and Xerri climbs in. He sits beside Lyle as Fred drives the seven blocks to the Blue Duck Bakery Cafe on Montauk. In the Village of Southampton, Montauk Highway briefly becomes a quaint stretch of shops the locals call "Hampton Road."

Pulled up in front of the cafe, Lyle peels off a twenty for Fred. Each twenty, on top of the rate the livery service charges Lyle's account, fosters goodwill and loyalty.

The Blue Duck's entry is easy, no steps. With no other customers now, there's room for Lyle's chair at a bistro table. Xerri takes a seat facing him and the waitress takes their coffee order, black for both. Xerri also orders an elaborately iced cupcake from the display case.

Gesturing at Lyle's chair, Xerri asks with sincere concern, "How long-eh?"

Lyle slaps the armrest of his new chair. "This baby is new. It's been a year since my car accident. But they're making great strides in spinal-injury research these days—especially regeneration through stem cells." Xerri's eyes narrow at the thought. "The specialists I see each week are very confident that I can benefit from new breakthroughs. I'm a candidate for a clinical trial."

Xerri seems absorbed in thought.

"Father?"

"Embryonic stem cells?"

"The best there is."

"Mister Hall-eh...I do not understand the meaning of 'peeling off Jacksons' or 'great strides' but I do understand the meaning of embryonic stem cells."

Uh-oh.

Xerri is blunt. "We believe the use of human embryos in such research is gravely immoral and unnecessary. Mister Hall-eh, you are not a Catholic?"

"Father, I'm a Christian, raised in a Presbyterian family. And please call me Lyle?" At least he can attempt to be informal—though he's growing increasingly anxious that he will never be on the same wavelength with this foreign priest.

"Okay. Lyle-eh. I hope you understand that Catholic bishops have studied this stem-cells controversy carefully. Their concern is human life—bioethics-eh. They are learned men and they are not socially or scientifically 'backward' as some people suggest. History is full of man's subjugation of the defenseless and we ask, Who is more defenseless than an unborn child?"

"Of course."

Lyle wonders why he's even going through the motions. The priest has more.

"Men of science-eh. Great thinkers of today. The more they uncover how nature works, how the world around us works, the more they think they've proven there is no God. It's ironic. In fact they're uncovering *how God works*. God invented science-eh."

The waitress comes to the rescue with their mugs of coffee and Xerri's cupcake, a chocolate thing that underscores this priest's youth. They take sips. Hot.

Lyle makes savory sounds. "Good, huh? I'm not supposed to have this," Lyle confides, "which makes it better."

Xerri takes in Lyle. "Yes-eh. I have passed this place, but did not understand it was a coffee shop." He blows across his cup. "So...Monsignor wants me to talk to you. About spirits of the dead."

"If you don't mind."

"And he informed you that the Church teaches that ghosts do not exist?"

"He did. He also mentioned that you have some experience with, uh, supernatural occurrences."

Xerri casts his eyes down into his coffee mug. "In a manner of speaking."

"But you don't believe in ghosts?"

"I believe in all things seen and unseen." He forks into his cupcake. Devil's food. "But not ghosts, per se."

Great, Lyle thinks. At least this is just a cup of coffee. Hannan has pawned him off on a young guy who does not believe in ghosts and thinks that stem-cell research involves killing babies. What else will they disagree on? He takes out his iPhone.

"Okay. Well this is what—I mean who—I saw. Late at night at an old house near where I live." Lyle clicks on the sketch of Jewel and places his iPhone in front of Xerri. "An artist drew her from my description. She calls herself Jewel."

The priest's features tighten with concern.

"Oh, my." Xerri studies the ghostly image. "That's an old girl-eh."

Lyle says, "Yes. She's an oxymoron."

Xerri surprises with a toothy smile. "You like the Greek language, Lyle-eh?"

Exploiting a break in the ice, Lyle says, "All seven words I know of it. Feta. Acropolis. Marathon. Mnemonic...uh, Olympics..."

Xerri gives a chuckle. "I had to study it. Most of the New Testament was written in Greek." He leans toward Lyle, confessing, "It is not easy."

Xerri refocuses on the sketch and sips more coffee. He grows serious. "A young girl wearing makeup. To look older than her age. A girl who's been through some serious trauma." He looks at Lyle. "How did you learn her name?"

"She told me, I heard a few words, kind of floating in the air."

"Interesting. She told you she's twelve years old? What else does she say?"

Lyle is encouraged by Xerri's questions. "I'm guessing at twelve. It sounds like she's whispering a secret in Italian." Lyle pauses.

Xerri lifts his gaze. "Lyle-eh, you speak Italian?"

"No, no...a friend translated what I heard as 'Help us.'"

Xerri meets Lyle's weary eyes. "*Aiutaci?*"

"Yes." Lyle decides to add, "I told Monsignor, I got intense sensations in my leg muscles. Then a stabbing in my abdomen, like a return of my crash injuries. My heart rate spiked. I thought it was a heart attack." He makes sure to leave Georgie out of this.

Xerri, deep in thought, seems to be far away.

Lyle continues, "I don't want to have a cardiac event and die in my chair. But I'm fascinated by this girl. I want to see her again."

Xerri's eyes return to Jewel's image. "I can see cause for fascination. But still..."

"She needs help. She makes me want to help her. I went to court today to stay the demolition of the house."

"Yes-eh. That could prolong this problem. If it is a problem..." Father Xerri pushes cupcake crumbs around his dish. "Lyle-eh, you're telling me a lot regarding this house and this girl." He gazes into Lyle's eyes. "But not everything."

A wave of nausea passes through Lyle and he looks away. The priest is right. Nothing about Georgie. Xerri waits for a response. Lyle signals for the check.

"Father," he finally says, "I wanted to ask you...the Monsignor said you were experienced in supernatural activity. Can you tell me about it?"

Xerri finishes his coffee. "Maybe at a later time." His eyes search Lyle's. "First I want to see this house-eh."

Lyle clicks to the photo he took of Old Vic with its glowing cupola.

"Here it is. She—Jewel—appeared on the porch. In the front doorway."

"No. I mean I want to go see with my own eyes-eh."

~~~~~~~

16. Taken for a Ride

Humberto Duvan's goatee is coming in nicely. Chantale was right; makes him look every bit the twenty-eight-year-old success he is today. Not the punk they once treated him like. Not the teenager who had to stand across from the Hampton Bays 7-11 hoping to get work as a day laborer. He was standing there one afternoon when the man known as "Sabado" pulled over in his black Escalade and rolled down a tinted window. His girls had singled out the handsome teen and urged Sabado to stop. Humberto ignored his uncle's objections and let Sabado take him for a ride. The hulking older man impressed the kid with his tricked-out Cadillac SUV, his fancy clothes and jewelry. And his two pretty teenage girls in the backseat in their short, sparkly dresses. Sabado offered Humberto drugs; he sniffed cocaine for the first time and smoked some strong marijuana. Then Sabado encouraged the boy to "have some fun," not with one, but both girls. It was a great idea.

The two young ladies giggled as they dragged Humberto over the front seat and back to them. His T-shirt was off immediately. Then more. Sabado parked the SUV in a secluded lot and watched them from the front seat. He smiled from behind his sunglasses and at one point, Humberto noticed, Sabado breathed heavily and grimaced at the ceiling. The teenage boy enjoyed it all very much. The girls were so pretty and carefree. He didn't want it to end. So much better than standing outside in all kinds of weather with his embarrassing uncle. That was publicly demeaning. Later, Sabado explained that this kind of life was possible for a young man like Humberto. Of course, he would have to "earn" these luxuries. And there could be more to come—nice clothing, good restaurants, independence from his family and, in time, even a fine car of his own. Maybe more.

In that first encounter, Sabado learned that his handsome new protégé was heterosexual. But Sabado thought both qualities could be adjusted.

Years passed and Humberto did perform many services for the Colombian man who named himself after the last day of the week. Services for Sabado's friends and clients, too; men and women alike. He did a lot of driving for Sabado; dropping off a package here, a girl there, always returning with a fat envelope. Humberto learned how Sabado made his money—cash only. "Sell the product, rent the girl." There were more mundane concerns, of course, like maintaining a front. His sham livery service delivered maids and nannies to the summer homes of city people; transported their kids to tennis and sailing lessons; brought drunk people home from bars. Sabado disdained the livery business and its meager profits, but it made his illicit enterprise possible.

Humberto learned it all, and well. He also learned how some men, maybe five or six men, who had worked for Sabado for years, resented Humberto Duvan. They snickered behind his back. Called him "Hump Berto" —a pretty boy who enjoyed the boss's generosity because the boss enjoyed him. And used him. In their eyes, Humberto was less than a man, much less.

As Humberto grew into his twenties, he developed a yearning for a sexy woman a few years older. Chantale, tall and sophisticated, was one of Sabado's big "moneymakers." Originally from Haiti, Chantale had smooth cocoa skin and intelligent almond eyes set off by a wild coppery hairdo that seemed to go everywhere at once. Chantale was well aware of Humberto. But what if she believed the lies those men whispered? What could he do? Shoot them? Give them all beatings?

About three years ago, Humberto settled on a solution. It was bold but made sense. He was proud he'd even thought of it. He didn't need to administer beatings or arrange messy killings. No, the solution was to deal with only one man. Once he was gone, the other men would understand. And they would leave. Chantale would become his lady officially. He'd give himself a big promotion. And a new name: Berto.

It's been three years since Berto learned how effective a simple knife can be. One night back then, parked in the Escalade, Sabado threatened Humberto with his knife. They had a disagreement; Humberto had gotten uppity and refused to perform for his boss. Sabado, drunk and high, tried to teach him a lesson; teach him respect. The blade grazed Humberto's chin, leaving a scar like Harrison Ford's. Humberto pretended at the time to be sorry for "making" Sabado cut his face. But that was the night the young man made his decision. Sabado's golden blade was beautiful, actually. And, Humberto learned it folded effortlessly into its mother-of-pearl handle.

It was Berto's knife now. And his goatee covers the scar nicely.

This evening Berto uses the knife to clean some white gunk from under a fingernail as he peers out the window of his livery cab office. Darkness gathers as he studies the car parked across the street. How strange, Berto thinks, that the police send a white car on a stake-out every night. Do they think he's *estúpido*? And a blond woman at the wheel. A *punta*. Is that an insult to his manhood?

Berto has a pair of binoculars. Squinting into them, he can make out her face in the soft glow of her iPad. Damn. She's good looking as well as blond. He'll have to think about this problem. His employees will start to talk.

~~~~~~

17. The Devil's Workshop

Another twenty in his shirt pocket, Fred pulls his MediCab up in front of 111 Poplar. Lyle is lowered to the pavement as Matteo Xerri exits the van peering up at the forbidding structure. Riveted by the decrepit place, his eyes are drawn up to the vacant cupola. Neither man speaks. Xerri sees the high pine branch rake the Mansard roof. Lyle feels a wave of sadness ripple through him. And something like a silent challenge.

It's late afternoon and shadows close in on the property. The sun's warmth has evaporated, leaving the weedy yard cold. The yellow police tape and new CONDEMNED signs clash with the building's sullen darkness. A new telephone book in its plastic wrapper lies incongruously on the front walk. Something black wings out from the porch, veering away from the hulking front-loader parked nearby.

Lyle Hall's senses open up. Can he feel anything out of the ordinary? Anything at all—maybe some tingles? No. Just another conflicting jumble of impressions.

"I want to go inside-eh," Fr. Xerri says quietly.

What a weird thing for a priest to say. "Seriously? Break into the house?"

Xerri smiles. "Who would be the victim? The Town of Southampton?"

"You could get hurt, or in trouble."

"I am a Maltese citizen. I will get my standby flight back to Rome any time now. Will they extradite me for trespass-eh?"

"Well I'm not going in. Look at the place! And what would you do in there?"

"Experience it. Perhaps learn."

Xerri impulsively moves off around the side of the house alone. Lyle is surprised by the young priest's impetuousness. *How old is this guy? Thirty, if that.*

"Hey! Father!"

66

Xerri is already behind the old house. Lyle throws his chair into gear, waves to Fred, still at the wheel, and rolls after Xerri. Then he hears a loud crash.

Bumping through the weedy debris field that surrounds Old Vic—glass shards, cans, shingles, fossilized plastic toys, a rusted bicycle wheel—Lyle maneuvers around the silent front-loader and finally reaches the back of the house.

"Father Xerri?"

Turning to face the rear wall, he sees it. Matteo Xerri has somehow taken down the old kitchen door. It now lies over the two back steps, serving as a makeshift ramp up into the kitchen. He grins at Lyle.

"Holy *shit*...I mean nice work, Father."

"Thank you. I studied carpentry long ago-eh."

"You're not old enough to have a long ago."

Xerri smiles. "Lyle-eh, can you make a light with your mobile phone?"

Lyle ignites the flashlight app and Xerri positions himself behind the wheelchair. He steers Lyle's chair firmly up the improvised ramp to the threshold of the murky kitchen. Lyle illumines the interior. It's not good.

"No. No, I don't like this, Father..."

"In we go-eh!" Xerri humps Lyle's chair through the doorway.

"Omigod!" Lyle clutches his chest, applies the brakes and waits for the attack.

Nothing. Yet.

"Shit!" Lyle grumbles, again forgetting who he's with.

"Are you okay, Lyle-eh?"

"Yeah. I guess." If he's going in, going with a priest should be his safest bet. He shines his phone around the kitchen. A dingy old sink from hell. A four-foot-high cylindrical icebox, door broken off, contains a big petrified dog shit. The ancient stove's doors are gone. Rat shit all over the floor. It stinks in here.

It gets worse. Lyle's light hits it and he freezes. Big spider.

Very big. It flinches in the beam of light, but stays put in a corner of its extensive web. The phone light shows the web, studded with mummified bugs, stretches across the kitchen at a height of about five feet. The spider's segmented legs, long as a man's fingers, bristle. Its gray, pulsating ass is the size of a peach.

"Oh shit," Lyle trembles. "I can't stand spiders! I hate 'em. *Hate* 'em!"

"I understand, Lyle-eh, but we are here for something else." Xerri swats at a corner of the web and it recedes, giving them enough space to pass underneath. The spider backs into a shadowy corner and fidgets as the men pass. As they exit the kitchen, Lyle's phone light shows it's guarding a big egg sac.

Outside, the sun has sunk behind a neighboring house, bathing Old Vic in dismal shadows. Only the cupola is touched by a lingering ray of sunset. As Fred sits in his MediCab working his handheld, an aging Saturn two-door turns the corner and stops at the curb. Its engine shuts off.

Old Vic's boarded-up windows keep the interior in perpetual gloom. The faint daylight that filters through cracks is gone. Lyle's iPhone the only source of light, he and Xerri enter a spacious parlor area. There is no furniture save some plastic milk crates. Stone gargoyles support the mantle over the big walk-in fireplace. Trash has been burned there for years. Beer cans are everywhere. More rat shit. The dry air is beyond musty, barely breathable. Like trying to inhale a spider web or snort a mummy. Lyle plays his light across the walls. The window frames are huge—the parlor ceiling is 14 feet high. A few of the fine Victorian window moldings are intact. Most became kindling. The old wallpaper peeled away decades ago and vandals have spray-painted the room into a palace of vile curses, profanity and satanic bullshit. Lyle is embarrassed for Xerri.

"This place is unclean-eh," Xerri whispers, more to himself.

"Filthy," says Lyle.

The priest bends to him. "Lyle-eh, are you feeling...any sensations?"

Lyle takes stock. "Actually, no. I'm struggling to breathe and dying to get out of here, but I don't feel anything, or anyone, like last night."

"I see." Xerri borrows Lyle's light and plays it around the walls some more, pausing on some repulsive graffiti accompanying a crude spray-painted cartoon depicting sexual deviance.

"Disgusting," says Lyle.

"But it's all English-eh. I see no use of a foreign or ancient language. This is the work of teenagers with too much time and idle hands...the Devil's workshop."

Xerri shines the light on his own face, projecting a Nosferatu shadow up to the cracked ceiling. He nods at the rotted staircase. "Lyle-eh, I feel a need to look upstairs."

"Okay. But you're on your own."

Xerri bends to Lyle's level. "I would need to borrow your light."

Lyle thinks about this. Except for a faint orange glow from upstairs, the parlor is nearly pitch black. The iPhone shines on Xerri's imploring expression.

"If you please-eh?"

"Father, I don't want to be alone in this place in the dark in a wheelchair."

"Of course-eh. I understand." Xerri hands Lyle his phone and stands up.

Lyle lights up the young priest's face. He has a change of heart.

"This could be our only chance to explore in here," he says, handing back the lighted phone. "Just *please* come right back!"

"I will, I assure you." Xerri shudders as an ancient groan sounds from the cupola.

Lyle, positioned in the center of the parlor, watches Xerri feel his way up the creaky stairs. Its banister became firewood long ago. The priest stops to swat at some invisible thing. He disappears at the head of the stairs and the light fades to a glimmer. Xerri's feet scuffle above, crossing the ceiling. Darkness seals the parlor. The pine scrapes the Mansard roof. Another deep groan radiates down through the house.

~~~~~~

Lyle is alone in the dark. Gripping his armrests, he tries to will Jewel to appear. She owes him an explanation—*Georgie* on her mom's headstone? And what about his legs? But there's no Jewel.

Instead, tingly things lower themselves down the back of his neck. He immediately starts swatting and scratching himself. *Shit!* The sensation makes his flesh crawl. Is it the creepy spawn of that big mother spider making a home inside a helpless guy's shirt? He scratches more as tingles radiate down his spine. The tingles spread around front to his chest and ribcage. Finally Lyle screams out to the ceiling.

"Hey, Xerri! Oh *shit!* Get me outta here!!" Probably not how to address a priest.

Now the tingles under his shirt morph into what feels like larvae burrowing aggressively into the pores of his skin. Cursing helps. This is Xerri's fault. He scratches blindly at the imagined worms. What the fuck do they want, blood? They're multiplying now, and boring deep under his skin, into muscle, where scratching won't help. What the fuck? Can't Xerri hear him up there? He thinks the worms are interconnecting—a network of squirming invaders. He screams *Matteo Xerri!* once more. Can he sue this priest? What's his problem? And then...

They *burn!* The damn tiny things light up like fire under Lyle's skin.

"Shit!! Yo! Xerri!" He scratches harder still to no avail. Whatever they are, they're spreading everywhere—even up to his face! He can't scratch fast enough. Are they visible? It's so dark. Are tiny little demons boiling him? Where's Jewel? Why won't she help? Where the hell is Xerri? What the fuck is he doing upstairs?

Scream! Get him down here! But shit, there's no oxygen. His throat's so dry, he can only produce a dry cough. Try to get the chair in gear. Roll out of this godforsaken place. That kitchen is a big problem. No light. Obstacles. Spider web. Lyle hates spiders.

The itches under his skin burn now like spreading acid, up to his face too. What will he be if he survives this? Imagine sitting in a steaming bath and watching baby worms squirm out of your pores, parboiling. But how can you survive if you cannot breathe? Cry out for that damn priest! Gasp for oxygen. But Lyle only gags on dust. The ugly walls pulsate.

He claws at his clothes. They feel unclean and moist. Is it blood? Pull off the sweater, it's too hot. Scratch more. Scratch everything, beard and face. Ears too. Neck. Eyes. Oh shit! If I die, Lyle realizes, there'll be no one to save my daughter! This *is Hell!*

~~~~~~

Fr. Xerri does not hear Lyle. The priest is entranced as he steps carefully down the second-floor hallway, lighting a succession of murky doorways opening on small rooms. All the doors were busted in long ago. Then his light hits one door that's intact. And closed. Xerri approaches it. There's no doorknob. He pushes the door and it creaks open. He must step in. He's been invited.

The flooring is soft underfoot so Xerri trains the light at his feet. The room exudes a cold malevolence. He can see his breath. He tries to get solid footing as a palpable dread floods his heart. Suddenly something he cannot see brushes his pants leg. Plaintive voices rise around him. Women. Swirling words. The language is garbled but familiar. Italian, but antiquated. Something about a pregnancy. And captivity. And despair beyond sadness. He shines Lyle's phone-light. The little room is full of arms! Thin, naked arms grasp for him like refugees seeking asylum. Like this priest is their last hope. But Xerri's light dims, it will not reveal faces, only swaying hanks of black hair and many flailing arms trying to draw him in. Strange, desperate voices coil around him, pleading.

71

Xerri instinctively utters a blessing in Italian. He blinks as the room goes quiet. Shadows surround him, and then transform somehow into faint globes of ethereal light. Orbs. Maybe a dozen. The orbs rise gracefully above the priest and flow into the hallway, then up the rickety stairs to the cupola. Dumbstruck, Xerri wants to follow. But there's a chilling scream from downstairs. He takes one step and the old floor gives way.

Down in the parlor, Lyle, scratching wildly and half blind, peers up as a creaking sound above is followed by a sharp CRASH. *What the fuck?*

A human leg, bare except for a black shoe, dangles down from the ceiling. A faint glow surrounds it. Clouds of caustic gray powder shower down into Lyle's eyes, nose, hair and beard, making breathing impossible. What does this mean? Is this, he wonders, how we die? Hallucinating, choking, scratching as thousands of little fire-worms gnaw you to death?

It is. The walls close in. They soften and turn a dark red. Hugging him, suffocating him, holding his burning pain close and deep so it cannot dissipate. Now strange moans well up from the floor. They are like the miserable voices he heard when his vision of Jewel abruptly vanished. And then a putrid stench envelops Lyle. It's like his impure soul is being drained out and exchanged … for something pure. Pure evil.

There's more noise upstairs, but Lyle Hall can no longer hear.

Xerri painfully extracts his leg from between the floor joists and more plaster dust showers down to the parlor. His misstep could have been much worse. But it jolted him back to the here and now. He hobbles to the head of the stairs and carefully starts down. He pauses at the landing and shines the feeble light on the man in the wheelchair.

"Lyle-eh?" Xerri stumbles. He chokes on his words. "Mother of GOD!"

~~~~~~~

18. Threshold

Lyle Hall does not react as Xerri half-stumbles down the stairs. He's somewhere else. Where hungry things writhe under your skin and burn you alive till you lose your will. Where your lungs need no air. Your heart need not pump. The threshold of Hell.

Lyle looks nothing like the man Xerri left moments ago. Head cocked upward, mouth agape, eyes unblinking, he appears catatonic. Or dead. Lyle's scratched up face is turning blue. His hair and beard are like a wild man's, powdered with plaster dust. Beads of dirty sweat pimple his brow. His ripped-open shirt reveals angry red marks across his chest. Lyle's hands are twitching feebly, pilling, picking at his sweater. It's like a stricken friend Xerri once visited back in Malta. Good God, all this is his fault!

The priest places Lyle's iPhone on the sweater on his lap so it lights his face. Then he slaps Lyle's face. Hard. His beard emits a puff of plaster dust. Then Xerri puts his mouth on Lyle's whiskery, spittle-covered mouth and blows. Xerri raises his head, cries, "Oh God, please! Please, no!" and draws in a lungful of dusty air. His mouth goes to Lyle's again. There's dried sputum on the unconscious man's lips. Force the dirty air into his lungs. Make the man breathe. Frustrated, Xerri slaps the other side of Lyle's face.

Suddenly, Xerri's got his attention. Lyle's eyes narrow to two red slits and focus on the priest. A guttural, accusing voice erupts, not from his mouth, from his throat.

"What the fuck are you doing here?"

"I'm...saving you, Lyle-eh!"

The man in the wheelchair laughs scornfully through gritted teeth. But he does not inhale the shitty air. He glares at Fr. Xerri with unbridled hatred.

"Fuck you, priest!"

"Lyle-eh! I am so sorry! I'll get you outside!"

Then Xerri starts to get it. The deep, horrid voice rises again—it's not Lyle Hall's. What he hears next could not be more terrifying. The rasping, hateful voice taunts the priest from Gozo, Malta...once a good boy. Once a very bad one.

"Γνωρίζουμε. Σας προκάλεσε μητέρα σας να πεθάνουν."

Xerri recoils. His jaw drops and his stomach churns with revulsion. *Greek.* He stares at the broken man before him. Close to death. Lyle Hall only knows a few Greek words. And he could not know Teo's appalling secret. Nausea rises in him.

Those who did know are dead.

Now Lyle's eyes close, and he slumps forward. Xerri feels some relief—whatever took hold of this man may have departed, for now. First thing is get him out of here, then call for emergency help. Xerri props Lyle up and feels for a heartbeat. He recalls his CPR course...that's not a heartbeat; that fluttering is atrial fibrillation.

Xerri steadies himself behind the wheelchair and starts to steer with one hand, trying to keep Lyle upright with the other. Back to that horrid kitchen with the huge spider web—where the fat spider waits. Xerri's best chance is to get this man out in the air, perform CPR on him, call 911. He rolls the chair forward. He's been very foolish. He never should have attempted this stunt. Something seduced him into coming here.

Back in the kitchen, Lyle's iPhone, still on his lap, lights the ceiling at odd angles. The blanketing web, Xerri can see, is already repaired. It stretches everywhere at chin level. Xerri tries to hurry under it. Disgusting strands of spider web trail across his eyes and mouth; some adhere to Lyle's face and beard. Suddenly the phone light hits the big spider above. Bigger than it looked earlier, it's on the move, casting weird angular shadows. The web tenses as the spider creeps toward them, all hairy elbows and fat spider ass. Xerri imagines its twitching jaws tipped with poisonous fangs. He hates spiders, too. He propels Lyle to the open doorway but the chair halts abruptly when it meets the edge of the old kitchen door now serving as a ramp. The iPhone flies off Lyle's lap and skitters down the ramp/door. Now it's dark.

Where is that damn spider? His injured leg throbbing, Xerri works quickly to coax the chair's front wheels onto the ramp.

They won't roll. The spider must be directly overhead by now.

The priest looks around desperately for an answer in the darkness. Is that horrid spider about to spring on him? Then he notices Lyle's twitching hand. His hand threw the chair into park. The chair, he remembers, is electric.

The priest toggles the chair into forward as a gust of fresh air blows in the open doorway. He imagines the spider leaping onto the back of his neck as he works the chair, heavy with Lyle Hall, onto the makeshift ramp and out into the night air. The sun down, it has quickly grown dark and cold.

Xerri applies the chair's brakes, but as the front wheels meet level ground, Lyle is ejected, face down, onto the backyard turf. Xerri, suddenly exhausted, pushes the chair away and devotes the last of his strength to rolling Lyle onto his back. Dead weight. The iPhone lost, he kneels over Lyle and inhales a lungful of night air.

With a silent, desperate prayer, Xerri performs CPR on Lyle's unresponsive body. A gust of fresh air into the man's lungs. Pushing down forcefully on his solar plexus. Again. Again. Now more air. As he works he becomes aware of strange flashes of light. Not the iPhone. What? Lightning?

Another flash stuns the priest.

"You guys all right?"

Startled, Xerri squints up at the dark outline of a portly man. He can make out a rumpled suit. And a camera.

"Are you guys all right?" the man repeats, louder.

"Moses, you FUCKING PIECE OF SHIT!"

Father Xerri gasps and looks down at his patient. It's some kind of miracle. He's cursing out a prominent Old Testament figure, but he's alive.

"Lyle-eh!"

The portly man distracts Xerri by extending his hand. "My card. Mose Allen, *Southampton Press*. I'm covering the Lyle

Hall haunting story. Are you Matteo Sherry? What did you find inside? Anything?"

Xerri can't find the words. The patient lying before him can.

"Mose Allen, you FUCKWAD! Get the fuck away from us, you two-bit pile of pig shit!" Lyle is now supporting himself on one elbow.

"Mister Hall, are you in your right mind?" Mose Allen asks coolly. He snaps photos just as Lyle flies into a wild rage, looking his absolute worst.

"You FUCKER! I know your game! I'll shove that camera up your fat ass!"

Mose snaps two more. "Gentlemen, I'll wish you a pleasant evening."

Xerri helps Lyle up to a sitting position and the two men watch the reporter waddle into the darkness between the old barn and the front-loader in the driveway. Xerri looks at Lyle in disbelief. He's gasping and coughing. And cursing.

"Go fuck yourself!" Lyle shouts after Mose, for clarity.

"Lyle-eh! Please, are you all right?"

Lyle draws a breath of cool air. "Sorry, Father. I dislike that man."

"I see that. I'm just glad you're all right! Lyle-eh, what do you need right now?"

Lyle looks at the priest and catches a breath. "Scotch."

Something is buzzing in the weeds. Lyle's phone. Xerri retrieves it for him. It's Georgie. Her name conjures pangs deep in Lyle's gut. Not now. Later.

~~~~~~

19. On Duty

Hampton Bays. Once a working-class enclave and home to service providers and the bay men who catch the area's fresh seafood, the old town seems to be diverging in two directions these days—gentrified or downhill. Detective Georgie Hall's unmarked Imperial is parked on Squiretown Road, a quarter-mile up from the railroad station. Her car is white, not black. It's after sundown, and after placing a futile call to her father, she looks across the road at a dilapidated taxi-and-limo operation. Tonight, like all week, she'll monitor comings and goings at this shady livery service.

Stories abound regarding some new boss man using the taxi company's cars to deliver prostitutes and drugs to summer people and, as a front, working-class locals to their jobs. Chief Queeley had gotten heat from above about the situation and, with summer over, now was a good time to stake out the suspected hub of iniquity—and put his new detective on a potentially real case.

Georgie's parking spot affords a good view of the office and its attached garage bays. People arrive in the back of the structure where there's a rutted parking area. And some leave, using a past-its-prime limo, from a garage bay. Such missions sometimes require two men.

Tonight a garage bay opens and a limo roars to life. It emerges slowly and pulls up alongside Georgie. Not too smart— she gets a make on the driver, with his shaved head, and the passenger, with his '50s pompadour. The two men sneer at her and then speed off toward Montauk Highway. Georgie taps into her iPad using the men's code names—"Mister Clean" and "Trini Lopez"—noting their departure time, direction and a partial license plate. She omits that the passenger was making an obscene gesture for her to see. She doesn't want to come off as overly sensitive.

Georgie is reaching for her coffee thermos when her cell phone moans.

"Hall speaking."

"Detective Hall, Sergeant Barsotti."

"I know. What's up."

"Are you at the observation point, Detective?"

"Parked and unmarked. What's up?"

"It's your father, Detective. Thought you'd want to know."

"My father? Know *what*, Frank?"

"Do you have Internet access?"

"Yeah. What's going on?"

"Well, Sergeant Swanson here at the station house, checking out the "Police Blotter" stuff the *Southampton Press* has online, found a story about Lyle Hall."

"Okay. What's it about?"

"He went to court today to stop the town from demolishing an old house near his neighborhood."

"Okay. His attitude has seemed a little odd recently, but I thought he was making some progress, getting out of the house and all. He was actually in court today?"

"This morning. The unusual part, what people are talking about, is he says he wants to save this old house because it's…haunted."

Silence.

"Excuse me? My father is fighting to save a haunted house?"

"Can you get online?"

"I'm there now."

"Detective, uh, there's something else."

"Like what?"

"Somebody here screwed around with your locker."

"You mean broke into my locker?"

"They didn't break open the locker. I hate to be the one to tell you, Detective, but your locker door has a…a balloon stuck on it. It's made to look like a ghost."

"You're kidding me. I'm trying to do professional work here and we have Animal House behavior in the locker room for Halloween?"

"Didn't want it to be a surprise."

Sergeant Barsotti disconnects with Detective Hall. "Big Frank" approaches Georgie Hall's locker and its prank display. The few women on the force have their own row of lockers but no real privacy. No one is nearby right now, though some cop is in the only shower making echo-y "ghost" noises. *Boooooo! Booooooooooo!* reverberates comically off the tile walls. Using his cell phone, Frank snaps a few pictures of the ghost balloon taped onto her locker door. Without touching it, Frank closely examines the balloon. It's small. It has eyes and a mouth drawn with a black Sharpie and crudely resembling the ghoul in *Scream* movies. The balloon itself is a sickly off-white in color.

It's a condom.

Back in her unmarked Crown Vic, Georgie's attention is drawn away from the livery depot as she cursors to "Court News" on the *Southampton Press* site. There's an article datelined this afternoon from Justice Court. Its byline makes Georgie recall a pudgy middle-aged reporter she's seen in court occasionally. Then her heart jumps.

His story is about her father. It's not good. There are photos. They are not good.

Across the road, the limo office is dark. But a shadow moves in the window. Once again binoculars examine Georgie's face, lit by the iPad she's intently studying. A long lock of blond hair slips down from her left ear and she tucks it back in place with her index finger. Hair out of the way, her pretty blue eyes can be seen. And her dark eyebrows, furrowed with concentration.

~~~~~~

20. The Princess Diner

Fred helped Xerri heave Lyle into his chair and then drove them to the Princess Diner in Southampton. Lyle, ornery and disheveled, insisted that was where he wanted to go. Upon delivery, a fresh twenty joined the others in Fred's shirt pocket and he went off duty. Father Xerri arranged to borrow Father Wozniak's car later to get Lyle home.

Right now Lyle is in the men's room hovering over the handicap-accessible sink which is full of sudsy water. He tries to deal with the plaster dust in his matted hair, vestigial strands of spider web, red scratches on his cheeks and around his eyes—it's no way to appear in public in Southampton, even at a diner. But the Princess does have a little bar.

The diner's practically empty. Seated at a booth bathed in fluorescent light, the young priest examines his paper placemat with its Acropolis design. He's transcribed Lyle's Greek-sounding utterance onto it. He needs to make sure of what he heard.

Γνωρίζουμε. Σας προκάλεσε μητέρα σας να πεθάνουν.

Two short statements. Xerri sounds the first Greek phrase under his breath.   *"Γνωρίζουμε."*

Then he whispers it in English: "*We know.*"

It's disturbing; including the use of "we." Xerri whispers the second phrase, the one that really made his heart skip an hour ago in that hellish house.

"Σας προκάλεσε μητέρα σας να πεθάνουν."

Simple words can be so devastating. He sighs deeply, his heart sinking. He folds the placemat. What has this Lyle started? He exhales the words in English.

"*You caused your mother to die.*"

"Hungry, Father?"

He's back from the men's room. The crippled man who opened Pandora's Box.

Lyle Hall does not register the priest's distress. Xerri composes himself and looks at this strange retired lawyer. He's cleaned up and got his navy sweater on. He's still unkempt, but the diner is nearly deserted and he's unlikely to be recognized. Lyle's mood has brightened. Since blacking out in Old Vic's parlor, he remembers only little bits prior to landing in the backyard where Mose Allen was waiting to snap pictures.

Both men crave food after their experience in the haunted whorehouse, and they order without menus. Lyle orders the burger platter and, upon hearing that, Teo changes his Greek salad to a burger and the waitress marches off.

"So, Father..." says Lyle. "What happened?"

Xerri tries to address the recent events from a professional viewpoint. "So, when you lost consciousness inside the house, you said certain things to me. In Greek. I heard it clearly. But you do not speak Greek, Lyle-eh?"

"No way. Just the seven words...Olympics...feta..."

"And, though it came from you, it was not your voice-eh."

"Then who in hell's voice was it?"

Xerri pauses. Peering into Lyle's tired eyes, he says, "Precisely."

This gives Lyle a cold chill. "So what did I say? In English..."

The priest looks away. "I can tell you this. It was talking to *me-eh*."

"*It?*" The chill creeps down his back and stops at his waist.

"Lyle-eh, did this episode feel different—compared to first seeing Jewel?"

The busboy sets down two ice waters and a small tray of disturbing gray pickles. Xerri spears an olive and pops it in his mouth.

"This was like a near-death experience. Excruciating pain—like a million fire ants were eating me alive. I was crying out, but couldn't breathe or make a sound..."

A black cloud seems to settle over Lyle as he relives the trauma, but then the waitress arrives with his coffee. Her badge reads BETH.

"Beth? Can I have a Dewar's? A double? Two cubes?" Lyle nods to Father Xerri but the priest indicates satisfaction with his water. Beth regards the odd couple for a second, then says, "Sure, Hon," and bustles away.

"You're not allowed coffee, Lyle-eh—but you are allowed alcohol?"

"Not with my meds." Lyle lifts his cup. "But then, I'm not taking my meds."

Xerri rolls his eyes. "Two wrongs. Or *three-eh*."

The busboy returns with two sizzling burger platters laden with crisp fries.

"This makes four," Lyle says.

As they set to work on their meals, Lyle can see the waitress speaking with the cashier/bartender guy in the black vest at the little bar near the register. They both glance at Lyle and turn away. The guy splashes Dewar's into a rocks glass.

Beth brings the drink and quickly departs.

Lyle holds up the squat glass of golden liquid. "Moderation in all things."

Xerri forms a faint smile. "You do appreciate Ancient Greek culture."

Lyle takes a gulp and closes his eyes. The elixir warms his throat and radiates through his chest. It's been a year. The alcohol hits Lyle's brain right away. This is why they invented scotch. This is why he drank. Lyle flashes on how some in the restaurant trade called him a "happy drunk." Non-confrontational. Generous tipper. Humorous. Bought rounds, even for strangers. Especially pretty ones. Would offer rides. Only thing was, he drank a lot and drove fast.

Xerri yearns to inquire about the deeply disturbing things Lyle said to him in the parlor. But not now—his eyes aren't even open.

"Are you okay, Lyle-eh?"

Lyle blinks. He meets Xerri's gaze.

"I am now."

The priest nods and cuts his burger in half. Juicy red meat, done perfectly.

The two men are quiet until they're halfway through their platters. It's after seven p.m. Lyle drains his rocks glass and holds it up, signaling to Beth.

"So Father, if you don't want to share whatever I said in Greek, want to at least tell me what you think was going on back there?"

Food has Xerri in a better mood to talk. "Well, I have a mixture of facts and impressions. Firstly, that you, Lyle Hall-eh, are a very sensitive man."

Lyle responds through a mouthful of burger. "From the waist up."

"And I'm not the only one who knows this. Second, that house is unclean. I am convinced that place was a house of prostitution at one time; that the rumor is true. I believe the parlor, where you waited..."

"Alone in the dark. In a wheelchair. Choking and possibly dying."

"But saved by a resourceful priest-eh. I believe the parlor served as a lobby where women were paired with the, uh, clientele-eh. Where transactions were made. The sexual acts, and worse, took place in the rooms upstairs. There are many rooms up there." He pauses, unsure how much he should share. "In one room I sensed the presence of captives. Women. Desperate, hopeless women."

Xerri has Lyle's full attention. Lyle wonders if these women might be the whisperers. Xerri looks into Lyle's bleary eyes. "And there's something very wrong at the top of the stairs. That...lookout."

"You went up into the cupola?"

"No, I only looked up the stairs. But I could feel evil. Still present. You know, if you burn your tongue with coffee, how your tongue reminds you, even the next day? I think acts of evil leave something behind that, uh, lasts."

"Father, did I dream it, or did your leg punch through the ceiling?" It feels weird for Lyle to call a guy Georgie's age *Father*; especially asking him such a question.

"It did. Hurrying back to you, as promised, I stepped on a weak spot in the floor." At this Lyle suppresses a grin. "And thank you for your concern-eh."

Beth drops off a fresh Dewar's. Lyle swigs some as she departs.

"Okay, prostitution. I think we knew that. But when you say 'something very wrong' in that house, you mean something worse than common prostitution?"

He does. Xerri's shoulders slump as he sinks into a dark place. His eyes lower to his plate and he toys with a French fry. "Women were subjugated there. For years-eh. Children too, I think." He looks up at Lyle. "Some never left."

"Never left?"

"Alive-eh."

Lyle winces at this. He downs more Dewar's. "Can we talk about me now?"

Xerri lightens just a little. "Yes-eh. Your experience may be linked in some way to all this. You told me you've been experiencing empathetic sensations. But your own reactions could merely be psychosomatic, given your surroundings."

"Then how was I speaking Greek? I only know a few words." Lyle indicates Xerri's folded placemat. "And not those words."

Xerri studies Lyle's eyes. The old boy is half tipsy now, *sakra* as they say in Malta. The priest unfolds the placemat and shows it to Lyle.

"You could see these words? Do you know what they say-eh?"

"No idea, Father. I just know that you wrote them down. I want you to tell me."

But Xerri can't. "Lyle-eh, who was that photographer you cursed?"

"Shitty local reporter. The fat loser has nothing better to do than write about me."

"What did he write about you?"

"Dunno, but it can't be good."

Xerri thinks for a moment, then leans in. "Lyle-eh, I am curious about the relationship between you and that old house. Why it seems to communicate to you...and why now?"

Lyle studies his drink. "Because I'm a real-estate lawyer?" He looks up. "What I want to know is, where's my little friend, Jewel?"

"Lyle-eh, the girl only you can see may not exist."

"Choking to death existed an hour ago."

"I was glad to be able to come to your aid."

Lyle looks at the young priest. "Oh. Right. Thank you, Father, sincerely, for getting me out of that house. Was that CPR you were performing?"

"Yes-eh. I learned it long ago in Malta. Thank God. You stopped breathing. Your heartbeat was fluttering. It's a miracle. You should be in the emergency room right now..." he nods at the food and drink in front of Lyle, "...instead of ingesting these things."

Lyle pops a fry into his mouth. It's still warm. He takes a swig. "You know, Father, after today, this is just what the doctor ordered."

"Really? Your doctor?"

"American idiom." The dark cloud returns to his demeanor. "Seriously, Father, thank you for taking care of me. You see..." he tries to find the words "...I can't die."

Xerri knits his brow. "Teenagers think that way, Lyle-eh."

"No, no, I mean I mustn't die. Before I fix something. Something important."

Lyle needs to change the subject. "Father, your history with the, uh, supernatural..."

Xerri looks down. "Oh. That's hard to describe." He pauses. "But I feel badly that I brought you into such an unclean place. I should tell you some...*things-eh*."

Lyle sips scotch and peers at Xerri.

"Lyle-eh, Malta is an ancient place. An ancient civilization." Xerri gazes off somewhere else. "You know, even today it is still possible for a person—or a child—to be...*occupied* by an unclean spirit." He looks at Lyle. "A demon."

"Possessed?"

"It happened in Biblical times. Why would it stop today? The Underworld has no calendar. It wants our souls. I heard you tonight curse me and speak in Greek. An ancient language. I believe that was not you, Lyle-eh." Xerri grins a little. "But that was definitely you cursing the man with the camera. Like you were reborn."

Lyle grins too. "Yeah—*I'm ba-ack.*" This is lost on the priest. "Well, Father, I think the possessed characters in the Bible had epileptic seizures or something. Or palsy. Or maybe Tourette syndrome."

Lyle examines Xerri's eyes. They're incredibly black and seem endlessly deep. Lyle takes in the priest's youthful good looks, his healthy head of black hair. Why didn't he marry? Xerri's striking features remind Lyle of Egyptian funerary paintings he'd seen once at the Metropolitan Museum of Art. In ancient times well-to-do Egyptians, even youthful ones, had their likenesses painted on the outside of their sarcophagi. Probably best not to mention that he looks like a mummy.

"Lyle-eh," Xerri finally says. "I have suffered like that. From epilepsy. But some people, my father, and some priests I know, believe the worst. That it was demonic possession."

Silence. *Holy shit*, Lyle almost says aloud, *this priest was once possessed?* He shivers and slugs his scotch, feeling repulsed, frightened and fascinated at once.

"You weren't an exorcist? You had an exorcism *performed* on you?"

Father Xerri nods solemnly. "Twice-eh."

<center>~~~~~~~~</center>

21. The Slow Season

Berto Duvan stood in his darkened office and watched his two lieutenants, Mundo and Ruben, roll out of the garage bay and pass the parked white cop car. He stared at the white car. And an obsession with its driver grew in his heart. Mundo and Ruben were older than Berto, and seemed loyal to him. They were Sabado's employees who'd grown disgruntled. They used to complain to each other about the boss and Berto knew it.

Each had dirty jobs to perform. The worst was the time Sabado ordered the two men to dispose of something. Sabado directed them to drive a limo to a swamp he knew of behind the Big Duck in Flanders. They had to carry two heavy parcels in doubled-up trash bags down a path to the swamp and throw them in. Sabado assured them the bags would sink. Mundo and Ruben worried over how Sabado let slip a phrase: "unlucky girl." They struggled with the weight of both black-plastic bags. Mundo felt nauseated when he noticed some long dark hair dangling from a rip in Ruben's bag. They both grew appalled as they discussed why this job required two separate bags. That night's deed united the two and still haunted them.

Berto believed Mundo and Ruben did not know or care about the jobs he had to perform for Sabado. Three years ago Berto made them good offers that they accepted. Sabado's other men, the ones who looked down on Berto, took off once it became clear that, wherever Sabado went in his Escalade, he wouldn't be coming back. They didn't want to be around when the authorities got curious.

That was fine with Berto. Those rough men could never deal with the sleek clientele from Manhattan the way handsome Berto did. Berto, who made it a point to speak with only a hint of a Nicaraguan accent. Who, one October morning, unexpectedly entered Sabado's office at the limo garage, took possession of Sabado's rolodex and had a locksmith install new locks. Who had Chantale's document forger add his name to Sabado's DBA—South Fork Transportation Services. Chantale convinced Berto to pose as Sabado's nephew, Humberto Pena, for documentation. Her forger did a good job. The driver's license looked perfect too. And the magnetic signs on the limos' doors and the phone number on the livery cabs could stay the same.

Berto also made it a point at that time to take Chantale out of circulation, transforming her into the proud fiancée of a hardworking local businessman.

The challenge was to manage growth. The summer was a crazy busy time of furtive drop-offs in lovely neighborhoods where city people with cash waited. Maybe behind a mini-mall, or at the end of a driveway, there they'd be with their cash. There were lavish catered affairs under the stars at beachfront mansions. Berto himself, in one of his nicer limos—minus the signage—would pull up past the valet losers in their red jackets. A cell phone buzz quickly brought the party person with the envelope out to the limo. Such a thick envelope for such a small package. Life was good if you were smart, handsome and had a set of balls. And it would get better—Berto wanted his own mansion someday, and to finally make Chantale his wife.

His business also served smaller, more private affairs—a bachelor party, a birthday, or no excuse at all. These would require a drop off in a secluded driveway. Not just a package, a girl too. Two girls sometimes. The city people would specify hair color and Berto would provide. What did they know? They'd be drunk already when the girls arrived in their wigs. One like Tina Turner. Sometimes a Kim Kardashian or a Beyonce lookalike. Specificity paid a lot more. Tina and Beyonce had been Chantale's specialty. The partiers would get high. Too high, usually, like the naked muscleman who went around one customer's porch punching out all the hanging plants like a prizefighter. It was important to collect the cash upfront—Berto's orders. The limo driver had to collect it—Mundo or Ruben were among the trusted few. The driver would remain nearby, just a text away, for the duration. If the number of males at the party was higher than expected, and it often was, the driver stayed put in the driveway.

But from October on, it was slow. Berto sent some limos into Manhattan—no signage—with small deliveries throughout the cold months. But he was relying too much on working-class locals for business in off-season Hampton Bays. These people had little cash, especially this time of year, so Berto would constrict his operation. His local girls handled the few clients during the quiet months. The classier girls like Chantale always headed south for the winter—Miami, maybe home to Haiti or Colombia—and that was okay. They'd migrate back in May.

But Berto had to keep buying drugs to keep his suppliers content. Cocaine, heroin and Oxycodone rip-offs. Pot, too, though bundled pot was obvious and odorous and a hassle. A jug of Oxy pills was much more valuable and easy to handle. So the runs into Manhattan were key. And they had to go smoothly.

With Berto's bloody coup, Chantale took him in and became his partner. But wintering with Berto in Hampton Bays was a far cry from Miami. And Berto had noted changes in her of late. Without her heels, she was not so tall. Without her makeup, a little less exotic. And the cold weather brought on weight gain and something possibly worse, a kind of restless dissatisfaction they both could feel. Maybe they just needed a vacation. Maybe they needed to get married. She wore her engagement ring, but Berto knew they had yet to bring in enough money to really "do it up right," buy a nice house and fly relatives up and all that. The couple kept their money, over $200,000 in cash, stashed in luggage.

And now there was this cop car outside every night, the unmarked white car. Plain as day. White. And a bitch cop. What the fuck? The cops were showing him disrespect by sending a girl to do a man's job. What if he fucked up this girl cop? No. Harming a police officer brought very harsh sentences, everyone knows that. Maybe he could scare her. Make her uncomfortable and unsure of herself. He's got to react somehow. She can't just park out there every night, disrespecting him in front of his men.

Chantale also knows the cop on his case is a woman. It's good when Mundo and Ruben drive by her and give the evil eye. For starters.

Berto needed to talk to Chantale about her voodoo dolls. She loves playing around with them but could they really work? She would know. Chantale had a kind of dark streak that, combined with her exotic looks and strange beliefs, still gave Berto a sexual charge. She would know.

~~~~~~

22. Inoculation

Sitting in the Princess Diner across from the Maltese priest, Lyle feels a little woozy from his reintroduction to scotch. Get it straight—this young guy's not an exorcist; he's a former victim of demonic possession. *Possessions.*

Lyle focuses. "So, why did you choose the priesthood?"

Xerri looks down at his coffee. "Oh, Malta is a very mystical place, you know?"

"Malta is mystical?"

The priest smiles. "Truly. As a boy I had a...*thing-eh* for mysticism and the spirit world. I am from Xagħra on Gozo, an island off Malta. The people of Gozo are very spiritual."

"What do the people of Gozo call themselves?"

"Maltese." Xerri pauses. "Gozo is famous for its prehistoric megalithic temples. *Ġgantija.* You know of them?"

"Not really. I must have missed school that day."

"I am sorry. Well, I grew up nearby and as a young boys my friends and I played in these giant temple ruins. To my friends they were frightening. We would sneak in and explore. The temples are prehistoric—five-thousand, six-hundred years old-eh. Over three-thousand years before Christ!"

"Impressive. Father, your uh, demonic experience, did it occur before or after you joined the priesthood?"

"Both-eh." Xerri pops another olive—a taste from home.

"*Twice.* Does that mean your...exorcism...didn't work the first time?"

Father Xerri's face darkens. "It did work. For a while-eh. But maybe a soul becomes susceptible. Like if you are susceptible to influenza, you know?"

"A relapse." Or, Lyle muses, maybe the demonic world has it in for Matteo Xerri.

"Perhaps-eh." Xerri now appears deeply sad on some level Lyle may never understand. The priest leans forward and speaks confidentially. "You see, I became a priest hoping nothing like that would happen to me again. My father sent me to seminary school praying the priesthood would inoculate me." He pauses again. "But maybe they wanted even more to reenter me because I became a man of God."

Lyle knows "they" means multiple demons. "How long have you been a priest?"

"Six years-eh. I'm still studying at university for advanced degrees. I've even studied construction engineering," Xerri shows a glint of a smile. "I always loved the way things were built, I think, ever since I first snuck into the temple ruins. And I've studied carpentry for building affordable housing. It's all about physics."

"Carpentry?"

"Yes-eh. That was Jesus' profession, you know."

"Jesus was a professional?"

"Oh, yes-eh. Teaching and healing came later. At home he worked with wood, like his father. And he died on a big piece of wood. A piece of Roman carpentry." Xerri studies Lyle's face hoping for a flicker of resonance.

Lyle says, "So the priesthood provided you with an education, an avocation in affordable housing and…a shield?"

Xerri smiles sadly. "You put it well. That and, I hope, more. God knows for sure."

"When did the demons first, uh, come to you?"

Xerri is easing into this line of questioning. "Oh, I was fourteen."

"What was that like? Can you describe it?"

The priest avoids Lyle's eyes, but then flashes a smile. "You really want to know. Okay. It is maybe like a seizure. Epileptic spasms. One thrashes on the bed or the floor. Helpless, in great pain. *Raghwa* comes from the mouth. One says things."

"The unclean spirits say 'Rag-wha'?"

"No. That is, uh, Maltese word for 'foam' at the mouth. I am sorry."

"You Maltese have your own language?"

"Yes-eh. Why not? Wales has Welsh. Maltese culture is ancient. Malta was once a crossroads of the world and our language is an...*istuffat* of many ancient tongues."

"Right. So when you, I mean *they*, say things, what exactly are they saying?"

"That is hard to know. They blaspheme, say filthy things-eh. Maybe an ancient tongue. They hate and they lie. They want to deprive God of our immortal souls."

"Why are they saying things we can't understand?"

Xerri again smiles briefly. "That's a good one. I think they want to scare us, you know? Let us know they exist. They are full of hate and want to drag us down-eh. The old languages are familiar to them. Hatred is ancient. It needs no translation."

"How ancient are we talking?"

"Older than civilization. Evil is at work in Eden in the first book of the Bible. Evil is described in the last book of the New Testament, Michael defeating the serpent, long before history. Evil preys on our pride and envy. The Eden story is about our false pride. How easily we choose to make ourselves like gods. Even today, so many decide God's children are inferior and deserve subjugation, persecution and worse. You know-eh?"

"Oh, I know." Lyle has only a melting ice cube left in his glass. He glances over at Beth, but decides two doubles should do it for tonight. After all.

"Father, when you had these episodes, did your parents intervene? Did they get a priest to help you?"

"The first time, my father was fishing. My mother knew our local parish priest was off the island. So she got this very old lady to come. I was stricken in the temple ruins. I fell to the floor in a dark chamber. My friends ran and brought them both to me."

An expression of profound sadness ripples across Xerri's features. Lyle can feel it himself on a deep level—he's beginning to be able to read this unusual man.

"So the old lady took care of you? Even though she wasn't a priest?"

Xerri comes back from somewhere far away. "Yes-eh. That worked, for a time. But the seizures and voices did return. When

I was finishing seminary school on the main island of Malta. The priests at the seminary helped me. Very devout men."

"They believed this to be demonic possession?"

"Yes-eh. The priests at the seminary knew the languages issuing out of me. And what the hateful words meant."

The busboy takes away both men's platters. Xerri continues. "Later, a medical doctor diagnosed me as epileptic. But on a practical level, those priests did save my life-eh. I nearly swallowed my tongue."

"That would be bad."

"That would be fatal-eh." Father Xerri looks at his watch. He folds his placemat and slides it into his jacket pocket. "Lyle-eh, I will study these Greek words and confer with my fellow priests about this. And I want to learn the history of that old house."

"That'll be tough, Father. The records are missing. But I have a good researcher working on it."

"I hope we will both share what we learn. I will be back in Malta soon but we can still communicate." He gives Lyle his card. It's in Italian.

"All I know is, I don't want that house to come down. Not now. Not till we know more about it. And about what I've experienced there."

"I must say, Lyle-eh, you have experienced something on the spiritual plane. Even if your physical sensations were psychosomatic. The rest is yet to be understood-eh."

Xerri calls Father Wozniak on Lyle's phone to ask for a ride and Beth brings the check. Lyle hands her four twenties.

"Thanks, Hon." Beth pauses. "Hey. We were just wondering. Didn't you used to be…?"

"Yes. I did."

As the two men wait outside in the dark for Wozniak, Lyle says, "You know, I get the sense that a lot more happened to you than you're willing to talk about."

Xerri spots Wozniak's car approaching. "And I get the same sense about you-eh."

~~~~~~

23. Self Loathing

Vitalis Wozniak drove Lyle back to Bridgehampton. Conversation was constrained as Lyle sat in the backseat with his folded chair. The two men in black sat up front. Like God-cops with a perp. Wozniak's shaved head contrasted with Xerri's black crew cut. Lyle could see Wozniak's eyes drift back to him in the rearview mirror as he drove—the new Lyle. No lawyer suit. A wheelchair. Wild hair, crazy eyes. And a little tipsy.

After about twenty minutes, Wozniak pulls up at Lyle's house on Ocean Road and Xerri works to get the wheelchair out onto the tectonic sidewalk. Wozniak waits at the wheel while Xerri helps Lyle up the ramp to his porch over slippery wet leaves. Before parting Lyle says, "Father, thank you for spending the time, and for the CPR. You're a lifesaver."

"Next time we should visit the ER after CPR."

"Next time?"

"I am sorry!" The priest smiles. "I would not wish that on you-eh. But I hope to get inside that house once more. Alone-eh." Xerri steps back to leave, then says, "Lyle-eh, you are the most interesting man I have met in Long Island."

"I try."

"We must keep in contact."

Xerri heads for Wozniak's car and Lyle opens his front door.

Inside it's dark and cooler than it should be after a warm October day. Lyle flicks on some lights and checks the thermostat; the air conditioner's off. He's exhausted, but before his bedtime ritual he rolls into his office and opens the email from Ray Linder.

Mr. Hall: please find finished rendering attached. It was my pleasure. –RL

Noting the absence of question marks, he opens the attachment.

Jewel.

Good God. The sketch is now fully rendered and just beautiful—two versions, including one with the full dress. Jewel's riveting expression, chin raised slightly, eyes aimed at the viewer, makes her even more stunning. She looks better still on Lyle's expensive monitor. Her hands seem to reach out to him, imploring. Like last night. Lyle fights off the scotch he drank and tries to will himself into a rapturous state. He wants his experience with Jewel to bring feeling back to his legs—any feeling at all. But nothing comes. His mind runs through various schemes to preserve Jewel and...*what?* Her way of life? Wrong. Her way of death? What if he'd actually died in Old Vic's parlor earlier tonight? Would Jewel be there—wherever there is—to meet him? Why would she? If he were to die at 55, how old would Jewel be? Twelve? One-hundred-and-twelve? Does your age matter when you're dead? Too thorny. Maybe Lyle should just stay home here and live with an artist's sketch.

The plain fact is little Jewel wants something from Lyle Hall. What if Lyle somehow did "save" Old Vic and succeed in purchasing it? Then what? It would require cost-prohibitive architectural and engineering work just to keep it standing, before even considering renovation. Restoration would include finding—or milling—new pieces of authentic molding to go all over the house. Mose Allen was right about that. To say nothing of the plumbing and heating and cooling. And Wi-Fi.

Would Jewel stand for all that? Or vacate? Then Lyle would have a supremely expensive former whorehouse that was formerly haunted.

And then what? Move in? How would Mose Allen cover that? What if Lyle did move in and Jewel remained in the house? Would she talk to him? Continuously? Just at night? Would she only know things from 100 years ago? Do ghosts take time off? From what? Would feeling return to his legs? What if he could walk when inside the house, but needed the wheelchair outside?

A sudden reality strikes Lyle hard. A sickening wave of fear and self-loathing floods his stomach, joining the big dose of Dewar's poisoning his gut.

What is wrong with you, Hall? Your daughter may be in mortal danger. It might be your fault! You've been handed an unmistakable, etched-in-stone warning. Your only daughter. Only surviving family member. What are you doing about her? Everything you do—everything! —should be about your daughter! What have you done today to keep Georgie safe? Keep her alive? If she knew, she'd have more reason to hate you! But then what if this threat to Georgie's life is not real? What if it's paranormal hogwash?

~~~~~~~

24. Becky Tuttle

Staring at his computer screen, attempting to quell his roiling thoughts, Lyle tries to focus on tangible next steps. Something Noah said resurfaces. Mose mentioned it too.

Lyle Googles Save-a-Barn. The org's home page features some old barn along with their slogan: *Save-a-Barn, Guardian of the East End's Farming Heritage*. Also pictured is Becky Tuttle, the contentious face of the non-profit. Under "Contact us" is a phone number.

"You have reached Save-a-Barn, Guardian of the East End's Farming Heritage."

Their outgoing message sounds more annoying than most, like a receptionist was forced to recite it. It's late now, Lyle plans to leave a message. The recording goes into a pitch for donations, then various irrelevant system-options. Finally, an alphabetical listing of staffers. Becky comes up early. She's away from her desk.

"Hi Becky, this is Lyle Hall. I wanted to talk to you about taking steps to preserve a property in Bridgehampton that I believe is a historic site. I just learned Southampton Town is going to knock the house down and I was wondering if we might talk about working together in some way to save it. There's a nice old barn on the property, too. Hope this call isn't too much of a shock for you. Please give me a ring back?" He leaves his cell number.

Fight annoying with a smile in your voice, Lyle thinks, hanging up. He then Googles Becky Tuttle hoping for more images. And there she is. Not bad for a preservationist prude. Mostly grip-and-grin photos with donors at local fundraisers. Becky's now in her 40s, Lyle calculates—the new 30. Disjointed memories flash back as he scrolls through her pictures. Then he sees it. A news photo credited to Mose Allen for the *Southampton Press*. Maybe 10 years ago, on the courthouse steps, there's the Lyle of old jawboning with a group of frumpy grumpy people. He likely had one of his liquid lunches before the foregone court decision in his favor. Front and center amid the protesters is a pissed-off Becky Tuttle. Young. Not frumpy. Prim but not exactly proper. Lyle takes in Becky's WASP-turned-community-organizer good looks—healthy head of blondish hair, nice figure, freckles. Weirdly appealing, despite her years of battling Lyle and Fraser.

At first he barely notices his phone vibrating. He picks up.

"Lyle Hall?"

"Becky Tuttle?"

There are awkward pauses in life. This is definitely one of them.

"Mister Hall, didn't you retire from practicing law?" Her tone is cool.

"Yes. Sort of. But you know how it is."

"How is it?"

Lyle clears his throat. He and Becky had faced off in court quite a few times over the years, Lyle on the side of development and modernity, Becky on the side of old. Her voice stirs up images from their shared past—Lyle getting histrionic in court; trying to pummel down Becky and her pro bono legal representation; making sly statements in court about preservationists' resistance to progress; gloating to reporters afterward. He conjures Becky's face in the courtroom, daggers in her eyes. He sees Becky and her supporters out on the courthouse steps reacting unhappily as he proclaims "Progress is our friend!" to local news media.

That was then.

"It's...well, things are fine, you know? But, uh, I got involved with this, uh, *house* near me. Helping people who don't want the town to bulldoze it. A stately Victorian..."

"You're talking about Old Vic?" Her tone goes from cool to cold.

"Uh, yeah. One-eleven Poplar."

"I'm reminded, Mister Hall, of a phrase you used once on the courthouse steps after we lost a ruling to you. I remember a group of concerned citizens demonstrating and chanting in favor of preserving our heritage—in that instance, a pre-Revolutionary schoolhouse in Watermill. You wanted a McMansion with pool house and tennis."

Schoolhouse to Pool House is how Lyle vaguely recalls a Mose headline.

"I'm sorry it didn't go well for you."

"Mister Hall, you weren't sorry at the time; you were both aggressive and defensive. You taunted the demonstrators—and me—saying the schoolhouse was 'an old piece of crap.' Now it's gone. So listen to me: Old Vic is an even *bigger* old piece of crap. That is *not* the type of building people get behind preserving!"

Silence. She just hung up? Shit. Lyle grits his teeth. He was that bad back then? That unprofessional? A text pings in his phone—Georgie.

Before disconnecting from Becky, Lyle sighs, "I am sorry."

There's a sound. Then a voice.

"You should be." Becky Tuttle. Still talking means there's still a chance. Regrouping, Lyle improvises.

"Becky, One-eleven Poplar may be the most controversial historic site on the East End. But the barn, you know, is pre-Revolutionary. And the main building's Second Empire Victorian design alone is stunning. Renovation could—"

"Spare me the bullshit, Lyle. I know that place better than you do and nobody—*nobody*—will get behind a preservation effort. Least of all one with you in the lead. You tore down a historic schoolhouse and now want to preserve a whorehouse! It would be funny if it weren't so sad. And by the way, don't bullshit me about your helping *people*, Lyle. There are no *people* interested in Old Vic. So you must have a hidden agenda."

Lyle finds it weirdly sexy of Becky to come at him at gut level like this. And it's titillating to hear this prim lady use the word *bullshit* on him. He recalls at this odd moment how she went through a divorce. No way out now, Lyle falls on his sword.

"Becky, I understand how unsatisfactory the schoolhouse ruling must have been for you. And I'm sorry I seemed disingenuous just now in describing Old Vic. I'm just beginning to work on the case. But I want you to know I'm no longer a man who tears down historic buildings—not anymore. Things have changed. I have changed. And I'm very sorry about that schoolhouse episode." Not bad, Lyle thinks.

"Epi*sodes*," Becky corrects.

"Plural." Lyle decides on a bold new direction. What the hell: "Becky, how about joining me for lunch tomorrow? Talk over this house problem? Could be a chance for me to…make amends. Say the Maidstone?"

The phone line is disconcertingly quiet again.

"Call me tomorrow morning. If you're ready to reveal your agenda."

"Fine. If you can get free, the Maidstone's nice in the fall. Quiet. We can talk."

Quiet indeed. Lyle waits a few beats.

"Becky?"

She's gone. And full of surprises. Swearwords, admonishments, guilt infliction, suspicion, yet open to a lunch meeting. He visualizes Becky seated across from him at the snooty Maidstone. Not chanting an anti-Lyle Hall slogan, she'll look pert in her sweater set with freshwater-pearl choker, season-appropriate wool skirt and modest heels. He'll trim his beard and make sure he's prepped-out in something Kennedy Democrat. It might be fun making up with her. She could be very helpful in his new crusade to save Old Vic. And it would be good to get out and have a business lunch again. Maybe even a white wine. Just the one. What's that political couple's name? Matalan and Carver?

Call me tomorrow morning.

He looks at his phone. It's not the number he dialed—it's Becky's cell phone.

Then something strikes Lyle——what did Dr. Susan Wayne say about libido? That he might experience a "phantom revival of libido." *Phantom* since Lyle could not do much about it. But she planted a seed of hope that he'd at least keep a libidinal pilot light burning until his spine is healed. Meanwhile, his lower body might not work, but his imagination did. For example, Susan Wayne reminded him of the lady psychologist who treated Tony Soprano on television. So maybe it was okay how his mind wandered as they sat through talk therapy. How he'd picture his therapist rising, locking her office door and gripping his wheelchair armrests, lowering her mouth to his, allowing Lyle to slip his hands under her conservative two-button blazer.

Becky Tuttle sits at her desk in her south-of-the-highway center-hall colonial in nearby Sagaponack. She'd decorated and furnished the house in "traditional elegance" before her divorce. Her daughter is away at college; her ex-husband is in Manhattan. She has vivid memories of Lyle Hall—especially her attempts to defeat him in court. She knows all about his career-ending deadly accident a year ago. Everyone in town knows. But by last spring, with the summer people coming back, Lyle Hall had diminished to more of a local curiosity. There were sightings, but few even spoke to the man who'd morphed into a strange, crippled version of the devil they knew.

Becky remembers the scintillation she'd get from being lambasted by Lyle Hall in court, in public and sometimes in the media. The notoriety prompted a kind of guilty pleasure. Here was this compelling, successful legal mind picking apart her homespun efforts to preserve local history. Lyle was impetuous and unafraid of the press; like one of those football coaches who brags to reporters that his team will win the big game.

Becky wonders what life could have been like for his wife. Or *wives*. She barely remembers the first; she was Lyle's age. Number Two was very much the younger trophy. Everyone erroneously assumed the worst—that Lyle divorced his cancer-stricken wife to bed this strenuous-looking woman with the raging hormones. Not demure in the least, she was Lyle's equal in impetuousness. You knew it when the two were seated in a restaurant—he'd be drinking and she'd be loud. Then they stopped being seen together. Then Dar, that was her name, stopped being seen at all.

All things considered, lunch with a new Lyle Hall might be…interesting.

Matalan and Carver indeed. Lyle, sitting at his computer, realizes asking Becky Tuttle to join him for lunch was pathetic. In East Hampton, no less. But he puts Georgie out of his mind for the moment and clicks "Becky Tuttle Images" again. Not bad.

~~~~~~

25. Lasagna

Googling Becky is weird but refreshing. Lyle starts to obsess about her. He Googles Matalan and Carver to read about them. The he remembers Georgie texted him during his negotiation with Becky.

Georgie had brought over lasagnas from Citarella while he was on the phone. And the mandatory orange pennant. Shit. The stuff is on the porch. She opted for drop-off-and-text rather than come-in-and-visit. Lyle imagines her saying she didn't think he was home/was on her break/had to get back to work. How do you fix that, he wonders.

Sure enough, out on the porch sits a styro cooler containing a selection of Citarella's fine lasagnas. Hard to miss, what with the orange safety pennant stuck in the Styrofoam. Good to his word, Lyle screws the whip-flag pole to his chair-back, the orange triangle wagging high above. He hates it. But he has a modern idea: take a selfie of it installed and text it to Georgie as proof. Smile sincerely. Don't think about the tombstone.

Tired and too full of diner food to eat lasagna, Lyle rolls into his bedroom for a nap before tonight's return visit to Old Vic. He's so tired, he blows off taking his meds. He blows off a text from Noah: *What time 2nite?* He also blows off his other bedtime routines, like getting in bed. His chin lolls to his collar bone and he falls into a deep sleep in his chair. His sleep is fraught with disturbing dreams. Not his dreams. Jewel's dreams.

Then the doorbell rings.

~~~~~~

26. Flo Hendricks

The front doorbell jolts through Lyle like a javelin. A visitor? At
9:30 at night?

He rolls cautiously to the front door and peeks from behind
the curtain covering the slender sidelight window next to the
doorframe. Talk about frumpy. It's a fat lady. Isn't it past
bedtime for fat ladies? Okay, she's not morbidly obese; she's
heavyset and doughy—like that lady in the sitcom *The Office*.
She's wearing a dark pants suit and a fake-pearl choker that's
pinching her jowl. Her brown hair is done up in a kind of Lynda
Bird Johnson and …

The woman abruptly bends down to eye level and peers in
directly at Lyle. Lyle jerks back, startled. She raps on the
window for good measure.

"Hell-oh-oooh!"

"Who's there?"

"Florence Hendricks. I'd like a word with Lyle Hall,
please?"

"Regarding?"

"It's regarding Old Vic."

Shit. Old Vic? Who is this lady? Lyle hesitates.

"What about Old Vic?"

"Are you Mister Hall?"

The lady's frame now takes up the entire sidelight window,
eclipsing the front porch light. What to do…

Punt. Lyle sighs, opens his door and there she is, briefcase in
hand. What is the meaning of this?

"Can I help you?"

"Lyle Hall." Statement, not question.

"Do I know you?"

"No, but I know you."

"How's that?"

"It's my job." She has her business card at the ready and hands it to Lyle. "I'm Flo Hendricks."

Lyle examines the card. Nice print job. Under her name there's an exotic job description: "Parapsychology; Paranormal Investigation Etiquette; Clairvoyance."

Positioned across the top, Lyle sees five symbols: a circle, a plus sign, a wave, a square and a star. Her contact information includes an address in Shirley, Long Island. The town's name makes him think of Shirley Booth. The bottom of the card reads: "Member, Parapsychological Association." The card also bears a confident slogan:

Professional help.

Lyle looks up at her. "I don't know what any of this means."

Flo Hendricks regards Lyle. He can somehow sense it—she is reading him.

After a pause she says, "You will. Can we talk? About that old house and what you've been experiencing?"

"How do you know anything about *that?* Were you at the courthouse today?"

The woman slides her iPad from her briefcase and brings it to life.

No. But he was..." She shows the screen to Lyle and he gasps.

"Holy *shit!*"

It's the online daily edition of the *Southampton Press.* Someone took a picture of him in his wheelchair filing papers in the courthouse lobby. *Is that allowed?* And there's a photo of Old Vic looking like total shit. Worse, there's a big, honking feature story.

"You should read it, Mister Hall."

Dumbfounded, Lyle takes her iPad, then looks up at her before he starts to read.

"It's Lyle. Lyle is fine..." Then the words on the screen sink in. Lyle is not fine.

Controversial Lawyer Moves to Save 'Haunted' House

Lyle Hall returns to court a preservationist
Hopes to renovate condemned Victorian for 'ghost girl'
By MOSE ALLEN for the *Southampton Press*
SOUTHAMPTON, NY – October 13, 2010

Most regulars at Southampton Town Justice Court today did not recognize Lyle Hall's return to jurisprudence. The brash, some would say aggressive, lawyer was a courthouse fixture for three decades until laid low last year by a catastrophic auto accident on Montauk Highway in Bridgehampton. The accident took the life of local resident Elsie Cronk, 85, and ended a legal practice known for its seemingly uninterrupted successes, particularly in the controversial area of land development.

But that career came back to life of sorts earlier today when Hall, now getting around in a wheelchair, transformed by a long rehabilitation and thinner, filed a motion for an injunction against the demolition of a decrepit Victorian house in Bridgehampton. Known to locals as "Old Vic," the structure was condemned recently by the Town of Southampton. Residents know the rickety place as an eyesore at best and a threat to safety and property values at worst.

Not so Mr. Hall, whose motivation may strike some as spooky.

"I believe there's a spirit of some kind residing on the premises," Hall said today in an interview at the courthouse. Hall, who was in a coma for nearly two months after his accident, has experienced this spirit intimately on a recent visit to Old Vic. It's a girl, he said, of about 12. Only Hall has seen the apparition. "I saw her face," he said.

One challenge Hall faces is the strongly held belief that the building was once used as a brothel. "That is a matter of conjecture and hearsay," he said, unconcerned with the ramifications and how a purported history of prostitution might affect his efforts to convince the Justice Court to spare Old Vic.

While most such preservation efforts are conducted by organizations with fundraising power and influence, Hall is unfazed by his lack of clout, political or otherwise. He plans to use his own money to fight the township and, if he succeeds, pay for the renovation from his accumulated wealth. Hall seems resigned to do so: "I think it's still a beautiful old place and I think it should remain standing and be renovated."

He added, "Our region enjoys a rich and unique history. We are working on unearthing the documentation that shows how this home is a little gem of Long Island history. But we need more time." It is unclear at this time who might be working with Hall on the unearthing.

The next move is the Town of Southampton's. One longtime clerk, Alpharetta James, went on the record in favor of Hall's return to court. "Things have been a little quiet around here without Lyle Hall. Everybody may not have loved his style, but you knew when he had a court case."

Besides his preservation motion Hall will be busy with other legal action. Elsie Cronk's family is suing him in civil court for her wrongful death. He is also moving to have his suspended driver's license reinstated. In addition, the New York State Bar Association is expected to disbar Hall, but that does not seem to perturb him. "I'm considering letting them disbar. At this point I might like to fade away into the sunset."

But before that, Lyle Hall will be busy in court soon, given the old house's imminent demolition. And who knows, maybe he'll bring along a co-complainant. One only he can see.

~~~~~

27. FEARcom

Lyle stares at Mose Allen's online story in disbelief.

"Oh. My. *God*." This escapes him as a sigh.

"Scroll down, Lyle. He updated it."

Lyle scrolls down. There are three recently uploaded color photos of Lyle. In two he looks totally insane, screaming at Mose Allen's camera lens. Father Xerri is in one shot, propping Lyle up. The second is a close-up revealing weird red scratches crossing Lyle's face. His shirt is ripped open and claw marks seemingly scour his chest. The third photo shows Lyle outside the courthouse earlier gesturing at Mose. Lyle's extended middle finger is discreetly blurred. All of it sucks.

Mose Allen wrote descriptive captions. Lyle decides not to read them.

He looks up at Flo Hendricks and surrenders, rolling back to allow her inside his house. He flips on some living room lights and motions the woman to the sofa, a large sectional. She places her briefcase on the sofa and sits, taking in her surroundings. How the first wife's traditional wall hangings and prints depicting New England-y farm scenes clash with the second wife's abortive attempt to update with pointy modernist furniture. There's Lyle's rack of lavender dumbbells. An extra wheelchair, folded closed, leans against an uninviting arm chair. Flo winces at the exercise contraption hanging limp from the dining room entryway, then levels her eyes at the man facing her.

"You're upset with this reporter, Lyle."

"No," he replies warily, "I was earlier, now I'm just numb."

"Why were you upset earlier if you only just read the story now?"

"Maybe I saw this coming." He flashes on the sordid scene out behind Old Vic.

"I see. Your priest friend—is he really a Maltese exorcist?"

"No, not really. He's just a priest I know, visiting from Malta…the article says nothing about him."

"You were thinking about him."

A chill creeps up Lyle's neck. She's right. He was. Lyle tries to pick up any signals at all from this strange lady. He can't.

"Don't try to read me, Lyle."

"I wasn't."

"You were. It's not considered professionally honorable."

He looks at her card again, particularly the odd symbols.

"Don't worry. Those symbols are not demonic. The pentacle, you'll notice, is point-up. The symbols were developed by Karl Zener, the perceptual psychologist, in the 1930s."

"I don't know what any of that means," he says, wondering how big a mistake it was to let her in his home.

"Zener created a deck of cards using those five symbols. He designed the cards to test a person's perceptual ability."

"Perceptual?"

"You, for instance, perceive the spirit of a dead girl. Doctor Zener would be able to quantify your clairvoyant acuity by asking you to name the symbols on the backs of the cards. A null-hypothesis subject would score about twenty percent—roughly getting one in five correct."

"How would you score?" he says, thoughts drifting to an exit strategy. Her exit.

"Last time I was tested I scored one hundred percent. And you can call me Flo. I know you're not interested in dead perceptual psychologists. And I know you're boiling about this online article. And I agree; it's not good. You want to kill this reporter. That's natural. I'm here to help."

"Yeah...NO!" Lyle starts and shoots up in his chair. "What? I do not want help *killing* anybody! I just...want to slap him. I mean with an injunction. I never should have...he caught me at a weak moment." He draws a breath, realizing that Flo is anything but a contract killer. "Back when I was a full-time lawyer I used to bust his..."

"Testicles..." she says, restricting a smile to one corner of her mouth.

110

"...because I though he was a low-rent jerk and not a real journalist."

"Journalists can pick up on that, even a null-hypothesis reporter."

"We never got along, but...but this..."

"He's getting his pound of flesh and then some. This is just the beginning. Which is why I'm here." Flo slips a folder of papers from her briefcase. "Don't get mad, get even. Freeze him out of the story. You need help dealing with the media. Professional help. I work for a company that will shield you from stuff like this and get your true story out in the best light."

"I don't want my story out."

"Too late." Flo taps her iPad and a big logo appears on a Web page:

FEARcom
Get Near Your Fear

"What am I looking at? Who wants to get near fear?"

"These days, just about everyone." Flo shifts into promotional gear. "Lyle, FEARcom is the premiere paranormal website, high-def cable TV programmer and global source for paranormal news. If we say it's real, it's real."

"*What*'s real?"

"Paranormal events such as those you're experiencing. Lyle, you think you told this reporter too much. I can tell you hardly gave him a thing and look what he did with it. Even the very best coverage you can expect will treat you condescendingly. They'll tag you as some old guy with autonomous sensory meridian response."

"Not *that*. Can you stop them from calling me 'old'?"

Flo sighs and calls up the horrid pictures Mose Allen snapped behind Old Vic.

"See, Lyle, the worse you look, the better he looks. That's why FEARcom sent me. As soon as we saw how unfairly you were being treated—and we see very clearly how bad this can go for you—we knew we could form a mutually beneficial partnership."

"A partnership to do what?"

"What FEARcom does best—get your story out, your real story, not just to paranormal buffs, but to the news-hungry public all over. Who says 'There's no such thing as bad ink'? Look again at what this Mose Allen did to you. With the considerable resources FEARcom can bring to bear, we ensure there will be good ink. We will control your story and you will come out of this in a much better place."

"Well, how come I've never heard of you?"

"If you are involved in paranormal—and, Lyle, you are now involved—you know that FEARcom is the CNN of paranormal news. The company is moving into mainstream media, TV and print much the way TMZ did with celebrity coverage. Only FEARcom provides high-value paranormal coverage to a public hungry for human-inhuman interest. Albeit dead humans."

"'Inhuman interest'?"

Flo leans toward Lyle and murmurs, *"People love this stuff."*

"So…you would take care of me, make sure I'm not misquoted, not made a fool of, present me in a positive light?"

"Correct. You and your ghost girl."

"What do I give you in return?"

Flo smiles. "Nothing. Except exclusivity."

Lyle gazes back at Flo Hendricks. This is all so sudden.

"And that's it?"

"That's it."

"I dunno. This could all blow over tomorrow. It's a bullshit story on a rinky-dink website."

"Lyle. Your story has legs. I know."

"Legs?"

Flo takes in Lyle's wheelchair. "Unfortunate choice of terms. Let me fill you in on something. We monitor paranormal blogs, Twitter feeds, all of social media. There's already an ad hoc movement growing on the Internet to organize a group of true believers to come here to Bridgehampton and camp out in a show of support for you, for the ghost girl and for Old Vic."

"You're kidding."

"I don't kid."

"Campers? How many?"

"There were 50 or 60 rabble-rousing online an hour ago. Sharing directions to Bridgehampton, to Old Vic, to this house. Things like that only grow. The media covers movements like that—big media—and it feeds on itself."

Lyle ponders this.

"Lyle, that's why I really want you to consider our offer. If your predicament is genuine—and this bears every sign that it is—you seriously need help from a professional organization that specializes in both paranormal and media events. So you might as well go with the best. Don't get slapped around by some hack."

Lyle looks into Flo's eyes. Is she for real?

"I'm for real, Lyle. And please stop comparing me to Phyllis in that *Office* sitcom. I am not Phyllis by a long shot."

"I wasn't..."

"You were. Lyle, I'd like to say sleep on it but tomorrow will be too late for you to think straight. I promise you, you will need the kind of shield we can provide much sooner than you think."

"Well who would I work with? You?"

"Me, yes, but I'm part of a news production team."

"You mean like on one of those awful ghost-hunting TV shows?"

"No. We only visit the sites of legitimate paranormal events. And we use high-definition production techniques. The team I work with is based in New England. I live on Long Island and our producer sent me right away to get ahead of this story."

"What would I do with you and your team?" Lyle's jawbone tenses up.

"We'll interview you, probably film a kind of reenactment, procure archival stills and shoot fresh footage. Deliverables will be ready-to-air TV news packages. We'll do a lot, but we won't wear you out. Remember, you'll only have to talk to us because we will have the exclusive."

"So you will interview me? On TV?"

"Silk will conduct the formal interviews. I offer informed commentary."

"You mean turn my personal issues into some televised bullshit masquerading as news? Sorry, ma'am, I don't do that. And what do you mean, 'silk'?"

"Not what, Lyle—*who*."

Flo taps her iPad and brings up a publicity photo.

"Silk is the paranormal-news world's consummate professional. Picture a cross between a young Barbara Walters and Angelina Jolie. Paranormal enthusiasts worldwide hang on her every word *and* she's about to break into mainstream media in a big way. She'll conduct your interviews. Up close and personal."

"Why should I care about any of that?"

Flo rotates the screen to Lyle. "You tell me."

Lyle goes numb. His taut jaw relaxes. He has not been around beautiful women for a long while. He stares at the image.

"Oh. Her name is?"

"Silk." Flo senses Lyle's hopeless yearning and a rising animal instinct as she slides a contract from her folder.

Lyle studies the screen. "Where do I sign?"

~~~~~~~

28. Djab

Pacing around his office, pressure building due to the police presence outside—and a bitch cop, no less—Berto finds himself reliving strange details from that October night three years ago. The night he emerged from a swamp a man.

No one would find this swamp, not in this lifetime, he assured himself as he slogged away from it on bare feet. Ironic how it was Sabado who had once told him, to get rid of something you never want to be found, go behind the Big Duck. Two hundred yards to the swamp.

That night, Berto made his way out of the scrub pine forest, his clothes dripping wet, feet numb, toward the stupid Big Duck and Route 24. The place sold eggs and shit—it was lit up now, but closed. He would wait behind a tree for Chantale and her little BMW. Staggering out of the woods to the gravel side road, he stepped over a trampled line of blue plastic tape, noticing it for the first time. The tape stretched into the darkness—past the swamp all the way to the bay. For most of that distance, it was suspended on stakes. Like somebody actually owned this godforsaken shithole.

Chantale soon pulled up in her BMW. She didn't mind the odd detour; even she had no clients on a Wednesday in mid-October. Berto slid in next to her. He stunk. What the fuck? Her car is only six years old and he would have to clean her leather seat. Chantale studied him for a moment, putting it together. Berto was not okay. He seemed to be in shock—shivering, barefoot, his shirt and pants soaked, ripped and smeared with mud. And possibly blood.

Berto was monosyllabic as she sped back to her place on the outskirts of East Quogue. She knew Berto had left with Sabado earlier in the evening. Recently, Berto had been to Chantale's place quite frequently. Sabado either didn't know or was too distracted or, in his fifties now, too old to care at this point. Chantale, the Haitian beauty who still held the top spot in Sabado's hierarchy, enjoyed the attentions of her boss's handsome lieutenant. He was better looking than any client. It was illicit and kind of kinky having him visit behind Sabado's back. Young Berto obviously loved it when they were alone and she spoke to him sternly, like he was a bad boy. And he was, after all.

Berto liked Chantale's rental house, decorated so prettily. He liked that her clients did not come to her—a limo took her to them. Recently, in pillow talk, Chantale had mentioned that Sabado should retire. No man his age could keep an operation like this going successfully. A few nights ago she reached down under the sheet and whispered to Berto how a younger man with a set of balls might retire Sabado someday.

Berto always left her place before sunrise. Until this strange night.

On this occasion Berto showered in the bathroom adjoining her bedroom. Chantale slipped into a nightie, as usual, then scooped up his wet clothes and went down the hall to the washer-dryer. The clothes were hopeless. Filthy. And they stunk. Chantale had her new single-cup coffee machine going in the kitchen—extra-bold West Indies Dark Roast. But these ruined clothes overpowered the aroma. They smelled like a swamp. Berto had no other clothing at her place, but that would be his problem. She chucked his wet stuff into her garbage can—and heard an odd thunk. She reached in and held up the ripped linen shirt. She removed something kind of heavy from the chest pocket and recognized it.

It was golden and had hung around Sabado's neck for years—the ugly head of a *djab*—a Haitian devil figurine. To some Haitians, a djab was simply a troublemaker, a rambunctious spirit. To others, those with generations of family who knew and truly believed, a djab could be more. It could hurt enemies. Ward off trouble. And it could reward people. Chantale had described this to Sabado once, years ago, when she was young and trying to impress him. And she used quite a bit of her earnings to purchase this gold-plated thing.

Sabado had smiled at his pretty girl that night she was so bold as to reach around his neck and clasp the gold chain so the djab hung just so at the midpoint of his collar bone. She whispered that the djab gave the wearer powers, including sexual power. He snickered. He would keep the unusual trinket. And Chantale.

Now Chantale rinsed off the talisman and inspected it. About the length of her thumb knuckle, it had twelve tiny eyes, six on each side arranged vertically, and a leering mouth. It had two projecting horns; each held a tiny ring at the tip to accept a link of a chain. Chantale washed her hands carefully and, back in her bedroom, fished a replacement chain out of a drawer. As she attached it, the shower shut off.

She could hear Berto toweling himself dry. She slipped on a pair of her naughtiest high heels. Now she was tall. Berto stepped out of the bathroom, a pink towel around his waist. He looked at Chantale and was struck with mixed signals.

"Sit down, Berto," she said ominously, motioning to her bed. He did as he was told and looked up at her. Chantale radiated the seductive command that put her in demand with clients. She stepped closer. Her tan, smooth legs looked so powerful.

"You have no clothes..."

He just gaped at her.

"I threw them out, Berto." She stepped so close that her legs straddled Berto's bare knee. "And I found something."

Chantale held up the djab, shiny now and dangling from a new chain.

"Do you know what this is, Berto?"

"Yes... I mean, no..."

"You need to know."

"Please tell me?"

Chantale fixed Berto with a penetrating expression. Berto could not tell if it was sexy or scary. Maybe it was both.

"It's from Haiti, boy. A mean little devil. But it gives the wearer powers, if he believes. Do you think Sabado had power?"

"Yes..."

"I gave him this little devil, Berto."

Berto's mouth fell open as Chantale brought her fingertips around the sides of his neck, the golden chain tingling his bare skin.

"You want power, don't you?"

Berto looked up at Chantale, transfixed. "I do..."

She was so close to him as she clasped the chain behind his neck. He felt her breath. She smelled delicious. Her legs locked his thigh. Her hair hung in complicated tendrils, tinged with a rusty golden color. She hummed something strange and rhythmic. Now the djab hung around his neck, heavy on his collarbone, leering back at Chantale.

"It can give a man power in bed too." She scratched his jaw. "If he believes."

Chantale poked Berto's chest backward firmly and he reclined on her big bed, gazing up at her. Then she pulled open the pink towel.

~~~~~~~

29. Kitchen

Flo Hendricks finally departed after setting up a meeting for Lyle with Silk in the morning. But now Lyle is much too tired to stay awake till three a.m. to visit Jewel and then face a new day of trials. He resolves to bathe, heat up one of Georgie's meals from Citarella, and grab a few hours' sleep. Since he's an insomniac, getting up at 2:30 poses no problem. Lyle almost falls asleep in the spinach lasagna before he drags himself into bed. Chilly, he pulls the comforter over himself and fades into sleep.

Hard to tell when the strange dreams started that night. He didn't used to dream. He'd anesthetized himself with scotch for years, more so after Belinda's cancer diagnosis, continuing through his sleazy relations with the future Mrs. Dar Hall, then the "loveless marriage" to same, followed by the loveless divorce, then the increasingly wild forays into risky behavior, much of it set in Montauk where Lyle was less known and less disliked, and finally, last year's purchase of the obnoxious Hummer from an automaker about to go out of business.

After Lyle violently put away the Hummer for good, dreaming was obviated by all the meds.

Not anymore. Tonight, after the most active day Lyle's had in ages, he sinks into a deep slumber. So deep he does not awaken. And the strange dreams come.

Some dreams are about a healthy, able-bodied Lyle. There's a fantasy of cute little Georgie and her doting father. Lyle, sadly, never doted. Other dreams are darker. The Lyle of old, in disputes with women. Sometimes beautiful women. Sometimes Dar. Worse, Lyle experiences poor, blameless Belinda Cheswick. A local girl who married an up-and-coming law student and presented him with a baby girl.

Then comes one that is so real and unreal at the same time. Jewel. That face again. Beautiful Jewel. A warm wave of hope is overcome by cold dread, pain and woeful cries. She recedes in fear back into that old house. What does she want? She wants him to hear the cries, a piteous chorus of women. See the splash of blood; see the big, sickening knife. See the baby, the silent infant, eyes closed, wrapped in a ragged cloth. Then more cries and more blood.

Finally Lyle's dream resolves to something that cannot be real. Must not be real. Belinda Hall's headstone with *Georgia Hall* etched into it. So cruel. So final. Two-thousand-ten. That's right now. It's a warning. And a cry for help from long ago.

There's more crying coming from somewhere. Where? Who is crying?

Lyle Hall is crying.

He opens his eyes, raises himself on an elbow and punches the cold, unused pillow to his left. *That was me? Me crying?* It's dark. What does his hated clock radio say? Five-thirty a.m.? *Five-thirty?* No! He missed seeing Jewel? Shit!

Or did he see Jewel? Did Jewel come here to see him in his sleep?

Lyle lies back and tries to clear his head. In the predawn quiet it's easy to hear the subtle tinkling sound. Strangely gentle. Where is it coming from?

Shit. It's coming from the fucking kitchen.

Lyle eases himself out of bed. Quietly into his chair. He's wearing a big T-shirt and a big Depends. There are some stretchy sounds his weight makes against the chair's faux leather. Unplug the battery charger from the outlet. Quietly open the drawer in the nightstand. Carefully extract the Glock 19 9mm. Lyle has never used it, except on a few visits to a firing range years ago. Check that it's loaded. He hears another clinking noise and his heart jumps. Gun's loaded, now he may have to use it.

There's a rattle in the kitchen. Then a sharp little drawer slam. Then the subtle tinkling resumes. Lyle rolls slowly into the hallway. His electric motor is nearly silent. Shit! He should call Georgie! But his phone is back in the bedroom charging—not a time to turn around and fetch it. The kitchen is at the end of the hall. There's more tinkling. What the fuck is making that sound? Or who?

Lyle rolls to the kitchen entrance, his heart is pounding. The stove hood light is lit, as he left it. Lyle reaches up for the overhead light switch with his free hand, pointing the Glock into the kitchen. There's motion. Something's there. It's big.

Lyle flips the switch on, blinding himself and the intruder. Both hands on the pistol, Lyle's heart rate spikes. He squints at his opponent. He's tall. He's got a knife.

"What the fuck you doing in here!?" Lyle shouts, his heart pumping hard. "Drop that fucking knife or I swear I'll blow you away! Drop it now!!"

The man looks confused.

"What? This?" He holds up a silver butter knife. Lyle's pistol is trained on the man's heart.

"Yeah, that! Fucking drop it, I said!" Lyle begins to recognize that this tall man is quite old. "You fucking stealing my fucking silverware, you fuck??"

The man makes a wan smile.

"Stealing it? Why no, son, I'm arranging it for you."

"*What??*"

The old guy gestures at Lyle's kitchen counter. There's a meticulously positioned placemat, on which is set Lyle's china, picked out long ago by Belinda, crystal stemware and a silver place setting. All but the butter knife.

"See that? That's the way to live. Especially when you're young like you are. You should enjoy the good that life gives you while you can. That's what my wife always told me."

Lyle's heart rate calms down some. His Glock in one hand, he steers into the kitchen peering around for any additional intruders.

"You broke in here, mister...?"

"Name's Glen Stanley. No 'mister' needed. And you're Lyle Hall."

"You broke into my house to put out a *place setting?*"

"You make it sound awful when you say it that way. But I guess that's what lawyers do. There's no harm done, you see..."

Glen Stanley gestures at the kitchen door. It's ajar. "I'm a retired locksmith. I didn't break anything."

"Why do you think you can be in my home? Are you all right?"

"I'd be all righter if you put your pistol down." Lyle relents and lays it on his lap.

"Thank you, son. You see, I'm following my orders from the Boss."

"And who might he be?"

"He might definitely be my wife."

"Is she here too?"

"Not exactly, son. She died a few months ago. But I have my orders."

"Must've been some marriage."

"Oh, it still is."

The two men regard each other. Lyle absorbs Glen Stanley's batty kindness. The old boy's plainly dressed for the outdoors, kind of like a New England farmer who shops at L.L. Bean. He's thin and has mussy gray hair.

"So, is that it? Can I expect you in here on a regular basis?"

"No sir, I did what I needed to."

"Did you? Question, Mister Stanley—why tonight?"

"It's Glen, son. Tonight was the night I read about you."

"Oh. You read about me. You know something, I have no fucking idea what you're talking about!"

"Well, son, I like to read about ghosts and such. Seeing as I'm married to one."

Lyle stares at Glen Stanley. "Okay..."

"So when I read all about you this evening, I saw you were unhappy and I felt I had to come out here and help you the way Maeve helped me. Still helps me, in fact."

"So you read about me and now you're helping me. Read what? That dumb story on the Internet?"

"Yes, I read about you on the computer. A man wrote about your career and all the bad things that happened and how you are so obsessed with the ghost of a girl that you want to buy her house. Sounds crazy, but I'll tell you, from my perspective, I get it!"

Fucking Mose Allen strikes again, Lyle thinks. He glares at Glen Stanley. Is this guy for real?

"Yes sir," the old man continues, "that's how we knew to come. You said you were a 'believer.' Well, we're believers too, you see. You've been given an extraordinary gift, Mister Hall. And we're here to help. Help you through this extraordinary time."

Lyle becomes dimly aware of flashing lights—red alternating with blue—blinking through his kitchen blinds from outside. He hears odd squawking sounds.

"Who's 'we'? You and your wife?"

"Well, me and my fellow travelers. We all passed around your story last night and got organized." Glen Stanley nods toward the kitchen window, its blinds drawn down.

Lyle is rattled and irritated but slightly more at ease now. Why, he doesn't know. He rolls to the window. "'Fellow travelers'?" He peeks behind the blinds at the street.

And freezes.

Holy shit.

Outside people are pitching tents. On his lawn. Out by the sidewalk. Across the street. A lot of people. Hard to make them out in the predawn light, but mostly younger people, like campers. Two Southampton Police squad cars are parked akimbo, their roof lights flashing but otherwise quiet. One car door is open and a really big cop, Sgt. Frank Barsotti, is out and shining his flashlight on people's ID cards. It's controlled chaos. Lyle has never seen anything like this. Not even during the Road Rally.

His heart sinks. That putz Mose Allen! Was that Flo lady right?

"Mister Hall?" Glen Stanley is by the kitchen door. "If it's all right with you, we would like to see the ghost girl, too."

Lyle turns from the window and stares at the old man.

Glen continues, "We'd very much like to see her. If we may. So I'll be right outside here if you need me. Good night." He smiles. "Should say good morning!" He exits and closes the door. Lyle hears it lock.

Lyle fights back nausea and acid reflux. He feels besieged and violated; his home is no longer secure. He rolls up to the counter. China and silver. Crystal stemware. Like Belinda would put out for special occasions. Nice. And all wrong.

Police lights flash through the kitchen door. Red hot anger suddenly flushes through him. Lyle grabs the silverware, as much as he can in one fist, and yanks open a drawer.

"*Shit*. What has fucking Mose done?" he says aloud. "What the fuck have *I* done?"

~~~~~~~

PART TWO

GHOST HAMPTON

30. Tent City

"*UH-ho!!*" That's Fraser Newton's derisive chortle. It signifies that mockery will follow. And it does.

"Mose *Allen??* I can't believe it! I thought he retired to Queens or something."

Lyle, seated at his computer, can tell Fraser has him on speakerphone. Josie is probably in early too, and can hear her boss having a field day.

"He didn't retire, obviously," says Lyle, exhausted already by 8:30 a.m. "They put his damn column online."

"They sure did! Nice photography, too."

"Apparently he's found a new readership, Fraser. And they're fucking camped outside on my property in some kind of Patagonia L.L. Bean city. One of them came to the door earlier and offered me a tin cup of coffee. They are fucking cooking out there."

"How was the coffee?"

"Not too bad."

"So what's the downside? Any pretty girls?"

"Well around five-thirty, an old man broke into my house. I almost shot him."

"Yikes. You're a ghost-whisperer *and* old-man-shooter! Wait—shot with what?"

"What do you think?"

"Lyle Hall has a *gun?* Good Lord, this gets weirder and weirder! I love this!"

"I hope you love this enough to help me. I filed my request for an injunction against demolition yesterday."

"I know. I read. I can't believe you gave that guy an interview!"

"Fraser, I did *not* give that guy an interview!"

"It reads like you did. Gotta run. Call me."

Fraser hangs up. Lyle Googles the *Southampton Press*. There's the story from last night. He scrolls down to the photos and the captions he's yet to read. There's Old Vic. It's credited to that rat bastard Mose. The house looks like total shit. The caption reads: *Reputed Bridgehampton brothel awaits the town's bulldozer.*

Lyle focuses on the photos under it. There's Lyle in the courthouse filing paperwork with Alpharetta. The photo is not credited because taking a picture in the courthouse would get you in trouble. The caption reads: *He's a believer. Lyle Hall files motion to halt demolition.*

Then there's Lyle outside the courthouse, giving Mose the blurred-out finger. *Hall, back in business, is now pitching for the other team: preservation.*

Further down are the crazy photos from outside Old Vic last night. Unbelievable that Lyle Hall can look that bad. The two-shot of Lyle in Fr. Xerri's arms is pathetic. Then there's crazy-looking Lyle in full rage, cursing out Mose: *Lyle Hall claims he saw a ghost at neighborhood knock-down.*

Lyle scrolls down a bit further. The he sees it.

Jewel.

Somehow that rump roast Mose Allen filched Jewel's picture and posted it. Lyle's blood boils. This beautiful, sad girl dragged into the digital 21st century.

As he goes through the chore of donning yesterday's sweater/shirt/khakis outfit, his heart suddenly sinks. A whole day has passed and he's done nothing to secure his daughter's safety. Lyle doesn't even have a clue what to do or who to approach about this appalling threat to her life. *No one* would believe him. Georgie least of all. But if the headstone date is real, only a few days away, God forbid, and he did nothing...

Ringing. Lyle has to take this call.

"Dad? What are you doing?"

"Buying a haunted whorehouse. What are you doing?"

"Taking a lot of harassment from my coworkers. Dad! What have you freaking *done?* You were in court yesterday with some cockamamie new crusade? You actually interviewed with that court reporter? You let him take your picture?"

"It was not an interview! And I did not *let him* take my picture!"

Georgie's voice lowers to a pointed whisper. "That drawing of a girl—is it by Ray Linder? Did you stop to imagine what would happen if it got upstairs that Linder was moonlighting on his lunch hour using a Town Police laptop for personal gain? And how about my involvement in arranging it? And you appear in the *Southampton Press* flipping the bird? And *then* you're photographed trespassing on Town property looking totally insane? I'm trying to start a career here, Dad, and you are so not helping!"

"Georgie, I'm telling no one about the artist."

"Great, Dad. I can see how it goes when you decide not to talk."

"I answered a few of that miserable shmuck's questions. I thought honesty was best at the time. I didn't know he was taking my picture."

"Pointing a camera at you is the first hint. Dad, we're skirting a much larger issue here. You are freaking telling people that you want to preserve an old derelict house because you think it's haunted? *Really??*"

"I told one or two people that, yes."

"One or two?? Dad! People at the stationhouse are harassing me over this and it's very uncomfortable! I'm newly promoted and this is all they need to have a field day."

"Like what kind of harassment?"

"Well somebody drew a cartoon ghost on the assignment board and wrote a big 'Booooo!' next to my name. I don't need this, Dad!" Georgie decides to leave out the inflated condom for now.

"That actually sounds fairly good-natured."

"And they took your dumb picture off the website and blew it up to eight-by-ten and hung it in the day room. With that stupid caption."

"Now that's going too far. Who do I get fired?"

"I'm serious, Dad, people are looking at me differently. Including the Chief."

Lyle recalls the day he twisted the chief's arm. "Queeley's a putz."

"You're *not helping*, Dad!"

"I recommend you go about your business and continue doing excellent detective work. Excellent work trumps all else."

"Easy for you to say. So did you talk to Frank?"

"Big Frank? No. He was out there earlier ID-ing squatters."

"Well he went off duty at eight a.m. He'll be back tonight. Dad, hear me now. This has to end. Today. *Now*."

"It will, Daughter, things like this don't last."

"You *have* to end it, Dad. If only for me. I'll call you later to make sure you took care of this. And when I call you, I expect you to pick up, okay? Dad, if you can't protect yourself, at least protect me!"

Lyle is about to beg Georgie to be careful but she disconnects. He shudders as the nauseating thought of Georgie's name added to Belinda's headstone hits him again.

Now Lyle has a call to make. Try to get some positive outcome from all this.

You have reached Save-a-Barn, the guardian of the East End's farming heritage.

Lyle keys in the extension and waits.

"Becky Tuttle."

"Lyle Hall."

There's that pause. Kind of gut-wrenching.

"Yes?"

"I'm calling about lunch? I suggested it last night?" He realizes he's up-speaking.

Another pause. Then..."Mister Hall, I don't think this is the time, what with all that's going on."

Where did "Mister Hall" come from? Is someone standing by her desk? Lyle hears some muffled chatter, then Becky's back.

"Lyle, it's not a good time. I'm sorry."

"That's okay, Becky." Pause. "So why is it not a good time? Because that guy wrote that dumb story making me look like a nut and I now have a tent city of wackos set up around my house?"

"Yes."

"Oh."

Becky opens up a little. "Lyle, you should see NewsChannel 12. I have it on now and I'm looking at your house."

"Really? Want me to raise the blinds and wave?"

Becky Tuttle stifles a giggle. "Could you? It looks like a kitchen window."

"Hold on."

Lyle rolls to the kitchen dinette and cracks the shade.

And there they are. Lights, camera, News12 doing a stand-up right from his lawn.

"Ho-lee flippin' *shit*..."

Up and down the block, on neighbors' lawns, in the gutters, across the street, a tent city of campers stretches beyond Lyle's field of view. Most are Patagonia-style dome tents. There's one GI canvas pup tent right outside Lyle's dinette window. Its occupant spots Lyle in the window and comes out and waves. He's tall, old and crazy.

"Mister Hall! How ya like that coffee?"

Stunned, Lyle makes the okay sign.

"Lyle?"

"Oh, sorry, Becky. I just...I just saw the extent of what's going on outside."

"It is startling. Your fifteen minutes of fame."

Another awkward pause.

"So Becky. About that lunch..."

"How can you think about lunch at a time like this?"

"I'm a man and I don't cook. And I need to get out of here. So, Maidstone?"

"No, not the Maidstone..."

"Why? You know too many people there?"

"Yes."

"Oh. Want to go someplace clandestine then?"

Becky thinks about *clandestine*.

"Lyle, I've got to go now. You might call me later. And good luck with all of..." Becky Tuttle stares at her computer monitor. News12 Long Island is streaming a live feed from Lyle's yard. A blond woman reporter gestures at Lyle's house and then points down the block. Camera shows the street is overrun with people, tents and weird homemade signs. Then the feed switches to another scene—111 Poplar Street. Also overrun.

"...all of...*that*." She hangs up.

Lyle doesn't turn on the TV. What he sees outside his window is more than enough.

"Jeez," he exhales. "I gotta get out of here."

~~~~~~

31. Believers

"Mister Hall?"

"I'll be right out, officer!" Lyle says this through his front door mail slot.

It's 11:00 a.m. and, because of the campers, at least a hundred people now, Georgie has arranged for two cops to escort her dad out to his MediCab for the ride to Justice Court. A rare telephonic victory for Georgie. Lyle is to return to court and rescind his wrongheaded request for an injunction against demolition. He had to admit that the occupation of his neighborhood by camping crazies and the late-night home invasion—well-meaning though it might have been—are unacceptable outcomes. He's also agreed to meet Georgie after he does his court business. She's taking time off from work to get him ensconced in a hotel room somewhere in Southampton until "all this blows over." She's also determined to obtain "additional therapy" for her father.

Still a little spooked by Glen Stanley's visit, Lyle rolls to the kitchen, makes sure the door is deadbolt locked. He chains it too. He notices the china and silver is laid out and is no longer sure if he'd put it away hours ago. On his way to the front door, Fred phones, frustrated that he can't get the MediCab near Lyle's house due to all the campers and hubbub.

"Okay, okay, Fred, I'm coming out. I'll come to you."

"Yeah, well there's a damn big van in the middle of the street too, so I give up!"

As Fred disconnects, the policemen knock again and Lyle opens the door to a young patrolman and a middle-aged sergeant. Peering past the two cops, he's hit by the chaotic scene playing in his front yard and the street beyond. Over a hundred people are scattered around pup tents in a makeshift campground. And their number is growing—a van down the block is disgorging a half dozen backpackers. He's struck by the surprisingly mixed demographic—from Glen Stanley's Greatest Generation to young, underemployed-looking people of both sexes. A kind of United Nations of weird.

Across the street, the large corner lot between Mr. Rosewater's house and the edge of the cemetery is now a kind of staging area with lots of colorful, newly pitched tents. Two creative-looking guys with dreadlocks are there banging on inverted plastic tubs. Lyle knows only a fraction of the homes in town are occupied after Columbus Day, and old Mr. Rosewater is one. The tub-bangers move right the fuck in front of the old bird's house and a dozen or more campers surround them. Lyle dimly notes that the banging—three throbbing blows in a row— jibes with an increasingly enthusiastic chant. It's unsettling— some kind of paranormal call-and-response thing. The group moves as one into the street, closer to Lyle's house.

Lyle looks at his two cops. "Gentlemen, is the street passable?"

"Not exactly," says the younger cop. His little name plate reads PETRY.

"We're trying," says the sergeant, a black man whose plate says MACKEY.

"Well I'm glad you men are here. Let's do this."

The two policemen help maneuver Lyle, who's forgetting his change of clothes, toiletries and various prescription meds, out to the ramp. As soon as the crowd spots Lyle in his pennant-flying wheelchair, they close in on his property. The cops carefully steer him down the ramp as more campers join in the chant. It coalesces and grows louder. Something from a pop song? The Monkees? That *Shrek* cartoon?

"Then I saw her face!"
CLAP CLAP CLAP
"I'm a believer!"
CLAP CLAP CLAP

The crowd chants, claps and repeats. And repeats. They're using Lyle's words, he realizes, from that damned Mose Allen story. Twisting his words. All these people are chanting some bullshit they read online! They're all here because of Mose Allen!

Lyle thinks again...no, face it: They're here because they must love haunted houses and Lyle did in fact speak to a reporter, however ill advised. That Lyle Hall does not love crowds of people who love haunted houses is now immaterial.

Once he's wheels down on the wobbly slate sidewalk, the pressure from the crowd is palpable. For one thing, everyone stands taller than him. Petry and Mackey flank Lyle's chair and a third cop joins in, creating a phalanx. Big Frank is off duty.

"Where to, Mister Hall?" says Officer Petry.

Lyle points down the street to his MediCab and the odd cluster starts to move toward it when Glen Stanley's wizened head pops in view between the blue uniforms.

"Mister Hall! What do you think?" he cries out, trying to be heard over the chant and growing commotion.

"I'm impressed."

"Me too! Exciting! Bigger turnout than I expected! We're gonna get results!"

Lyle involuntarily rolls his eyes at whatever "results" might mean at this point. A video camera pokes at him, and a News12 microphone. It's the blonde.

"Mister Hall! Have you seen the ghost girl again? Will you save her house?"

Lyle silently waves her off and the cops do a good job of blocking her out.

Glen Stanley reappears. "Mister Hall?"

"Glen, please stop calling me Mister Hall? Lyle is fine!" Lyle snaps at him.

"Sure." Glen turns to the campers near him and, cupping his hands like a megaphone, hollers, "Lyle is fine!"

Some in the crowd turn and repeat the phrase to those out of earshot. The words somehow become a new chant—"Lyle is fine! Lyle is fine!"—creating a weird counterpoint to the initial chant: "Then I saw her face! Lyle is fine! I'm a believer!"

Lyle can see the News12 blonde reporting on-camera with the chanters behind her. "Oh my God..." he says to no one. "What have I done?"

The three-man police force is slow clearing a path for Lyle to the street. Campers swarm around the wheelchair. Lyle gets young Petry to take down his orange pennant, hoping that helps. Random heads pop in between the blue uniforms as they inch Lyle away from the house. The campers want a look at Lyle Hall. As the plastic tubs throb on with their three-beat riff, some campers blurt out cockeyed questions.

"Lyle! Do you want to adopt Jewel? Or marry her?"

"No! Too young! And too old!" He elicits a sort-of chuckle.

Some want to share their own ghost stories.

"Lyle! I got your ghost story beat, man!" This from a disturbingly scruffy man. "Come by my tent if you want to hear it!"

"Later, dude." This guy doesn't even know my ghost story, Lyle thinks.

He's making a little more progress when Glen reinserts himself. "Lyle, are you going to see Jewel tonight? We want to go see her too! There are many Believers camped at her house already!"

"I don't know that she likes crowds, Glen." Lyle tries to be more civil. "Do you know any ghosts who like crowds?"

"No, Lyle, but we'll be quiet."

It sinks in that these strangers all know Jewel's name. Of course they would.

The sense of chaos intensifies as the press of bodies builds. A boney, elderly hand thrusts a Sharpie pen at Lyle. What for, an autograph? Unbelievable!

Then it happens.

Something to write on lands on his lap. Something totally unexpected.

Jewel. Her beautiful face on a sheet of photocopy paper.

Lyle's stomach churns. He goes into a convulsive fit of anger, mumbles a curse, crumples up the paper and tosses it back into the crowd. The Sharpie, too.

A hush falls over the group. Except for a tub being beaten three times somewhere. The crowd doesn't know how to react to Lyle's hostility. There's some murmuring. Did Lyle just make a bad mistake? What kind of ammunition do the police use for riots? Rubber bullets? Lyle feels very faint. Very short of breath. Very short.

"C'mon, folks, give us some room here! A little room!" says Sgt. Mackey.

Then Glen Stanley pipes up. "Hey! Believers! It's okay! We've got plenty more! Hundreds more!"

Shit, Lyle thinks, *hundreds more*. Jewel, his troubled, secret friend, is no longer his and his alone. Linder must have sent his sketch to somebody who sent it to somebody and then Mose Allen attached it to his haunted whorehouse story.

Glen Stanley tries to lift the crowd's mood with his Lyle chant. A few campers tentatively pick it up.

"Lyle is fine! Lyle is fine..."

The campers relinquish some space to the six-footed, two-wheeled grouping and they make more progress away from Lyle's house.

Then a tall young man with dark curly hair looms into view.

"Mister Hall? Mister Hall?" He shows the policemen his news media ID badge and they allow him access. "Mister Hall, Josh Berendt. With FEARcom. I work for Silk."

"I don't know what that means."

"Silk is here to meet you. For your interview. Flo Hendricks texted you."

Lyle shrugs at the cops. "Right. Look what my last interview did for me!"

"I'd highly recommend doing it, Mister Hall." Josh points to the street and Lyle can see the FEARcom news van parked obnoxiously. Two women are standing by it. One is dowdy Flo, working her iPad. The other is speaking into her Bluetooth headset. Lyle realizes it was her picture Flo showed him last night. Wow.

~~~~~~

32. Silk

She's gorgeous—kind of like Catwoman, in black leather and heels. Only better looking. Very striking rich, dark hair. Lush, sell-your-soul-for lips. And mysterious dark glasses. Silk is talking animatedly into her headset as she signs autographs for mostly male college-age losers. A big young guy in a FEARcom T-shirt is lining them all up. Flo makes eye contact with Lyle.

"So that's...?" Lyle begins to say.

Josh, moving with the cops, leans down. "You signed the agreement last night," he reminds the befuddled wheelchair guy.

Lyle returns Josh's gaze.

"It'll never stand up."

"Your signature?"

The cops continue to steer Lyle toward the MediCab, but the FEARcom van stands in the way. Now the crowd breaks into their "I'm a believer!" chant again. It's sunny and unseasonably warm near midday. Lyle feels sticky and sweaty. As he gets closer to the van, Flo Hendricks approaches.

"Good morning, Lyle!"

"Hi," he says as the cops halt again. He takes in the van. It's new. The van's rear window is tinted, but he senses it's full of video and computer gear and luggage. A huge, gleaming FEARcom logo is applied to the side panel. Under it is the company slogan: *Get Near Your Fear*. Lyle has to tell Flo about his change of heart. Now's the time.

"You got my text?"

"Listen, Flo, I'm sorry you all came here and everything, but I spoke with my daughter and came to a decision..."

Flo moves closer to him. "And now you have cold feet. Second thoughts. Family dissuaded you. You're giving up. You don't think the contract you signed has merit."

"Uh, yeah, actually. But I wish you'd leave my feet out of it."

The cops look at each other. Mackey says, "Mister Hall? Shall we proceed?"

The chanting seems to get louder. Now Glen Stanley reappears, thrusting his face down to Lyle's.

"Lyle, are you going to be on FEARcom? How exciting! Now I know we'll win!"

"Uh, Glen…" Lyle says as Glen turns to face the chanting campers.

"People! Lyle is going on FEARcom!" There are general grunts of approval. "That means WE are going to be on FEARcom!!"

The crowd erupts into whoops and cheers. Lyle cringes and regards his police escort's skeptical expressions. He notes Flo's self-satisfaction and the smug look on the puss of the tall young guy, Josh or whoever. No. Absolutely not. Georgie was right. He doesn't need this. She doesn't either. A normal life is a good life. Out of the public eye.

The crowd takes up an impromptu chant. "FEARcom! FEARcom! FEARcom!"

Over the chants Officer Petry tries to get Lyle's attention. "Mister Hall? Mister Hall?" Time to go.

There is sudden quiet.

Everyone—crowd, cops, FEARcom staff, everyone except Lyle—turns toward the FEARcom van. The chants quiet down to a hush. Someone is coming.

"Mister Hall?"

The voice is youthful but throaty, redolent of late nights and getting one's way. Lyle looks up at her and waves of untapped emotion and sexual energy flow through him. His jaw drops. A soft sibilance envelopes him. People are whispering her name...*Silk.*

She's coming straight toward him. The crowd murmurs excitedly. The policemen give way as she strides forward on stiletto heels, dark sunglasses, black leather pants that look like technicians sprayed them on, and an outsized motorcycle jacket, also black leather, its belt cinched tight at her small waist, yet big and powerful-looking around her shoulders. Lyle recalls that zipper. He saw it, he saw Silk, last night on Flo's iPad. The oversize metal zipper is nearly halfway down. Inside the zipper is a curve of femininity.

"Mister Hall?" Her voice is husky, needful and teasing at the same time. Lyle wants to hear more of it. A lot more.

"It's Lyle," he manages. "Lyle is fine."

Silk comes to a halt close to Lyle, violating his personal space. He gets a major charge of weird energy from the violation. She crouches down to his level. Her red lips protrude below big sunglasses. She's maybe 26. There's a Marilyn Monroe-style beauty mark. Her long fingers, adorned with shiny black nail polish, pull away her sunglasses so Lyle can see her incredible green eyes.

"I'll bet Lyle is fine," she says, coyly, like a purr. Lyle's block is crowded with strangers and weirdoes and cops and camper equipment. *I'll bet Lyle is fine.* That one half-whispered statement ushers Lyle into a sultry, private dream world. Didn't they say that Bill Clinton had the ability to make individuals feel like they were the only person in a crowded room? Why the fuck am I thinking about Bill Clinton right now, he wonders.

Lyle doesn't need to read Silk. She's someone who gets what she wants and she wants him. Any fool could pick up on that.

She smiles a knowing smile. The kind that makes Lyle fantasize.

She holds out her hand.

"Silk."

Lyle takes her hand. It's very soft. Her perfume, too much, is mesmerizing.

"Pleased to meet you," he says from a daze.

"Are you? Well, Lyle Hall, you're going to get a lot more pleased."

"I am?"

Silk looks at the cops standing around Lyle. Focusing on young Petry, she says, "May we have a minute?"

The cops shrug and back away a little. Now Silk gives Lyle her full attention.

"You're used to making money, aren't you," she says. "Well, we're going to put you on a celebrity skyrocket. You will be in demand nationwide. All over the world, Lyle, not just here." Her white lower teeth show when she says his name.

The hyperbole helps to shake Lyle out of his dream state. "In demand?"

Silk cocks her head and pouts at him. Dark tresses slip across one eye.

"Celebrity has value, Lyle, an exciting new career for you. National television, book deals, paid appearances, speaking engagements, endorsements." She nods at the people crowding around them. "See this? Your friend Jewel is just the beginning."

Silk forks her sunglasses into the hair atop her head. Her bangs free themselves and flop over one arched eyebrow. Both hands come to rest on Lyle's armrests. *Just the beginning*, Lyle muses. He imagines sucking all the red gloss from her lips to see them naked. Silk blinks and he notes how long and dark her lashes are.

"Lyle, you want your Jewel story covered the right way? That hatchet-job on the Internet is only the beginning if we don't take control of it. Is that court reporter a paranormal expert? No, he is not. His was a pathetic, twisted attempt to write about what could be the defining supernatural occurrence of our time."

Silk turns to Flo. "You have that photo of Lyle that's on the Internet?"

On cue, Flo steps forward with her iPad displaying Lyle Hall at his very worst—Mose Allen's shot of him wild-eyed crazy, shirt ripped, face scratched, hair and beard powdered white. Lyle winces as Silk takes it in with some satisfaction.

"Oh, what's that character from Shakespeare? King...uh, Hamlet?"

"You're thinking of King Lear," Flo offers.

"Yes. A tragedy, right?" Silk looks at Lyle. "We know how to avert tragedy."

"Uh, Silk," Lyle tries to make a point. "I don't really think there's a future in this, uh, this apparition stuff."

Silk pouts again. Those fascinating red lips seem to have a life of their own. His eyes fall to her jacket zipper and her cleavage, like a baby's butt, nestled under that jagged metal. Suddenly it's gone. A cold wave of despair washes over Lyle.

Silk thrusts herself upward using Lyle's armrests and stands to face the crowd, her quadriceps bulging beneath her leather pants at Lyle's eye level. Officer Petry watches her work.

"Hey people!" She cries out to the crowd. "How many of you believe in Jewel?"

There's an instantaneous response. "I'm a believer!" repeats from all corners. Many wave Jewel's picture overhead. Glen was right; there are lots of copies.

Silk smiles and looks down at Lyle Hall. She addresses the campers again. "And how about Lyle Hall?" she cries.

First Glen Stanley starts with "Lyle is fine!" Then many of the campers join in. They continue as Silk, her point made, crouches down to her prey.

She plants her palms on his armrests again. The crowd noise dissolves into random whoops and cries. From this vantage point, Silk's cleavage is fuller still, just out of Lyle's reach. Did she plan this?

"This is just the tip of the iceberg, Lyle. A big one, I promise you. I know you're not afraid of success. And I know success when I see it." She whispers, "Think about it."

He does.

Silk falls silent and looks into Lyle's eyes. Her smooth hands on his armrests are so close, almost touching his elbows. Glen gets the crowd repeating its dumb "I saw her face—I'm a believer!" chant. The perfect background for Lyle's faulty decision-making. That tall young guy, Josh, orders the big kid in the FEARcom T-shirt to hand out an armload of black FEARcom T-shirts. His name is Chad. Josh starts to move around the crowd, capturing digital video of the chanters, who eagerly demonstrate their enthusiasm.

Lyle decides to attempt to read Silk, her background—where? beauty school?—and the kind of woman she is—aggressive, self-centered, anyone could tell that—but the variety of pressures blocks out a good read. He's new at this, he reminds himself. Silk's lips alone are so enticing. Lyle flashes on a range of erotic acts while her dark eyelids lower just slightly, intimating the intense focus she will afford Lyle Hall once they start to work together. That chanting. Will it ever end? And there's that fat lady standing there. Flo Hendricks…okay, she's not obese, but compared to Silk…Lyle can sense how Flo is somehow inside his consciousness, snooping around. While he picks up gorgeous waves of eroticism from Silk, he also feels dowdy Flo examining his thoughts like a psychic hall monitor. Are my thoughts not my own? He protests. What the fuck! He closes his eyes and his imagination runs free…

He can now stand up. And walk. And take Silk in his arms. They're in some swank hotel room in…New York City…maybe L.A. He unzips her black leather jacket. His hands slide under it while she opens his expensive jeans. She bends, slowly lowering his jeans to the floor. She stands and unbuttons his tailored shirt. He unzips her form-fitting black skirt, exposing her red thong and round rump. She writhes away, turning her back to him. He sinks to his knees and massages her bitable glutes. Her leather jacket slips down, revealing bare shoulders. She reaches back and her black nails talon his ears. She directs his mouth on a tour. He realizes his beard is shaved off. His face feels so soft against her skin. His hands roam. He inhales her leather, her earthiness, and…

And a neighborhood full of squatters resounds with a stupid chant. A fat lady has observed everything he just imagined. The sun is beating hot and there are cops and he has a beard hiding scars and he's been plagued by visions and nightmares for two days. He's in a wheelchair and has no feeling from the L4 vertebra down. But Silk still looms right in front of him.

"Lyle?" He hears his name in a husky whisper. "Lyle?" What was that John Lennon "dream" song back in college…where "John" is whispered repeatedly…

Silk, Lyle now realizes, will help him get to Jewel again. And Jewel will help expose whatever danger Georgie faces—unless it's just a hoax. And the spinal-injury clinic will return strength to his legs. He will be a new kind of celebrity, traveling, helping fearful people everywhere and enjoying intimacy with Silk. He opens his eyes and there she stands. His new partner.

There's a thrumming sound close by. A phone.

"I have to take this," says Silk, putting on her sunglasses. She connects the call and pats Lyle's hand. Pats it like a nurse pats some old geezer's hand in a nursing home. Silk steps back, talking into her Bluetooth.

"Yes, Gregg," she says to the caller. "He's right here." She listens, then says, "Oh yeah, we've got him," and turns her back to Lyle. He watches her behind sway, sheathed in black leather, as she moves toward the FEARcom van.

Flo Hendricks is standing there probing Lyle's eyes with her own. He finally looks her way. A sly little smile pokes the corner of her mouth. He can sense her strange thoughts—ironic, even vindictive, but accurate. *You just got Silked.*

"Mister Hall?" It's Officer Petry. "Will you be needing further assistance?"

Cop. Lyle suddenly remembers Georgie is a cop. He's given her his word he would end this. She's suffering at work. Her very life may be in danger. However... working with these paranormal experts may very well solve the riddle of *Georgia Hall* etched on her mother's tombstone. Georgie will understand the special circumstances...

Flo smiles at the cop and waves him off. "Thank you, officer. We'll take it from here."

Chad appears, all his T-shirts now distributed to the faithful.

"Chad," says Flo, "push Mister Hall over to the van and we'll get to work."

Chad's strong hands grip Lyle's chair handles but Lyle throws the chair in gear. "It's motorized," he says, and steers it in the direction Silk took. She's now out of sight behind the van. Lyle, Flo and Chad move together toward the shady side of the big FEARcom van. Meanwhile, campers close in around Josh's camera—except for one scraggly coot with Civil War sideburns. He's been camping with Glen Stanley. Lyle glances back at Josh as he rehearses the campers in their new FEARcom T-shirts spouting, "Get near your fear!" in unison for the camera. A promo, Lyle muses. There must be big money in fear.

Silk, still in conversation, emerges from behind the van and addresses Chad.

"Have Lyle sign those pictures of Jewel."

"Sign how many?" Chad asks.

"All of 'em."

Silk turns back to her caller and Lyle gets a sinking feeling. Like he's a piece of meat. He feels possessed. But it feels kind of sexy.

Chad hands Lyle a black Sharpie. "Okay, Mister Hall..." He rotates the chair to face the crowd. "Let's meet your public." Lyle sees how many campers now wear FEARcom shirts and hold pictures of Jewel. Josh is videotaping them as they converge.

"I don't do autographs," Lyle says for Chad and Josh to hear.

"Chad," Josh says, one eye in his lens, "tell him it's in his contract."

Lyle gets it. He autographs one picture and hates it right away. He also notes the FEARcom logo is printed on each sheet. He's a kept man. Suddenly a wrinkled photocopy is thrust before him—the one Lyle angrily crumpled and tossed earlier. Lyle looks up. The coot with the bushy sideburns.

Their eyes meet and Lyle gets a fleeting read from the old guy:

This Lyle Hall character is going to hurt somebody.

~~~~~~

33. Milk This

The cops keep working the crowd outside Lyle's house, asking suspicious-looking persons for ID; calming the tub-bangers; explaining local laws regarding lawful assembly and answering questions from campers. The campers—who number over 120 now and call themselves Believers—mostly want to know about any nearby public restrooms.

Finally done signing, Lyle and Flo move behind the van. Silk is there, talking into her Bluetooth.

Flo looks at Lyle. "It's Gregg. FEARcom VP of marketing."

Josh joins them as Silk disconnects. Chad walks over. She faces her team.

"We're a go. National television. Two networks are bidding."

"Woohoo!" says Chad. Josh regards the big kid like he's a mental defective.

Silk focuses on Lyle. "Are you familiar with our work on FEARcom, Lyle?"

"Sort of…but I'm already near my fear as it is."

Silk bares a dazzling smile. Lyle wants her to bite him. Bad.

"That's good. Lyle, one thing we need to do is make absolutely sure that your story and Jewel's story are told with clarity and fairness. Do you want to appear in those awful checkout-line tabloids with 'space-alien babies' and 'two-headed dogs'?"

"How do you stop that?"

"We don't stop that. We fight back by getting your true story out there and telling it our way—the best, most professional way."

"What if I don't want my story out there?"

Silk nods toward the crowd of campers. "Too late. They're assembled outside Jewel's house too. What we're talking about is managing the story. Do you want to appear with Barbara Walters? Katie Couric? The big cable news outlets?"

"Uh, no."

"Incorrect. You do. You actually have to. That's where FEARcom comes in." With a nod to her team, Silk draws a bead on Lyle. "We have the supernatural-story-management expertise to handle big television networks, handle your story and handle you, Lyle."

Lyle imagines Silk handling him. "How?"

"You will interview on national television with me, and *Lyle Hall* will become a household name."

"What kind of national television?"

"Gregg is working that out as we speak."

Josh and Chad groan at the mention of the FEARcom vice president.

"Is he good?" asks Lyle.

"He's effective. He called to make sure you signed our exclusivity agreement."

"Last night, Silk," says Flo. "I have it."

"I'd like a look at that document," Lyle says weakly.

Silk turns all business. "Then we're agreed. All Jewel-related stories and interviews, for television, radio, print, Internet or other media, go through FEARcom. On your behalf, we will negotiate with and charge fees to the major television entertainment-news programs and talk shows and their ancillary outlets. Free-market, fair and square."

"They pay for content?"

"They'll pay for our content."

"And you'll be with me?"

Silk stoops to pat Lyle's hand. "Every step of the way, Lyle." Patronizing.

"How long will this last?"

"Well your story, as I've said, has all the earmarks of becoming a defining event. It has legs. In the future, the world may mark paranormal episodes as Before Jewel and After Jewel. To put it another way, we know how to milk this thing."

Lyle realizes that Fred the driver, who's been sitting in his MediCab chain-smoking cigarettes and calling Lyle's cell to no avail, is now approaching on foot.

Silk continues. "You don't actually work anymore, do you, Lyle?"

"No. Not really. Some pro bono work."

"Perfect. Pro bono sounds good."

"Mister Hall? Mister Hall?" Fred joins the group. "I have other fares waiting."

"I'm sorry, Fred!" Lyle says, flashing again on his promise to Georgie—that he will return to court and drop his dumb motion.

"I waited a half-hour—want me to go?"

"Uh…"

"Yes, thank you," says Flo, stepping in. "We've got him from here."

Lyle beckons Fred closer. Fred smells like cigarette smoke. "I'll call you later." Lyle slips two twenties in his shirt pocket. Fred glances at Silk and heads back to his van.

Silk gets back to business. "Flo, I have to work the phone. I need to use the rental car and have you ride in the van with Lyle."

"Okay," Flo says, handing over the keys.

"Get to know Mister Hall while I nail down the interview segment. Take Lyle to lunch and bring him up to speed on the paranormal world. You got us a hotel?"

"Yes, it's a motel, really. Montauk, off the beaten track. The Memory Motel."

"It's okay? Not a dump?"

"I think it'll be okay, Silk," says Flo, a little unsure she's met Silk's requirements.

"Hey," ventures Chad, "as our official clairvoyant, shouldn't you know?"

"The place is old school but okay," Lyle offers.

"It's private," Flo says. "I think that's important."

"You got four rooms?" says Silk. "One for Josh and Chad; one each for the rest of us?" At this, Josh squints at Silk but she ignores him. Silk's phone starts ringing again and she speaks rapidly to the group.

"Flo, make sure my room has the amenities. Chad, make sure all my stuff—wardrobe, makeup table, everything, is in my

148

room. Lyle, try to get some rest, you're going to have a big night. Remember, a big splash on television will put more pressure on the judge in your court case to do the right thing for Jewel."

Lyle nods but a wrench in his gut reminds him all this is in direct violation of his agreement with Georgie. His phone throbs and he peeks at it. Shit. Georgie again.

"Now Josh," Silk says, ignoring her own phone, "we need stills of Lyle shot from all angles for the reenactment. Use your Nikon. Gregg guaranteed the package we're offering will be high definition."

"Yes, Boss Lady."

Reenactment? Lyle broods.

"We need Lyle and Jewel both looking their high-def best," Silk says.

"Is that *all?*" says Josh.

"No. Finishing the graphic ID is key. We need to 'own' the piece. Do that first."

"I'm going to do a bunch of things first. Where's my staff?"

"Standing to your left. Chad, this is high def, you know? Remember, that's no good without high def audio, right?"

"You want surround sound?"

"No, no, just make it really pristine. So we can edit the shit out of it." Silk's incoming phone call went to voice mail. She looks at the caller ID. "That's Gregg again. Gotta call him back. Josh, think 'Emmy' when you light the set, got it? See if the hotel has a library or a den we can use. I don't want the setting to be a skeevy motel room."

"I'll make it nice," Josh says.

Addressing the group, Silk adds, "This is about to get interesting, people. I will inform Josh when I know which network we're going with. Later, after we upload the segment, we'll have a take-out dinner and watch the broadcast. Then, late tonight, we're going to shoot Lyle at Jewel's house."

Flo notices Lyle react. Lyle at Jewel's house. Tonight. On camera. This has really lurched out of his control. But Silk's bossy confidence makes him want her even more.

Silk's phone starts ringing again. "Gotta go. Ta-ta and play nice." She hurries toward Flo's rental.

Josh watches Silk get into the car. "Next time I definitely want a job description," he says under his breath.

Lyle looks to Flo. Someone is coming up behind her.

"Okay! Where's Lyle Hall?" A brash male voice intrudes. A tall, loud, blond-haired man in a suit holding a microphone and trailed by a cameraman and an audio guy. The little sign on his mic reads WFSB-TV. "Silk?" he calls over to her. She's in the car on her phone. "What a *surprise*. She's on the *phone!* So where's the paranormal lawyer?" He looks down and recognizes Lyle Hall. "I call we're next!" To Josh, he says, "We have to upload right away so, would you mind, you know, giving us some room?"

Larry Anders is a reporter for Channel 3 in Hartford, Connecticut. Flo gets in his face and Josh and Chad automatically take positions flanking Lyle.

"Larry," Flo says firmly, "FEARcom has an exclusive on Lyle Hall."

"Oh *shit!*" Larry Anders says in mock dismay. "*Great.* So he won't talk to me? This could end my brilliant career!"

"That could please your dozens of viewers," says Flo.

"That stings, Flo." He looks down at Lyle and winks. "At least I *have* viewers."

Larry Anders directs his men down the street, intending to interview campers, locals, policemen and so on. They only go a short distance before realizing that a large number of campers wear FEARcom T-shirts.

"Oh *shit!*" He turns back to Flo. "*Really*, Flo? T-shirts? I can't get a crowd shot!"

Flo smiles sweetly and Larry's men set about cajoling campers to remove the offending T-shirts if they want to be interviewed on television.

The chanters and percussionists create a crazy background cacophony as Chad helps Lyle into the van's backseat. He folds up Lyle's chair and stows it in back with the video equipment. Flo gets in next to him. Lyle is theirs.

Behind the wheel now, Chad asks "Where to?"

"Do you have headquarters somewhere?" Lyle asks.

"Yeah," says Josh from the front seat. "Connecticut." He glances back at Lyle. "Paranormally, it's a busy area. Hence that jerk from WFSB."

Lyle thinks this over. "Right. Okay, so you want the Memory Motel? Get onto Montauk Highway and head east."

With direction from Officer Petry, the FEARcom van slowly makes a tight U-turn through the crowd in the street. Chad is careful to avoid wandering campers and backpackers. Then there's a rap on a side window and Glen Stanley's face appears. He's trying to make out Lyle in the backseat.

"Lyle? Lyle, we're going to Jewel's house tonight, right? What time? Late?"

Chad gives it some gas and Glen is left behind. As they pull away, the van comes up on Fred, who's carefully backing his beeping MediCab away from the scene.

Chad cuts him off.

~~~~~~

34. Out of Town

As the FEARcom van moves through Bridgehampton—sans
Silk—Lyle Hall wonders what in hell he's gotten himself into.
National TV? What national TV? Prior to anything like that he's
got to call Georgie and fess up. No, begging forgiveness after the
fact will be easier. Deciding to go with Silk—where'd she go,
anyway? —is one of those go-with-your-gut things. How often
does a 55-year-old get to work with someone like Silk? This is
all so surreal—little Jewel, the courthouse, Fr. Xerri, fucking
Mose Allen, the Believers, the gorgeous Silk, television. Lyle
tries to convince himself that something good has to come from
it. The perfect result would be Jewel tells Lyle how to avert his
daughter's death. Georgie would have to accept that. Everybody
wins…

Lyle feels a stab in his gut. *What's wrong with that scenario?*

"Can we drive by Old Vic?" Lyle suggests. "I want to see if it's
okay."

"Already shot an intro there with Silk," Josh says, adding,
"It's too congested there now." He glances back at Lyle. "But we
have good footage."

Chad pulls the van onto Montauk Highway. "What's the
name of the hotel?"

"The Memory Motel," Lyle responds. "Past Amagansett.
About twenty minutes from here." Lyle ponders a moment. "So
who's this VP? Greg who?"

"Chilton Gregg," says Flo, "of the Hartford Greggs. Old
money."

"Chatsworth Osborne, Junior," Josh sneers.

"Huh?" The snarky nickname strikes Lyle as vaguely
familiar.

"Gregg discovered Silk a few years ago," Flo says. "He used
family money to bankroll FEARcom. And put her on the map."

Lyle chews on that.

Josh glances back at Flo. "This motel. They had vacancies?"

"It's October," Lyle points out.

"We're not the only TV crew looking for rooms right now," Josh returns.

As the van rolls through town heading east on Montauk, they approach the Y-shaped intersection with the "Founders Monument" war memorial. Chad pulls up at the traffic light near the carved granite block Lyle crashed his Hummer into a year ago.

The pizza slice of turf in the intersection supports a tall flagpole bearing Old Glory and the impressive mausoleum-style granite that was first unveiled in 1910 on the Fourth of July. Originally it commemorated the 250th anniversary of the hamlet's founding and its residents who fought in the Revolutionary War, the War of 1812 and the Civil War. Since then, Bridgehampton has had to include World War I, World War II, the Korean conflict, Vietnam…and counting.

This is the first time Lyle has been in close proximity to the monument since the crash. He peers at it from this unusual aspect. Is it slightly off kilter? Please let that be an optical illusion. Fact is, the granite looks unscathed. Healthy new sod covers the tire gouges from last year. He looks at Flo.

"That's where I crashed my SUV…"

Then Lyle feels a twinge of discomfort. Then a lot. What was Dr. Susan Wayne's warning?

Suddenly all the wind flushes out of Lyle's lungs. He doubles over in a violent convulsion. Paralyzing pain forces itself up through his abdomen, even into his jaw.

"Lyle!" Flo cries. She unlatches her seatbelt and embraces Lyle's upper body. His face almost between his knees, Lyle has unknowingly stretched his seatbelt across his throat.

"Lyle!" Flo can sense the convulsions roiling through him. "Chad! Get us out of here! Hit the gas! Please!"

"We're at a red light, Flo!"

Flo squeezes Lyle firmly. He starts coughing deep and hard, unable to speak. She locates his seatbelt buckle and releases it. Lyle is coughing but he is not breathing.

"Chad! Just do as I say!"

"What is the *problem?*" Josh says, annoyed.

Chad groans and pulls out from behind a pickup also stopped at the light. He hits the flashing emergency lights and creeps over white-paint hash marks on the shoulder. Now even closer to the big stone memorial, Lyle stops coughing and goes silent. Flo fears a near-death experience. Hugging Lyle, she tries to tell if his heart is beating.

"Chad, you have to get us away from here. Now! Drive the van!"

"What do you *want* from me, Flo? I could get arrested!"

Lyle Hall is the driver of the 2009 H3 Hummer that crashed here. And now he's back. His old injuries rip violently through his body and face again. Like a sadistic torturer's return visit.

But now he's outside, floating above the scene. He sees his own Hummer come screeching out of nowhere. It strikes the Ford with shattering force, spinning it backward. The Ford bounces off a telephone pole and comes to rest on its passenger side. But it did avoid that old guy walking his dog. The dog is going crazy. The Hummer's horn is honking steadily somewhere. The Ford's driver is caught up in the seat belt. Elsie Cronk. She's not in pain, but her 85-year-old heart has stopped beating. How long can you go without a heart? Her son's homemade birthday cake is everywhere. What a shame. The wax number-candles said "50." There was a fire truck decoration, for Jimmy's promotion. Sirens wail out on the street. Time running out. A face looks down through the driver-side window. Oh, God, it's Jimmy! Jimmy goes into shock seeing his mother like this. Men pull him back. Men try to open the door. In a great wave of emotion, a mother's heart reaches out to her son. The years flash by. And time is up.

"Get us out of here now, Chad!" Flo growls. "Our man could be dying—we have to get *away* from this place!"

"Just do it, Chad!" says Josh, his foot pumping an imaginary gas pedal.

"Oh, *shit!*" Chad cries. He rolls into the intersection with his hazard lights flashing and cars and trucks left and right halt and start honking. "Guys, this isn't a freaking ambulance, you know!"

Sickening gurgling sounds form deep in Lyle's chest. Josh rotates to face the backseat, trying to assess the crisis level. As Flo hugs Lyle's upper body, sharp flashes of terror, pain and violent death stab her heart. She experiences the injuries Lyle's body suffered—his back, his internal organs, his face…

The Hummer H3's executive steering wheel, leather-wrapped, fine-grain-wood, a $400.00 option, is rammed under his ribcage. So is the deflated airbag that exploded on impact. His broken jaw on the dashboard, his forehead is wedged under the spider-webbed windshield. The wipers flap ineffectually over the convex glass. The blood is on the inside. Sirens. First responders try to free old Elsie from her big old car across the street. The Hummer swerved away from the Ford Futura at the last second. One second too late. And now, if the rescue men don't come over to Lyle's obnoxious SUV, if they don't come soon...

Angry hollering joins the honking at the FEARcom van in the intersection. One driver swerves around the van, and Chad defensively jerks his wheel away. Unconscious Lyle bites Flo's finger and she pops back into the here and now.

She knows he's not breathing.

"Chad, please!" she cries.

"I'm *trying!*"

A big TV news truck, satellite dish and all, screeches to a halt perpendicular to Josh's window. Josh looks out to ascertain the threat. It's some asshole from NewsChannel 12 at the wheel—he leans on his horn. Just then Chad sees daylight ahead and hits the gas. As their van lurches forward, Josh slaps the back of his hand against his window, middle finger extended upward in salute. The news-truck driver honks wildly and yells something out his window.

Heading out of town down Montauk Highway now at 50 miles per hour, rather than 30, Chad says, "Should we stop and give him CPR? Anybody *know* CPR?"

Flo looks up at Chad in the rearview mirror. "It's most important now to get him away from here! I mean it, Chad. Gun it." He guns it. Flo closes her eyes. She sinks back into Lyle's private hell. He's reliving the accident again from the old lady's perspective.

Elsie Cronk's late husband, Ed, purchased their big Ford Futura, defying the invasion of the Japanese midsize, back when Lyle was attending NYU. An aircraft carrier of a car with two massive doors. It's beige. Trapezoidal rear passenger windows. Pimply black Naugahyde roof material that peeled up randomly over the years. Jaunty front bucket seats upholstered in a huge Scotch plaid.

Elsie and Ed's son is a crack handyman who became so in-demand locally the summer people fight over him. Jimmy Cronk, who'd served his village for decades as a volunteer fireman and first responder, was recently promoted to assistant chief.

It's October, traffic is light. That old guy walking his dog stops halfway into the intersection. His dog lunges forward on its leash, and Elsie gives them a wide berth, making her right-on-red into the intersection, heading west. In the early sunset all Elsie sees are Lyle's two white headlights coming fast, the sun low and orange behind them. She never feels the shock of impact. Just the spinning. And her lovely cake—Jimmy's cake—flies off the passenger seat. The car spins backward, skidding onto the sidewalk and into a telephone pole. The cake explodes, icing and decorations flying.

Flo can feel it all now. Lyle's split-second decision: hit Elsie head on, or plow into the granite monument. Yeah, he was accelerating to beat the amber light. His brakes locked and he swerved toward the monument. But he clipped the Ford's front end, bumping it violently counter-clockwise. The rest is physics.

Sirens now. Flo knows Lyle is in excruciating pain. Everything hurts. Except his legs. The steering wheel really hurts. Damn airbag. Can't breathe. Get away. Die. Dying would be good right now. More sirens. Maybe those rescue guys can help Elsie Cronk. Dying would be good now. The pain would stop. It needs to stop.

The FEARcom van leaves Bridgehampton behind and Flo returns to the present. She feels Lyle's body relax. And he's breathing, albeit weakly. He's been sweating profusely. She sits him up and looks into unfocused eyes, a bloodless face.

"Lyle, can you hear me?"

Lyle nods and closes his eyes. The van speeds east toward the Memory Motel. His head lolls onto Flo's shoulder and he exhales something barely intelligible.

"Gurney's. Take me...to Gurney's."

~~~~~~~

35. The Memory Motel

Lyle's eyes are closed when the van zips past Gurney's Inn, a resort hotel in the classic mold overlooking the Atlantic. Flo rouses him as they pull into Montauk.

At the no-view Memory Motel, Josh gets everyone's rooms sorted out. Lyle, complaining that he wants Gurney's, gets the one handicapped room. There's a motorcycle parked next door to it, but it's close to the bar. Silk gets a "nice" room with a big bed she's going to hate. The kid at the desk informs Josh that there are still a few vacancies. He texts Silk and receives a directive to block out all remaining rooms on the FEARcom account. The new rationale is to keep rival news organizations from getting close to Lyle Hall. And now Josh has his own room, as will Gregg the VP, when he comes down to oversee, to bask in the limelight, to watch Silk work.

Before Flo takes her room, Josh takes her aside.

"He's not going to Gurney's, Flo. Silk will freak."

"It's his own money, Josh."

"Not the point—we need him here. We need to photograph him now looking distraught and disheveled; not relaxed and put-together. We need to shoot the first interview, too—all on deadline. When Gregg cuts his deal, air time will fall in the access time slot, the seven p.m. hour. We'll need something compelling to air in a hurry."

Ultimately they compromise—Josh will shoot high-resolution stills of Lyle straightaway looking his worst. Then Flo can take him and schmooze over lunch someplace while Josh works up broadcast graphics and fiddles with the digital imagery, including his download of the Jewel drawings that will figure in the reenactment.

"Flo," Josh emphasizes, "we absolutely must have our broadcast package together by five p.m. to make the 7p.m.

'access' time slot. It must be kick-ass. And Silk doesn't want a refreshed Lyle. The worse he looks the better."

~~~~~~

Popping her head in Lyle's door, Flo dangles lunch at Gurney's as his reward for going along with the photo shoot. And he must remain disheveled looking for *vérité*. Thinking it's only a few shots, Lyle reluctantly agrees and Flo heads off to her room.

Josh has chosen Lyle's room for the shoot and he and Chad arrive with special gear. First they hang a sheet up on his wall.

"You're photographing me and a *sheet?*" Lyle says.

Josh checks light levels. "The sheet will be replaced with a background."

"What kind of background?"

Josh squints through the lens of his costly Nikon DSLR seated on its tripod.   "Looking pretty disheveled. What kind of background you want?"

Chad tries for levity. "How about equestrian? This is the Hamptons."

Josh shoots Chad a look.

"How about surfing?" Lyle throws out. "This is the Hamptons."

Josh looks up from his camera. "The background will be appropriate. I was at Old Vic today and got some good stills."

"So you're going to place me in a scene in front of Old Vic?"

"Something like that. I first have to erase some demonstrators, two homemade signs and a backhoe."

"What do the signs say?"

"They say 'I'm a Believer.' Hold that grimace." Josh clicks.

After a half hour Lyle is exhausted. The more drawn his demeanor grows, the better Josh likes it. Flo knocks and enters.

Lyle notes that Flo is in a fresh outfit. Lavender.

"Josh, about done with our man?"

"Yeah. Think I got him at his worst."

"Hey, I rented another van! Enterprise dropped it off just like on TV." Flo smiles at Lyle. "C'mon, Lyle, we have a lunch reservation."

As Lyle rolls toward the door he glances at Josh's laptop, lying open on the bureau. Curious. He sees a black silhouette of a Victorian house with a quarter moon hanging above.

Plastered large across the image, in a sickly yellow:

GHOST HAMPTON

~~~~~~

36. Pranks

It's midday when Detective Georgie Hall enters the stationhouse in Southampton and passes the desk sergeant. Swanson, pretending to be intently focused on some bullshit paperwork, quietly whistles a tune—the first five notes of "Georgie Girl"— just loud enough for Detective Hall to hear. Walking on, Georgie notes that the duty board, a white board listing all officers' duty schedules, has been cleaned up. The "Booooo!" scrawled in black marker above Georgie's name is gone.

As a detective, Georgie does not have to acknowledge Swan Song and she emphasizes this by passing him brusquely. She will take on the harassment problem by confronting Chief Queeley. Queeley will—or should—deal with underlings appropriately. If he does not for any reason, Detective Hall can go directly to Internal Affairs. There are also certain experienced lawyers who specialize in workplace harassment in law enforcement. Hiring one of them is an option, but Georgie does not want to start her detective career by suing everybody if there's any other way. If there is a harassment case, Swan Song, a devious pudge who, despite being old enough to be her father, has seen almost no action on the street in his career, is a person of interest. If anybody knows about someone placing inappropriate graffiti on the duty board, it would be him. It stands to reason his knowledge would extend to harassing pranks in the locker room as well.

Georgie enters the locker room. It's quiet now. She turns down her row and approaches her locker. It seems clean. Placing her briefcase on the bench, she leans against an adjacent locker to catch the light. From that angle, just below her door's vent, she glimpses a barely visible rectangular smudge suggesting clear tape that was recently removed. Tape that held an inflated condom. A few inches below that she can make out a similar smudge—more tape. The prankster wanted his balloon to stay put. And he walked around with a tape dispenser along with his condoms and Sharpie marker. Using her iPhone she takes pictures of the locker door from that angle, but the results are indistinct.

A locker door opens in the row behind her and she freezes. Was she so absorbed she didn't hear a man approach? There's whistling. But it's aimless, easygoing whistling. The locker door slams shut and heavy feet move out the door to the parking lot. *Why is she so apprehensive at her own locker*, Georgie admonishes herself. This isn't right.

She flicks open her briefcase and extracts her fingerprint dusting kit. Listening for any more movement around the locker room, she decides now is the best time. She carefully dusts her upper door with white latent powder—all the lockers are gun-metal gray. She gives special care to the area around the tape marks where the miscreant may have pressed a finger while applying tape. She plans to dust the locker handle too, in case the guy—and it was *so* a guy—tried to open her locker. But then she sees it.

The powder exposes a right thumb print. Nice and big—a man's. A left-handed man who steadied himself with his right hand while applying the tape last night. Under the thumb, less distinctly, there's an impression from the heel of the right hand. Excited now, Georgie takes a number of pictures with her phone. They look good—especially the prints' position in relation to the tape marks. Then she lifts the prints with clear tape from her kit. She applies each tape to fingerprint cards and labels them— CONDOM BALLOON PRINTS 10/14.

Satisfied, Georgie starts to pack up her kit. She should wipe down her locker door. She reaches for a fine cloth from her kit but stops. Wait. Leave the dusting powder right where it is. Unnerve the bastard when he comes back. Make him think twice.

Georgie leaves the locker door as-is and walks off, briefcase in hand, to Chief Aiden Queeley, Jr.'s office.

~~~~~~

Aiden Queeley, Jr. is Lyle Hall's age. The two went through Bridgehampton's public school system together with Noah Craig. "Junior," as kids called Queeley, was the son of a Southampton Police Captain and that, along with his extra-large physique, afforded him some respect growing up in the 1960s. It also inspired him to inflict bullying tactics on smaller and younger kids in school. Junior's football career would eventually take off in high school, but in grade school he'd sometimes stoop to hanging around with the two annoying know-it-alls, Lyle and Noah. Junior's size and unpredictability made the boys uncomfortable around him, but young Lyle had convinced Noah it was best to just go with it. One activity in autumn was to ride bikes to the haunted house on Poplar after dark. The old place was said to have *whores* wandering around inside. Dead whores, if you could believe it. The boys threw every rock or piece of debris they could find in attempts to break the remaining glass in the windows and, possibly, scare up a whore. They'd remain on their bikes in case a pissed-off whore did emerge, so they could outrace her.

One night the three brought their own rocks and bottles, since every loose object in the area was already inside Old Vic. After they ran out of projectiles Junior acted on impulse. Noah, the really brainy one, had school books in his front basket. In one motion Junior Queeley grabbed one and scaled it like a Frisbee through the nearest window. Noah winced as he heard it skid across the floor inside the abandoned house and clunk into something. And then a horrifying realization. That was his homework binder. And the biggest bully in school just threw it away to a horrible place.

Noah looked up at Junior Queeley's ugly, freckled face in the half light. He was smiling. Noah was not.

"That was my homework!"

"So?"

Lyle did not like where this was going.

"You're getting it, Junior."

What? Skinny Lyle Hall giving orders? Junior turned to him.

"You kiddin' me, Hall?"

"I said you're getting it, Junior," repeated Lyle. "That's my friend's homework binder. Get it or I'm telling."

"Oh? I'm *so afraid*," said Junior. "You're telling *who*?"

"Parents, school, the police, everybody. Unless you go get it."

Noah was getting upset; he saw no way out of this.

Junior sneered at this kid. "The *police?* You know who my father is, jerk-off!"

"That makes it worse for you, Junior," said Lyle, getting steamed. "If you're such a big boy, I dare you to go in that house and get Noah's book back. I *dare* you, Junior."

Junior Queeley glared at Lyle while he processed the ramifications of the dare.

"You afraid of ghosts, Junior?"

"No. No way."

"Afraid of whores?"

"What? No!"

"So that leaves your parents."

Lyle had struck a chord and Junior decided to negotiate. What they settled on that night was fairly elaborate. Junior would retrieve the binder only if Lyle and Noah would help him and never speak of it again. The window in question was first-floor, but awkwardly high up. Each boy rode home and, unbeknownst to their parents, returned to Old Vic with equipment—a short aluminum step ladder, a flashlight, an old rake. Lyle climbed up his ladder to the window sill and Noah handed him the flashlight he'd brought. Lyle shined it inside and spotted the binder, lying open on the disgusting floor amid rocks, debris, spider webs, broken bottles, and maybe rat shit. He decided to omit those findings.

"Okay, Junior," he said quietly, "it's right there on the floor."

Leaving the flashlight balanced on the warped windowsill, Lyle descended the ladder and looked at Junior.

"You're big enough; you can reach it with your rake."

Junior, sneering like this was no big thing, climbed up and shined the flashlight inside. He was struck by how disgusting the room really was. He muttered *shit* to himself as Lyle prodded him with the rake. Junior trained the flashlight on the binder and, with the rake in his right hand, stretched to make it reach into the room.

"Shit. I can't reach it!"

"Yes you can!" whispered Lyle. "We'll help you!"

"What are you gonna do? Make my arm longer?"

"We're gonna hold your legs," Lyle said, his eyes meeting Noah's.

This was not part of the plan, but Lyle and Noah stepped a few rungs up the ladder and grabbed Junior's big legs, bringing them horizontal. Junior grunted and squirmed further through the window straining to reach the binder. This made his T-shirt ride up, exposing an expanse of white skin—Junior's lower back. As the two friends awkwardly held the big boy's thighs, something came between them.

A spider, fat from a summer of feeding. It dangled down between them, hovering over Junior's bare back. Noah could see Lyle gasp in the half light. Lyle hated spiders. He flinched and involuntarily gripped Junior's thigh hard, digging his fingers in.

"Hey! Hall! Is that you?" cried Junior, struggling with his own issues. "You feeling up my leg? Are you a *queer?*"

The spider touched down, all dark, fat and hairy, on Junior's exposed flesh. Lyle and Noah could take no more. Junior squirmed more. "Hey! Don't touch me there!"

Physics took over. He dropped the flashlight. It thunked to the floor inside and rolled. Junior was more than halfway inside, propping himself up with the rake.

"Shit!" he cried as weird shadows played across the dirty old walls and spider webs. "Get me out!" he cried, kicking his legs. *"Pull me out!!"*

As the spider explored Junior's lower back, Lyle whispered to Noah, "How bad you need that book?"

"Not so badly..."

Lyle jumped to the ground and grinned up at Noah.

"Hey! Hall!!" came Junior's strained voice from inside the window. "What the fuck are you doing??"

"I let go of your leg like you wanted, stupid!"

"What *are* you doing?" whispered Noah.

Lyle smiled up at his friend. "Get off my ladder, Noah."

"But..."

"Hey, you two shits! Pull me out! Pull me out or I'll... Hey, you guys!!"

Noah got it. He jumped to the ground. Both boys giggling nervously, Lyle folded shut his dad's stepladder, hooked his arm under it and got on his bike.

"Gotta run!" Lyle said and both boys sped off to their homes leaving Junior's legs flailing pathetically in the window.

Lyle and Noah could still hear Junior Queeley plead and threaten from a block away. Junior eventually lowered himself from the window. He couldn't reach the homework binder but he did come away with Noah's flashlight, which he kept. Lyle and Noah agreed the incident should remain their secret, much as Lyle wanted to tell the world. Junior Queeley's parents had forbidden him from ever visiting Old Vic so he never told anyone, especially his father, about the predicament Lyle left him in.

Queeley did not speak to Lyle for years after that. Not until they were out of high school. Home from college for Thanksgiving one night, the two encountered each other in Hardy's, the "old man's bar" in town. Lyle bought Junior, now a very large football player at Hofstra, a beer. On their second brew, both young men started to laugh.

~~~~~~

37. Chief Queeley

Southampton Police Chief Queeley looks at the young detective seated across from his big desk. She has a businesslike, graduate-degree air about her: honey-colored hair pulled straight back; gray pants suit; no jewelry; tall, even sitting down; the right weight for her height; blue eyes framed by dark lashes and a none-too-happy knit to her brow. That pain-in-the-ass Lyle Hall's smart daughter.

"So, how pissed are you?" Asks Queeley. His pink, meaty face is framed by a nimbus of short ginger hair, his pudgy hands sprinkled with freckles.

"Chief, I don't need this. No one does. Not in the workplace. Not anywhere."

"Right. What do you want to do about it?" He lowers invisible white eyebrows.

"Stop it. It's stupid, hateful and insulting."

"Right. So you want Internal Affairs?" Mentioning this route makes him squint.

Georgie looks at Chief. "The guy likes ghosts. I want to scare him. But I will go to IA if he keeps it up."

"Well this is the kind of thing that can get worse if you try to expose it. I find that you can let it pass by itself." He relaxes visibly to suggest a desirable resolution.

"Like a kidney stone? Chief, did you have any forensics done on my locker?"

"No. When I got in today the locker was clean. I told Swanson to clean the bullshit off the white board too."

"I took lots of pictures if you get curious." Georgie weighs whether to mention that she dusted her locker and left it dusted. "And my secret admirer is in for a little surprise if he visits my locker again."

"Really? What, a booby-trap?" Queeley's face reddens—is that now considered a sexist term? Just talking has gotten so politically charged these days.

Georgie plows ahead. "It's not a big deal, Chief." She fixes him with a look. "But if it continues, I'll have to make it a big deal."

Queeley does not like feeling intimidated, even in the subtlest way. He looks in her eyes and sees determination. He switches gears.

"Speaking of a *big deal*, Detective, your father's, uh, escapade is drawing increasing attention. Has it occurred to you that once your father's issues resolve, this harassment issue would run out of steam on its own?"

Georgie sees where this is going—Queeley obviously doesn't like the whole ghost thing and now there's an unsubtle quid pro quo on the table.

"I'm aware of the cause-and-effect, Chief. This morning I got my father to agree to rescind his legal action. He'll do that today and it will die down."

"That's probably for the best. I'm sure you're aware of the costs—in patrolman overtime alone—that your father's adventure has already incurred the township."

"Chief, I understand the additional police presence in that neighborhood has a cost. But I assure you I have my father in line and he's going to cease and desist."

"That's good. I...*we* need the media coverage to cease too. It's not good for the department. It gets in the way of real police work. It's not good for Bridgehampton. Our community is not about squatters and wackos. And I hope you understand, Detective, we do not need *you* appearing on some television broadcast associated with this ghost thing."

"That will not happen, Chief."

"Good. Now I've seen some recent photographs of your father. May I ask, is there some prescription medication he should be taking? Or should not be taking?"

"I'm looking into that, Chief. My father sees many doctors."

168

"Do you need time off from your case to focus on your...on him?"

Uh-oh. Georgie's ongoing drugs/prostitution investigation is her first real case. Queeley was just waiting to dig that "offer" in—let other personnel take over her case while she unplugs to spend quality time holding hands with an old nut in a wheelchair. Not a good career move right now.

"No, sir. I can handle my hours and my father."

"You sure?"

"Positive, Chief," she says stonily.

Queeley looks at Georgie, trying to gauge her. He slaps his desk.

"Well. Glad we talked. I agree that this will all blow over soon enough." He stands and she rises. He's as big as she's tall. "Without further embarrassment."

Georgie's tension resurfaces. "Right, Chief. Just want it clear that I view my harassment and my father's exploits as separate issues. If the harassment stops I won't have to go to IA..."

"Of course," he cuts her off. "We want you focused on real police work."

Queeley steps from behind his desk. He is a jumbo-size man and his uniform works hard to contain his girth. Georgie reaches for the doorknob and Queeley adds, "You know, I've known your father a long time. Since childhood."

Georgie responds with a bland "Yes, sir."

"Interesting man. Detective, see Swanson; he's got a new locker for you."

Outside Queeley's office, Georgie decides to leave without signing out and seeing more of Swan Song. She uses the side door to the lot and her white unmarked Crown Vic. Maybe drive by the Hampton Bays livery cab location and observe it in daylight. Maybe talk to some dirtbags. At the least get away from the damn stationhouse.

Her remote makes the car chirp to life. She opens the door and stops dead. There, on the driver's seat. A stupid "ghost" balloon. Made from an inflated condom, its approximation of a

"Scream" face drawn with a black marker. It's obscene, taped to the seat-back so it stands tall, its face leering up at Georgie. The airflow from opening the door makes the balloon tremble.

Georgie looks back at the stationhouse. What does she expect to see? The fucking sickos who did this hanging out a window waving? She turns and photographs the damn thing a bunch of times with her phone. Angry, frustrated and a little shaken, Georgie doesn't know what to do so she bats the balloon away with her briefcase—it bobbles onto the passenger seat. Georgie is done with dusting for latent prints; she peels the scotch tape off the upholstery and plops into the seat. Starting the car, she looks over and sees the balloon shrivel, releasing the breath of the sexual harasser. Pulsing with rage, Georgie punches her father's speed dial number. No answer. No fucking answer.

She starts the car and pulls out of the lot. Call Big Frank. He'll know what to do.

~~~~~

38. Both Sides

Gurney's Inn, just west of Montauk, is an old seaside spa/resort in the classic mold. All rooms overlook the Atlantic. Open year-round. Nice restaurant and bar. The top-notch fitness and massage facility, with its saltwater pool and various hot tubs, is called the Sea Water Spa. Lyle has had work done on his broken body here, off and on, in recent months. Pleasant, but none of it lasting.

After a soak in the handicapped shower, two muscular staffers, ignoring the shocking array of scars across their client's upper body, helped him into the bubbling hot whirlpool. That, a stint in the salt water pool and then the 180-degree sauna, helped restore Lyle. His self-inflicted scratches calmed down, too. The masseuse was off but he got a good rubdown with hot oils from a masseur. His back and shoulders. Then Lyle donned a sumptuous Gurney's bathrobe and hit the Spa Shop. Here he picked up some needed toiletries and a branded Gurney's Dopp kit for travel. He let the Spa Shop girl, whose complexion was disconcertingly perfect, pick out Lyle's new outfit from the limited selection of menswear: a white polo shirt (collar folded down), pearl-gray sweatpants, fresh white socks, spa sandals. And a Gurney's sweatshirt in unisex peach.

That took over an hour, but now a refreshed and groomed Lyle greets Flo at the entrance to Gurney's Sea Grille. There's time for a quick lunch.

"Lyle Hall," she says with a smile. "You clean up well. Maybe too well."

"It takes a village."

Entering the restaurant, Flo is pleased to be in a place bathed in sunlight and offering sweeping views of the sparkling Atlantic. The lunch crowd, sparse in October, has mostly dispersed. As the waiter shows the two to a table, Flo decides to put aside Lyle's crisis at the war memorial for now. She sets her iPad to the side of her place setting. Across from her, Lyle reexamines Flo's card.

"So...how come there's no FEARcom on here?"

"FEARcom is one of my professional clients."

Lyle looks at Flo. She's close to him in age. Kind of white and doughy, like she comes from a world where people never discovered exercise or the outdoors. Flo should not wear lavender sweaters that show a lot of upper arm. Her small eyeglasses and tinted schoolmarm hairdo still remind Lyle of "Phyllis" from *The Office* on TV.

"Lyle, see where my card says that I'm a clairvoyant?"

"Oh. Yeah."

"Among other things it means I can often tell what people are thinking."

"Right..." Lyle feels a weird chill. "Oh. Sorry. I didn't..."

"You did, but that's okay." She forms a tiny smile. "Just don't make a habit of it."

Flo takes him in for a moment. "So. You've been experiencing clairvoyant episodes yourself."

"I've had brief moments. 'Empathy.' My therapist has been helping me understand it. Is clairvoyance like one step beyond?"

"Could be. If you are consciously embracing the spirit world. If you are perceiving things beyond the natural range of the senses. In the early stages, your extra-sensory perception may be intermittent. It may hit you in flashes of understanding. You may want to turn it on and turn it off but cannot find the switch."

"If I can't turn it off will I be subject to every feeling everyone has ever had?"

Flo winces. "No, I hope you'll eventually learn to control it—to have it take you where you want to go." She grows serious. "So tell me about last night inside Old Vic. You and your priest *broke in?* Looks like a rough time, based on those photos."

Lyle opens up a little. "Okay. The place is over a hundred years old. Nothing inside but graffiti, garbage and rat shit..." He looks at Flo. "And something else. Something felt like it was itching, then burning under my skin."

"Like something was getting a taste of you. It made your skin crawl." She looks in Lyle's eyes. "The priest. I know he's not an exorcist. Why was he there?"

"He's interested in this sort of thing. I thought he could help me figure out..."

"Figure out what? Jewel? He's just a priest, no?"

"He's into mysticism. I wanted his take on, you know, the house, maybe the girl."

"But there was no girl. Lyle, you're blocking something. That's unhealthy."

Lyle isn't ready to divulge his ugly outburst at Fr. Xerri. And no way he can share the crazy revelation of Georgie's name materializing on her mom's headstone. The busboy brings a basket of bread and Lyle changes the topic to Flo's bare ring finger.

"So...were you married at one time?"

She tenses. "A long time ago. Why do you want to change the subject?"

"Well, did you know everything *he* was thinking?"

"Suffice it to say he wasn't thinking enough." Flo forms a wan smile and lets up a bit. She takes in Gurney's Sea Grille and its pleasant surroundings. There's one table left of ladies who lunch. Out the big salt-sprayed windows, dune grass ripples in a breeze; beyond that, bright sunlight glints off the waves smacking the beach. It feels summery, though the sun hangs low in the autumn sky.

The waiter, a tall gay man who knows Lyle, automatically delivers Lyle's six Montauk Pearl Oysters. He takes their orders—the catch of the day: healthful grilled sea bass prix fixe for both. Lyle reflexively suggests a white wine for Flo. She opts for iced tea and watches the waiter move off.

"He used to look forward to your coming here..." she smiles.

"He was in the minority."

"And you knew it."

"But did not act on it. Would you like an oyster? They're good and good for you."

"No, thank you, I don't eat shellfish."

Lyle senses Flo's mood shift again as he knocks back a few oysters. She needs to get down to business. He decides to preempt her next question.

"So thanks for getting me through that, uh, episode back there in Bridgehampton."

"You're welcome. We need you alive," Flo deadpans. "For now."

"Agreed." Another oyster. Lyle dabs his whiskered mouth with his napkin.

"Enjoying?"

"Can you tell? This is a month with an *R*." Flo looks disinterested. "Months without an R are not so good for consuming shellfish. Because they're hot months..."

"Lyle, based on your traumatic reaction when passing the scene of your accident, I'm concerned how draining and difficult today and tonight may be for you. You experienced violent convulsions the first night you visited Old Vic. Something attacked you on your next visit. Then today in the van you went to a very dangerous place. Your heart rate..."

"Well my therapist has instructed me to stay away from the site of the accident. And it's true I've experienced some uh, extreme discomfort recently."

"Your therapist was right. And your experience of empathy has been much more acute recently as well, am I right?"

"Yeah. So FEARcom knows everything?"

"They do when I'm on the case."

"And I'm now your case. Myself and the dead girl."

Flo leans in and lowers her voice. "I'm serious. You could have died back there. You stopped breathing. Our next step was to take you to the ER."

"The ER is far enough away that I would have stopped breathing for good before we got there." He meets Flo's eyes. "So, whatever you did, I appreciate it."

She nods. "Describe for me what was going on at the intersection."

Lyle turns somber. "I was experiencing the crash again, including the pain. From both sides this time." His eyes drop to his oyster platter. There's one left.

"'From 'both sides'?"

"I experienced Elsie Cronk's death. That was something...new."

Flo feels like she was there, too. She takes on a sympathetic look. "That poor woman you struck." Lyle suddenly glares back at her. She's hit a nerve.

"*She* caused the accident!" Lyle sputters. "She made a wide turn into my lane! And I was *not drunk!* And if anyone *can* drive drunk around here, it's *me!*"

"Lyle..."

Lyle lowers it and leans in. "That old lady blundered into the intersection against the traffic light! Yeah, I hit her big old Ford, but I was swerving hard away from her to avoid a head on collision—that's how I wound up hung up on the monument!" Lyle hisses, "That's how I wound up *like this!*" The lady diners glance over.

He adds quietly, "They thought I was dead."

Lyle gives his last oyster an angry shake of Tabasco and downs it. "The first responders had one Jaws of Life. They used it to free the old girl, but it was too late. They were subsequently surprised to find I was not dead. I was surprised too."

Flo is gratified she was able to get Lyle to react emotionally. That is her job. But now she slides her hand across the white tablecloth, close to his hand. Like when she was holding him earlier in the van, she picks up emanations from the catastrophic accident. Bright red blood spatters his windshield. Firefighters restrain a rescue worker in a fluorescent vest from the old lady's car.

She sees that Lyle has calmed a bit. "You experienced Elsie's death. Can you tell me what that was that like?"

Lyle is absorbed in repositioning some crumbs on the tablecloth with his finger. "It was...it was actually okay, in a way. It was a terrible shock, but she was kinda ready to go." He looks up at Flo just briefly, then back down. "And something surprised me…it felt maybe like…*love*." He looks at Flo. "There was this big, amorphous glow that touched everything. Her son, Jimmy. He was one of the first responders. It touched the other men there too. Then she died. And it faded out."

"Interesting." Flo types a note in her iPad. "A mother's love is strong."

They both stay quiet for a moment. Lyle seems drained, his eyes lowered.

"You know, Lyle, it's good to let it out. You have to, for your own health. Your therapist's name?"

"Susan Wayne."

Flo considers for a moment. "It does seem that a preponderance of your issues involve women."

Lyle rolls his eyes and nods at the waiter. "A 'preponderance,' huh? I think I'll have a scotch."

"Don't, Lyle. I know you're not supposed to have alcohol." Flo touches Lyle's hand and holds his gaze. "Tonight could be tougher than you imagine."

"Scotch is our friend." The waiter approaches and Flo releases Lyle's hand.

"Mister Hall?"

"More iced tea, please." The man heads for the iced-tea station.

"Good choice, Lyle," Flo smiles. She's got a lot of work to do on this guy and cameras roll soon.

~~~~~~~

39. Frank Discussion

"You're *kidding* me." Sgt. Frank Barsotti sounds more than a little surprised over the phone. "On the seat of your car?"

"Standing upright on my seat, Frank. Held with scotch tape," Georgie says, her voice stone cold. "Same unmarked car I've been using the past week. Disgusting."

"That shows determination. Boldness."

"Stupidity."

"Which leaves us pretty wide open. Do you want to go to IA?"

"I don't know. Part of me thinks this just got way worse; part of me thinks it was one last prank and it's now over."

"It's escalation. This crosses a line. And if you do nothing, that sends a bad message. Did you dust your locker for prints?"

"Yup. And I got some. Didn't inform Queeley yet. But he'll know—I left the dust on the door. To send a message."

"Nice. Maybe next you can capture some of the evildoer's breath from the, uh, balloon."

"I'll leave that for you. As far as the prints, I lifted a thumb and partial fingers of the right hand. Like the guy was leaning on the locker with his right and positioning the balloon and tape with his left."

"What I'd do is ask Swanson for a pen. See if he hands it to you with his left."

"I'll just watch him write in his ledger."

"Bingo. Why you made detective. And he's never away from that desk, since Queeley lets him pad hours."

"You really think that putz is doing this?"

"It's a putzy thing to do. But it also shows some nerve—like he grew a pair. Sorry, I mean feels emboldened somehow. Obviously, this is tied to your father's adventures in that derelict house. Have you gotten him to calm down?"

"He promised me this morning he's going to court today to rescind his motion. It remains to be seen how much calming down there'll be."

"That *Southampton Press* story and those wild pictures really got around. Does he take prescription medication?"

"Lots. Except when he doesn't."

"That tells you something. So you know, our men in blue are all over his property. The neighborhood's overrun with ghost-lovers camping out, chanting and so on. News-twelve went over looking for Lyle. Did you know there was a break-in last night?"

"What? Where?"

"Your dad's."

"What happened??"

"An old coot let himself into Lyle's kitchen. A ghost aficionado. Nothing happened and your dad did not press charges, but we're watching the situation."

"Omigod. He did not tell me about that."

"He doesn't have to if you have access to TV or Internet—News-twelve interviewed him. Sweet old guy. Mostly what's happening in the neighborhood is just a lot of peeing in bushes at this point. A little marijuana use, disturbing the peace. But we need to watch all the residences." Frank returns to the inflated condoms. "Detective, if you will, I want to think out loud about this condom guy—and we agree it's a guy? No way it's Jonesy?" Roberta Jones is one of the very few female cops on the force.

"It's not Jonesy."

"Okay. Let me run through this guy: Keeps weird hours—weirder even than yours. Is around the stationhouse when no one else is. Has access to the fleet's car keys. Has access to office supplies such as scotch tape and Sharpies. Left-handed. Can draw or cartoon a little. Likes the movie *Scream*…and is not an active-duty cop."

"How do you know that?"

"Because I'm an active duty cop. Idle hands are the devil's workshop."

"Uh, okay."

"Where was I... Oh. The weird part: Feels emboldened for some reason, inspired to do this. May have an urge to entertain or impress his fellow cops."

"Impress his fellow cops who are active-duty which he is not?"

"Right. Though we active-duty cops are above this type of stunt. Way above. What stumps me is his inspiration. Maybe he found himself alone while sitting around the stationhouse for sixteen hours and acted on an urge. Or maybe someone motivated him or challenged him. Again, someone he wants to impress."

"You get a lot out of one condom, Frank."

"Don't spread it around. Another thing. He does not like you."

"You think?"

"Insecure about a younger woman who's successful at police work."

"Unlike you."

"Very. And, given the condoms, he might visit prostitutes."

"I'll keep an eye out for him. What if he just likes to make balloon animals?"

"Condoms are contraceptives that can also ward off sexually transmitted disease."

"So they have three uses."

"That we know of. So—we have a left-handed, lonely-guy putz. It's pretty obvious. And Swanson is divorced, by the way."

"Thanks for being attentive to his private life."

"You're welcome."

Frank and Georgie both go quiet for a moment.

"Detective, where are you now? Want me to swing by?"

"No. No thanks, Frank. I don't want to draw attention. But you've been helpful."

"True."

Frank inexplicably stifles a chuckle Georgie can hear.

"Frank? Are you *enjoying* this? I thought real cops were above this stuff!"

"It just occurred to me. Maybe you let it out that the condom size was *extra small*. You know? Just to gauge reaction. Bust the alleged perp's alleged chops a little."

"Condoms come in *sizes?*"

"So I'm told."

"And what if my coworkers got the idea I was familiar with such things?"

There's silence over the phone. Then Georgie and Frank burst into laughter together.

~~~~~~

40. Grilling

The bus boy delivers the sea bass entrees. Lyle digs in and Flo can see how hungry he is. She needs to dig into what he really saw and felt at Old Vic two nights ago. And what really happened to him inside that house with the priest last night? Lyle's definitely withholding something, but she's confident she can break through.

"Lyle, that first night, your legs…" She peeks at her iPad as Lyle chews. "Did you truly feel a return of function? Could you move them? Walk?"

"I didn't try to stand. The stabbing pains came right after I started to get feeling."

"What was your strongest emotion at the time? Fear?"

"No, awe. And excitement."

"Oh? What about sexual function? Sorry, I have to ask." Flo flushes, then forks her own sea bass.

Lyle is mistrustful of this question; Flo may be snooping around his subconscious. But it's best to respond. "Believe me, that'd be the last thing on your mind at a time like that. I thought my heart was going to explode."

Her eyes meet his. "Did you feel attracted to the ghost girl?"

"What? No! No I did not! Where are you getting this stuff, Flo?"

The lady diners look over at Lyle. He sees Flo is working from a list on her iPad.

"You understand I have to ask, don't you, Lyle? If you tell the world that an apparition revived feeling in the paralyzed lower half of your body, and you were seeing a beautiful young girl who once lived in a brothel…people will make that connection."

Lyle lowers his voice to a growl. "I didn't tell the world anything of the sort!"

"You told this reporter Mose Allen something. The rest is an inference away. And the world loves to infer."

"I'm telling you it was *not* that way. This girl's only twelve. Or was. I wish I could prove it. I simply thought, until the stabbing pains came, that maybe my legs would work again. I'm *not* some sicko."

"Lyle, you know all too well how your own neighbors demonized you after your accident. You should be prepared. The media, and the blogosphere, thrive on sensationalism and the girl's age is a sensitive topic that we think will come out. FEARcom will help control the message but imagine all the lousy websites and cheap tabloids having a field day with this."

"But you people will shoot all that down, right?"

Flo smiles faintly. "Controlling the story is part of what we do. Occupy the high ground. Maintain credibility. But sensationalism feeds on itself and, Lyle, the girl in the artist's rendering looks more sophisticated than twelve years old. That poses a problem."

"Is Silk going to ask me about that? About Jewel?"

"She is. You need to be ready with your response. You have no record of…interest in underage girls, so that's good."

"So you vetted me."

"Had to. If you were a child molester, we couldn't have you under contract. You know, forgetting the girl for now, it's clear to me that your encounters with the paranormal have sexualized you in the living world."

"As opposed to the necromantic world?"

"Psychologically, that is. Your stimulating otherworldly experiences have given you hope that you can return to full health. That hope engenders an inner yearning that expresses itself in freely sexualizing women you encounter, like Silk, in your imagination."

"Oh? So is that Freudian?"

"Everything is Freudian. But to casual observers you can come off as a creepy old man. We're going to work on that."

"I wish you'd get out of my mind."

"Be glad someone knows when you're occasionally truthful."
Flo glances at her iPad. "We'll be asking you about last night in
Old Vic. You and the priest. The big problem with Mose Allen's
photos of you, by the way, is not that you look totally mad."

"Oh? What could be worse?"

"Fakery. Plenty of celebrities detest being photographed. The
problem is your scratches are self-inflicted. As if you're trying to
fake supernatural contact. That's bad."

"Did you just say 'celebrities'?"

"I did. You're transitioning." She nods at Lyle's plate. "I'll
let you enjoy."

After a few minutes of trying to enjoy his meal, Lyle says, "You
know, those obsessed campers want to go to Old Vic tonight
and...and basically ask Jewel to come out and play. They want
me there to make it happen."

Flo swallows. "That's not going to happen."

"Did you know that a crazy old man broke into my house last
night?"

"Yes..." Flo Googles the burgeoning list of Lyle Hall, Old
Vic, Jewel, Ghost Girl stories and clicks on the latest. "Here.
Mose Allen's been busy." Lyle stiffens. "He interviewed this
older man. A Glen Stanley."

"Let me see that."

Flo rotates her iPad for Lyle. "Looks like they got him to
write a positive story. Wacked-out Lyle Hall confronts a fan
who's broken into his kitchen and, instead of shooting him, chats
with him and sends him off without pressing charges. Later they
enjoy coffee together..."

"I can read," Lyle snips. "And I was there." He glances up at
Flo. "Sorry."

"That's okay. See what this story conveys? It softens your
image slightly, but gives their website another reason to run your
Wild Man of Borneo picture from last night. The newspaper
wants to establish the reporter's human side. And show that there
are other nutty people in the world. Besides you."

"And that I'm attracting them to my house."

"See, releasing a soft, human-interest story sets up this reporter to come out guns blazing next time. Now tell me, you in fact have a gun at home?"

"Glen only says here that 'any other man' could have shot an intruder."

"Again, softening your image." Flo knows he's got a gun stashed somewhere, but lets it drop.

After more bass, Lyle asks, "Flo, what broadcast or TV show am I—are we—supposed to be on tonight?"

"Not sure yet. We'll shoot the interview and Josh will make it part of a 'package' including the reenactment—"

"Including more bad pictures of me your man shot?"

"Don't worry, Josh will do you justice. He also needs to present Old Vic's backstory, but that's proving hard to come by, so we're relying on some informed third-party conjecture."

"Sounds like more bullshit."

"Only as a last resort." Flo checks a new text from Silk. "Lyle, the outlet most likely to pick us up is *Entertainment Tonight*. Silk and Gregg are working it. There are multiple bids for the first installment."

"First?"

"If this takes off like we think it will. There's always 'more to come.' Think of it as your bully pulpit—rally support to save Old Vic."

Lyle pushes some rice pilaf around his plate. *Shit.* Rallying support would be a big problem. "Well, despite all the bullshit, I still need to go back to that house. I need to see Jewel. In private. Hard to explain."

"It's natural," Flo smiles, "or should I say supernatural, that you want to see her again. You'll be with us at Old Vic later when we shoot—Josh and Chad have to keep the campers away somehow and deal with the police. Their problem." Flo looks into Lyle's eyes. "Here's my problem: I need to know how many spirits are really present in that house. From my experience, they're not all...*good.*"

He looks away. Can't admit to cursing out Fr. Xerri in Greek. Or seeing Georgie's tombstone.

"Lyle, last night's break-in-scratching-yourself episode strongly suggests multiple spirits. Talk to me about Jewel's voice—was it youthful? What did she say to you?"

He returns her gaze. "She said 'Help us' the first night. In Italian. Nothing last night.

"Italian. Really."

"Are you reading me now?"

"I am. You're afraid of something, Lyle, and it's not a twelve-year-old girl."

"Fine. Her voice was a whisper. How should it sound after a hundred years?"

"Lyle, I'm getting a mixed message. Pleasure and pain. Hope and fear. More than one entity is trying to communicate. Be truthful now, you'll do better on TV later."

Lyle knows he'd better give her more. "Okay. Father Xerri felt there *were* other spirits. Upstairs. Like captives. I believe Jewel wants me to fix something in the living world. She said 'Help us' to me. And you're right, there was another, hostile voice. Okay? But I cannot let that house come down."

This sets off a *Georgie* alarm in Lyle's head. "Not yet," he adds.

Flo nods. "Even though something wants to harm you. There's more at stake here than giving a ghost a place to continue being dead in. The hostile voice, it sounded male?"

"Yeah. And not nice."

"And what did 'he' say?"

"He said 'You.'"

"In response to what?"

"I asked Jewel what exactly she wanted when the male voice intruded."

"So the nice girl wants your help and the evil male voice wants *you*, and wants to hurt you." Flo knows she's finally gotten somewhere with this difficult man.

"Kinda, maybe. Look—they're knocking down Jewel's house and she asks a real-estate lawyer for help. Makes sense, right? And I don't want the dumb playground the town plans to put there to be haunted. What if that thing does to kids what it did to me?"

Flo types into her iPad. "So a dead girl knew the house would be demolished and knew you were a real-estate lawyer. And she has an evil co-habitant. It doesn't add up. You're holding something else back. Something important."

Lyle frowns at this as the waiter appears at the table with a check.

"I didn't ask for the check," he says testily.

"Of course, Mister Hall, this is blank. The ladies at the table behind me asked if you would be kind enough to autograph it."

Lyle flushes, signs the chit, and glances over at the three well-dressed older women seated nearby. Good—he doesn't know them. He gives a tiny wave.

Flo bites back a smile. "Celebrity. Now, as I was saying, you're hiding something. When people hide something, it's usually bad."

"Why don't you just move into my psyche?"

Flo turns serious. "It's something tangible, rock-hard. Like that monument."

Lyle can feel Flo watching him think. He tries to stop thinking.

Mercifully, Flo's cell phone tinkles with a text. It's Silk demanding to know why they're not back at the motel preparing for the interview.

Their prix fixe tiramisus sit in styros on the backseat of Flo's rental as she drives him back to the motel. She thanks him for lunch.

"Any time, Flo. And thanks again for whatever you did when I blacked out back there in Bridgehampton. Could have been a near-death experience."

"It *was* a near-death experience. This is quite a rough patch, but we'll make it through." She extends her right hand to Lyle and makes eye contact. "Friends?" They shake hands and jumbled images of Flo's past life flood Lyle's mind, then vanish.

Back to business. "Lyle, speaking of multiple TV engagements, we'll need to get your priest friend on camera for the next segment."

"I don't think Father Xerri will be so easy for Silk to rope in."

"We'll see." Flo drums her fingers on the steering wheel. "Recalling your experience today at the monument, what image remains the most vivid?"

Lyle exhales. "Well...I think I saw the last thing Elsie Cronk saw."

"Go on."

"Her son looking in the car window at her. As she died."

Flo sighs and stares at the road ahead. "There will be multiple TV segments."

She can see what Silk will do with all this on camera. And what Josh can do with his computer. She knows this will be the biggest paranormal event in her career. She smiles to herself as she drives along a stretch of beautiful, deserted beach road. She was right, of course. It's not just a sad-eyed girl in that house—there's something else lurking there, and it's not good. But Flo's got her exclusive scoop for FEARcom. And he's sitting next to her now, screwing with his cell phone.

As they drive Lyle delves into his voice mail. Shit. Missed call after missed call from Georgie interspersed with Manhattan and Los Angeles area codes. And Noah Craig, Susan Wayne, Fraser Newton, the physical therapist, Becky Tuttle... Wait. Becky, huh?

Instead of listening to Becky, Lyle finds a text from Alpharetta: Judge Sloane has scheduled an expedited hearing for tomorrow morning. Georgie expected Lyle to rescind today. Flo and Silk expect him to make a dramatic televised plea to save Old Vic today.

Feigning interest to his iPhone to keep Flo at bay, Lyle reviews their lunch chat. He'd withheld his cursing in Greek at Fr. Xerri inside Old Vic—hoping to spare him. Denied the gun thing. Withheld Georgie's dreadful headstone. It's only fair that

Lyle keeps personal concerns to himself. Flo isn't showing all her cards either. Clairvoyance, what a pain.

~~~~~~

41. Taproom

Josh Berendt has been busy at the Memory Motel. He'd secured the taproom as the set for the first segment and lit the place moodily, especially a conversation area he set up for Silk's interviews. The barroom is popular with young hipsters in summer and its walls are festooned with posters, photos and wacky old memorabilia. Josh plans to shoot his subjects with the bar's reflective bottles as a crystalline out-of-focus backdrop. Now he sits at a table tapping away at his laptop. Chad is running some wires. Silk is in her room getting ready and Flo is in hers, changing her sweater. Black is the order of the day.

Lyle rolls to the handicap-accessible room FEARcom provided him. It's near the taproom, a short spin along the flat walkway. There's a big motorcycle parked in the spot next door. Once inside, Lyle places his new Dopp kit on the sink in the roomy bathroom. He looks at himself in the mirror. So changed. But if you didn't know the Old Lyle, you might think New Lyle was somewhat intriguing. He's seated, but so what? You can barely see the scratches across his cheeks and forehead now. Maybe Silk will hit him with one of those makeup powder-puffs. He decides to trim his salt-and-pepper beard—scissors are in his kit. Lyle feels a need to distance himself from Mose Allen's photos, all wild and covered with plaster dust. This will be the groomed, civilized Lyle. The spa-casual Lyle. The fucking crazy Lyle. Just look at whatever is going on behind those haunted eyes. Can the camera guy get that on video? He'll damn well try.

Josh has given Rooney, the taproom's longtime bartender, a hundred bucks to post a sign on his door: OPEN 5PM. Happy hour. Rooney doesn't mind since patrons are sparse this time of year and a TV interview could be good for business.

Rolling into the bar at the appointed time, Lyle is treated to a booming greeting.

"Well, *Mister Lyle Hall!*"

"Hello, Mister Rooney."

"Been a while! How the hell are ya?" Rooney is drying beer glasses the old fashioned way, with a sloppy towel. He's an older man whom modern times seem to have left behind—his hair slicked back; white shirt cuffs tucked under; his very long belt circumnavigating an extensive gut. He momentarily turns his back.

"Still loving life," says Lyle. "Just from a lower altitude."

"Ah-huh," says Rooney. He turns and plants a big double-Dewar's-rocks in front of Lyle. "Your usual. On the house, sir."

No one else is paying attention to Lyle. The golden drink, ice cubes glistening, is within easy reach. It would be offensive to refuse Rooney's gesture. What the hell. Lyle picks up the drink. The rocks glass is surprisingly heavy. And cold. He barely remembers breaking doctors' orders last night at the Princess Diner. Today at Gurney's he refrained manfully. He's about to do an in-depth television interview about a ghost girl and the probing interviewer is the most attractive, desirable young woman he's ever seen up close. Rooney has a little something for himself—a squirt of draft Bud in a short glass. They both raise their glasses.

"To old times," smiles Rooney.

The scotch goes through Lyle like a gunshot, as if drinking is something new. And it is—the Dewar's he had yesterday was his first in a year but that was only to steady his nerves after the bad episode at Jewel's house. Today's scotch makes Lyle woozy after only a sip—most of the stuff is still in the glass. He realizes another day of almost no rest has passed, adding physical weakness to his psychological strain and lack of prescription meds. With the TV interview ahead of him, maybe he better nurse this.

Rooney points his clicker at the TV. "Hey, you see any of this?" The same blond news lady from NewsChannel 12 is standing in front of Lyle's house, blabbing. The sound is off, but the graphic at the bottom of the screen is embarrassing:

Bridgehampton Lawyer Fights to Save 'Haunted' House

Silk's men look up at the TV. Josh takes it in briefly then returns to his laptop.

The scene switches to a live feed—a news crew set up in front of Old Vic. Another blond reporter starts blabbing and gesturing at Old Vic. Then she turns to an expert interviewee.

"Holy shit!" Lyle exclaims. Everyone looks over at him. "That's *Becky Tuttle!*"

Rooney turns up the volume. Becky, wearing a mauve sweater set with her pearl choker, is on camera in front of Old Vic talking with the reporter. Old Vic looks like hell in daylight. Worse than ever. Campers, now fully invested in their "Believers" moniker, are milling around in the near background; some in FEARcom T-shirts, some mugging for the camera and waving. Inverted plastic tubs are throbbing rhythmically off camera. Led by old Glen Stanley, a couple of Believers start up a tepid "Lyle is fine!" chant. A graphic appears briefly onscreen.

REBECCA TUTTLE, Save-a-Barn

"People sometimes do inexplicable things," Becky says over the background racket. "Trying to preserve a house because one believes it's haunted is unusual but trying to save a...a known *brothel* goes far beyond what our community will support."

The reporter gestures back toward the old barn. "You're in the barn-saving business, what about preserving this one?"

Becky turns to assess the barn and Lyle assesses this view of her figure.

"Well that's a much, much older structure," she says, "and a different story." Camera takes in the 30-foot-high shambles. "I think its pre-Revolutionary War historical significance can be proven and it could be saved. Renovation would be costly, but the historical value is—well, it's about preserving our community's farming heritage."

"But for Old Vic your verdict is demolition?"

Camera captures Becky solo. "In this case, yes."

Camera closes in on the reporter. "As for Lyle Hall, the real-estate lawyer turned preservationist is going to have a lot of explaining to do at Southampton Town Court tomorrow." As she nods toward Old Vic, Glen Stanley instigates an energetic "I'm a Believer" chant. Raising her voice, the reporter says, "And these demonstrators have a lot of chanting to do to convince Judge Gerald Sloane to halt the bulldozers."

Camera pans to the house. A front-loader sits in what passes for the driveway. The chants and tub-beating rise in volume and vigor.

> "I saw her face!
> BAM BAM BAM
> I'm a Believer!"

A few Believers add, "Lyle is fine! Lyle is fine!" As the reporter signs off, camera pans to a chanting Glen Stanley—the Pete Seeger of haunted houses.

Rooney silences the TV. Lyle realizes that all four FEARcom members had assembled behind him to watch the coverage. There's a black leather jacket over his right shoulder brimming with feminine allure.

"*That* is going to be easy to beat," says Silk. "We have the one thing they all want, right? Lyle Hall. *And* we have *Entertainment Tonight*!! Let's get to work, people!"

The group heads to the interview set and Chad whistles the *Entertainment Tonight* theme. Lyle stays back by the bar and watches Silk seat herself so she can face her two guests, Lyle Hall and Flo Hendricks. He flashes on Becky. Why did she call him?

He considers playing her message when his phone starts buzzing.

"Dad? What are you doing?" Georgie calling from her condo in Southampton.

"Georgie, I'm sorry." Lyle, immediately on the defensive, keeps his voice down.

"You're *sorry?* Try *crazy*, Dad! You were supposed to rescind that cockamamie request for an injunction and then come and meet me! *Remember?*"

"Yeah, well I met some people..."

"Oh? Some people? How nice! Living or dead? I had a frigging police escort for you and you went off with strangers! Where to? Dad, are you all right in the head??"

"I'm staying in Montauk for a few days till this blows over."

"Really! Your favorite un-Hampton. When were you going to tell me about the change of plan?"

"Georgie, you don't understand...it's just, it's been very difficult..."

"Oh? Difficult? You want to hear difficult? This job you helped me get? Well somebody here is sexually harassing me now. In the workplace!"

"Sexually?"

Georgie's voice grows quiet. "It started yesterday with the cartoon ghost on the assignment board and *booo!* written by my name. But then someone went to my locker..."

"And?"

"And they stuck a white, uh, balloon with a ghost face drawn on it." Georgie grows silent.

"A balloon, Georgie?"

His daughter's voice falters, as if she's trembling. "Okay. Dad, it was a condom. Okay? An inflated *condom* taped to my locker door. Then today there was another one taped to the driver's seat of my car..."

Lyle feels a nauseating gut punch. He caused this.

"Georgie Girl, I am so sorry! This is *terrible!* I'm so sorry you have been hurt by all this. It's all because of me! Did you report it to Internal Affairs?"

"Not yet," she says quietly. Lyle hears her sigh heavily. "I took pictures of the thing with my cell phone. I dusted my locker for prints. They gave me a new locker. Like that helps. Dad, I really, *really* don't need this shit in my life right now."

"I know. I know, Girl. I'm so sorry! Georgie, does Queeley know about this?"

"We talked. He made me promise you would end this B.S. you're into."

Lyle tries to think as Chad moves a table, revealing more of the interview set—and Silk's shapely legs. She's wearing a short black skirt and heels with her trademark leather jacket. She crosses her perfect legs, appearing very fit and trim. Josh adjusts a special light aimed at her.

"Dad. I'm working all hours surveilling, seeking informants, gathering evidence against this drugs-and-prostitution ring. I don't need additional shit in the workplace. I do need you to stop the bullshit with the haunted whorehouse and just relax. Wash your hands of this. Retire for real. Work on your health. Take up water colors. Or cooking..."

"I don't want to burn my arms."

"So make salads. Or smoothies. *Something*, Dad. But not this. Please. *Not this.*"

Josh beckons Lyle with his index finger. Lyle stays put, so Josh sends Chad over.

"Georgie, I was going to rescind today but..."

"Do it tomorrow, Dad. Swear to me you will."

"Mister Hall? You're needed on set," says Chad.

Lyle nods to the young man, who then returns to his audio mixing board. Lyle peers over at Silk. Made up for TV, she's so gorgeous his heart skips a beat. He wants to bite her.

"Okay, Georgie, tomorrow."

"Okay. And answer your damn phone when I call!"

"I will. Good luck. And please *be careful* out there! I love you."

She disconnects without further comment. He puts his phone on silent.

"Whenever he's ready," says Josh as if Lyle is wasting his time.

Head pounding now, Lyle first rolls back to Rooney. Somehow his glass got empty. Flo, now in a black silk blouse, takes her seat and Josh gets busy lighting her.

"Everything okay, Mister Hall?" Rooney inquires.

"Could be a tad better, Mister Rooney." His glass and a twenty land on the bar.

"A rerun?"

Amid the conflicts tearing at Lyle's consciousness right now, he gets a long-buried flashback. Of course Rooney the bartender knows Lyle Hall. The Memory Motel. Lyle remembers. The lady bartender from the Shagwong Tavern at the far end of Montauk. How she was a bodybuilder. How one night she agreed to a private showing just for Lyle. This place is, after all, a motel. Her name, *her name*...began with an *F*...

"Yeah, one more. You make it just right."

Rooney pours scotch with a flourish into Lyle's rocks glass and the cubes tinkle.

"Hard to mess this up. Only the one ingredient." He hands the glass down to Lyle, adding, "Excellent choice."

Lyle takes a good swig. Dewar's. Yeah, he remembers.

"Lyle Hall! Paging Lyle Hall!" Josh is going for ironic. The two women are seated and looking at him. Chad is clipping a Lavaliere microphone onto Flo's collar. There's one perched on the open zipper of Silk's leather jacket.

Lyle rolls over to the set, glass in cup holder, and takes his position stage right.

~~~~~~~

42. First Interview

If Silk looks gorgeous at 10 yards, she's drop-dead up close. As Chad clips on Lyle's microphone, he drinks in Silk and some more scotch. This is obviously her time to shine. Her dark hair is blown out and looks even more lush now. Josh has some kind of purple gel backlighting the hairdo. Lyle notes the tiny beauty mark on her cheekbone. Her lips are red and full—approaching Angelina Jolie plumpness level.

Then there's Flo. She's looking at him oddly. Lyle nods to both women and takes another swig.

"What do you want me to do with him?" Josh asks Silk.

"Don't show him drinking on camera."

Lyle realizes he's getting used to being referred to in the third person. Silk glances at Lyle and then looks over at Josh's laptop on a nearby table. It shows the live feed from the camera trained on Lyle. He can be seen raising his glass to his mouth again.

"Josh, is your laptop color-correct?" Silk inquires.

"Yes. What you see is what you get."

She ponders. "You know, I think he's going to be okay as is." Silk studies the laptop image. "The peach sweatshirt...looks weird on video. But a good weird."

Josh bends to look at his laptop straight on. "It brings out the red in his eyes."

"Actually, I wish he didn't 'freshen up' at that spa. You're going for close ups?"

"Yes, ma'm. I'm recording all four camera feeds including the three stationaries. There'll be plenty of coverage. When I edit I can, uh, tweak him in software."

Silk looks at Josh. "Well there isn't much time for tweaking or editing. *ET* expects a tight package on deadline."

"I *know*." Josh sounds irritated. "Done this before."

"Not for *Entertainment Tonight*." She turns to Flo and Lyle. "Let's do this."

Chad makes a shushing sound. Since this is not live, Silk will simply make introductory remarks to her camera. Josh is also on her with his handheld. He can cut to some tighter shots later along with cuts of Lyle and Flo reacting to her. As she begins Silk sounds a little formal, but her tone is that of the cat who ate the canary—Lyle Hall. For Lyle this tone is very suggestive. And now he experiences Silk as her fans do.

"A long-abandoned Victorian mansion in the tony Hamptons that many believe to be haunted…a secret revealed by a tortured spirit…and a damaged man's dramatic quest for answers. We'll find some answers tonight, on 'Ghost Hampton.'"

"That's good, Silk," says Josh from behind his camera. "Keep going."

Silk gazes into his lens and, warming to her subject, delivers without notes.

"Widely rumored to have been a brothel long ago, Bridgehampton's ramshackle 'Old Vic' now awaits the wrecking ball. There are no records of Old Vic's ownership, its history only rumors, and the local Southampton Township plans to transform the site into a playground. But *one* who could shed some light on Old Vic and its past, we're told, is a twelve-year-old girl. A pretty little girl who's got this town in an uproar." Silk sucks her teeth seductively for the camera. "Because she's been dead one hundred years."

"Good. That was real good, Silk," says Josh. "I'll smooth over any rough spots as we cut away to stills."

"Okay. On with the show," says Silk. "Keep rolling."

Now Silk shifts to her news-anchor style.

"She calls herself Jewel. Appearing late at night in Old Vic's doorway, she has spoken only to our guest. Yesterday, that man, a retired lawyer, went to court to prevent the Town of Southampton from demolishing the ghost girl's dwelling place. Today, we have a paranormal standoff for the digital age. Ghost lovers have flocked to Bridgehampton, staging a vigil in hopes of glimpsing Jewel. They now plan to stand in the way of Southampton's wrecking crew. Last night, our exclusive guest, despite his confinement to a wheelchair, bravely entered Old Vic with a friend—an exorcist from Malta—by his side. He's here now with his incredible story."

Silk smiles and makes a welcoming gesture. "FEARcom's exclusive guest, the man who discovered Jewel—Mister *Lyle Hall!*"

Shit. As Josh moves in on Lyle, he wonders what to do. He makes a dopey wave.

"Along with Mister Hall tonight," Silk adds, "we have FEARcom's paranormal expert, clairvoyant Florence Hendricks."

Flo nods grimly, then details the widely held belief that spirits who have found no place in the afterlife cling to locations that were central to their lives—aka *haunting.* When they encounter a living person who is susceptible to the paranormal— she nods at Lyle—there can be an intense desire to communicate with him. Sometimes more.

The two women chat easily about Old Vic and its camp of demonstrators. Silk refers to Lyle's successful career in real-estate law. She brings up the unlikelihood of a favorable court decision when Judge Sloane hears Lyle's complaint tomorrow. Then both women turn to Lyle.

"Lyle," Silk says, "your picture of Jewel seems to be everywhere. Where did it come from?"

This makes Lyle visibly uncomfortable. "Oh, I hired an artist and described her from memory. Not bad, huh?"

Josh cuts to Linder's sketch of Jewel and Silk agrees.

"It's a beautiful rendering. People are even wearing T-shirts with Jewel's image now. Someone said it has elements of the work done by police sketch artists." She pauses. "Isn't your daughter on the police force?"

Shit. "She's a detective with Southampton Town, not a sketch artist."

"Jewel's voice," Silk moves on, "what was it like hearing it that night?"

"Oh, well I didn't hear very much…it was like a whisper."

Flo asks, "It was definitely a girl's voice?"

198

"Yes."

Flo's job is to get Lyle to open up about his terrifying experience.

"We understand Jewel implored you for help. But there could be more than one spirit. Didn't you sense another presence? Not a girl, perhaps something malevolent?"

"Well, all I could see was this girl, Jewel. But then I heard this older voice, sounded male. It triggered an intensely painful reaction, even in my legs, which are paralyzed."

Silk asks, "And what did this older male want?"

Lyle hesitates and appears uneasy. Finally, he says, "Me."

"*You.*" Silk says, "They're keeping Lyle pretty busy at Old Vic."

"Indeed," says Flo. "Lyle, you've had no feeling in your legs since your car accident?"

"That's right. A year ago. But we're working on it. I see specialists."

"As you've recovered," Silk says, "you've found that you're susceptible to empathic sensations. Particularly at places where painful events once occurred?"

"Yes. Something new for me."

Silk smiles slyly. "Lyle, can you feel my pain?"

"I don't think you have any, Silk."

"Let's hope you don't feel anything else I have!"

The women cluck at this light moment and Lyle blushes awkwardly.

"Lyle," Flo says, "describe your physical reaction when you first encountered Jewel."

"I was afraid, but fascinated. I felt like my whole body was tingling, even my legs, which was a surprise."

"Even your legs. And then what?"

"Jewel asked for my help, but then turned into, uh, smoke when I heard the other voice. Then I felt sudden, sharp pains where I had my old injuries. They were strangely accurate. And my leg muscles were in agony. My heart pounded so hard I was afraid it was a cardiac event."

"Fascinating," says Silk. "Let's talk more about Jewel. How'd you know she's just twelve—or died at the age of twelve?"

"That's hard to explain. I just knew."

"But she could be older."

"About a hundred years older." This amuses the ladies. Lyle smiles, but it fades.

Flo says, "A sexual reaction is possible sometimes when a living man communes with a spirit—a *succubus*. Did you experience a reawakening in that regard?"

Lyle's expression turns dark. He looks down at his drink.

Silk teases, "Now Lyle, your secret's safe with us." Both women smile. "And honesty is the best policy when you're sitting next to a clairvoyant!"

Lyle takes a swig from his scotch. The ice cubes have nearly melted. He's afraid he's about to lose his mind on national television—*Jewel's twelve, dammit!*

"Josh, keep shooting!" orders Silk.

"I am, Silk."

Silk leans toward Lyle. "Lyle, the reason we ask you this highly personal question...and believe me, it's a perfectly natural, or should I say supernatural, reaction to encountering a beautiful creature from the spirit world. The reason we ask, is to get to the bottom of your fixation. People don't usually risk as much as you have because they've seen a ghost. Viewers want to know why."

Lyle looks her in the eye. "She's a *girl*, Silk. I in no way had any attraction."

Flo asks, "Well did you feel you were capable of functioning sexually at the time?"

"What? What kind of question is that?" Lyle looks from Flo to Silk. "You can't ask that on national television! Especially not on *Entertainment Tonight!* This isn't going on *Entertainment Tonight*, is it! *Is it?*"

"Josh, keep shooting," Silk says. "Lyle. Lyle. Calm down. This interview will be on *ET*, assuming you get through it soon enough for Josh to edit the segment. It will air tonight at seven-thirty. Now I'm sorry if some questions seem too personal or distasteful but you need to understand that from this footage we'll also provide exclusive content for FEARcom."

"I don't even know what fear-fucking-com is!!" He exaggerates to clarify.

Silk looks at Josh. "Cut." He stops the cameras. She turns back to Lyle. "It's a website and Internet TV channel, silly. You know that. Look—the primetime stuff is going on *ET*. The raunchier, I mean, more private stuff is going on the website. The material is drawn from subscriber questions. We're asking you what they're asking us, get it? The point is to dispel any doubts about you—get it all out in the open."

"Silk, I get it, but I don't want it. Who would? I'm not some kind of paraplegic exhibitionist here."

"I understand, but you've become more than you know in the eyes of the paranormal world. They want to know everything about you, Lyle."

Chad pipes up. "Silk's right! I'm on the site now; the questions are pretty hot."

"Look here, Silk, is this some kind of porn site? If it is, all bets are off!"

"Lyle, this is *not* porn. This is how people talk in the twenty-first century."

Josh throws in, "Privacy is overrated."

Silk shifts her chair closer to Lyle. He can smell her perfume. Her legs are incredible and perfectly tan. Must be spray-on. Her thick bangs flop over one eye as she cocks her head and takes his hand in both of hers. Her lips are very shiny.

"Lyle. You're in good hands. We know what we're doing. We can't give you the right to approve the edit. You're going to have to trust us. And relax, okay?"

She massages his hand. Her hands are so soft. She closes her eyes meditatively. Lyle doesn't relax. His gaze falls from her lush eyelashes to her jacket zipper. How sweaty is Silk's skin inside her leather jacket now? It makes him crazy that they asked about sexual function on camera. But...

"Okay..." he says quietly, his imagination at play. "But I'm not answering any question I deem inappropriate."

Her eyes open and she catches the direction of Lyle's gaze. He instantly redirects his line of sight, but he's busted. Silk responds by giving his hand a patronizing pat—Lyle thinks of it as the nursing-home pat, he hates it. She pulls away from him. She won.

"Fair enough, Lyle," Silk says for all to hear. "Josh, let's roll 'em!"

"Deem away!" Josh says, switching on his cameras, staying with ironic.

The two women ask Lyle a few more questions. Based on the dumbness level, he surmises they're from "subscribers." One that stirs some discussion is: "How does a ghost know a bulldozer is going to knock down her house?"

"Because it's parked in the driveway," Lyle answers.

Silk promotes Lyle's expected appearance tomorrow at Southampton Justice Court, promising an exclusive report tomorrow night. She adds that tomorrow's installment of "Ghost Hampton" will feature another exclusive guest—the "Maltese exorcist" seen in the *Southampton Press* photo with Lyle Hall.

Finally Josh yells "Cut!" and everyone relaxes. Everyone except Josh—for him the hard work is just beginning. By 5:30 p.m. he needs to upload a kickass five-minute segment to *ET*'s client site—including digitally enhanced reenactment imagery illustrating Silk's description of Lyle's experience. Gregg has also promised a standard :60 "backgrounder." Then the *ET* producers will pass judgment. They may ask for last-minute changes—they are, after all, FEARcom's client. Josh heads off grumpily to his room with his laptop, leaving the equipment breakdown to Chad. It's already 4:30.

Silk strides up to Rooney's bar. Lyle swivels to watch her. In heels she seems unattainably tall; it makes him want her even more. Worse, he's completely deflated by the way the women picked him apart on camera.

Then Flo bends down to Lyle's face and speaks confidentially.

"Lyle, I'm sorry we made you uncomfortable. You understand the reasons why?"

"Yeah, and I don't like them. What happened to 'Sensationalism is bad for credibility'?"

"The more personal content is only for the website."

"There's no such thing as 'only for the website.' Even I know that. And what the hell happened to 'friends' Flo?"

"We are still friends," she smiles.

"Oh? By a twenty-first-century stretch of the definition? And what happened to 'the power of a mother's love'? You forgot that?"

"It's multiple segments, remember?" She stands. "See you later. On national TV."

Flo leaves for her room. Rooney mixes some fruity drink for Silk. Lyle watches him sneak peeks at her. He refuses payment. She turns and faces Lyle, drink in hand.

"Whew. I need to relax. You should too, Lyle."

"I'd like to. But I have some phone calls to make. This thing airs at seven-thirty?"

"If all goes as expected. Josh is very good at what he does."

"That's nice. He won't make me look like a crippled sex pervert on TV?"

"He'll do his best," she winks. "We'll watch *ET* together at 7:30 in Flo's room, then grab a bite and have a production meeting. Later we need to get you onto the Old Vic property to shoot." Silk starts to leave with her drink. "And thanks. You were a good sport. I think we'll all be very happy with the segment once Josh works his magic."

Silk departs and Lyle rolls to the bar. Rooney returns from taking the OPEN 5PM sign down from the door. Chad, working in the "set" area, is packing away the cameras. Josh's lights will remain hanging from the drop ceiling. The masking-tape X's stay on the floor where Lyle and the two ladies sat. Multiple segments.

Rooney pours Lyle another Dewar's.

"That was extraordinary, Mister Hall."

"Mister Rooney, I don't even know what ordinary is anymore."

Lyle leaves another twenty on the bar and takes his drink with him.

~~~~~~

43. Beyond the Grave

Seated at her vanity tonight, Chantale has applied more makeup than usual—eyes, lips too. Like back when she worked nights. And a nice slinky dress with high heels. She primps her hairdo, a sproingy collection of lush, rust-colored coils she calls "the sexy mop." For a second, she sees in her reflection the gutsy 17-year-old Haitian girl who traveled to Manhattan to become a supermodel. Fifteen years ago. Also reflected in her mirror is Berto sitting on her bed. Not bad. Not exactly George Clooney, but an improvement over that pig, Sabado. And in the three years since she and Berto became partners, she's socked away some decent cash. But not good enough to buy her dream house; they're still in her rental.

Chantale rises from her vanity and approaches Berto, who is wearing his usual black suit/white shirt combo. Tonight she looks as good as ever—even better.

Berto is watching her television. He seems transfixed. It's some bullshit about a local man and a haunted house. An unusually seductive-looking TV reporter is interviewing him. Chantale takes in the reporter for a few seconds. She watches some talk shows hosted by women—like Wendy Williams—and they may show leg, but they don't show cleavage like this. And the reporter's manner, directed toward the old guy in the wheelchair and to the audience, seems unusual for TV. Chantale turns to Berto.

"So? Where are you taking me?"

"Taking you?" Berto keeps watching, the TV remote on his lap.

"It's Thursday night. We're going someplace nice." Her expression hardens. "You were going to surprise me. *Remember?*

Berto pretends well. Eyes on the TV, he says, "Yes, I wanted to take us for nice steaks tonight, but now I have to work."

Chantale widens her stance; her hips block his view of the TV. "How did I guess?"

"I don't know, maybe you're psychosomatic? I didn't even know myself." He looks up to Chantale puppy-style for sympathy. "It's that police bitch. Chantale, she's parking across from the garage every night watching who comes and goes. It's creeping me out. And my men too. And she's a woman. The cops are dissing me, sending a *girl*."

She steps closer to him. "You should be glad it's only a woman cop. That means they don't suspect you of much." She looks carefully at Berto's face and into his eyes. "You've been doing cocaine."

"Just a little. It's the pressure, Chantale. It's the slow season, I have to make us money and there's this fucking police stakeout."

Berto hears Silk's voice on the TV and peeks around Chantale's hip to see.

Chantale stoops to Berto's level and her real and present cleavage eclipses the screen. She sinks a hand between Berto's thighs, grabs the remote and mutes the TV. Now it's quiet. Her hand returns to his lap while she slides two fingers under the gold amulet that rests on his collarbone on a short chain. Chantale now has his full attention.

"So this is not working for you, Berto? It works for you in bed." She fondles the amulet. "You need to focus on reality. Not reality TV. Your problems may really be about vengeance."

"Vengeance?"

"Vengeance *against you*, Berto—from beyond the grave."

This thought triggers a flashback to Sabado's death that gives Berto a chill.

"It may be," Chantale says, "we have to deal with both the living and the dead."

Berto takes out his ebony cocaine case. It resembles a cigarette case, but features a mirror and holds an impressive supply of coke. Chantale stands straight and watches him scoop some with his elongated fingernail and snort it. Sniffling, he looks up at her.

"Want some?"

Chantale places her knuckles on her hips. "No. I am not afraid, like you."

Berto snorts loudly and snaps the case shut. Acidic postnasal drip spreads through his sinus passages. He always got off on this bossy pose of hers, but not tonight. Not the disappointed way she's looking at him. She steps closer, one leg between his knees, and takes his face in her hands. Her bare arms look firmer since she joined the local Planet Fitness. Her perfect fingernails tingle Berto's face as she speaks.

"You know my mother was a powerful mambo in our village back home, Berto. She practiced Petro Loa Voodoo and people with troubles came to her from all around. She had spells and curses that could make bad people very sick. Make them stop hurting you. Everyone knew. She made good money. She was beautiful, too, and strong. All the men wanted her. I knew that even as a girl. She sent me away to New York to become a fashion model. And you know, one day, when my visa ran out, there was Sabado waiting near the Immigration Office. He offered me work, and a place to stay."

"I know."

"Then you know I brought my mother's skills here with me. Sabado liked that." Chantale's thumb runs over Berto's chin, the spot where his goatee hides the scar from Sabado's knife. She whispers, "He liked that very much."

Berto is high now and feels less fearful. He's entranced by Chantale all over again. He loves to watch her lips move. He pockets his cocaine case. He pulls her gently by her smooth arms down to his lap.

Now they're eye to eye. Berto notes how high up her skirt has risen. She undulates slowly on his lap and looks into his black eyes.

"Berto, you need my help again." She strokes his throat just above the golden djab she gave him. "Tomorrow night, Berto, you will see, will be different."

Her mouth envelops his lower lip and she bites briefly. Then, with one finger, with a perfect finger nail, Chantale prods Berto's solar plexus and he reclines backward. He stretches out on her bed and begins to unbuckle his belt. He's done this before. She stands up and looks down at him, hands on her hips. Then a surprise. She turns and stalks toward the bedroom door.

"Tomorrow, Berto," she says, pausing in the doorway. "First blood."

The screen door to the driveway slams shut. Chantale's BMW 321i convertible starts up.

Shit. Berto lies there, the TV silently showing that dark-haired woman in leather playing to the camera. What does Chantale mean, *first blood?*

~~~~~~

44. Entertainment Tonight

Lyle napped a little in his room. But he saw Georgie's sickening headstone again. Then a bloody knife; a silent baby. Then woke up with his first hangover in a year. A bad one. He scrolls through his phone messages. Many are from people he knows: Georgie, Fraser, Becky—shit, he forgot to call her and now she's screwed him on TV. Then there's Noah, Susan Wayne and, over and over again, Fred the Driver. Must be pissed. One number is definitely that of the Town Justice Court. And...Shit! Florida! Dar left a message. There are many calls from New York City and Los Angeles and God knows where else.

Georgie. He must call her. But Lyle gets a new text: He has to join everyone in Flo's room now to watch *ET*. There will be pizza. And a production meeting. Lyle still has some scotch in his rocks glass. He places it in his cup holder.

"Ghost Hampton" actually aired. Lyle watched it in Flo's room with the group. It's five minutes. Josh Berendt did a good, un-ironic job using visuals to quickly lay out the story under Silk's voice over: the old house, the court-ordered demolition, the "controversial paraplegic lawyer" who wants to stop it, the vision of a beautiful girl, the demonstrators occupying the neighborhood. The footage looked really good. As did Silk. She did her standup outside Old Vic, the house looking appropriately bad. Josh used moody "reenactment" images depicting Lyle's encounter with Jewel. When Silk described Lyle, Josh showed cringe-worthy stills by Mose Allen but, in a surprise, Josh piqued viewer interest by segueing from the wild man photos to a civilized Lyle Hall seated on set with Silk and Flo. At that point the piece shifted to "up close and personal."

On TV, Lyle clearly appears to be wrapped around Silk's finger. Silk looks so good and comes off so professional that this "Ghost Hampton" gig is unquestionably her stepping stone to a bigger TV career. Her risky choice of black-leather jacket halfway unzipped, short black skirt and heels, speaks loud and clear to the paranormal "subscriber base" as well as a much larger TV audience of young males and haunted-house fans.

Josh used a brilliant lighting scheme for Silk and a more dismal look for Lyle. Flo's lighting was middle of the road. Josh kept one camera on Lyle's sagging face as Silk asked a question and, as he started to respond, flipped to Silk's reaction—always very attuned and sympathetic. This, Lyle concluded as he watched, is a star maker.

ET wraps up with longtime host Mary Hart promising more "Ghost Hampton" tomorrow and, for Lyle, a disturbing new wrinkle: "Tomorrow we'll go inside Old Vic to expose its dark secrets and the mortal threat to the life of the man trying to save the place." The screen dissolves to Mose Allen's still of Fr. Xerri, dramatically supporting a deranged-looking Lyle Hall. "And," Mary concludes, "meet the mysterious young exorcist who saved his life!"

ET goes to commercial as everybody in Flo's room claps and hoots. Except Lyle. He really has to do it all again? They're bringing in Xerri, too? Lyle, so smitten with Silk from the start, now vaguely recalls that the agreement does not specify the number of on-camera interviews. Silk performs a victory gyration as Chad pops the plastic cork on some Champagne-like beverage from White's Drug Store in Montauk. It foams over the plastic motel-room cups Flo has set out. Silk's people raise their drinks for a toast.

"To 'Ghost Hampton'!" Silk cries. "'Ghost Hampton'!" the team responds. They drain their room-temperature "Champagne." Clutching his scotch, Lyle watches Silk throw her head back and down the cheap sparkly in triumph. Wearing a black sweat suit and flip flops for now, she still looks great. Flo observes Josh watching Lyle watch Silk. Then Flo passes out cool rubbery slices of pizza on paper plates. Both Josh and Chad take sloppy bites of their slices. As if it's any good.

"Now team!" Silk asserts while the glow is still on, "We are only as good as our next broadcast! We were lucky to have Mary Hart host our piece tonight. She conveys gravitas."

"We're *so* grave!" Josh says, keeping it ironic.

"That was Mary Hart?" says Lyle.

"It was," says Silk. "She's hosted *ET* forever. It's like having Maury Povich do you."

Flo closely observes Lyle's thoughts: *"Maury Povich do you." Hmmph. Silk's idea of middle-aged greatness. If I weren't like this, if I were in top form like in my court-case days, if...* He finishes his scotch as Silk answers her phone.

Flo wants to acknowledge Lyle. "I think Lyle did a good job on-camera. It's good to have a subject who looks like he's been through the mill—it adds vérité. People identify more strongly with a man who's suffered, and looks it."

Josh says, "After I edited the hell out of the footage. I hope I can keep his rocks glass out of frame tomorrow."

Silk looks excited as she disconnects. She goes into marching-orders mode: "Okay people! Speaking of tomorrow's shoot, we're going *live!* Gregg is working with people at Fox News on a live five-p.m. slot. They want the local-haunted-house angle. They want to air us—and our man Lyle—live at five discussing the latest on Old Vic as a whorehouse, the sad little ghost girl, Lyle's legal options, his accident-empath story, and that cute exorcist priest. So we need lots more footage. Josh, we can start with your reenactment imagery, but we'll need stills of Victorian-era prostitutes. Get permissions for stock photos; Gregg authorized budget. Chad, get better background music. This is not *Chiller Theater*. Think gravitas.

"Tonight we're going for the best vérité footage we can get of Lyle at Old Vic. Tomorrow, we cover Lyle's court appearance and the judge's ruling. Josh will cut a new opener updating our story and pumping up the drama. Before we go 'live at five,' Josh will have a window to edit tomorrow's exclusive segment for *ET*, incorporating the day's new material with the graphics and everything. *ET* will tell Gregg how long they want the segment. A longer run time tomorrow will mean tonight's viewer response was strong. And we'll get paid more."

Silk regards Lyle, who is not in the moment. "Lyle, in addition to shooting on site at Old Vic tonight, I also want footage of you at your wife's graveside and at the war memorial on Montauk Highway where you had your accident."

Lyle starts, "What?"

Flo intervenes. "Silk, that monument is a very dangerous place for Lyle. Based on his reaction to merely passing through that intersection earlier, we can't put him in that jeopardy. I actually thought Lyle's heart stopped at one point."

Silk thumbs her cell. "So we'll pump up the empathic angle with voiceover, without Lyle in the shot." She looks up at Josh. "Josh, figure it out. Get police photos."

"Okay. And I already have high-res stills of him from the reenactment."

"Make it work. You've got the night-vision camcorder for shooting at the gravesite and Old Vic?"

Josh seems to enjoy being challenged by Silk. "We have the technology, Silk. Infrared. If *Ghost Hunters* can do it, we can do it better."

"Good. This is national broadcast TV, team. The real deal."

"Silk," Lyle says, "what's this about my wife's grave?"

With that Silk draws close to Lyle and adopts a favorite pose, crouching in front of him. "Lyle, we need to show you as an empathic man in the present day—we need to *show it* to television audiences, not just tell it. If this is compelling for viewers it's because it's about you—you and a beautiful dead girl named Jewel. It's about what you once were and what you are today."

Lyle absorbs Silk's essence. Some heady perfume. That dark, healthy hair. Those lips, those eyes. That halfway unzipped sweatshirt. But he cannot read Silk's heart or mind. Silk continues, "And we need photos of you as you were. The dynamic, successful lawyer reshaping the Hamptons from old fashioned farmland into the high-end vacation destination it's become—a playground for the Steven Spielbergs and the Ira Rennerts. Developing a new Gold Coast out of a potato patch."

"If you say so," Lyle responds. "But I don't have any photos for you," he lies.

Silk grows fake-needy. "No?" She pouts. "Not one itty-bitty picture of handsome Lyle Hall is anywhere to be found?"

This is exquisitely uncomfortable for Lyle, especially with these FEARcom people standing around watching, including a woman who is probably reading his mind right now as he imagines wildly hopeless erotic acts. Silk pretending to come on to him is so perverse, he ignores her implication that he is no longer "handsome Lyle Hall."

"Sorry, Silk," Lyle finally musters. "Can't help you there. And Father Xerri, I can tell you now, will never go on camera."

Silk is used to getting her way. She stands up, cat-and-mouse time over. "Chad. Dig up archival stills of Lyle Hall tomorrow. Josh. Get me that priest."

The thought of filming Belinda's grave sickens Lyle. And what if a new name has somehow been added to her headstone? "Silk, I won't be visiting my wife's grave with a camera crew. I've never visited it before and I'm not going to start now."

Silk stares down at Lyle with an odd expression. Then she adopts another favorite pose. Hands on Lyle's armrests, her face at his level, she half-whispers, "Lyle, you signed a production agreement, remember? It states that you will participate in the production and not impede completion in any way." A real whisper: "Re*mem*ber?"

Part of Lyle wants to prolong this moment.

"Silk, I did not sign away my late wife's dignity."

"Oh, Lyle," Silk continues very quietly, as if she's already won this one. "You know this project's profit potential is directly linked to your performance. And your signature ensures that you will make every effort." She gives a hint of a pouty smile. "Jewel is just the beginning, Lyle."

Lyle breathes in Silk's scent. He also perceives Flo Hendricks somewhere in his consciousness, observing. He wants to tell Flo to get lost and she probably knows it.

"Silk," he whispers, "I do not want Belinda's grave a part of your coverage."

Silk tsks in frustration and rises, turning away from Lyle.

"Josh, shoot Belinda Hall's headstone and environs tonight. Light it dramatically. Add Lyle in software."

"*Jawohl*," Josh sighs with a German accent.

Silk opens Flo's door. "Later, people." End of meeting. She looks back at Flo. "Flo, we need to talk."

Lyle excuses himself and heads to his room. He has to return some calls. And he has to put the thought of them filming Belinda's headstone out of his mind.

~~~~~~

45. Florida Calling

Flo's cell rings. Silk calling from her room.

"Flo. You alone?"

"Yes. Just cleaning up."

"Listen, you have any idea how big this is becoming? Besides national television and global Internet hits, Gregg says we have print media requests out the wazoo. Including *People*. And now top-tier newsmagazine shows are calling—like *20/20*."

"But they don't pay."

"You're kidding, right? *60 Minutes* doesn't pay but the huge boost we get in national recognition skyrockets our value as content providers. Then there are books, documentaries, maybe feature films. Remember *Blair Witch*? You follow me?"

Flo Hendricks is following Silk. She's also developing a soft spot for the difficult old scotch-drinking mess that is Lyle Hall. She's even been quietly envisioning him as a New Lyle who's able to walk. An interesting, though remote, possibility.

"Flo?"

"I follow you. A high tide raises all boats."

"Listen to me. Lyle has made his money in life, now it's our turn. We are working our butts off on his story and it's only fair to expect our share of this phenomenon." Silk pauses for effect. "So, Flo. I need you to butter him up tonight. Get him feeling jazzed about his special place in the paranormal world. Maybe in history. This story's getting too big for him coming off as a sketchy, unpredictable drunk on camera."

"I'll work on his attitude, Silk." Flo stifles a weary sigh.

"Gregg is worried about him. We can't have all our eggs in one basket."

"Our 'eggs'?"

"Flo, that exorcist priest is trending online. What's his name?"

"It's Sherry or something. He's trending?"

"Check it out. Young, handsome, mysterious. And heroic—there's that picture of him with Lyle at Old Vic. He's celibate, but Twitter is really heating up, lots of women want to change his mind. I need you to rope him in for tomorrow's show."

"What's in it for him? He is a priest after all."

"You'll think of something. You did with Lyle. Later." Silk disconnects.

Tomorrow. Flo looks around her room at the fake Champagne bottles and pizza boxes. Lyle only signed on after seeing Silk's promo photo. Flo calls up the infamous two-shot of Fr. Xerri and Lyle on her iPad. Silk's photo won't work on this guy.

Alone in his room, Lyle's mind is swimming when he's struck by an unearthly thumping coming through the wall he shares with the owner of the motorcycle parked outside. A racket like that can't go on forever. It better not—it's aggravating his hangover.

Looking at his list of voicemails, the latest is from Fraser. Lyle clicks on it.

> Lyle! You're famous! The whole planet saw you on TV with that babe! And there are reruns on the Internet. She is too hot! You know how to pick 'em. You looked a little peaked though, did they sedate you? You drinking again? Whatever, can't wait for tomorrow's installment. And I like the pink sweatshirt—brings out the red in your nose. Call me!

Lyle's phone vibrates with a live call. Shit. It's Florida. Dar. Better take it.

"What do you want now, Lyle?"

Lyle hears his name pronounced with two syllables. He knows what he's in for.

"Didn't you call me?"

"I'm responding to a text message from that scummy partner of yours saying we need to talk. So here I am. I called you earlier, but you didn't have the decency to return my call, which actually *is your call.* Whatever it is, Lyle, I know it can't be good as I sit here in my nice condo overlooking the Gulf."

216

Dar must not know about the TV segment. Yet.

"I actually did want to talk about your nice condo."

"Listen to me, Bud, I am not vacating my home under any circumstances. *Comprende?* Sell that stupid old house you live in if you don't have the cash to keep me in the style to which I'm accustomed. Oh, and by the way, *everyone* down here saw you on TV with that slut bullshitting about a ghost. If you try to put me on the street now it'll backfire on you in public!"

Lyle is sick of the public already. And his house is not stupid. Well, maybe it is.

"I'm not putting anybody on the street. I do want to talk to you about the condo, and about me. Since I got out of the hospital..."

"Oh, sure. Let's *chat*. So...you have a 'naughty nurse' every night now, huh?"

Bringing up "naughty nurse" is a low blow—a stunt Lyle tried back when he started fooling around with Dar when poor Belinda was in decline. He conceived of this supposed role-playing frolic while drunk late one night. Perusing an adult costume website, he ordered an elaborate "naughty nurse" outfit, complete with white high heels and some spurious medical instruments, for Dar to wear one special night. He got it a lascivious size too small, knowing Dar was big-boned. The gift did not go over as intended, and it became one of the things she would hold against him.

Darryl Albright first met Lyle Hall in court. She was a legal assistant working for one of Lyle's frequent adversaries. Eventually, Lyle and Darryl entered into a steamy secret dalliance. Georgie, a teen living at home back then, grew suspicious, and Lyle made himself look like a total shit in her eyes. Dar became public knowledge once Belinda passed. Lyle's only real defense was that he was drunk at the time. He's paid for that in many ways since.

"Dar, I'm done with the nurses now and get by pretty much on my own."

217

"Yeah? Did you finally learn to cook a meal?"

"No, I don't want to set my arms on fire. In fact, Georgie comes by and drops off reheatable meals for me once or twice a week."

"She's keeping you alive? What, she leaves them on the porch so she doesn't have to speak to you?"

"Yes, actually, but we are on speaking terms."

"Hard to imagine. So. What do you want, Lyle?"

"Dar, I want to buy your condo and give it to you outright. It will be in your name; and I will pay its maintenance and taxes."

There is ominous silence.

"It's something I want to do," Lyle adds.

"Bullshit. You're *drinking* again. I know what you 'want to do,' Lyle! Don't have that scheming Fraser or his slut assistant contact me again! How *dare you* do that to me!"

Lyle is saying "Dar, no, really—" when she abruptly hangs up. At least I've planted the idea in her head, he thinks. Maybe I should just tweet her...

~~~~~~

46. Salt Marsh

With Chantale off somewhere in her BMW, Berto got to his limo office prior to the police lady's arrival. Keeping the office dark except for News12 on TV—hoping to catch more on that haunted house and the gorgeous babe—Berto stares at the spot across the road where the she-cop parks her white car. He bends at the waist and snorts up a mountain range of coke off a mirror. Dipping into the wares, just like Sabado did. So what? He muses about his old boss and what he might do in this situation. He thinks back to the last time he saw Sabado—October three years ago, the salt marsh outside Flanders, back behind the Big Duck. Where he sank the fat man's Escalade. The old guy with his sparse hair dyed black, well over 50, had told Berto about the site once—if he "ever needed to get rid of something." A horrific night. But you cannot succeed if you are afraid of risk.

Berto remembers driving the Escalade up to Flanders, up Route 24 northwest of Hampton Bays, that chilly autumn night. Blood was...everywhere. His linen shirt was ripped open, exposing his boyish chest. His boss, in a heap next to him, would slump onto Berto when he made left turns and stain his creamy slacks with more dark blood. Then Berto made the sharp right turn onto a gravel side road just before the monumental, stupid Big Duck. He drove back behind the scrub oak and pines to a place where no one went. No fishing, no dirt bike trails, no interest from anyone. No roads, just a vague path. About two hundred yards into the scraggly woods lay the mucky salt marsh. One section was surprisingly deep; Berto had measured it earlier with a rock on a rope. But now, he realized, without a change of clothes, he could be seen in public, his clothing ripped and bloodstained, on the night of Sabado's disappearance.

Berto was not going to drag the fat old guy through the woods. Headlights off, he gunned Sabado's Escalade right between some spindly trees. Breaking a stream of blue tape marking a property line, the SUV lunged down a narrow deer path that led to the swamp. Tree branches scraped at its windows and sleek paint job. The side-view mirror popped off and dangled as Berto jolted over the rocky, branch-strewn forest floor in the dark. He blew out a tire on a sharp stone, making progress increasingly difficult. And Sabado was still busting balls—his thick body kept repositioning itself in the passenger seat, forehead clunking on the dash, sliding left onto Berto as he tried to steer. At one point, after hitting a downed branch, the corpse's head sank down into Berto's lap. It was disgusting. Berto halted and pushed the body up into a sitting position. The head was very wobbly due to the ear-to-ear gash Berto had inflicted. Sabado's head had been in Berto's lap twenty minutes earlier when he received the knife wound. The last time for that, Berto swore. That was when Berto slipped the knife from the fat man's silk blazer. Opened it. Ran the fingers of his left hand through Sabado's thin hair. Slipped the blade under the big man's repulsive double chin. Pushed the head down.

After one clean slice Sabado had less than a minute to live. At first he showed shock and disbelief. Then a flash of anger; he would kill this little sonofabitch he'd rescued off the streets. He grabbed Berto's shirt. But he had no strength. He could not speak. No breath. He slumped over and bled out in the soft leather passenger seat. On the console and the floor. On Berto, who wondered how much blood a body could hold.

Earlier that night Berto had driven Sabado, as usual, and parked the Escalade in a corner of a deserted parking lot behind some tile-and-masonry delivery trucks. So they could "talk." Berto knew this lot, off Montauk Highway outside Hampton Bays, was secluded enough to do the deed. Sabado was drunk again and deep into cocaine. As usual Sabado had offered Berto a sniff from his elongated fingernail.

Once certain Sabado was dead, Berto zipped up his fly and tried to make himself presentable. But his expensive cream-colored slacks were soaked with black blood. He couldn't button his nice shirt; Sabado had ripped it open in a futile gesture.

Adrenaline pumping, Berto dismissed the idea of securing a dead man's seatbelt. Just drive.

Head up Route 24 to Flanders. That was the plan. To the deserted swamp behind the Big Duck. Do not speed. Get pulled over and it's all over. Maybe he should have seat belted the fat tub after all. As he drove, a memory surfaced unexpectedly. A comical American movie about rich gringos in the Hamptons. *Weekend at Bernie's* was one of Sabado's favorites. He made Berto watch it once, early in their relationship. Sabado laughed and laughed while Berto failed to see the humor. This night as he drove to the Big Duck, Berto realized something strange— Sabado was now Bernie.

~~~~~~

47. Diversion

It's 2:00 a.m. Friday and the FEARcom team and their dupe, Lyle Hall, return to Bridgehampton in two vans. Chad is alone in the FEARcom van and Josh is driving Silk, Lyle and Flo in her rental. Lyle is dull and hung over after an hour or so of disturbing dreams interrupted by bursts of infernal heavy metal from the room next door.

Silk's plan is for Chad to distract the campers with the branded FEARcom van so the unmarked rental can get the team close to Old Vic to shoot video.

A hardy handful of Believers, hangers-on now cold and frustrated, have returned to Old Vic to mill around. Sgt. Frank and his detail had cleared them from Lyle's block and then from Old Vic earlier that night. That went peacefully until News12 returned—the same crew that almost struck the FEARcom van in the intersection earlier. TV cameras inspired chanting and sign-waving but it took on an ugly tone. To Frank, the campers are like iron filings and the damn cameras are magnets.

Now Silk's van hangs back and they watch the FEARcom van pull in front of Old Vic. Chad attracts stragglers who want a glimpse inside the tinted windows. This is Chad's first job since college. He's a big, Channing Tatum-looking guy who got his dream job: working closely with the gorgeous Internet sensation Silk, producing paranormal news content for TV and social media. It's especially dreamy if you're okay with very low pay, driving all night, taking the team's deli orders and shit from Josh.

His foot on the brake in front of the house, Chad feels a weird, unexplained chill. He likens the Believers approaching his van to zombies from his favorite videogame. But these folk are harmless. A girl with dark, lank hair and wearing a large FEARcom T-shirt over her hoodie is at the passenger window. He lowers the window.

She looks in the van and her expression darkens.

"Hey! Where's Silk? Where's Lyle?"

Chad is flustered as more Believers gather round the open window. These outliers are more like vagabonds than the telegenic folk News12 preferred. They're unhappy. The star of FEARcom and the crippled ghost guy are not in the van. And where is Jewel? Is Jewel even real? They've been deceived. Chad can't raise his window with the girl's fingers on it. She's standing on the running board. He decides to proceed according to plan, having attracted some ratty Believers, and rolls slowly, foot on the brake, away from Old Vic at about one mile an hour.

Suddenly a large hand reaches in the window and grabs Chad's T-shirt collar, scaring the piss out of him. It's the grimy hand of a big creepy guy who leans halfway in the van. He's replaced the girl on the running board.

"Hey! What the fuck, man? You hear the lady? Where the fuck is Silk? We came a long way, man! Stop the fucking van!"

Chad wants to drive much faster but he brakes instead—there are Believers in front of the van now. He tries to pry away the guy's hand. The window won't raise with the big guy there. He resumes creeping forward at walking speed and the demonstrators move out of his way, complaining loudly. Chad turns the van left onto a side street. Where the fuck are cops when you need them?

Chad raises the window some, compressing the big guy's chest, and he finally lets go. Chad gives it some gas. The group lets out a collective cry. The grimy guy writhes out the window, hits the pavement and runs alongside for about twenty yards.

"You really *suck*, dude! Stop the van so I can fuck you up!"

Strobing red and blue lights finally make Chad stop as Sgt. Frank pulls in front of the van. The threatening guy scrams and the rest of the campers disappear up the driveways of summer homes.

Big Frank gets out and asks for Chad's license and registration. As Chad extracts his wallet he realizes he's wet his pants. Frank smells urine. Then he sees movement down the street. A suspicious van has pulled up by Old Vic. Chad offers his license with moist fingers.

"Look, kid, stay right here," Frank says. He heads back to Old Vic on foot.

As far as Silk is concerned, her decoy plan is successful. Josh may get some decent new footage after all. Even though Lyle Hall has turned into a depressed lump.

Josh brings the rental van to a stop. They're scoping out the old mansion wrapped in yellow tape when a flashlight signals them. A big cop approaches Josh's window.

"Was I speeding, Sergeant?"

Sgt. Frank points his flashlight into the van. That TV lady's in the passenger seat. That fat lady is in the back with Lyle Hall.

"Evening, Mister Hall."

"Hi, Frank," Lyle says glumly from the backseat.

"Mister Hall, this here is town property. It is unsafe and is under police protection. You and your friends will have to leave."

"Okay, Frank. Just wanted a look-see. We'll move on."

"And tell your friend in the other van to move along too, Mister Hall."

"Okay, will do. Thank you." That's the way you handle this, Lyle thinks.

Big Frank steps away from the van and Josh proceeds slowly forward. Silk rings that idiot driving the FEARcom van.

Lyle peers intently at Old Vic's planked-up front doors as they pass. Nothing. But he realizes he truly wants to communicate with that girl and understand her needs, her story. Jewel. Not the T-shirt; not the TV reenactment. The real, 12-year-old dead girl. Excruciating pains, death threats and cardiac stress notwithstanding.

Again Lyle marvels at the upheaval he's caused. People really must yearn for something to believe in, he thinks. Then dread for a living 30-year-old girl hits his gut again. He needs to communicate with her. Understand her needs. Keep her alive. But he's way off course now, and he knows it.

~~~~~~

48. The Barn

"This sucks," Josh says, as he pulls the van away from Old Vic.

"Lyle," Flo asks, "did you feel anything at all as we passed the house?"

"Sad that I caused all this trouble." Lyle cannot verbalize the dire threat Georgie is under. "Shit, maybe I just dreamed all this. Might as well have. There's no ghost and the house is gonna get bulldozed."

"Not true, Lyle," says Silk. "Josh, make the right up here."

Josh turns the corner.

"Lyle," Silk asks, "can we get onto the property from the back side of the block?" Before he responds, she says, "Josh, make another right."

Sure enough, from around the block you can see Old Vic's cupola poking up behind a closed summer house. A dark driveway leads to an old picket gate, beyond which lies Old Vic's scrubby backyard. It looks doable.

"Park here, Josh," Silk says. "We're going up that driveway and onto the property. Bring your low-light camera. Cell phones off, everyone."

"Okey dokey," sighs Josh, sounding drained.

Josh and Flo quietly set up Lyle's chair on the pavement. Lyle seats himself and, looking up the driveway, feels a sickening wave of fear. The dark structure, Old Vic, looms behind the summer house. Pressures haunting his real life intensify his nausea. He knows something is very wrong here. Preservation would be a bad mistake.

In silence, Silk leads the group single file up the driveway. Soon all four are through the picket gate and into the weeds of Old Vic's backyard.

As his wheels contend with the terrain, Lyle says, "At least tick season's over," trying to dispel his private gloom. Josh shushes him.

From the yard they can see the back of Old Vic is as tightly wrapped with yellow police tape as the front. The kitchen door is nailed up with planks. Josh shoots low-light video.

Old Vic's ancient barn is close, the remaining lot being a half-acre. It seems the local police have ignored it. A sudden outburst on the sidewalk in front of Old Vic makes Lyle's heart jump. Big Frank dealing with stragglers? Silk leads the group out of sight behind the old barn. There's a warped old door. Josh tries it. It creaks open.

"Quiet people," whispers Silk. "Let's get inside the barn. We'll shoot here. It's not the mansion but at least we're on the property."

"And at least we're trespassing," whispers Josh.

Inside, Flo immediately is struck by a profound sense of despair. An ancient dread seems to hang in the musty, unbreathed air. She notes how out-of-it Lyle seems. Silk has Josh close the door for more concealment and the rickety walls seem to close in on them. Silk's iPhone flashlight pierces the dark seeking a suitable backdrop.

"There!" She indicates a dense, tunnel-like spider web the size of a table cloth running along the sidewall. A thing like a hairy hand is crouched at its mouth.

"You want to do your standup *there*?" Josh says, impressed. He lights up his camera and plays it across the web, focusing in on the fist-size spider.

Silk turns to face Josh's camera. She's wearing her motorcycle-jacket-and-skirt outfit. "It's good television. Just don't let that thing jump me while I'm delivering."

Lyle tries to pull himself out of his funk. He activates his phone's flashlight and is instantly confronted with two sickly pink eyes near the floor.

"Oh, shit! *Thefuckisthat!*" Lyle whispers harshly.

Everybody freezes. The creature is low to the ground, big, ugly. It glares at Lyle with beady eyes. It turns and ducks between two clapboards dragging its hairless tail.

"A big old possum," says Flo.

"Hope they don't bite," says Josh.

226

Lyle shudders at the thought.

"Okay, people," says Silk, "we're going to shoot fast. I'll do my intro. Then Flo, you join me. I'll introduce Lyle. We'll talk about his empathy and his dramatic attempt to contact Jewel yesterday by breaking into Old Vic with his exorcist friend."

"Silk," says Josh. "He's wearing the same clothes he wore for today's segment." Josh shines his camera light on Lyle in his peach-colored sweatshirt.

"Shit. Lyle, you have to take off the sweatshirt," Silk says hurriedly. "Otherwise we look like a one-day-only story."

Lyle Hall is not concerned with what the story looks like now. Being in this old barn is not at all like connecting with Jewel outside her front door, being invited into her long-dead world. This is different. Something horrifying happened in this barn. Children, babies, blood, screams. And it's still happening, even now. He pays no attention to Silk and her reporter business. Something in here is paying attention to him.

"Josh, we gotta move," says Silk. "Get his sweatshirt off."

Josh hands Flo his camera to light the man. Lyle does not resist the process. The sweatshirt goes over his head and pulls up his white polo shirt with it.

Flo gasps at what she sees.

Lyle's bare midsection is illuminated. He's obviously had extensive lifesaving surgery. Subsequent surgeries. A huge vertical track like a deep purple railroad line is crisscrossed by a stunning network of angry wounds and sutures—puffy folds of white skin overlap sunken gashes. Flo envisions the cataclysmic car crash and the broken ribs and pierced organs. Rampant internal bleeding. Hours of lying opened up on a Southampton Hospital operating table undergoing emergency surgery. Non-vital organs, his spleen and gall bladder, removed entirely. Flo marvels that Lyle survived at all. How can he look at himself in a mirror this way? Lyle closes his weary eyes tightly. Flo feels an urge to help him. Somehow heal him.

"*Dude*," says Josh as he pulls Lyle's polo shirt down and stows the sweatshirt in his basket. He takes his camera back from Flo and fiddles with it.

"Hey, Flo, you were recording video."

Silk looks up from her text messaging with Gregg. "Good to go, Josh?" She steadies herself to deliver her standup. The camera's built-in microphone is all there is to capture sound. The big hairy spider cringes behind Silk when Josh's light hits it. Perfect.

"Rolling!"

"We're standing tonight in the ancient barn adjacent to Old Vic, Bridgehampton's reputed haunted brothel. Dating back to the Revolutionary War, this creaky structure bore silent witness to whatever went on in Old Vic and surely keeps its own secrets…"

Silk notices Flo and stops. Her jaw slack, arms limp, Flo is staring unblinking at Lyle. She's in a trance. Silk doesn't think this is good television.

"Flo? We're rolling!" She's unresponsive. Silk follows her empty gaze. Shit—her star has passed out. And he's bleeding from his ears.

"Oh God! Josh! Help Lyle!" Silk says. "I'll take the camera! Flo! Get *with it!*"

Flo cannot hear her. Silk…her concern for Lyle Hall is just an act. Silk could never care for this wasted mess that Lyle has become. Her perfect body is meant for some dumb stud. But Flo could care. She wishes Lyle could walk. Ask her out on a date. It could be nice. Gazing now at the ravaged man slumped in his wheelchair, Flo can see into Lyle's darkness. It's terrifying. A great bloody cocoon, like giant bat wings, envelops him, sealing out the actions of living people—the meaningless minority. The cocoon's walls are leathery. They pulsate around this catatonic man. Whispered moans well up though the filthy floor—deep voices and high-pitched wails swirl around him. No point in struggling. He's passive as ugly sounds and images of blood, terror, hatred lash at him. Flo senses a searing pain that makes

Lyle cringe in his chair. Orange flames glow somewhere—Lyle's future home. Two hands appear, grappling for control of an old carbon-steel kitchen knife. One hand is small and white, one is big, strong. She hears hateful curses. A woman's desperate cries in a foreign language. The knife stabs into human flesh. Blood flings everywhere. The knife turns on Lyle Hall. Flo screams as it thrusts into the crippled man's midsection.

His eyes shut, Flo knows Lyle is in another place. She blinks at her surroundings, tries to return to the living world and her job. In Silk's inexperienced hands the camera's light swings at wild angles—the barn floor, the walls, up at the roof. The light runs across a row of bats hanging from a rafter above. All their eyes turn red. Flo hates bats, hates them. She is standing in their dried poop…the product of bugs they eat and God knows what else.

Steadying Flo with her free hand, Silk's strident voice tries to bring her back into the moment.

"Flo! C'mon, Flo! I can't hold you up! We gotta move! Listen to me. If you fall there's bat shit all over the floor, okay? So don't fall. And behind you is a big web with a huge spider! There are bats everywhere! We're going out the door—now!"

Flo blinks again. She focuses on Lyle. He's unconscious, black blood in his ear. Josh obviously has no idea how to help.

Finally Flo gets her bearings. "Oh my!" she cries. "Get him out of here!"

Josh takes his camera from Silk and places it, still recording, on Lyle's lap. He attempts to push Lyle's wheelchair across the dirt floor to the doorway. It won't move.

"Now, Josh! Do it!" Flo cries.

"I don't know how to drive his wheelchair, Flo! It's fucking stuck in park!"

The bats grow agitated. Silk starts pulling Lyle's chair by its armrests as Josh pushes. The camera captures Silk's face grimacing under duress—not composed for once.

Suddenly all the bats take flight. "Shit!" Josh cries. Both women squeal in terror.

Flo briefly illumines the ceiling with her cell phone just as dozens of little black wings flutter around her head. Tiny, filthy little mouths kiss her face, try to bite her white skin. There must be a hundred bats. Sharp claws attached to featherless wings hook her hair and her sweater.

Lyle slumps forward as Josh and Silk work the chair to the doorway.

Flo reaches the barn door first, just as a bat gets caught in her hair. She screams and bolts out across the yard, swatting at the winged thing tangled in her hair. It bites Flo's soft hand, then flits away into the night sky. Josh finally gets Lyle's chair going and it rolls stubbornly outside and into the bumpy yard. They all head for the old gate.

Flo, her matronly hairdo a wild mess, makes it across the yard first. She gasps for breath as Silk and Josh steer Lyle through the gate and onto the driveway. Josh halts the chair and Silk sits Lyle upright.

"Oh my *God!*" says Flo, looking at Lyle. "I'm calling an ambulance!"

He's breathing. He's stopped bleeding but blood has collected in both ears. Josh takes his camera from Lyle's lap. It's still recording.

"Flo!" Silk says harshly, "You are *not* going to call..."

Bright lights hit Lyle. He opens his eyes and works to hold his head up. A large, dark figure approaches briskly. Sgt. Frank Barsotti.

~~~~~~~

49. Big Frank

"Mister Hall?"

Lyle Hall cocks his head and squints into the beam of a big police flashlight. Behind Big Frank is his cruiser, parked in the summer home's driveway. Its headlights add more light to the scene. Flo crouches by Lyle, dabbing his ears with a tissue.

"He's fine, officer..." Silk begins.

"I hope so," Frank says flatly. He shines his light on each face in the group. Tall thin young man: wise ass. Pretty TV reporter. Fat lady with wild hair. Circus is in town.

"You people aware you were trespassing on Town property?" Frank says, tired of this shit already. "There's a reason it's cordoned off in yellow police tape."

"Officer," Silk adopts her smarmy sexy-needy mode. "You see, we're a news organization on assignment..."

Josh produces his ID badge as Silk continues, "...I'm a television reporter." She sidles up directly in front of Big Frank. "My name is Silk."

"Uh-huh..." Frank knows her full name. He nods at Flo. "And you, ma'am?"

Flo stands, done with Lyle's ears. "Florence Hendricks, Officer."

"Uh-huh..." Frank holds his light on Lyle; two fingers tap the handcuffs hanging from his big belt. He's thinking. Voices squawk from his car radio as he crouches to look into Lyle's bleary eyes. Georgie's dad is pretty beat up.

"Hi, Frank."

"Mister Hall, how you tonight?"

"Lyle is fine," he sighs.

"You sure about that? Certain people need to know."

Lyle nods yes. Frank knows he has to tell Georgie about this. Not telling her would be problematic. He stands and faces Silk.

"Officer, I assure you," Silk says confidently, "Mister Hall was never in any danger. He was fully complicit in our newsgathering effort and..."

Frank raises a hand for quiet. "Look, lady, whatever you're trying to do here is unlawful. This is not how we do things in Bridgehampton."

"Officer, I..."

Frank cuts her off again. A rarity for Silk. "I saw that you sent your branded van one way to distract your fans while bringing Mister Hall here in an unmarked van. Your employee is parked down the block now." He looks at each of the FEARcom people. "I want your word that you will not attempt to pull a stunt like this again. And that Mister Hall will get any first aid he may need immediately. Otherwise..."

"You have our word, officer," Silk says solemnly, going for sexy-yet-sincere.

"It's okay, Frank," Lyle adds weakly, inured to people talking about him by now.

"In addition to caring for Mister Hall, you'll want to get your van driver—observing local speed restrictions—to the nearest restroom. Based on his odor."

Silk squints, uncomprehending.

Frank bends toward Lyle. "Mister Hall, a Southampton Police detective will be visiting you. Get home, or wherever you're staying, safely and get some rest."

Lyle nods assent. Frank stands to the side and shines his flashlight on the odd group as they move from the driveway out to the street and their two vans.

Once seated in his squad car, Sgt. Frank watches Silk conduct an impromptu team meeting, including a drained Lyle, under a street lamp near the FEARcom van. Chad, looking very uncomfortable, remains in the driver's seat. He rolls down his window and Silk orders him to roll it back up.

"First off, Josh, did you get any useable footage? I need to know now."

Josh plays back some blurry, shaky images on his camera's flip screen. They see the camera's light whip up, down and side-to-side. Sometimes a compelling image pops up: a row of bats here; a huge spider there; a large rat-like animal hissing; Lyle's horrific scars; a chaos of bat wings. Screams. Silk in close-up looking fearful.

"Yeah—dumb luck but definitely some useable vérité, Silk."

"Good. Vérité is good. Edit B-roll from that for the teaser. We'll also cut away to it when we go live tomorrow. Our big follow-up interview."

"I'll do it in my spare time," says Josh, back in ironic mode.

"I'm serious. Gregg texted me. We all need to be in top form tomorrow for this. This will be the big one. And it *will be live*, campers."

"You mean later today," Flo says, obviously sapped. "This afternoon."

"Correct. Today. Friday is a news day. Saturdays are not. Remember we're taking Lyle to Southampton Town Court this morning—that will be critical. And we'll need to discuss what the hell happened in that barn. I want us all on the same page."

Silk looks at Lyle with sudden, temporary concern. "Lyle, you're going to be able to do all this, right? You sure you're okay?"

Lyle looks up at Silk for a long moment. She's always beautiful. He feels like Quasimodo. Then he makes the first demand anyone's heard from him in quite a while.

"I need scotch. Now."

"Unambiguous," says Josh.

Silk goes for self-preservation. "Right. Well it's very late and I am going back to the motel. We have two vans. Flo, why don't you oblige Mister Hall."

Flo nods yes.

"Josh," Silk says, "help Lyle into Flo's van."

Silk glances over at Chad in the FEARcom van. He appears perfectly miserable and embarrassed. Josh and Flo get Lyle situated fairly quickly. Flo gets behind the wheel and as they pull away she and Lyle hear Josh complaining in the FEARcom van. "*Shit, Chad!* What the *fuck?*"

"Where to, Mister?" Flo says as they move off.

"I need a change of venue," Lyle sighs. "Hardy's is the nearest gin mill. Probably still open. Make the next left."

Flo passes Sgt. Frank's squad car and she waves to him. Frank is dialing his cell phone. Lyle notes the small, puffy wound on Flo's hand as she steers away.

Georgie Hall, sitting in her cruiser across from the limo depot, answers her cell phone.

"What's up, Frank."

"Don't mean to call so late but, your dad..."

"*Now* what?"

~~~~~~~

50. Swamp Water

Berto Duvan watches the blond bitch cop talk on her phone.
Everything about her makes him crazy. He paces his office,
trying to calm himself with more cocaine. But then his recurring
vision returns. Disposing of a big body on a moonlit night three
years ago.

From the marsh's edge, the stupid Big Duck was two hundred
yards away and obscured by scrawny woods. Berto finally
lurched the Escalade away from the grasping tree branches and
stopped short of the water. Lowered all the windows. Plan was to
gun the SUV into the spot he knew to be the marsh's deep end
and slip out as the swamp water engulfed dead Sabado. He
looked across at Sabado one last time. The fat, dead face. The
ugly mouth that had touched him. The open sport shirt, collar tips
spread outside the blazer. And the strange gold amulet that
always hung tight around his fat neck. It was bloodied by the
gaping wound. It still glinted on its gold chain. And it called to
him.

On an impulse Berto reached for it. The amulet was moist
and it slipped from his fingers. But a dead man would not
prevent him from collecting a souvenir to go with his new knife.
Ignoring the wound, his fingers hooked the golden trinket and
yanked it from the necklace. The dead man's heavy head fell
toward him again. Berto jammed the trinket in his shirt pocket.
Time to get out of here.

All the windows were open. He tossed his cell phone out onto
dry ground. He remembered to dig out Sabado's phone—for
client contact numbers—and lobbed it near his. He took a deep
breath and floored the gas pedal—the SUV lunged forward, but
halted abruptly in the muck. Cursing, Berto threw it violently
into reverse and, Sabado's corpse reacting wildly, skidded
backwards to a halt. Berto switched on the headlights. No

obstructions ahead. He revved the motor in neutral, then popped it into drive. The dead body slammed forward as the glorified truck jumped ahead. Swamp water splashed up and outward left and right of the front end. Berto became terrified that the Escalade would sink only partially and not be hidden by the swamp water. But then the heavy thing began to settle into the sludge as cold dark swamp water gushed in the windows. Just what Berto wanted. But now a new shock. He couldn't get out. The steering wheel had locked into a position that seemed to pin him to the seat.

The dark water was startlingly cold as it rushed in. It smelled of something awful. As if other men like Sabado rotted beneath the surface. Berto was a thin young man. Strong and smart. He tried to remain calm as he writhed in the driver's seat, swamp water gushing up to his ribs. Somehow he was reminded of Sabado's amulet in his shirt pocket. He grabbed it through the shirt fabric and held it to his heart and vowed he would not join his overweight benefactor/tormentor in this swamp.

And he didn't. The shitty water welled up and flushed Berto out from under the steering wheel. He flowed easily out the open rear window and took a gulp of air. Not fresh air, but it was air. And dry land was close enough to get to. The SUV made deep glugging noises as it swallowed muck and was swallowed by the muck.

Berto dragged himself out of the swamp, at first using a slimy, dead pine branch as a lifeline. The muck sucked off one of his nice loafers. Fuck it, just keep going. Finally reaching solid ground felt like some kind of miracle. The dirt floor was carpeted with pine needles. He stooped a moment, shivering, and caught his breath. He turned and looked into the water. It was some kind of miracle. The dark swamp water was indeed deep enough here, more than six feet, enough to conceal Sabado's Escalade for a long time. Berto scaled his other loafer into the swamp.

So strange. The engine died but somehow the headlights and tail lights remained on. They gave the most ghostly glow under the brown water. It was entrancing. He knew the submerged electrical system would give out soon. And the swamp creatures

236

that lived on dead flesh were already invited through the open windows to a feast.

It could be argued that Berto had done a noble thing this night. That he was brave. That it was well past time for a new leader. One clever enough to use the Internet and cell phones, to network among spoiled city people who thought the Hamptons owed them a good time. And find more and more of those people. Until Berto would not have to work anymore. He could marry Chantale. He'd hinted to her that a turn of events was coming. And Chantale had hinted that great rewards would come with such a turn of events.

Berto needed his cell phone. It was somewhere in this fucking forest of scrub pines. On the ground amid the litter of pine needles and deer shit. Where the fuck had he thrown it?

Then another miracle. It lit up and rang. Right over there by the trunk of a spindly pine. Berto was stiff, cold and wet, but made his way to it quickly. Picking up the phone he felt a rush of satisfaction. Its little screen read *CHANTALE*.

Berto told her she needed to pick him up by the Big Duck right away. Yes, the Big Duck. What does she not understand about that? Okay. He calmed himself, said he'd explain everything as soon as she came for him. He'd be waiting. And hurry. Please.

Berto disconnected and then located Sabado's phone by dialing it. Then something drew him to the edge of the swamp one last time. He peered into the dark morass at the strange lights glowing below. He wanted to thank God for getting him through this. Then it dawned on him. You don't thank God for helping you kill a man. Even a man like Sabado. You thank someone else.

Tonight in his limo office Berto snorts more coke. There's a reason he's recalling Sabado's death. He looks out at the cop car. That bitch has been sitting there for hours. He sees her end a phone call, start up her car and drive off abruptly. Why?

~~~~~

51. Bum's Rush

Hardy's is in fact still open. It's a classic workingman's bar—a year-round rarity in this summertime economy studded with celebrity watering holes. Hardy's regulars are no fans of Lyle Hall, but Joe Hardy, Jr., the manager and son of the owner, won't be on hand at this hour, which is key. And they surely have Dewar's.

Parked outside the bar, Lyle un-wads his peach sweatshirt and puts it back on. Flo struggles to get Lyle's chair ready for him at the curb; Lyle helps himself down into it.

"Getting back in the van is another matter," he says to Flo. "But I can roll home from here."

"Stop," says Flo. She gets a water bottle from the van and moistens a fresh tissue. "There's still dried blood in your ears."

Flo crouches and dabs inside Lyle's ears. For Lyle, this kind of intimacy, even with Flo, is oddly titillating. Her hair is completely wild; the moist tissue is cold, but this triggers weird, fleeting erotic images he tries to dispel.

"Lyle, what *happened* to you in that barn?" Flo gasps. "Once again, I should be taking you to the ER," she admonishes herself. "*Not* to a bar."

"In olden times bars were emergency rooms. A noble tradition."

As Flo cleans Lyle up he receives random flashes—disjointed snippets of pain Flo has experienced. A young man long ago. Death of a pet dog. Loss of her mom. Some kind of surgery. Frustration with and jealousy of...*Silk*.

She brushes back a lock of his hair. "Don't try to read me, Lyle. Unprofessional."

So now I'm supposed to be a professional empath? Lyle thinks.

"You have to work toward it," Flo says. "Okay," she stands up. "That's as good as you'll get without the staff at Gurney's."

238

She looks at the front of Hardy's Tavern with its old neon sign and cheap brick face and sighs. "Let's do this."

The peculiar couple cross Hardy's threshold. An aging cripple in a wheelchair and a fat lady under an explosion of dyed-brown hair. The dimly lit joint smells of stale cigarette smoke. People, men mostly, have been drinking here for generations. There are only a few patrons hunched by a TV at the end of the bar which is tended by a mistrustful-looking older woman with blond hair and dark roots. She smokes indoors after 3 a.m. The old-school TV is playing *Matlock*.

"These are my people," Lyle says sotto voce as Flo leaves him at a sticky table.

Flo deals with the barmaid and brings back two drinks. Hers is a white wine spritzer with a straw and a tainted lemon peel. His is a double, two cubes. She sits across from Lyle and watches him down a gulp of scotch. He can feel her eyes.

"Thanks." He holds up his glass. "Stuff is the same the world over."

"Consistent. Like you. So Lyle, what *happened* in that barn?"

He thinks. "There's some...*thing* there. Felt like it enveloped me, wanted to hold me there. I couldn't see any of you in this darkness. The air reeked. There was screaming and crying and cursing. Flames somewhere. There was a fight over a knife. Spurting blood. A woman cried out. Then the knife came at me. I came to when you screeched."

"You're welcome. Could you understand any of what was said?"

Another gulp and Lyle is finished with his double.

"No. Like listening to my ex-wife."

"Lyle, if you learned one thing from that experience, what would it be?"

"The *really* bad stuff took place in that barn." He pushes his empty glass to her.

"Another drink will total more than four ounces of alcohol."

"If we can trust the barmaid. All the better to interrogate me."

Lyle watches the barmaid's eyes follow overweight Flo and her wild hair as she returns to the table with more scotch. The old girl's on the phone, lit cigarette in the corner of her wrinkled mouth. He wonders what kind of tip Flo Hendricks leaves. It's good young Joe Hardy works days. It's been years since the protracted court debacle he involved the Hardy family in, and Lyle is unsure if the dad, Joe Hardy, Sr., is still living.

Flo sits down and holds onto Lyle's rocks glass. Their hands touch. Lyle feels a strange transference of energy between them. Not unpleasant.

"Thanks for bringing me out of that experience, Flo."

She was waiting for that. Flo releases Lyle's scotch. "I was there for you."

"Could you actually see the fight over the knife I saw? You can do that?"

She shivers. "I did. It was terrifying. And I saw it lunge at you."

"That was something new. Worse than my earlier visions with Jewel." Lyle blocks out the terror of being shown Georgie's headstone. Keep that from Flo.

She nods, sips her spritzer. "Did you experience anything else new?"

"My eyes were drawn to the floor." He takes a swig. "Disturbing."

"The floor. Why? That possum?"

"No. I saw a big black puddle on the floor. It rippled. Something was dripping down into it. Despite the screams and the knife fight, I needed to look down at this puddle..." He blinks at Flo. "My face was reflected in it."

"How disturbing." Flo sips again. "Lyle, I want to know what the spirit world wants with you. Why not...oh, that barmaid?"

"I could see the spirit world not wanting that barmaid. Maybe the spirit world wants a crack real-estate lawyer."

"Listen to me, Lyle. Tomorrow—I mean today—is a huge day for you. And us. You've already started out with a demonic encounter and two big glasses of scotch."

"Kinda go together," he says.

Flo sips through her skinny red straw. "Let me contrast tonight with your earlier experiences. This time there was no Jewel. No fire ants burrowing under your skin. You felt held captive. Moaning voices started to scream. Flames burned somewhere. Your eyes were drawn to a strange puddle on the floor. A desperate struggle over a big knife. An adult woman cried out, in a foreign language, I presume. Possibly pleading for the stabbing to stop. The knife cut into a body, then it went after you."

Lyle considers her recap. "That's about right. I definitely felt someone else's terror and...despair. It felt like that was my own fate, too."

Flo peers at Lyle. "Don't go there."

His spirits sink. "I couldn't see Jewel. Like she was locked away where I could never help her." He mutters, "Bloody hell," looks into his drink, and swigs some more.

Flo's hand goes up to her hair where the horrid bat was entangled. Her hair extends in many directions. "Maybe it's a good thing all those bats went crazy." She drinks. "It means something. You had glimpses of some atrocity that won't fade away."

As Flo sips more of her spritzer, unmindful of how bad it is—50 percent dead club soda from a gun, 50 percent white wine from a box—she's hit by a realization: *People who come in contact with this man get hurt. Some die.* In a way this makes Lyle seem even more intriguing. As the wine takes effect she decides to loosen things up.

"So. Lyle. You know any celebrities? This is the Hamptons, after all."

"It is, but I don't know too many, Flo. None that you'd know."

"How can someone be a celebrity that the public is unaware of?"

"Out here, it can be done."

Down at the corner of the bar Lyle sees the barmaid, off the phone now, lean furtively to an old patron nursing a beer who then glances over his shoulder at Lyle and Flo.

"How about Alec Baldwin?" Flo asks.

"Never met him."

"Paul Simon?"

"Sorry."

"Alan Alda."

"Nope." Lyle thinks. "I'm friends with Jerry Della Femina. We were supposed to have dinner before all this started."

"Is that a male or female?"

"Very male. Big Madison Avenue advertising executive. I did some legal work for him once and we hit it off. He gets me."

"Kindred spirits." Flo knits her brow. "Lyle, regarding Silk," She looks him in the eye. "You know she's a consummate professional."

Lyle stares back at Flo. "Yeah. *So?*"

"So you should also know she's not *available*."

He looks down and swirls his scotch with a red stir stick.

"Lyle, I can perceive how you feel about people. It's something I'm good at. I know you're given to...unbridled fantasies."

"They're actually pretty bridled. And I'll thank you to stay out of my private—"

Flo looks up suddenly at a large red-haired man.

Two hairy mitts grab the wheelchair's hand grips.

"Closing time!" the big man grunts. He easily sweeps Lyle away from the table and toward the door.

"Hey!" cries Flo, standing up. "You can't do that! He's an injured man!"

Lyle knows who is giving him the bum's rush. And he can see Joe Hardy, Jr. in the bar mirror, propelling his chair. Lyle gets a flood of emotions from young Joe. Anger, loss, frustration. His father at home, health failing. Bouncing this bad lawyer feels good.

Hardy's even larger pal holds open the old door with its diamond-shaped window. Lyle's chair bumps over the threshold and in a second he's out on the sidewalk. He'd be embarrassed, but no one's around. Maybe he should feel shame. His drawn-out court action years ago was meant to take the fight out of the

Hardy family so that their location could be taken over by a Manhattan-based partnership bent on building a high-end Greek seafood restaurant that would be open six months of the year. The Hardys surprisingly won the case but their legal costs were devastating. They'll never get out from under the debt. Joe Jr. raised the price of beer but...hey.

Flo brushes past Hardy, rushes outside and crouches next to Lyle.

"Oh, my God! Lyle, are you *okay?*"

"Yeah. Been thrown outta much better places."

"People have clearly defined attitudes toward you. To put it euphemistically."

"I'm a man of many euphemisms."

Lyle hears Hardy lock the door. He starts rolling down the street and Flo walks along. Quick reflexes preserved the rocks glass in his cup holder. It even retains some scotch. "Flo, I need to get my meds and personal items from my house, now that the neighborhood is free of campers. It's only a few blocks. I can roll there and get some air."

"I'm going with you," Flo says, ignoring for now how they need her van to get back to Montauk. This could be an opportunity for meaningful talk.

~~~~~~~

52. A Walk With Flo

Lyle and Flo cross Montauk Highway and turn right onto Hull Lane. It leads to Ocean Road and his house. The cemetery is on their right. Lyle notes how Flo's demeanor seems odd, otherworldly, like she's viewing him from orbit. A spritzer can do that?

"Lyle, forgetting how an irate man just threw you out of a dive bar, your issues really do stem from your inability to relate to women on their terms."

"Guilty," Lyle says. "I am a man." They move down the street in the gutter.

"Beyond Mars/Venus stuff, Lyle. I believe you treated women as objects when you were younger and never really grew past that. Then your accident and long recovery forced you to look at things—and your daughter—differently." Flo eyes Lyle's profile. His rocks glass jiggles in his cup holder as he rolls. Some scotch has splashed onto his pants. "You should benefit from your newfound empathy and your contact with Jewel. It should improve how you relate to your daughter as well."

"You're saying Jewel reached out to me because I'm a better person now?"

"Well, we don't know what prerequisites a supernatural entity harbors—usually it just wants you to go away. Maybe 'waiting for you' is more accurate. Jewel did not reach out to just anybody—not your barmaid for instance. You are...unique."

"I'd rather be plain vanilla at this point."

Ocean Road lies ahead. The homes are dark, a few have lit porch lights and pumpkins. A dog barks irritably somewhere, echoing across the murky cemetery.

"It bothers me," Flo says, "that we may be dealing with something other than a girl. Something that can trigger horrific experiences in certain susceptible people." She looks at Lyle again. "Lyle, I saw your wounds and the scarring from your accident when Josh removed your sweatshirt."

"Lucky you."

"It's serious stuff. I could sense some of what you've been through. You feel guilt for causing the death of the other driver. And there was a celebration...curtailed."

Lyle looks straight ahead in silence as he rolls. Suddenly he blurts harshly, "Okay. Elsie had a birthday cake on her passenger seat. For her son's fiftieth birthday." His tone softens. "Her son Jimmy was a first responder. He left his own birthday party to answer the call. Found his mother in her car." Lyle grows agitated again. "And by the way, what happened to the 'mother's love' I experienced being so 'interesting'? Instead you accused me of being a child molester on TV!"

"Lyle, we followed our subscribers' questions. We'll get to the love thing soon."

"Yeah, Elsie's 'love thing.' Meanwhile her family is suing the shit out of me."

Flo walks on quietly beside Lyle for a few moments. Finally, she nods toward the cemetery and asks, "Is Elsie Cronk...here?"

Lyle exhales, does not look at the cemetery. "Her remains are here. She's wherever you're supposed to be...when you live well."

Lyle's house is about two blocks away.

"How about your family members' remains? I'm wondering what life's like as an empath with a cemetery down the street."

Lyle sounds tired now. "My father's interred in Queens with his siblings. Mother is in assisted living in Florida near my sister."

"Your first wife Belinda is here." Flo senses a sudden wave of emotion. Again she's hit a nerve. Lyle is hiding something deeply serious.

"She's in heaven or whatever," Lyle spits. He halts, grabs his rocks glass and drains the scotch.

Flo crosses her arms. "What are you hiding, Lyle?" Sometimes blunt works.

"I have a goddamned personal life, dammit!" Lyle blurts. "Not *everything* is available to you! Or FEARcom! Or your executive producer!" Lyle stows the glass.

"Fair enough. But I sense something very serious going on involving your wife's grave. Even now."

"Sense all you want," Lyle says testily as he throws his chair in gear. *Sense all you want,* he thinks. Lyle fights a powerful urge to go look at Belinda's grave. He envisions her headstone, their daughter's name freshly engraved. The cold terror of it. Is Flo there too, damn it? Snooping?

They move on in silence for a bit, then Flo asks, "How long have you lived here?"

"Growing up, we lived north of the highway with the normal people. My father was your basic small town lawyer. Bridgehampton was—and is—a small town most of the year. I bought this house in the '80s once I started to make some money."

"Are we near the ocean?"

"Not very, but I have winter water views."

"You what?"

"I can see my neighbor's pool when the leaves fall."

"You don't have a pool?"

"I do. I stopped opening it when my second wife left. I was busy with work and don't sunbathe. Maybe someday I'll have reason to use it. Or just sell the damn place."

"I see. Do you belong to a country club?"

"Two. They let me freeze my membership."

The two turn right onto Ocean Road.

"Lyle, I should talk to you about Silk. Your feelings for her may be unhealthy."

"I am not unhealthy! They're making great strides in spinal-injury research, you know. Stem cells. Regeneration. Electronic stimulation. All kinds of stuff."

"Can they make you twenty-five years younger? What I'm saying is you should find someone who appreciates you for who you are. What you are. Don't hurt yourself."

Grim silence.

"Last topic. What is going on between you and your daughter?"

Lyle grudgingly opens up a bit. "Georgie is my only child. She's thirty. Her mother died when she was fifteen. She's a Southampton Police detective. I got her promoted."

"But there's some kind of issue."

"Isn't there always? I'll tell you this—I just learned she's being harassed at work. Sexually harassed. And it's linked somehow to this 'Ghost Hampton' shit."

"Oh, I'm sorry for her. It's terribly difficult to do quality work under those conditions. It ties the two of you up in a messy way. She shouldn't fault you but, I can see how..."

"Oh, she faults me, all right. But misogynous resentment for a female detective would be there regardless. This was just the trigger mechanism." Lyle glances at Flo as they move along. "Somebody's inflating condoms, drawing ghost faces on them and putting them on her locker. And in her car."

"Oh God, no. Her fellow policemen? I'm so sorry for her."

"It's tough, but she's a big girl, she'll get through it. They may have Internal Affairs in on it at this point. But I worry about long-term recriminations. It's not a good work environment for her right now."

"Your daughter must really need to talk to you at this point."

"Indeed. She just called, demanding that I cease and desist with the ghost stuff."

"You should tell her you are under contract to cover ghost stuff for FEARcom. But I keep sensing there's something more important that you need to tell her."

"It's unprofessional to try to read a fellow ... whatever it is I am. Remember?"

"The amateur doesn't read the pro. That's backwards. Now, one more last topic?"

"This better be the last, last topic. We're almost at my house."

"Okay. Lyle. Tell me. What are you planning to do with your gift?"

"My *gift?* You mean the empathy? How about send it back."

"You might be able to do some good...for a change."

A white 2004 Crown Victoria suddenly comes alive across the street. Headlights. Red-and-blue grille lights flashing. No siren. It crosses diagonally and rolls straight toward Flo and Lyle. It jolts to a halt in the gutter directly in Lyle's path.

Driver's door swings open. A woman in a dark pants suit gets out, leaving the door open and the lights flashing. She storms toward Lyle Hall. Flo sees this tall, determined young person with honey-blond hair clipped behind her head approach. She strides past Lyle without comment and confronts Flo.

Flo is hit with waves of jagged anger, pain and frustration radiating from this dead-serious woman. She's pretty good looking, too.

"Florence Hendricks?"

"Detective Hall." Flo makes a tiny smile of recognition.

Georgie nods at her father. "I need a moment."

Flo gestures maitre'd-style toward Lyle and backs away. She stands under a tree by the tectonic sidewalk and observes the two interact. And there's something weird beyond them, up the street. Amorphous, ghostly white, billowing in the trees.

~~~~~

53. Gutter Talk

Georgie stands facing Lyle, her arms folded across her chest. They are both parked in the gutter of Ocean Road, the street where she grew up. Flo observes the encounter from a respectful distance. Georgie does not stoop to go eye-to-eye, but a rush of fatherly emotion flows through him at the sight of her.

"Dad. *Really?*"

"Georgie, it's all right..."

Georgie spits her words through clenched teeth in a ferocious whisper. "It is *so not* fucking all right, Dad. Not for you. Certainly not for me. Have I not explained to you what I'm going through?"

"Yes, but..."

"Don't 'yes but,' Dad. You are going to go to court and undo the trouble you started by rescinding that embarrassing motion you made. You promised you'd do it today. You did not. You *will* do it tomorrow, Dad. Understand?"

It's obvious to Lyle how upset his daughter is, but the sense of ultimatum in her voice triggers his innate lawyerly defense mechanism.

"Georgie, I need you to understand what's in play here..."

"No. You do not need that, Dad. You need to be good to your word on this. For *real* this time. Do it. Do it tomorrow."

"Georgie..."

"Tomorrow. On your honor. If you ever had any!"

Lyle peers up at his daughter. She is so impressive when she's angry. And beautiful. There's no way out. Lyle can sense the pressure being brought to bear on her at work. Who from? Is her job even worth it? Is Lyle making Georgie's job even tougher?

"*Dad...*"

Got to respond. "Okay. Okay, Georgie. In the morning. I'll do it. On my honor."

The two stare at each other. There are no Believers around. Just a patrol car up the street past Lyle's house. A neighbor's porch light backlights Georgie's hair. Lyle is desperate to tell her about his premonition. She relaxes her stance and shakes her head.

"Georgie, I am sorry about the guy hassling you at work. He's obviously a sociopath. And an ass."

"Don't tell me about what I'm experiencing."

He points his chin at the Crown Victoria, lights blinking, engine running.

"That your car?"

"Only thirty-six more payments," she deadpans coldly.

"I mean, is that the one with the—"

"That's the one."

"You do stakeouts in a white car?"

"Want to paint it for me?"

Lyle grins a little. "I've been thinking about this guy at work. He's a cop?"

"Yup."

"Do you have any idea...?"

"Yeah. Desk sergeant. About to retire. Pulls sixteen-hour shifts. Not married. Lot of free time on a quiet night."

"How does he get all the overtime?"

"Queeley."

Lyle vaguely remembers the desk sergeant from occasional visits he's made to see Chief Queeley over the years. "That pudge at the desk? Queeley lets him pad hours?"

"It's not that uncommon."

"How would that guy ever have the nerve to...to..."

"Name's Swanson. He's never been respectful to me, especially since my promotion. And he assigned me the only white car in the fleet."

"Why'd you accept it?"

"Didn't want to act up. It is my first case, Dad."

Lyle ponders. "Some people might behave like this if they felt threatened. Or were trying to impress someone. And felt shielded somehow. Could someone be encouraging or enabling him?"

"Dad, I don't know yet. But Queeley called me in this morning and indicated that, since the harassment is specific to your haunted house debacle, it will likely end when you cease and desist. Which you so failed to do."

Lyle gazes up at his daughter and detects just the hint of vulnerability. She's playing a man's game. He considers Queeley's suggestion. There's something fishy.

"If this—then that?"

"Huh?"

"Quid pro quo? The harassment might end if I end my..."

"You are going to end it, Dad. No ifs."

"Right. It's just...*Queeley*..." Lyle blinks. For a flashing second he has a vision: a very old cabinet somewhere, a forgotten file. "Georgie, could there be police files on One-eleven Poplar? Maybe hard copy filed away somewhere? Never digitized? Maybe documented police cases involving the former owner?"

"Dad, *what for?* You're not pursuing the case. On your *honor*."

"Right. But I can still be curious. Could you check it out for me?"

"Maybe. Quid pro quo."

Georgie lowers herself to Lyle's face, her palms on his armrests. Her left thumb almost dips into his rocks glass. She looks so grown up. So not the round-cheeked baby he's holding in his arms in the framed photo in his living room—taken back when he was a drunk. Lyle flashes on providing the baby's name for her birth certificate and how Belinda, whose father's name was George, later had to correct it. Lyle, real estate always on his mind, had reflexively spelled it *Georgica*.

Now she's a professional. She nods in Flo's direction.

"Dad. What's with *her*? You're not planning any more paranormal bullshit are you? No more horrid television. It's not good for you. It's gotta end. Understand me?"

Lyle looks into her blue eyes. How many days left to live? Two?

"I do. We're just talking. She's interesting. We're…friends."

"You make friends pretty quick these days."

"You have to in the paranormal business."

Georgie rolls her eyes and stands up. Right then it all wells up in him. He has to tell his daughter something hugely important. So important he could explode. Can't put it off any longer.

"Georgie, wait a moment."

She folds her arms and cocks her head in an impatient *I'm listening* pose.

"Georgie…" Lyle's head starts to shudder. Tears well up. He's afraid he can't speak. "Georgie, you know something? I love you!"

It comes out a whisper. As if he could prevent Flo from eavesdropping. Better try again.

"I love you, girl!"

Georgie's face drops in emotional shock. She has no recollection of ever hearing those words before. Lyle looks like a shuddering wreck. She suddenly cannot speak, there's a lump in her throat. His eyes are wide and fixed on her. She bends to him. One hand steadies his scruffy face while she plants a big kiss on his cheekbone.

"And you gotta swear to me you'll be careful in this job of yours!" he wheezes.

Georgie stands back up, her head wagging almost imperceptibly in a silent *I cannot believe you* gesture. She blinks back a tear.

"We both gotta do what we gotta do, right, Dad?"

He stares at her like he's memorizing her face.

"Dad, I gotta go. You know what you have to do in court tomorrow. End it with Judge Sloane. Then we'll talk about looking for some old mystery file. And no more alcohol, Dad. You smell like a distillery."

Georgie nods to Flo. "He's all yours. Just be careful with him."

"We will," she says, a little unsteady after the exchange she just witnessed.

252

Watching Georgie pull away in her Crown Vic, Lyle feels at war with himself. He'll never solve the threat to Georgie's life if the old house—and Jewel—go away. But he's promised her he'll let the house fall. Even though she may only have a few days left. Or is it all just paranormal bullshit?

Off duty and driving west on Montauk toward her Southampton condo, Georgie reflects. She did not like Flo's *we will* shit. Who's *we*? Flo and that repulsive Vampira TV reporter.

~~~~~

54. Lyle's Porch

Flo and a brooding Lyle, chin buried in his chest, are quiet as they approach his house. A streetlamp cuts some of the gloom. The gutter has wet leaves. Flo holds off calling attention to the massive white thing waving in the trees ahead.

"That's quite a girl you have there," she says after a moment.

Lyle gets the impression Flo has no children. "*Oh*, yeah. You know, it's hard to discipline them when they're police detectives."

"She's good at disciplining you." Flo smiles at him. "You've been hiding something from me. Now at least I know who."

"Please."

"And now I want even more to know what you're concealing about her."

"Nothing to do with you and your fear business."

"Oh, no?"

Suddenly a fat, ugly creature scurries past, low to the ground, on quick little feet. It crosses a lawn and wriggles under a nearby porch, dragging its disgusting hairless tail.

Lyle cringes and they both stop in their tracks. "See that? It was that possum!"

Flo grows serious again. "Lyle, do you know about paranormal attachment?"

He looks up at her. "Should I?"

"You should. It's a proven phenomenon."

"Lay it on me," Lyle sighs. He frees his rocks glass from his cup holder and derives a few watery droplets as Flo speaks. The dog resumes barking in the distance.

"It's like this. When a living person spends time investigating a place inhabited by a presence, it may 'attach' itself to that person and go on to dwell at the investigator's own residence. The person's own home becomes haunted."

Lyle feels exhaustion coming on. "It can piggyback? It's contagious?"

"It may be conveyed by an animal. Have you experienced anything like that?"

"No. How about you? You've hung around a lot of haunted places." He looks at Flo. "Ever bring a ghost home?"

Flo doesn't respond. Lyle follows her gaze upward—to a stunning sight.

"Lyle, I have never seen a house so spectacularly *toilet-papered.*"

"*Shit!*" More woe for Lyle. "No wonder Georgie's unhappy. She grew up here."

Lyle's block is transformed. While Big Frank was busy herding the campers from Old Vic, local teenagers raided Lyle's street, chucking reams of toilet paper over tree branches. Now, in the predawn, white toilet paper dangles everywhere like ghostly Spanish moss—the majority concentrated on Lyle's property.

A cop car pulls to a quiet stop across the street, no lights. Too late.

"Nice work," says Flo, slightly in awe of the vandalism. They move closer.

"Damn kids. They knew the cops were at Old Vic. Who do you call to remove toilet paper from your trees? ServPro?"

Lyle's house received careful attention. Toilet paper hangs from the tree limbs over his front yard. His bushes are wrapped like mummies. Even the rafters under his porch roof are thoroughly TP'd. The house is a 1950s ranch, updated now and then, but still dated by any standard. With its porch dark, the place looks sullen. Lyle didn't think to turn on the porch light when he left. But he can make out shaving cream and DayGlo goop sprayed everywhere, too. Some dope scrawled *Wear's Jewl?* with it on the porch wall.

Now they both hear something up on the porch, like muttering. There's an unnerving hiss, followed by a heavy thud. The toilet paper on the porch flutters.

Lyle gets spooked. "What was *that?*"

"Let me check it out," Flo says, turning coolly professional.
Lyle pulls onto his sidewalk and right away hits a rut.

"Damn slates! Flo, help me!"

Flo helps propel his chair forward to the foot of his ramp.
Something's on the porch. Georgie's meals in a sack? No, much
too big. It's quivering. What is it?

Flo whispers, "I want a closer look."

"Me too. I live here, dammit."

Flo helps steer Lyle up the ramp and onto the porch. The
toilet paper sways in his face. From here the big lump looks like
a sack of potatoes with a T-shirt pulled over it, a sort of blue. The
shape twitches in the dark. Old boots protrude from it. One boot
is trembling. The barking dog has gone silent and Lyle can hear a
throaty hiss coming from the shadows on the porch.

He flips his iPhone to flashlight mode and suddenly they both
can see it.

"Oh, SHIT!"

It's a man.

"Omigod!" Flo blurts.

But two pink eyes are glaring back at them. It's that vile
possum from the barn. Standing on the man's chest, like it's
challenging them. Its pointy little fangs flash as it exhales a
wicked hiss.

"Good Lord!" Flo cries, "What do we do? That poor man!
He's alive!" She claps her hands, trying to shoo the possum.
"Scat! *Scat, you!!*" It digs its claws dig into the blue T-shirt,
wrinkling an image of…Lyle's face. A goddamn Lyle Hall T-
shirt.

Flo dials 911. Lyle takes in the animal's beady eyes, its dirty
white face, its pointy snout. Possums are not supposed to be this
big. Not this aggressive. He rolls forward to see the man. One
hand is visible. It's that of an older man. Is he alive? His boot has
stopped trembling. Why the fuck is he on Lyle's porch wearing
that stupid T-shirt? What is this primitive monster doing to him?

Lyle tries to rouse him. "Hey! Mister! You all right? Can you
hear me?"

No reaction. The possum's position blocks a view of the old guy's face.

"Yes, Ocean Road!" Flo says to the dispatcher. She glances at Lyle's front door. "Forty-nine Ocean Road. The Hall residence. An elderly man collapsed on the porch. No, not Mr. Hall. He's here with me. And there's a big, rabid possum. Yes, that's what I said! I think it has rabies, it's threatening us! We need help right away! Please hurry!"

It occurs to Lyle that Flo is a smart girl.

He feels an eerie kinship with this fallen man—and senses a strange peacefulness. Lyle needs to see his face. He rolls closer, despite the threatening animal. It's something worse than just a big possum. It's grinning. What does it want? Why doesn't it run away? Part of Lyle revisits the possum's dark corner in the barn. The tortured cries of a woman. And all the blood...

Flo hangs up as Lyle approaches the fallen man and the pissed off possum.

"Lyle, no! Stop! STOP!"

It's like she's crying out in a dream. But this is real. A real man. This obscene, hateful animal. Pink stuff froths in its grisly mouth. Why is it grinning? Squatting there on Lyle's face! Only a few feet away now, Lyle is afraid to see the man's face.

"Lyle! No closer!" Flo steps in front of his chair, blocking him. She's even closer to the prone man. She turns her back to the possum and faces Lyle. The animal lets out a shrill screech and launches itself at Flo.

Then Lyle comes *loose*. He seems to float above, able to see it all. He sees the possum attack as if in slow motion. It seems so powerful and heavy. Flo wears sensible shoes and a pants suit. The possum rips into her ankle, tearing her Achilles tendon. Its spiny jaws actually rip away flesh and Flo screams pitifully. She topples onto Lyle, rolling his chair backward. She sinks to her knees between him and the possum. He can't reach the animal, can't kick it. Flo's eyes register shock and terror as she slumps into his arms. The creature circles to get a piece of Lyle next, making its sickening hiss. Right then, Lyle returns to his own tensed-up body.

Cradling Flo, he frees his left arm and grabs his rocks glass. He flings it hard at the creature and actually clocks it sharply on the head. Stunned, the possum backs away. Flo lets out a sob. Then silence.

"Flo! *Flo!*" Lyle cries.

Kneeling, Flo's head comes to rest on Lyle's chest. Gasping for air, she clutches near her heart, her eyelids fluttering. It's gotta be a heart attack. But Lyle can't think. He spots the possum's repulsive pink tail as it slinks off the porch.

Desperate, Lyle speed dials Georgie.

"Hold on, Flo! Georgie will get emergency services! They'll come right away!"

His call goes to voice mail. But the lone patrol car down the street lights up and rolls to a stop in front of Lyle's house. It's Petry, the young cop from yesterday. He gets out and approaches the porch, flashlight playing on the whole gruesome scene.

"Officer!" Lyle gasps. "Two people down here! An old man and a middle-aged woman! There's been some kind of rabid animal attack!" As if Lyle would know.

Somewhere Flo can hear Lyle trying to help. *A middle-aged woman* indeed. That's what it's come down to. Her middle-aged heart has stopped. She has only the air left in her lungs. No more will come. One hand clutches her chest. One hand grips Lyle's arm. Face to face. He squeezes her other hand. The light in her eyes fades. She's dying.

Officer Petry stops at the porch steps. "Mister Hall?"

There's a high-pitched wail somewhere. Far away or near, what would it matter.

"Flo!" is all he can think to say. "Flo, my friend..."

Lyle hears her voice, inside his head. *Take care of your daughter...*

Flo's last breath escapes. Her head, wild hair and all, rests softly on Lyle's chest.

Embracing her, he hears a strange whispered phrase. *"Σας θέλω."*

Did Flo say that? Once again: *"Σας θέλω."* Sounds like *sustain low*.

258

It feels so expressive. How can Flo speak? Lyle tries to think of a prayer, but none comes to him. His own eyes close. Then he knows. Her spirit has left her body.

"Mister Hall? What's happened here?" Mounting the porch, Petry's flashlight scans the scene, coming to rest on Flo Hendricks, her face pale, eyelids half-closed.

A second patrol car pulls up in front of the house. Then a third. No sirens, just rooftop light bars flashing red and blue. His own eyes shut tight, Lyle senses more men hurrying toward him. He squeezes Flo. She does not squeeze back. Flashlight beams and cop-car spotlights play on the porch. The hanging toilet paper ripples and sways.

"Mister Hall?"

Frank's voice. Frank's beam finds the prone man's face. Glen Stanley. Peaceful, like he's dreaming. His blue T-shirt bears Lyle's crazy face. And words:

Lyle Is Fine.

~~~~~~

55. A Ride With Detective Hall

Time passes slowly when you have two deaths on your porch. Sgt. Frank Barsotti was as good as could be expected with Lyle, given the circumstances. EMS arrived right after the police cars. Flo was still positioned on her knees, Lyle cradling her, when the technicians carefully separated them and placed her on a stretcher.

Checking her over, one EMT mumbles "heart failure." Lyle, his face in his hands, knew that. They take her body away.

Glen Stanley lies where he fell, under a sheet now. Two cops roll Lyle back down his ramp, away from the scene. He sits on his uneven sidewalk, eyes closed.

Big Frank approaches him. "Mister Hall, did you know a Glen Stanley?"

Lyle blinks at Frank.

"Mister Hall, the deceased man on your porch."

"Yeah. Well, sort of. Glen camped on my lawn with the others, you know? He uh, introduced himself."

"How so?"

"Well he broke into my kitchen. But he was a kindly old guy. Meant no harm."

Frank glances up to the porch and corpse. "That's the old man who broke into your house?"

"Yeah, he's a locksmith. Was a locksmith. He was the first of the campers to come here. Sort of the organizer. A big supporter of my, uh, cause."

"Uh-huh. Well the EMTs think he had a stroke. Shortly before you and Miss Hendricks found him. What's this about a rabid possum?"

Lyle describes the possum on his porch, leaving out that he'd seen one just like it earlier in the old barn. Sgt. Frank takes some notes, then puts his pad away.

"Mister Hall, Detective Hall is on her way here. Since you've given a preliminary statement you can be, uh, remanded to her custody. We're going to take a look around inside your house, Mister Hall. Make sure things are all right."

Georgie's coming back. This will be difficult. Lyle removes his house keys from his fanny pack but notices a cop on the porch opening the front door. It was unlocked.

"Mister Hall," says Big Frank, "Mister Stanley left you a note."

~~~~~~

The sky is lightening. Another damn day dawning.

By the time Georgie's Crown Vic lurches to a diagonal halt near Lyle's curb, many more police and emergency vehicles are on the scene. One EMT guy seems oddly familiar and Lyle catches what seems like an unfriendly glance. That's nothing new.

Georgie gets out of her car and Lyle's heart jumps. He never gets to see his girl this frequently. As she walks over to him he remembers why she's here.

"Dad. What the hell happened here?"

"Georgie, I, I had no involvement in these deaths. I assure you."

"Oh. So why didn't they go die across the street on Mister Rosewater's porch?"

"Georgie..."

"Dad. You promised me you would stop. Does this do it for you? Loss of human life? Tell me it does."

"Yes. This does it. It was terrible. Terrible."

"The deceased woman was Florence Hendricks from that TV show. The man was one of the campers?"

"Correct."

"You know how often two people just collapse and die, minutes apart, on the same front porch?"

"No. They keep records of this sort of thing?"

"Dad." Georgie crouches in front of Lyle. "We talked about this. The bullshit TV interviews with Elvira are over. The ghost thing, over. The court case, over. Living in this house is over. It's all got to stop." She sniffs. "The effing *scotch,* Dad—over."

"I fell off the wagon."

Georgie stands and looks around her. Big Frank's on the porch. "Frank, you took his statement?" He nods. "Is the house open?" Two cops exit the house via front door.

"Think so, Detective."

Georgie looks down at Lyle. "Dad, you can't stay here."

"I'm staying at the Memory Motel. Don't tell anyone."

"I'm going to bring you out some stuff—change of clothes. Toothbrush. Your meds. Personal items."

"Personal items" is code for his hygienic medical supplies. Georgie goes into the house, leaving her dad alone on the front walk. He notes how Big Frank follows her inside. More vehicles converge at his curb. A light is on over at Mr. Rosewater's.

Soon Georgie comes out with a shopping bag containing Lyle's stuff.

"Dad. I confiscated your scotch. And you now use Mom's china? How weird."

"Oh, that's Glen Stanley. He was the table-setter."

"I don't understand. The deceased?"

"Uh...yeah. Long story." Lyle thought he put that fancy silver away last time but it's hard to be sure of anything these days. Maybe Glen let himself back in.

The street is now congested with official vehicles, including a medical examiner van. Georgie and her dad move to her white Crown Vic. Yards of damp toilet paper dangle down onto it. Lyle gets into the passenger seat fairly easily. Georgie unplugs the heavy batteries, collapses his chair and lays it in the backseat. There's a shriveled condom back there too. With a face. Once behind the wheel Georgie lights up her car, no siren, and pulls out. The toilet paper waves goodbye.

"You really brought out the crazies," she mutters. "You obviously stopped taking your meds. And you removed the orange safety pennant I got for your chair."

"It was attracting the wrong sort of people."

"I didn't mention this earlier because Ms. Hendricks was listening, but I'm beyond pissed that you didn't return my calls."

"She could tell. But that doesn't matter now."

"It really sucks when your own father won't return phone calls in an emergency."

"Not just *your* calls, Georgie. These past few days have been very difficult."

"Tell me about it. And by the way, Frank told me all about the dangerous bullshit you got involved in overnight. That shitty barn is off limits—it could fall down on you, you know. Then where would you and Morticia be?"

"If you're referring to Silk..."

"Dad. She is bad news and everybody knows you're puppy-dog infatuated with her. Millions who haven't seen you on TV watch video clips online. And at *your age*."

"I'm famous?"

"Try pathetic."

The conversation goes like this until they reach the Memory Motel. Georgie pulls up at Lyle's room. The eastern sky is pink. There are three police cars parked by Flo's room. Its door is open, lights on. Silk and Josh stand outside, answering questions from policemen. Georgie nods in Silk's direction.

"Dad, if you don't tell her you're out of the paranormal business, I will."

"Yes, Ma'm. Are you on this case, Georgie?" Lyle needs to know.

"No, thank God."

As she exits the Crown Vic, hellish heavy metal music bursts from the room next to Lyle's. A curtain ripples and suddenly the racket stops.

"Is that one of your new friends?" She starts to wrestle his chair to the pavement.

"No. A motorcycle enthusiast. I think that music relaxes him."

"I'll bet it does. Want me to knock on his door?"

"He'll just wait for you to leave." Lyle watches her set up his wheelchair. "Georgie, I'm really sorry about all your difficulty at work."

"They moved my locker next to the other female cop's. Like that helps."

"Is Internal Affairs involved?"

"Possibly. And someone might come in and conduct 'sensitivity sessions.'"

Lyle snorts a laugh reflexively. "I'd like to see Big Frank attend one of those."

"Funny, Dad." Georgie grabs her dad's shopping bag, minus the Dewar's.

Lyle swings into his chair and they enter his room. The music booms again.

"Shit! That racket is even louder in here! How can you stand it?"

"I try not to spend too much time in my room."

Georgie bends and gives Lyle's forehead an unexpected peck.

"Remember everything we talked about. You agreed to all my demands."

"I did." Lyle's Georgie premonition makes his heart break for her.

Pausing in his doorway she scowls at the music from next door.

"Get some rest if you can. We'll talk later. And I'm sorry about your friend."

"*Friends*."

Lyle fights back a sudden wave of emotion. Now is the time to tell Georgie about her name appearing on her Mom's headstone. Tell her how each time he speaks with her or sees her could be the last. It'd be criminal to keep it from her. Especially if it's true. And if it's supernatural bullshit, so what? He can't sink any lower in Georgie's esteem. She's leaving. She gives Lyle one last look. Here goes...

"Georgie...good luck at work. And be careful. Please."

264

Failed again. From his window Lyle watches Georgie go speak with the cops in Flo's room. Then she drives off. Silk and Josh must be back in their rooms. He forces himself to check voice mail; maybe return some calls. His mailbox is full of media outlets calling for interviews. Even Dan's Papers called. Delving in, Lyle finds some VMs from people he actually knows. A lot of irate messages from Georgie, but he can delete them now. Fred the MediCab driver is another story. He'll require twenties. There's Noah Craig: Does he owe Noah for research on Old Vic? Nah. And Becky Tuttle: Nah, scratch that. Josie: Hmm, interesting—save that one. Mose Allen: Asshole. Alpharetta: A considerate reminder call—Judge Sloane at 10:00am. Great. And there's Matteo Xerri. Got to get back to him. He might know what "*sustain low*" means.

Then Lyle's heart sinks. Two good people dead. And the sickening threat to Georgie's life—could it come from the job he got her? He decides to play back Fraser:

> Dude! You're a TV star! The next 'Ironside.' Is that reporter babe your new squeeze? Into leather now? Or are you doing the fat girl a favor? Sorry I didn't get around to purchasing Old Vic for you, but good luck convincing the judge that you intend to move in with a dead, twelve-year-old prostitute. Making it your primary residence is the only way he'll even listen to your complaint. By the way, I hear it'll be Sloane. Oh—I actually called Dar. She didn't pick up but I bet she was listening. I left a voicemail that you wanted to talk about the condo. See what I do for you? Call me.

The head-banging music stops. The door next door slams. The motorcycle roars to life. The cops outside ignore "Harley" as he rolls out of the lot. Peace for a while. It feels good. Before using the handicap shower, Lyle turns on the TV, volume off.

It's a News12 blond reporter. She's in front of Lyle's house doing live standup. Camera pans to her right and there's Police Chief Queeley, Georgie's boss, looking big, red and asinine under a fluttering bunting of toilet paper. Shit. Lyle enters the handicap bathroom and turns on the shower. As it heats up, he ponders his lot.

His daughter is in terrible danger. His house kills people. And it's his fault.

~~~~~

PART THREE

JEWEL

56. Precinct

Detective Hall enters the Southampton stationhouse shortly before eight a.m. She's got her briefcase and wears a fresh pants suit, conservative dark-blue, like something an FBI agent would wear. Like Frank's Internal Affairs friend suggested. Having only showered at her Southampton condo following two frustrating hours with her troubled father, Georgie is in a foul mood. She has not yet had her coffee.

The desk sergeant looks up. Swanson is the only person around. Like Pavlov's dog, he reflexively whistles "Hey there, Georgie girl."

Something clicks in Georgie's head and she veers toward Swanson's desk, startling him. Georgie, in her sensible two-inch heels, has some height and can lean in to his face. The sergeant recoils a little as Georgie goes eye-to-eye.

"Swan Song. Looking forward to retirement, huh?"

Swanson's eyes shift around the room. No one else is present.

She continues in a steely tone, "I'm going to tell you this once, Sergeant, so pay good attention." She looks into his bleary eyes. "I'm preparing the paperwork. My hearing with IA is scheduled. You sure you want that? Or you want a nice, quiet retirement?"

Swanson's pudgy mouth forms a response but Georgie cuts him short. She lowers her voice to a menacing whisper. "You like giving people a hard time. Know what? *So do I.* Now listen to me. I hear a peep out of you—anything even remotely disrespectful or inappropriate, and you get your own page in my report. I'll make you famous. I promise."

Perspiration has formed on his upper lip. He stares at Georgie as she pulls away and stands back, still facing him.

"And I keep my promises," she adds.

Georgie turns to the hallway leading to her office. In a lighter tone she says, "By the way, Sergeant, a heads up: IA will be interviewing anyone who requires an extra-small condom."

Swanson registers shock and disbelief. "And," Georgie adds, bullshitting, "they have a sample of the perp's breath."

Walking away, Georgie hears Swanson say calmly, "Chief wants to see you."

~~~~~~~

57. Captain Cyrus Milford

The nightshift kid in the motel office has never seen such activity; and it's October. All those cops. Silk. The TV camera guy looking for cigarettes. That wheelchair guy who came in late and sucked all the twenties out of the ATM, then complained when it ran out.

After his shower and a fitful nap, the sun is up and Lyle is trying to regain some control of his life. The idiot next door is quiet, so Lyle is free to obsess on the deaths of his two new friends. Just hours ago. And how tomorrow is his daughter's day to die and he's been helpless to stop it. He dresses himself in fresh clothes that Georgie retrieved—his khakis, white oxford-cloth shirt and navy sweater. She forgot socks. Not that socks matter. He reworks in his mind how to tell Georgie about the damn tombstone. Hey, maybe she'll surprise him and take him seriously! Wrong. She'll have even more reason to send him away for psychiatric evaluation. The TV tuned to News12, sound off, awful motel coffee dribbles into a plastic cup. A reporter's doing a live standup outside his fucking house. Again. He can't watch. Reporters can't begin to know what went on there last night. Those poor people on his awful porch. Lyle truly hopes they are now at peace, whatever that is. He calls Fred. Despite having blown him off for Silk's FEARcom van, Lyle persuades Fred to rearrange his morning and take him to court. I've still got it, he thinks, trying to psyche himself up. He's also got many twenties.

Fred is at the Memory Motel by 8:30 a.m. Lyle notes that Silk's room is dark, curtains drawn. Good. He imagines Silk "milking it" when she learns Flo breathed her last in Lyle's arms. The FEARcom van is gone. Maybe Chad hid it so as not to attract crazies. Five twenties in his shirt pocket, Fred maneuvers out

271

onto Montauk Highway. Lyle has him until noon. As they ride, Lyle leaves a voice mail for Xerri on Wozniak's phone. His cell phone, the ringer off overnight, has been popping with calls and texts from concerned civilians and media outlets. It will all end soon. The MediCab moves west through the sandy, largely undeveloped stretch of the highway known as the Napeague and Lyle is struck by how numb he feels. Numbness follows shock. Then a surprising pang of guilt—he must dial Noah Craig. No point in the old boy continuing his research.

Ready to deliver his conciliatory voicemail message, Noah actually picks up. It sounds like he's in a busy place with clattering plates, maybe Gertie's.

"Two deaths at your house and you choose to return *my* call? I'm flattered."

"I was trying to leave a voicemail."

"Well I'm very sorry for those people. It's shocking. I hope you're dealing with it all okay." Noah refrains from adding *for a self-obsessed neo-celebrity asshole.*

"Like they say, 'You can't go home again.'"

"Thomas Wolfe."

His brain still swimming, Lyle says, "I liked *Bonfire of the Vanities* …"

"Right. Lyle, have you listened to any of my messages?"

"I'm saving them for posterity."

"To be concise, I have news for you. And so does Becky Tuttle."

It's hard to care about anything these two might do now to save an old house that needs to be destroyed. Noah doesn't know it yet, but they're working at cross purposes again, like the good old days. But there's a note of excitement in Noah's voice: "Becky you need to talk to. What I have you need to *see*."

This piques Lyle's interest, even though the whole stupid game is over.

"It's important, Lyle. Meet me at the library before your court appearance."

"Wait, you know *when* my court appearance is scheduled?"

"Anyone who watches News12 knows."

Lyle heaves a sigh and agrees to stop by Noah's "office."
He'll tell Noah to his face that he's given up on Old Vic. That all
his research work was for naught. Hanging up, he's too drained
to call Becky Tuttle now. She might answer her phone.

Librarian Sheila Dowd gives Lyle a frigid nod from her desk.
Entering the elevator, Lyle has to compartmentalize the deaths of
Glen and Flo for now. And the looming threat to Georgie's life.
Tell Noah you're rescinding in court and get out. The elevator
opens to the basement reference room and Noah looks up from
his table, already laden with history books, periodicals, old charts
and file folders. And his laptop. He looks excited.

"Ah, you've come."

"Noah, I came because I have something to tell you."

"Me first. You'll note, I'm putting aside the sad fact that you
took a stranger, a *priest* no less, inside Old Vic and not me. A
gross violation of our agreement."

"He made me. I'm weak."

"Very. So what'd you see inside? Evidently it threw you into
convulsions."

"Saw cobwebs, graffiti...your homework binder." Lyle
doesn't want to address what may have been demonic
possession. "And the place really was a brothel."

"You found evidence?"

"No guest ledger, but Father Xerri had a strong sense. So
what do you have?"

"Still nothing on Old Vic per se, though I do have something
on the girl. *But first!* Did you know a much older house stood on
the site before Old Vic? That house and the barn behind it go
back to the seventeen-hundreds—pre-Revolutionary War. It was
a farm, later it became home to a sea captain. Cyrus Milford. The
turn of the nineteenth century."

"Two-hundred years ago? Why do we care?"

"*We* care because *we* have no records on the current
structure. And some of us worked very hard to dig up centuries-
old documents that no one alive today has seen."

"You are the best." Lyle sees it's a terrible time to tell his bad news as Noah warms to his subject.

"Records show that, in the eighteen-twenties, this Captain Milford's whaling business was failing. He was in danger of losing his house, as well as his three-masted whaler, the *Harrier*, which moored in Sag Harbor. Apparently other captains were more skilled, more dedicated, more sober. So Milford got into something more lucrative. He started returning runaway African slaves."

"He was a drunk, into catching slaves… Wait, Sag Harbor was a real harbor?"

"Lyle, it's one of our country's first major ports. So Milford began quietly transporting runaway slaves back to their owners in the South. In the North, fairly few landowners kept slave laborers; the practice was frowned upon, especially here in New York. Some runaways would flee up here hoping to find work on the farms and blend in with black freemen. Milford owed money to some unsavory people out here involved in rounding up runaways. So he provided transportation." Noah frowns. "They'd also seize free blacks to round out their quota. Additional profit, no retaliation."

"They would capture runaway slaves...like bounty hunters?"

"Basically. It wasn't illegal, not yet. But not a respectable business model." Noah opens an old folder and adds, "Especially the way Milford did it. The State of New York made slavery illegal on July fourth, eighteen-twenty-seven. That same day the *Harrier* was set ablaze in Sag Harbor. Locked in its hold were twenty-four purported runaway slaves. That evening Cyrus Milford's house burned to the ground as well."

Noah peers over his reading glasses at Lyle. "You probably want to know that."

"Fascinating. Chilling. Noah, you know I have a court date this morning."

"This is why the historian is held in disregard today. People don't have the time to learn their own history." Noah reboots. "Typically, once Milford had enough so-called slaves, about

274

eighty, he'd sail the *Harrier* to Charleston, South Carolina, to 'return' them to their owners. He'd get a cut of the profit."

"Noah, does this mean there's evidence that Old Vic is a historic property?"

There's a sudden noise. Lyle starts, then notices a young blond woman down an adjacent aisle paging through a book. It's Ginny.

Noah proudly holds up a scan of an ancient-looking document. It looks like a ship's manifest. Lyle sees columns of handwritten names and numbers and at the bottom a signature – *C. Milford, Capt.*

"To the Sag Harbor historians this looked like a list of crew," says Noah. "It's not crew. It's human cargo. The twenty-four captives trapped in the *Harrier*'s hold."

"Wow. So how did historians get hold of Milford's old records?"

"The barn. When they built your One-eleven Poplar in the eighteen-eighties, they cleaned out the old barn and found things, like ship's manifests and empty rum bottles. Milford likely stored them there so the missus, Goody Milford, would not see what he was really up to. The manifests eventually made it to the Sag Harbor Whaling Museum. They assumed the logs merely documented the *Harrier*'s whaling expeditions."

"So the house prior to Old Vic was owned by a monster."

Noah drinks from his water canister. "Bank records we found show Milford was about to lose his house that July."

"The old boy was a bad man and a bad businessman. What does that have to do with Old Vic and my, uh, issue with the house?"

"I'm trying to get Old Vic 'historical' as we discussed. There's more."

Lyle needs to tell Noah he's rescinding his motion, but now is not the time.

"Proceed."

"As New York's emancipation approached, Milford's crew had to know he didn't have enough 'cargo' to pay them. They abandoned the *Harrier* at its mooring with twenty-four men chained in its hold. When emancipation day came on July fourth, Milford and his human cargo had to be out of New York State waters or he'd be arrested. Jail was not nice back then. With no crew he couldn't set sail. He must have lost his mind. Lyle, Milford set his own ship ablaze in the harbor with twenty-four souls trapped below decks. He fled the scene. The *Harrier* burned and sank, somewhere in the deep end of Sag Harbor. It was never found.

"The local paper has Milford at home later. Passersby reported loud arguing before the house caught fire. Goody had to be distressed to see him back home, probably drunk, and not on whatever expedition he'd bluffed her about. A whale-oil lamp fell or was thrown and the house went up in flame, taking Goody Milford with it. The next morning they found her remains in the ashes. The barn was still standing. They found Milford there."

"Found him?"

"Hung himself from a joist. He left ship's records and empty rum bottles, no note. Took sixty years for people to forget all that and for someone to build on the property."

Lyle ponders this until Ginny makes another noise.

"Lyle? Do I have your attention?"

"Listen, Noah..." Lyle is about to reveal his plan for court today when Ginny emerges from the stacks with more old record books for Noah. Exhausted Lyle just stares at her cute face framed by straight flaxen hair. She places the books near Noah and sips from her own water bottle. She removes her glasses and stares back at Lyle Hall, currently the most controversial man in Bridgehampton, maybe all the East End.

"Lyle, you've met Ginny Schmidt, my assistant."

"Hi," Lyle says, snapping out of it.

"Hi Mister Hall," Ginny responds, taking another sip. She watches News12.

Noah says, "A student can get college credit doing research work for a noted historian such as myself. Ginny's a lucky gal."

"So lucky," she deadpans. "Noah, there's nothing else from the time period in these stacks. Want me to hit Rogers Library again?"

"Okay...is the staff there working with you?"

"Better than Sheila upstairs." Ginny nods upwards. "She caught me using a pen."

"That's a no-no. So try Southampton again and check back with me later."

Lyle's eyes follow the college girl as she heads for the elevator with her backpack. She wears skinny jeans. The elevator doors close on Ginny Schmidt.

Noah looks at Lyle. "She is a find."

"For a second there I was afraid she might be some ghost-loving whacko or a reporter." Lyle feels another pang of guilt. "Noah, if you employed an assistant on my account I need to reimburse you."

"Not necessary. She's working for college credit. Anyway, when I shifted her focus from nineteenth-century farming issues to One-eleven Poplar, she got psyched. She can tell her friends she's researching 'Ghost Hampton.' A comparatively sexy area of study right now."

Lyle notes Noah's use of "Ghost Hampton." "My issues are 'sexy' now?"

"Compared to potato farms. Especially if you're young and connected to the Internet or television."

"I get it." Maybe now's the time to tell Noah. "Look, I've gotta head to court..."

"So let me wrap up. We now know that the Old Vic property has a bad history. And there's probably a good reason there are no records on Old Vic itself. Relevant copies of the old *Star Press*, which predates the *East Hampton Star*, are missing. We've searched old deeds, bank records, museums..." He looks at Lyle. "Now, with the untimely deaths at your house, it's as if that bad history wants to extend its reach to the present."

"You do have a weird streak, Noah."

"Actually, Lyle, this is the most fun I've had in years."

"Ginny is cute."

"I meant professionally." He looks at Lyle. "Now, that sketch of Jewel that's everywhere. There's something curious about it. I need to show you."

Noah clicks his laptop. Lyle is shocked to see Noah has access to the same drawings of Jewel that he has. Did Ray Linder wallpaper the Internet with them?

"This went viral," Noah says, staring at the image. "Artist did a good job."

Noah clicks between Jewel's head shot and the full-body image.

"Lyle. We know that the house is eighteen-eighties Victorian, right?"

"Second Empire style."

"Right. Now look at this girl. The hair and the dress are Edwardian."

"Who?"

"English king after Victoria. First decade of the twentieth century. Teddy Roosevelt was president. People over here copied English fashion."

"Why do we care?"

"Because we want to know when this girl lived and died. It's a widely held belief that spirits maintain the look and style they wore at the time of death. They don't get haircuts or new shoes."

"She doesn't have feet."

"If this girl lived in Old Vic, it was after the Victorian era. Based on her hairstyle and dress I'm placing her death around nineteen-ten, allowing the style a few years to make it from London to New York to Bridgehampton."

"A hundred years ago."

"Correct. Here's the problem—you're sure she was twelve years old. Why?"

"Hard to verbalize. You just know when someone's a girl, you know? What I saw and heard was an adolescent girl."

"Fair enough," Noah says. "Now. Edwardian times were proper times. When a girl came of age—say seventeen years old—she commenced wearing her hair swept up like Jewel's here. A rite of passage." Noah gestures at the drawing. "This style is called 'Crowning Glory.' She even has rats."

"*Rats?*"

"Yeah. You save the dead hair from your brush and wad it together and pin it under your living hair to support this frontal pompadour." Noah cursors to it. "See?"

"I'll have to try that at home. Noah, what is your point?"

"Lyle, this is the Gibson Girl look. It was considered sophisticated in its day. Sophisticated women wore their hair like this, not twelve-year-olds. Capice?"

Lyle frowns in thought.

"Then there's her long dress," Noah continues. "Girls wore dresses that showed their lower legs. When they came of age, they wore long dresses that came almost to the floor. No woman wore a short dress and no girl wore a long dress. You see the problem, counselor?"

Lyle is quiet for a moment. Then he sighs. "Yeah. Jewel was made up to look older than she really was." The thought has sad implications.

"More evidence suggesting the house was a brothel. That's one reason I like history. Sometimes rumors are based on fact."

Lyle doesn't like this history. Poor Jewel had no childhood.

He looks at the clock. "Shit. Noah, I gotta run. I'm late. Can't thank you enough for your efforts." Lyle rolls purposefully toward the elevator. "I'll return the favor!"

"We'll talk more over lunch," Noah says. Lyle doesn't hear as the elevator doors close. Noah sneaks out his phone and sees a new text from Becky Tuttle. Lyle has been ignoring her calls. She's irritated but still wants him to join them for lunch, as planned, after his court appearance.

On the main floor, Sheila Dowd, ensconced at her oaken desk, deflects Lyle Hall's salute as he rolls for the exit. There must be something wrong with that Noah Craig if he's working with the likes of Lyle Hall. Noah Craig and that insolent college girl.

~~~~~~

58. Chilton Gregg

This morning Chilton Gregg, VP at FEARcom and, truth be told, the guy who bankrolls the operation, is excited. Gregg sits at his desk in his office at Gregg Industries' corporate headquarters, his father's company in Hartford. But he can't focus on his father's business now, he's totally immersed in his FEARcom side project. Gregg is also justifiably nervous. His protégé Silk scored a monster, career-making hit last night with her "Ghost Hampton" segment on *ET*. He could not imagine a better outcome if he'd scripted it himself. FEARcom will finally turn a profit, he's sure, just gotta play his cards right going forward. Of course, he's had Silk buttoned up under contract for a couple of years. Then there's this guy Lyle. A wild card. Not very sympathetic. Not a team player. You don't build a business plan around him. But Silk promises to trot new talent before the cameras, like this handsome exorcist. So that's a hopeful thing.

What scares Gregg is that people are dying. Florence Hendricks was a service provider but still, death is so final. Last night's deaths in Bridgehampton take the story to a whole new level. Hard news. But your business plan cannot hinge on your on-air talent dying. Not for long.

He's got newspapers opened to "Ghost Hampton" coverage, a clip of Silk's TV segment running on his laptop and his office TV tuned to local news. FEARcom has been an expensive hobby, but he can spend money. He wears his usual Brioni suit, dress shirt, no tie, no socks, Firenze loafers. He is not a tall man, Silk is taller. He's thin but shy of handsome. His hairline, at age 33, is making a retreat. He's dialing Silk for, oh maybe, the thousandth time this week.

Silk is luxuriating in her Egyptian sheets. The sheets travel with her, she's no stranger to sketchy motels. She still feels the glow from last night's televised triumph, but it conflicts sharply with the cold chill that's formed around poor Flo and her gruesome death. Silk had gone back to sleep after all those policemen questioned her. Emulating what she'd once heard about Marilyn Monroe, Silk sleeps in the nude. She's stretching her legs and deciding whether to shave them or go with pants this morning when her iPhone vibrates.

GREGG.

"Silk."

"Hi Gregg…" She uses her warm-and-cozy voice.

"So? Am I hallucinating or did Flo Hendricks actually have a heart attack and die last night while on the job for us?"

Silk clears her throat and turns businesslike. "It was terrible. But I have someone new to replace Flo."

"Well it's going to have to be somebody who kicks ass. Have you seen the outpouring of condolences for Flo? The server has slowed way down trying to deal."

"Oh it's somebody kick-ass, you'll see. I maintain a database of the best talent."

"We need someone telegenic, you know. Especially since your friend Lyle the Lawyer is so *not* telegenic."

"We were going for vérité with Lyle."

"Well keep in mind this is national TV and people, men and women, like something good to look at."

Silk tries a different tack. "Did I give the men something good to look at?"

Now it's Gregg's turn to clear his throat. "You did. Off the charts. And not just men. But maybe too much of a good thing. Try cooling it tonight. This has to play in Peoria. Speaking of which, do you have the handsome exorcist sewn up? We can't let some other media entity steal our fire."

"Flo is all over…" Silk recovers just a second too late. "I mean I have the boys all over him," she lies. "We're making an offer he can't refuse."

"Hard to imagine. We don't pay anything. And you're not authorized…"

Silk employs her sultry, I'm-in-control tone. "You'll see, Gregg. Trust me."

"Well you have to keep me informed of any contracts or agreements. We must stay in constant contact." Gregg can hear Silk sigh with impatience. He adds, "Tonight has to be better than last night or we, and you, are one-hit wonders."

"I'll make it happen."

"I'm counting on you. I'll see you later at your skeevy motel in Montauk. I'm getting the ferry."

Silk stretches her legs again and arches her back.

Gregg adds, "So how come I don't hear any excited crowds, honking horns, general hubbub? Are you at the courthouse now?"

Silk cranes her neck to see her clock. *Oh, shit.* Flo the mother hen typically woke everyone. And after everything last night… However, being who she is, Silk has a ready response, even for this.

"Gregg, we'll be there momentarily. Now let me work."

She disconnects, kicks off her good sheets and rises from the bad motel bed. Call Josh and Chad. No shower. Pants suit. *Shit!*

~~~~~~

59. Judge Sloane's Court

Fred is barreling toward Southampton Town Justice Court. Lyle fends off yet another call from Becky Tuttle. And another from Silk. He's trying to figure how best to play this court appearance. He knows Judge Gerald Sloane from many court cases. A no-nonsense jurist, he's been no fan of Lyle's courtroom antics over the years. So what. Lyle swore on his honor he'd drop his motion to save Old Vic. Simple. He'll just say "never mind." Like Emily Litella on *Saturday Night Live*.

Turning into the court parking lot, Lyle and Fred get a dull surprise. News media are everywhere. Satellite news trucks, production trucks, vans, reporters for print, radio, Internet and television. All Silk's competitors. And there's no FEARcom van in sight. A young man in a suit grasps the nature of Fred's MediCab and starts jogging alongside it, tossing questions at Lyle through the window.

"Mister Hall! How did the deaths at your home affect you? Where did you relocate? You really hope to live in Old Vic? Has Jewel appeared to you recently?"

Two more men and a young woman fall in beside the running journalist and shout similar questions. Lyle instructs Fred to head for the side entrance, but it's also clogging with people. Time to call Alpharetta.

By the time Fred lowers the MediCab platform, Lyle Hall is swarmed by pushy reporters, cameras and thrusting mics. Thanks to Alpharetta, the building's side door opens a little and a cop— the same one from the other day—sees the problem. He and a second cop come out and make way for Lyle and his chair.

Cries of "Lyle! Lyle Hall!" well up as cameras roll, trying to capture the man of the hour—crazy guy or philanthropic preservationist—for today's news reports. They fire essentially the same questions at him as the cops help him wheel through the doorway. Inside, it's just as crowded and louder. Mose Allen pushes toward him.

"Lyle!"

"Get lost, Mose. All this is your fault."

"You look a *little* more with it today. What are you going to say to Sloane?"

"Fuck off."

"That won't work with him."

Lyle turns and steers toward the courtroom. The two cops open the doors for him. Before he passes inside, Lyle glances toward Alpharetta's desk. Alpharetta gives Lyle a wink while maintaining her otherwise inscrutable expression. The cops hold the doors and Lyle rolls into the courtroom.

The place is buzzing. He's never seen the court packed like this. All eyes are on him. A prickly nimbus forms around him—there are way too many people to read. Instead he feels the suffocating pressure of a throng trying to read *him*. They are mostly reporters—overdressed strangers and some local Mose Allens. But no Silk. Lyle spots the white beard and straw hat of Dan Rattiner from *Dan's Papers*. Dan lives in Bridgehampton and his weekly newspaper operation has been headquartered right on Montauk Highway forever. There are gawkers. A few Believers wear their dumb yellow T-shirts or even dumber blue "Lyle" T-shirts. Lyle recognizes some well-dressed real-estate brokers in the pews. One cadre, seated in a row in their trademark all-white outfits, turn heads in unison and regard Lyle. Some of the attendees were once competitors of Newton Hall. They must crave media in October. Maybe this is more of a real-estate event than Lyle figured. But there's no Fraser. No Josie. They wouldn't have time for this bullshit. Lyle is alone here.

It dawns on him that this is the first time he's appeared before a judge since his accident. First time in a wheelchair. First time not in a tailored suit. With no briefcase. And no briefs. Lyle stops directly in front of Sloane's bench.

Oh, no. Across to his right Lyle sees Becky Tuttle ensconced at a table with her Save-a-Barn lawyer. Why? Becky, the only person ignoring Lyle, looks extra prim in a somber gray sweater set, staring straight ahead. It occurs to him that prim, along with ignoring him, can actually be sexy. She couldn't know that he's returned no one's calls the past few days, not just hers. He nods at her profile just as the bailiff shouts "All rise!" All rise except Lyle. Judge Sloane sweeps in from chambers clad in his black robe.

With his hawk-like visage and ingrown scowl, Sloane is not a friendly-looking man. As he seats himself, he glares down at Lyle in his wheelchair and casual clothing. The courtroom is buzzing and Sloane glowers at the packed house, rapping his gavel three times. The buzzing stops and the judge reads from some papers.

"The Court will now hear proof in support of plaintiff's motion to enjoin the demolition of the derelict structures at One-eleven Poplar Street in Bridgehampton upon allegations that said property is in fact of historic significance and deserving of preservation. The moving-party plaintiff, Lyle Hall, Esquire, is acting as a private citizen." Sloane peers down at Lyle. "Mister Hall, are you prepared to proceed with proof of the premises' historical significance or designation at this time?"

"No, Your Honor. I...we..."

"Let the record show that plaintiff is not prepared to proceed with its proof. Mister Hall, there is only one way this court will consider any new motion for injunction against demolition of the house on this property given the apparent lack of historical status. The plaintiff—that's *you*—must file a new motion including an affidavit stating that the house and property on which it is located is to be purchased for the sole purpose of title-owner occupancy—provided it is brought into full compliance with the Town Code. Not to 'flip' the property in a business transaction, but to move in and live there upon such condition. Now, Mister Hall, can you tell this court that you would purchase and occupy that property and house and bring it into full compliance?"

The courtroom goes dead silent.

"Your Honor, I would..."

There's a collective gasp and Sloane raps his gavel three times.

Lyle continues. "...I would if I could, Your Honor. But in light of recent events, I've come to agree that the structures should be razed."

Waves of whispered surprise roll across the room. Sloane gavels four times.

"So, Mister Hall, you're here today to tell this court that you've had a change of heart and wanted to express that in person—and at great expense to the Town of Southampton—rather than simply filing a letter withdrawing your motion?"

"Your Honor, I just arrived at my new position this morning."

"So now you will be at odds with your only ally in this case?"

"I'm sorry, Your Honor?"

"Mister Hall, surely you're aware that the historical-building-preservation organization, Save-a-Barn, has joined you in your application to stave off demolition."

Lyle's ears turn red. He gasps quietly. Becky Tuttle's eyes are boring into his temple. He sneaks a bug-eyed peek at her. She is pissed. Lyle turns to Judge Sloane.

"Your Honor, in light of events just last night and early this morning, in particular the deaths of two people associated with the movement to preserve One-eleven Poplar, I must respectfully withdraw my motion to enjoin demolition."

There. That should do it. Sloane looks at some more papers in front of him.

"Then I'm prepared to rule now." He looks down at Lyle and then over at Becky. "Based upon plaintiff's statement on the record today, the plaintiff's motion shall be marked withdrawn. The house at One-eleven Poplar, posing a danger to the community, will be demolished by the Town without further delay. However, the barn, given the motion filed with this court yesterday by the Save-a-Barn organization, will remain standing pending a full hearing at which said organization shall have to prove the structure's significance to our region's farming

286

heritage. Ultimately, any such preservation will be contingent upon the collection of sufficient funds to pay for the barn's renovation and upkeep as an educational and historic site. In addition to that effort, Ms. Tuttle's organization has promised, in conjunction with its motion, to enhance the property by constructing a child-safe preschool playground adjacent to the barn. Such hearing will be in thirty days on a date and hour the parties will be apprised of by my clerk."

Judge Sloane cracks the sound block with his gavel. The bailiff cries, "All rise!" As Sloane makes his way back to chambers the courtroom erupts into chaos. Everyone is in motion. A few voices defiantly chant "I'm a Believer!" Lyle is now their opponent.

Lyle's eyes meet Becky's. He tries to read her expression. Haughty victory over Lyle? Yeah. Smug? Definitely. Lyle realizes he actually likes her haughtiness. She's succeeded: turned the tables on Lyle Hall, despite his betrayal! His thoughts are racing so fast he settles on the weirdest one: the tightness of Becky Tuttle's otherwise prim sweater set.

~~~~~

Outside the courthouse, Silk is also pissed at Lyle. She overslept. Then she discovered Lyle had absconded from the Memory Motel without her. Then the FEARcom van stopped at Msg. Hannan's rectory only to be turned away. Then she and the crew reached the Town Justice Court, but it was already too crowded to park anywhere near the court, let alone get inside for the proceedings. Cut out of the action, Silk then learned, third-hand, that Lyle did a surprising about-face before the judge. *Demolish Old Vic now?* Betrayal. Hell hath no fury like Silk scorned, but her thoughts turned coolly professional as she calculated how to save today's interview with Lyle Hall on national TV. She'd have to tell Gregg about this. And that she was not present in the courtroom. Shit, he must already know. And after he did all that work scheduling today's live segment on Fox. And now Lyle suddenly has no cause. And Flo suddenly was unavailable. But

Silk was not about to let this crazy crippled guy fuck up her career trajectory. This could still be the most-covered supernatural event for years to come. The show must go on. Today. Lyle signed a contract.

The deaths at Lyle's house, followed by his courtroom surprise, are today's stories, but Silk's arrival still draws the most attention from the crowd outside court. People want to see her, in her tailored black pants suit, up close. Some hope she'll put them on TV. Becky Tuttle emerges from the courthouse and Silk heads straight for her, like the shark in *Jaws*, Josh following with his camera. She catches Becky on the steps. Meanwhile Chad screens "real" people for possible on-camera comments following FEARcom guidelines.

Lyle has made it outside too, ignoring the scrum of jabbering reporters and hangers on. He halts at the handicap ramp at the far end of the courthouse steps and watches the two women interact on camera from forty feet away. Becky's lawyer is steadfast at her side. Then he sees it. Smugness personified. Lyle feels his own jolt of betrayal as Chad leads Mose Allen over to Silk. Chad holds up a finger indicating *She'll be with you in a moment.* Silk finishes with Becky and turns to Mose.

Only a few questioners can get at Lyle due to his position atop the ramp. He tunes them out, instead broiling as Silk interviews that shit Mose Allen. *Fuck me!* he thinks, as Josh focuses on Mose, the jackass who'd do anything to discredit and embarrass Lyle Hall. *Mose!* He observes Silk's body language and gets another jolt—she actually uses her *might be available but not just now* body language with that doofus! Same as she did with Lyle! He struggles with this. Could he be just as pathetic as Mose Allen in Silk's eyes?

Lyle starts down the handicap ramp and Silk briefly meets his gaze with a cold look of contempt. Lyle just said in court that the "haunted" house Silk is using to boost her career should be torn down. Even from this distance he reads a flood of feelings in her eyes: especially a seething lust for revenge. He did sign a contract, after all. But Lyle finally fulfilled his promise to his daughter. Silk could never understand. Her job is to "milk this."

Josh's camera rolls as Mose Allen spouts off about the case. Lyle is certain Mose will be asked to speculate about his state of mind. He should record this when it airs. Maybe sue Mose for defamation of character. Lyle rolls down the ramp.

Fred's MediCab is positioned behind the Sabrett cart, as planned. On level ground now, Lyle must work through a whorl of traditional and online reporters gathering around his chair, shouting questions, poking their mics at him. He rolls slowly, tuning them out.

"Lyle! Did Jewel cause your friends' deaths?"

"Mister Hall! Did you intend to move in with a ghost?"

"Lyle! Where will Jewel go when her house is torn down? Your house?"

And so on. One last time, Lyle makes eye contact with Silk up on the steps. She holds the mic as Mose blabs on camera. Silk is beautiful when she's angry. Surprisingly, she mouths "three o'clock" at Lyle, holding her wristwatch aloft. Report time for the live broadcast she and Gregg worked so hard for. Three o'clock. He did sign an agreement…

Some Believers near Silk launch into "I saw her face! *CLAP CLAP CLAP* I'm a Believer!" for Josh's camera. Lyle dearly hopes they go away soon, and for good.

Now, as he inches to the MediCab, the Sabrett guy spots him and makes a big show of Lyle being "my best customer!" Cameras turn on him as Lyle realizes he's never before heard the man speak. Fred lowers the MediCab's lift and hops out to shoo people away and secure Lyle's chair on the platform. Cameras roll and cell phones click until the van's side panel slides shut and Lyle is insulated once more from the hubbub. Fred informs Lyle he's late for his noon pickup.

"My house, Fred," says Lyle, totally drained. As they roll, he considers a nap during the ride back to Bridgehampton. No, better work his awful backlog of voicemails.

~~~~~

60. Voice Mailbox

Monsignor Hannan is making the steeple with his fingers this morning as Xerri takes a seat across from his desk. He shifts uncomfortably as Hannan clears his throat.

"Matteo, you know we very much wanted you to return to visit our parish this summer." Xerri nods cautiously, knowing bad often follows good. "And I fully admit it was my thought to have you meet with Lyle Hall and discuss his...issues." Xerri clenches his jaw. "But what's transpired...those photos, last night's television show," Hannan shakes his white head, "and those terrible deaths...it's beyond the pale." Xerri feels a brick in his stomach. Hannan continues, "A young man from that TV show was here earlier asking for you." Xerri nods; Wozniak told him about Josh. "And I've received calls from news organizations. You understand we cannot have this."

Hannan grits his teeth and pushes an envelope toward Xerri. "I'm sorry. Your flight to Rome leaves tonight. The parish has paid the extra charge for the last-minute booking. A parishioner will drive you to JFK this evening." Hannan looks sincerely upset about sending Xerri home abruptly. "I phoned your father. He knows."

Matteo winces and takes the envelope containing his ticket to Rome with connecting flight to Malta. He bites back emotion and stands.

Speeding back to Bridgehampton, Fred is now late. But he's provided Lyle with a styro cup of hot coffee, earning a twenty. Lyle is opening his dreaded voicemail when an incoming call rescues him. It reads **VITALIS WOZNIAK** but the voice is not Polish.

"Lyle-eh! It's Matteo...can you talk?"

Right away Lyle senses a different Fr. Xerri. Not just the use of his first name, there's a palpable sadness in his voice. Xerri makes sincere expressions of shock and sorrow over the two deaths, concern for Lyle's wellbeing and personal apologies for making Lyle's crisis even worse. He says everyone in the rectory saw him on TV last night and Lyle envisions Hannan, Wozniak, even the housekeeper watching him make a fool of himself. Xerri says they are all praying for him and the souls of his dead friends. His voice grows shaky and trails off. He stops short of revealing his new travel plans.

Xerri's emotion makes Lyle forget the courthouse scene, Silk, Becky, Mose, the Sabrett guy. But the two horrid deaths wash over him again like a frigid wave.

"I only wish there was something I could do..." Xerri adds.

Lyle thinks a moment as the hamlet of Water Mill rushes by. He can feel it quite clearly. He is part empath, part self-centered shit. There's a palpable boundary, like a membrane. Then the scene on his porch last night hits him hard in flashback. Flo died in his arms, trying to speak to him. That alone is worth months of therapy.

"Father," Lyle says, matching Xerri's sensitivity, "Flo Hendricks whispered something to me last night. Just before she...before I felt her soul leave her body."

"What was it?" Xerri says in a hush.

"Don't know. A foreign language. Sounded like *sustain low*. She said it twice."

"'Sustain low'?"

"Yeah. Then her head came to rest on my chest. And she breathed her last." Xerri is silent on his end, thinking. Lyle grabs at a straw. "Father, there is something you could do. My house. I'm afraid it's possessed. There was this rabid possum. It attacked Flo. I think it attacked Glen Stanley too. Could you come and take a look? I'm...I'm scared."

"A *rabid possum?*" Xerri whispers. That was not in the news report this morning.

Never has Lyle Hall told anyone he's *scared*. Emotion wells up in him. It'd been a rough night. Day. Couple of days. His voice catches. "Father, I'm very afraid. Please?"

Xerri's running out of time but he agrees to go meet Lyle—
he'll borrow Wozniak's car. Hanging up, Xerri can sense
something deeply disturbing coming, as if it's awakening. He
whispers "sustain low" to himself. It's Greek. It's not good.

Lyle finally looks at his phone. Seeing the cascade of calls and
messages forms a hard knot in his gut. Georgie, Silk, Dr. Susan
Wayne, Becky Tuttle, Noah Craig, a Southampton detective, the
spinal injury clinic, and they're just people he knows. Lots of
repeat callers. Lyle has never seen a pile up like this. With his
phone rejecting new calls, he's got to delete most. Including
Fraser Newton.

There are the many calls from Georgie Hall—sometimes she
left a message; sometimes she hung up. He plays back a few and
decides, despite her obvious rage, he should save them all. If
anything *happens* to his daughter this could be all he has left:

Dad! What are you doing? You have to call me back right away!

Dad! That online article! And those pictures of you! Are you alright?
Call me back!

Dad! You're on TV? Really? With those women? Listen to me. I am
getting harassed here at work. Sexual harassment, Dad. It stems from
your haunted house adventure, understand? If you can't call your own
daughter back at least stop hurting her!

Dad! You were supposed to go to court and rescind! Remember??

Then there's hang-up after hang-up. He has to call Georgie, tell
her he rescinded his motion. But he can't dial. What if the next
time he hears her voice is the last time?

Calls from media outlets, newspapers, magazines, radio,
television, online sources and more clog his phone. Lyle knew
them by their alien area codes and he expected FEARcom to
handle all that since he signed a piece of paper. He jettisons them
all.

Then there's a local number Lyle recognizes but cannot
place. Who is that?

He punches it and listens.

Lyle, it's Josie. Look, we're getting worried about you. Can you please call somebody back? Anybody. Me. You need help. Okay? Lyle...?

The recording concludes with a sigh as Josie disconnects. Josie, who always had a good sense of humor. Such a good sport. Lyle decides to save her message when his phone rings—caller ID shows **EDWARD HENDRICKS.**

Shit. A family member. Lyle can't take anymore—he sends the call to the digital compost heap. There's no room in his voice mailbox. But the caller redials. **EDWARD HENDRICKS.** Lyle fends it off again.

Fred turns onto Lyle's block to deliver the empath and self-centered shit.

~~~~~

61. Candles in the Rain

Flo and Glen. Lyle keeps picturing their bodies on his porch last night. What if they're just the beginning? What if Georgie's next? She's a cop. Anything could happen to her.

He dreads this, but driving right up to his house is the only choice. He needs to know what the hell is going on here. Is it possessed? A threat to Georgie? What if that damn possum were on his porch when she dropped off meals? He needs something from his bedroom. Going in with a priest should help. But this will be the last time, ever. Lyle imagines Fraser putting this toxic house on the market. How the bullshit would fly.

Fred parks at the curb. Two squad cars idle in the middle of street, driver-side windows facing each other; last night's toilet paper dangles in shreds around them from the branches above. The vandals did quite a job. More cruisers and unmarked cars are parked nearby. The number of tents has increased following last night's deaths. Lyle's front porch is draped in a billowing blue tarp. Crime scene.

It's started to rain. On Lyle's lawn there's an improvised shrine devoted to Flo—flowers, candles, signs and homemade posters, some with pictures of Jewel. Childlike but fervent sentiments include "Watch Over Us" and "Ghost Hampton Loves Flo." They've co-opted Silk's "Ghost Hampton" title—more viral brand penetration. Flo's candles crowd the slate path to Lyle's porch. A Believer couple tries to light their candles but the rain is making that difficult. The guy wears a black trash bag.

As Lyle positions his chair on the MediCab's lift, the clouds really open up. Fred hands him a courtesy umbrella. Lyle hands Fred a twenty. As the van door slides open, strange faces come out of the rain. Cold raindrops pelt everything and Lyle opens the black umbrella as the lift delivers him and his wheelchair to street level. His breath grows short and he experiences intense anxiety—like Charles Laughton at the end of *The Island of Lost Souls*—as the Believers close in.

They've been attracted here by dead people. Sadly, Lyle Hall's arrival in an ambulette seems to make their day. But he hesitates to roll off the lift. More Believers crowd the front of his house, trammeling the yellow police tape meant to cordon off his yard. From his chair Lyle can see only those closest to him. Some are weirdoes—and they press closer. They're not very clean and are now getting wet with rain. Hands reach to touch Lyle. He does not move forward; instead he recoils from the barrage of strange feelings these people give off.

"Mister Hall! You need to get off my platform!" says Fred. "Sorry, but I gotta pick somebody up!"

Lyle desperately wants the van to envelop him and take him back to the Memory Motel bar. People start pawing him—men and women, young and old and weird. He feels nausea coming on. When did he eat last? Was it that awful FEARcom pizza?

Some Believers beckon their cohorts.

"Hey! It's him! In the wheelchair!"

"Lyle! Lyle!"

Others start badgering him with questions.

"Where's Jewel? Is Jewel here?"

"Can a ghost make you walk again?"

"Do you want to marry Jewel?"

"Who killed Flo? We love Flo!"

"Is there an evil spirit? Are you possessed?"

A few on the street initiate the damn chant again, including banging tubs:

I saw her face!
BAM BAM BAM
I'm a Believer!
BAM BAM BAM

"Mister Hall!" Fred pipes up. "I really gotta go, you know? Like, now?" The MediCab's wipers slap back and forth against the rain. An ugly-sounding generator is grinding somewhere close by. Rain is drumming on the umbrella. Everything sucks.

Suddenly big arms in raincoats part some of the people crowding Lyle and his chair. Three Southampton police officers in Hi-Vis yellow slickers spread the crowd enough for Lyle to roll forward. If he goes back into the van now he'll be a total coward.

"Fred, I'll call you!"

"Mister Hall, I'm booked all day..."

Not the response Lyle wanted. Not enough twenties. It starts raining harder. The platform rises behind him and now it's about how effectively the cops can keep Lyle safe until he makes it to his dreaded porch. Where they died. Where is Xerri? The three cops, saying things like "Give the man some room!" and "Back off, people! Nothing to see here!" make enough space for Lyle to progress. His objective is the entry ramp but it will be a challenge. The cops help inch the wheelchair, man and umbrella forward. Lyle recognizes one cop as Petry from last night.

The dumb chant peters out but Believers continue to pepper Lyle with embarrassing questions. So weird how strangers interpret events in your life.

"Do demons live in your house?"

"Where's Silk? We want Silk!"

"You hot for Silk, Lyle? She's so hot!"

"Are you really gonna let them tear down Old Vic?"

Lyle jumps when the old man with the yellowed muttonchops insinuates himself between two cops. "Lyle Hall. I was Glen Stanley's friend. We camped here together. Where's his body? What're you doing for Glen? He's got no one, you know!"

This is sickening. Lyle did get to know Glen a little, what with his gentle home invasions and strange ways of showing he cared, but still. What was his late wife's name? What *is* he doing for Glen? Unclaimed bodies go to the morgue in Southampton...

"I said, what are you doing for Glen Stanley?"

Lyle has no answer as he stares back at the geezer in his old hunting cap and plaid hunting jacket. He perked the coffee. Lyle crumpled up his picture of Jewel. Cops jostle the old guy away.

The rest of the crowd is concerned with Flo, Jewel and Silk. Fred's van is beeping as it backs away. Then it pauses. Lyle looks back and sees a big cop in a hooded slicker—Big Frank—having a word with Fred through his window. He hands Fred something. Fred resumes backing up and Lyle realizes he's made a big mistake. Alone as he is, he can't accomplish a thing here. Are the places where the bodies fell outlined in police tape? Poor Flo died on her knees. How do you tape that on the floor? Lyle's own home terrifies him. It's become a house of horror. And where in hell is Xerri?

Old Glen's old friend intrudes again between two Southampton PD slickers. "Did Glen leave you something? He said he would!" Then he recedes. Lyle's entourage presses forward. Shit. Why did he even come here? Georgie already picked up his damn meds. Oh yeah. Conduct a demon search. And grab something from his night table.

The policemen help Lyle reach his ramp. It's wet and has slippery leaves on it. The fat candles lit for Flo have fizzled out, their black wicks submerged in drippy reservoirs. The stupid wet toilet paper swings overhead in wind-driven rain. It's starting to plop here and there in clumps.

Now a hooded head pokes between two policemen. Lyle squints through the rain at the face: young and intense, a five o'clock shadow, swarthy complexion, dark eyebrows arch over black eyes drawing a laser-like bead. The man's hoodie sweatshirt makes him look like a dirtbag. He reaches for Lyle. Why don't the cops stop him?

"Lyle-eh!"

One cop fends him off.

"Wait! Officer! This is the man I came to meet!"

The cops get Lyle up onto the porch the hard way. The ramp looks too slippery so they pick him up, chair and umbrella and all, and deposit him on his porch near the fluttering blue tarp. It seems to glow. The generator is louder here, angrier. Lyle thanks the men and stows the umbrella. Then the creeping dread of Flo's death sinks in again. Why just Flo's death? Why not old Glen's too? Maybe the heart can only bear one at a time.

It's a relief as Xerri steps onto the porch. "Father, thank you for coming!"

Xerri forms a flicker of a smile. "No problem. I borrowed Father Wozniak's—"

"Mister Hall?"

Sgt. Frank Barsotti, worn out from his double shift, climbs the porch steps. The tarp blows open and some plainclothes detectives and evidence people glance out at Lyle. The generator he's been hearing is powering floodlights. The cops are drinking coffee from the luncheonette where Gertie works. They don't react to seeing wheelchair-and-priest. Lyle introduces Big Frank to his new friend. Frank recognizes Xerri from Mose's photos.

"Power's out?" says Lyle.

"Yup," Frank says. He nods toward the guys inside the blue tarp. "Detectives'll want a word with you."

Cold rain is running off the porch roof. The Believers are dispersing again, back to their tents or crummy cars. Lyle looks at Fr. Xerri, then at Big Frank.

"Can we have a few minutes inside? I need some more of my meds," he fibs.

Old Sideburns suddenly calls out from the lawn. "Look! He brought a *priest!*"

To the remaining Believers this is a portentous sign: a priest appearing at a house where there have been two unexplained deaths. They erupt into a disorganized chant: *"Priest! Priest! Priest! Priest!"* but it quickly fades.

Big Frank looks at Lyle. "Going inside is problematic. The deaths are considered suspicious, at least for now." He nods toward the tarp. "They'll want to take a statement. Then you should leave."

"Frank, can I just run in and grab my prescriptions?" He nods to Xerri. "I wanted Father Xerri with me. I'm uncomfortable around the house now. After last night."

Big Frank mulls this. He knows Georgie picked up Lyle's meds last night.

298

Looking up at Frank, Lyle changes the subject. "So what do you know at this point, Sergeant?"

"I can't comment on this case, Mister Hall." Frank lowers his voice and it's masked by the generator. "But the medical examiner says so far the deaths look like stroke and heart failure. Respectively. The detectives want to know the how and why." Frank turns and looks at the lit up crime scene. A rainy gust blows the blue tarp and it hugs the backs of the detectives like a plastic shower curtain.

"We won't touch anything but my meds," Lyle stresses.

Against his judgment Frank mutters, "Door's unlocked. And Mister Hall, I have something for you." Frank goes and joins the detectives. The tarp hugs his ass, too.

The creak of Lyle's door opening is drowned out by the grumbling gas generator.

Entering his house, Lyle looks back at his chaotic yard—the wet toilet paper, the soaked shrine to the dead, the straggling Believers. Wind whips the tarp. Two cops in slickers step up onto the porch—to bust him? No, they turn and face front, for security.

Lyle looks at Xerri and says, "Shall we?" A gust of cold rain lashes both men as they enter Lyle's expanded 1960 ranch house. A back draft slams the door shut behind them. It's quieter in here. The house feels clammy as it sinks into darkness.

~~~~~~

62. House of Horrors

A musty chill envelops the two men in the gloom. If you have to do this, Lyle tells himself, do it with a priest. Better yet, a Maltese exorcist or whatever.

All the shades are drawn. It's oddly cold. The heat's off. How long has Lyle been gone? It feels like years. No longer a familiar place. His fingers find the light switch. He flicks it. Nothing.

"Father Xerri?" Where the hell is he?

There's a sudden hard thud against the front door. The shock makes Lyle's heart jump. There's scuffling outside—a struggle on the front porch? Peeking out the front door's sidelight Lyle sees the two policemen manhandle poor Old Sideburns down the porch steps. His muffled expletives blend with jeers from the Believers on the lawn. Why does this have to be so weird?

Best to get out of here ASAP. Hopefully Fr. Xerri can quickly tell if the place is possessed—and a threat. There's a real clause in home sales covering haunting. Maybe demons too?

Lyle flicks the hall light switch again. Right. No power. He jumps suddenly as a cold, black presence appears beside him.

"Lyle-eh, did you pay your electric bill?"

Lyle steadies himself. "I think so. But the power's out."

"It's okay; I prefer to work in natural conditions. I want to sense what is here. Or was here." Xerri winces when he spots Lyle's Torquemada sling hanging in the gloomy dining room entry. "Will you guide me, please-eh?"

"Where to first?"

"Your bedroom. If this is all right with you."

Lyle has little choice—he leads the priest down the hall to his bedroom. The priest steps into the room alone. After a quiet moment he's back out in the hall.

"Did you sense anything...evil?"

"Oh, it's hard to say. You were once married..."

"Yes. Twice, actually. You could tell?"

"I sensed unhappiness-eh," Fr. Xerri peers down at Lyle. "Nothing demonic."

"Good. My second wife left years ago." Lyle rolls past Xerri into his murky bedroom. Central is the big, hand-made Scandinavian bed Dar replaced Belinda's with and then decided she hated. On the hope chest at its foot rest two five-pound lavender dumbbells from the set Lauren the physical therapist made him buy. On the dresser stands the big screen TV that, post Dar, displayed Fox Business, the Golf Channel and occasional soft porn. Lyle proceeds to his nightstand. Its drawer has a cool feature—a hidden compartment. Lyle opens it and extracts something heavy. Maybe this will calm his nerves. He slips it into the canvas pouch that hangs from his wheelchair and rolls out to Fr. Xerri.

"May as well pick up a few things while I'm here. Okay, next?"

The men can hear chanting outside in the rain. It sounds weak and distant. Some Believers have been corralled across the street near Mr. Rosewater's.

"Let's see the kitchen," Xerri says. "Then the basement."

As Lyle leads them to the unlit kitchen he feels a cold damp breeze.

There's a sharp *SLAM.*

Lyle's heart jumps in his chest again. "Jeez! What the hell was *that*?"

The priest moves to the kitchen door. It's locked.

"Lyle-eh, did you lock this door?"

"Yeah, but the police might have opened it. And Glen, the old man who died here last night, was a locksmith. He let himself in on at least one occasion, but he was harmless—I didn't have to shoot him."

"You have a *gun*, Lyle-eh?"

"I've never fired it, Father."

"Hmmm…" says Xerri, losing himself in thought. The people outside, the generator, the rain on the windows all seem hushed. The blinds admit fading light.

Xerri turns to the kitchen table and sees two picture-perfect place settings—silver, china and crystal goblets—waiting for a meal.

"This is very nice-eh...but why?"

"Oh, that? Old Glen said his wife insisted on using the good china and silverware and I should too. Said you only go around once in life..."

"Go on..."

"So he arranged my late wife's good stuff for me. And Georgie."

Xerri stares at the table setting. "When did he do this?"

"Uh, well, maybe last night...before...it's hard to know." He muses, "This stuff was Belinda's. My first wife. Dar hated it. Never used it."

Instead of responding, Xerri says dreamily, "Of course. Maeve."

"Yeah. Wait—you know the old girl's name?"

Xerri blinks. "Glen Stanley's story was on the TV-eh. Now the basement. Is there a flashlight? I know you wish to keep your phone on your person."

"Yeah." Wondering about this Maeve now, Lyle opens the kitchen junk drawer, hands Xerri a flashlight. "I'll have to stay up here."

Xerri flicks it on. Its beam strikes his unshaven chin and face Boris Karloff-style. Lyle is taken by how young Matteo looks and, at the same time, how old.

"I will be brief, Lyle-eh." The basement door is in the hall. Opening it, the light bobbing ahead of him, Xerri creaks down the old stairs. Then silence.

Lyle fidgets in the dark kitchen. He finds another flashlight in the drawer. It emits only a feeble brown glow. He wants to get back to the motel, and Rooney. There's some shuffling down in the basement.

CRASH!

Lyle's heart jumps again. Shit—is there some kind of demon lurking in the basement? He rolls to the head of the stairs and is reminded of Richard Widmark.

Sounds of a paint can rolling and more shuffling. Muttering in a strange language.

Lyle flashes on a scene in *The Exorcist*, the priest at the bottom of that long flight of stairs, and whispers harshly down to Xerri. "Father! Are you all right?"

"Lyle-eh!" Xerri cries, "I stumbled on some paint cans. Something startled me."

"What kind of something?"

Xerri's black figure emerges from darkness—climbing back up the stairs.

"I dropped the flashlight and it went out."

"Father, what was down there?"

Xerri reaches the top of the stairs.

"An...opossum, I think."

"There's a possum down there? Are you sure?"

"Yes-eh. It ran off. It squeezed out through a broken basement window."

Lyle flashes on last night. "Flo and I saw one here last night—oversized, horrible; actually standing on Glen's chest, hissing at us, frothing at the mouth. Then it attacked us. Flo got in its way and it bit her. Moments later she..." Lyle is struck by a thought. "Father, Flo stepped in its path—that rabid thing was going for *me*."

Xerri considers this. "She did not have to do that. Where I come from, if someone does you such a great service, you owe them a great debt-eh."

This thought makes Lyle's heart hurt. "It'll be tough paying that back, Father." He holds his feeble flashlight up to see the priest. "How did it feel, down there?"

"Again, it's hard to verbalize, Lyle-eh. I sensed sadness. But any house can harbor unhappiness over many years. It's not like there was a death down there."

"Did you see my wife's furniture?"

"Well, yes, an unusual amount of furniture for a basement. And...*moffa dwar il ghamara tal*. I am sorry to say."

"Really? Some kind of demon?" Lyle's brown light grows dimmer.

"My English is imperfect. It's how you say... *mold...mildew*. On the upholstery."

After Belinda, Dar started to redecorate the house. She made a poor decision and had the movers store Belinda's homey upholstered furniture in the cellar. That was 13 years ago. After the design-y modern furniture arrived, Dar announced that she still "hated" Lyle's old ranch house and wanted to move.

"I've got a possum and mildew down there. And that's *all?*"

"That's all I saw. Unfortunately, nothing can be done. About the mildew."

Lyle sighs his relief. "Let's get out of here. Have you had lunch? I'm starved."

~~~~~~

63. Follow-up Conversation

The rainfall has stopped, but now a bitter wind rustles tree branches. The toilet paper dangling over Lyle's front yard is plopping to the ground in soggy clumps. Except for the thrumming generator, things are quiet. The two cops in slickers are gone. The paranormal yahoos must have moved over to Old Vic. A squad car parked at the curb, a wad of wet TP on its hood, has its searchlight trained on Lyle's porch. Flo's shrine is a sloppy mess.

But as Lyle rolls out onto his porch, he feels a great weight has been lifted. A mystical Maltese priest who's had run-ins with the netherworld has pronounced his house free of evil spirits. Apparently. This is good—way easier to sell the place.

Sgt. Frank peers out from behind the tarp and catches Lyle's eye. He shouldn't have been inside unescorted but Frank will look the other way.

Lyle rolls to the top of his ramp, Fr. Xerri moves protectively alongside him.

"Mister Hall?" says Frank, approaching. "We need a follow-up conversation."

Lyle feels increasingly lighthearted, almost playful. He looks down his long ramp, wet and leafy, leading to the slate sidewalk. He gives Frank an odd grin.

"Any time, Sergeant!"

With that Lyle launches himself down the ramp at surprising speed. His wheels skid down the ramp kicking up water droplets and wet leaves.

"Lyle-eh! Oh, my Lord!" Xerri cries, lurching down the porch steps after him.

Lyle hits the sidewalk at speed and almost does a header out of the chair. Instead, giving a falsetto whoop, he manages to pull a one-eighty on the slate walk; he spins out, coming to a stop facing the porch, the priest and the sergeant.

He smiles broadly for what feels like the first time in ages. "My house isn't possessed! I can *sell it!*"

Big Frank stifles a grin as Fr. Xerri hastens to the paraplegic man's side.

"Lyle-eh! Are you all right?"

Lyle's smile fades as he spots Old Sideburns watching him from behind the neighbor's rhododendron. Last night's sickening events on his porch replay vividly in his mind. And he's reminded of the thin membrane separating empathic Lyle, who just lost two friends, and greedy Lyle, who wants to sell his old ranch house.

"Yeah, Father," he says, gloom setting in, "Lyle is fine."

Sgt. Frank joins them on the sidewalk. He looks Lyle over carefully, especially given the abrupt mood swing.

"Feeling frisky, Mister Hall?"

Frank eyes Lyle's canvas pouch. It's unzipped and hangs heavily from the chair's arm, supposedly full of meds. But Frank catches a glint of metal and a sinister shape bulging inside. He decides to do nothing about it, for now.

"No evil spirits inside," Lyle says. "That's good. Thanks for letting us go in."

Frank knits his brow. "Sir, letting anyone inside would be against orders."

Lyle gets it, feeling more embarrassment. "Oh. Right."

"Mister Hall, please stay in the local area and be available via your cell phone. The detectives will have questions for you."

"Okay. Want my number?"

"Got it." He hands Lyle a folded sheet of paper. "Here. This is a photocopy."

Lyle unfolds it. "What is this?" It's a few handwritten lines. It almost blows away.

"The original was on your kitchen table. Signed by Glen Stanley."

Frank heads back up onto the porch. He pauses on a step and turns. "Oh, and Mister Hall, Detective Hall said that you can return her call at any time."

"Will do, Sergeant." Lyle turns to his guest who's still not getting much of this. "Want some lunch, Father?"

Xerri cracks a smile. "Americans love to eat."

"I'll buy if you drive."

They approach the Wozniak mobile, a black, five-year-old Camry. Despite the toilet paper, the neighborhood seems less disorderly minus the chanting campers. Lyle looks across the street and pictures Mr. Rosewater observing from behind a curtain.

Xerri is startled when Old Sideburns steps into their path and confronts them again. He seems even more embittered now.

"Lyle Hall. Glen Stanley came here to help you. And he died. And you don't care. You don't get it."

The old guy returns to his rhododendron but adds, creepily, "You will get it."

"That man is resolute and adamant," says Xerri as he opens his car door.

Lyle swings into the passenger seat and the priest collapses the wheelchair. Its canvas kit bag flops heavily to one side as Xerri wrestles the chair into the backseat.

From Lyle's porch Big Frank watches the priest drive off with Lyle. He dials Georgie Hall's cell number and steps down from the porch, away from the detectives.

"Detective? Sergeant Barsotti. No, no problem. Things are pretty much okay, given the circumstances. May have to take this nutty old guy into custody. No, not your father. So listen, there's one thing...does your dad have a permit for a handgun? Yeah, a handgun. He came out of his house with it in his pouch. Doesn't know I saw it. I'll need to run a check for a firearm permit. Just so you know. Yeah, another worry for you."

Frank pauses, then adds, "How are things at the office?" He listens, then stifles a chuckle. "You returned fire at Swan Song? He deserves it. You know my friend from Internal Affairs? Well, he's coming by the stationhouse tonight. Chief Queeley knows. Even one visit should put the fear of God in Swanson."

Frank hears a strange request from Detective Hall.

"A hundred-year-old mystery file, huh? One-eleven Poplar?" he says, thinking it over. "May be some old file cabinets in the records room I can look in later." He pauses. "Oh, and sorry I missed last night. Thursday being Chinese night."

Big Frank disconnects. The rain starts in again. He rejoins the detectives.

Running east along Montauk Highway, Lyle tries to separate empathic Lyle: trying to save Old Vic, Jewel, school kids playing near the Barn From Hell and, above all else, his own daughter— from pragmatic Lyle: trying to be sure his house can be sold, trying to win over his object of desire, Silk, and trying to walk again. He wants to show Fr. Xerri the right Lyle over lunch.

As he drives, Fr. Xerri urges Lyle to recount all he can of Silk's ill-considered break-in at the old barn. He's intrigued by Lyle's blackout experience, his intense hallucination, the bloody knife and all. And how that was followed by two deaths. Heading down the rain-swept road, he can sense how fragile this man Lyle is.

"Lyle-eh, I did not say your house is clean," he finally says. "I merely did not detect the presence of an unclean spirit at the time. But last night, two innocent people died at your house. That tells us something. And last night in that barn..."

Lyle's spirits sink further. "Yeah, you're right." He absently unfolds the note Big Frank photocopied for him. It's wet. And the ghost of Jewel's face is vaguely visible. He realizes the original was neatly written on the back of a Jewel flyer. By a dead man.

> Dear Lyle,
> Thank you for accepting us ragtag campers into your life.
> We are genuinely excited about your contact with Jewel. I believe something good will come of it.
> I've visited haunted houses before, but yours sure is a doozy!
> I know you are feeling a lot of pressure and that's why you get a little touchy.
> We hope for the best for you and for Jewel. I know a good man when I see one and, like they say, Lyle is fine!

I hope you have good times to come with your own daughter. Maeve and I sure enjoyed our time with ours!

Yours truly,

Glen Stanley
PS – Hoping you will find your way to introduce me, and my friend Herb, to Jewel. It sure would be an exciting way to cap off a long life!

~~~~~~

64. Impressions

Rooney's Memory Motel bar is nearly deserted this stormy afternoon, but he's turned up the heat prior to the scheduled TV shoot. Josh's lights still hang from the ceiling. Two local men are hunched over beers at the bar. They glance over as Lyle rolls in with a gust of rain and a young priest in a wet hoodie sweatshirt.

Lyle takes a table near the interview set and Xerri removes his hoodie. He's got a black sweatshirt underneath and his white clerical collar protrudes above it. The big bartender dries his hands on the towel that hangs from his expansive waist and approaches their table.

"Ain't a fit day out for man nor beast!" he says warmly. Lyle's tipping has made Rooney extra warm. "What'll it be, gents?"

Lyle, his mood sour, orders his usual, and Xerri asks for a menu. Rooney explains that the kitchen will reopen in six months and suggests seafood take out.

"A seafood diet is the best. You see food and you eat it!" Rooney waits for some note of appreciation.

"Mister Rooney, my friend here, Father Xerri, is from Malta. They have lots of seafood, but probably don't have that joke."

"Malta, huh? That's a real place? Not just a Bogart movie?" Rooney looks at Xerri. "So what'll you have, Father?"

Xerri knits his brow. He doesn't drink, but makes today an exception and orders a cognac. Lyle asks Rooney to call out for lobster salad platters. Rooney says they don't deliver but will try to get somebody to bring over the food. "Seeing as you have a Maltese priest with you and all." Lyle says he'll take care of whoever drops it off.

Xerri holds Glen Stanley's letter. He studies it for a moment, then looks up.

"How well did you know this man?"

"Not well and not for long but he acted like we were somehow close."

"He was the man in your kitchen," the priest says. "I will pray for his soul." He pauses. "And the woman, Flo? How well did you, uh..."

"I was getting to know Flo over the past few days. She was a professional clairvoyant—if you believe in such things.

"Catholics are taught not to."

"Really." Time to ask Xerri again about the two words. "So Father, what Flo said to me as she breathed her last...*sustain low*. Any idea what that might mean?"

As with the words Lyle spit out at him in Old Vic's parlor the other day, Xerri knows well what they mean. But Flo's words might be too disturbing for Lyle right now. Xerri shrugs. "I have to think about that..." He's glad as Rooney returns with drinks.

Lyle raises his scotch and thanks Xerri for his help. They both sip. He wants more from the priest on assessing his house. But, after the tragic deaths that occurred overnight, he's relieved that, when he sells the house, he won't have to say it's haunted.

Both men sip their drinks and begin to warm up. Lyle speaks first.

"Father, did you see your picture on the *Southampton Press* website?"

"I think all of Malta has seen it by now."

"I'm sorry you've been linked in that way with me—at my worst, no less."

"Lyle-eh, that was my fault. I am sorry for you. I put you in a bad place."

Lyle sees his opening. "Father, at the diner the other night, you weren't ready to tell me what I said—when I cursed you out inside Old Vic. Was it really Greek? I mean, shouldn't I know what I said?"

Xerri knows there will be no good time to discuss it. "Yes, you probably should." He looks Lyle in the eye. "You said 'Fuck you, priest' in English." Xerri peers down into his cognac. "You...You then said in Greek you knew I caused my mother's death."

311

Lyle feels a cold shock in his heart. He sorely wishes he'd never asked.

"Oh, Father, that's terrible. I'm so sorry! I didn't...I couldn't have..."

Xerri looks up at him. "It's okay-eh. It wasn't you speaking, Lyle. That's the real problem. It's good you are letting that house be torn down." Xerri swigs his drink and changes the subject. "Your home, I thought, was lovely."

Relieved Xerri moved to a more pragmatic topic, Lyle tries to picture something Dar decorated as *lovely*. Then the bar door opens and cold air rushes in.

"That table there!" Rooney informs the seafood guy. "Wheelchair and priest," he adds helpfully, though no other table is occupied.

Lyle pays and gives the young guy a twenty. He and Xerri dig wobbly plastic forks into their partitioned styros full of lobster salad, coleslaw and French fries. The fries are crisp and hot. Both men's cheeks bulge as they feast. Last thing Lyle ate was cold pizza...when was that?

"Good stuff?" Rooney calls to them.

Xerri nods appreciatively and chews. Lyle lets him enjoy his meal.

As Xerri's assault on the lobster salad slows, both men drink and feel the warmth. Lyle figures he'll ask another question.

"Father, have you gotten what you were looking for out of the priesthood?"

"Have you gotten what you were looking for out of...jurisprudence?"

"Money," Lyle shrugs.

Xerri grins. "I hope we both found what we were looking for." He raises his snifter and they clink and drink. "I've found bringing the Word of God to people is a challenge-eh." Lyle notes how the priest's accent grows more pronounced as he tipples. "I believe there is a battle raging deep inside every person's soul, just as there once was a battle long ago in Heaven. Lucifer versus Michael. Michael won-eh. Then good faced evil in the Garden of Eden. Evil won that one. Today one force is still trying to pull us down. The other, raise us up-eh." Xerri sips cognac and smiles at Lyle. "It is ironic."

"What is?"

"What we learned from the Tree of Knowledge is how *mutu*...how stupid we are."

Lyle punctuates that by draining his glass and raising it so Rooney can see it.

Rooney brings a fresh Dewar's and collects the styros so they can concentrate on drinking. "You need another one there, uh, Father?"

"No, thank you. I am good." There's some pale residue in his snifter. Xerri smiles as Rooney moves away. "I like that. I have heard that only here in America."

"That what?" says Lyle.

"*I am good*. When you have your drink, you are good. If you have no drink, you therefore are *bad*."

"Mister Rooney?"

"Mister Hall?" Rooney replies from the bar.

"My guest here is in fact not so good. Got any good stuff?"

"Yeah. And I have the really good stuff."

"Good. Please bring over the good stuff. So my friend will be good."

Rooney returns with a fresh snifter and a dusty bottle of Remy Martin XO. The beer drinkers at the bar, two middle-aged men, turn their heads to follow him. Rooney pours the XO with a generous flourish.

"This, Father, is the good stuff." The cognac flows halfway up the snifter. "And don't worry; it's on Mister Hall here." He departs and Xerri raises the snifter tentatively.

"Thank you. Now I am good. But I really shouldn't. This is rare."

The two men clink and drink.

"Why is this rare? I mean besides the cognac being rare."

"Lyle-eh, I'm not really supposed to drink. Doctor's orders."

"Oh? Well you don't *have to* drink that, you know."

Xerri ignores that. "Are you supposed to drink, Lyle-eh?"

"Well, one a day, maybe. I'm negotiating with my doctors."

"So you will be taking two weeks off from alcohol after this? Mathematically speaking?" Xerri smiles warmly. His teeth are big and white.

"Yeah. After this." Lyle swigs his scotch, then pauses. "So I'm really hoping that whatever went on at my house over the years is small potatoes."

Xerri thinks about Lyle's house. "Oh, I hope so, too. Or perhaps no potatoes. But those deaths are big potatoes. Tragic." He sips his cognac. It is better than good. "What I think about your house-eh..."

Lyle grips his rocks glass tightly.

"...The kitchen and the bedroom are two places where negativity can build up in a home. I could sense it in both rooms."

"Oh? Demonic negativity?"

"Lyle-eh, we do not know this. Yet. But I can tell you about general sensations I get from the house-eh. Bedrooms and kitchens are supposed to be places of peace, warmth and nurture. For sleeping and sharing meals."

Rooney is listening from his position behind the bar. "Hey!" he calls over to their table. "My first wife? I wanted her to be a whore in my bedroom and an angel in my kitchen." He waits a beat. "But I got the opposite!" Rooney cracks up at the old gag.

Xerri nods solemnly to Rooney. "I will pray for her."

Lyle gives Rooney a look and then refocuses on Xerri. He seems a bit woozy.

"Lyle-eh, in some homes these two rooms become a nexus of unhappiness, argument and worse-eh. Did you know most murders occur in the kitchen?"

"*Really.*"

"Yes. In Malta this is true. The long knives are in the kitchen."

"Did anyone die in my kitchen?"

"No. No. Then there is my impression of the bedroom..." The priest leans toward Lyle. "Are you sure you want...?"

"It's okay. Let me have it." Lyle notes that Rooney is still eavesdropping.

"There was unhappiness in that room. Harsh words. Infidelity." Xerri lowers his voice. "Commandments were broken." He casts his eyes down.

From behind the bar Rooney whispers, "Go, Lyle." Lyle really wishes Rooney would mind his business. But who was the infidel in his bedroom? Belinda? No way. Dar? Possibly. *Lyle Hall?* Oh, maybe there were a few drunken romps. Like the lady bartender from Montauk—bodybuilder, indoor-tanning enthusiast, accomplished wrestler. What was her *name?*

Xerri resumes. "In the kitchen, another story. I felt there once was acrimony. Promises broken. Things broken...am I getting too personal?"

"No. Please go on." If Lyle can withstand hearing a Maltese priest describe Commandment-breaking in his bedroom he can handle some dish-breaking.

"But today I sensed something new and unusual, at odds with the bedroom. Something bringing harmony and peace."

"Glen Stanley was breaking into my house. Does that count as 'things broken'?"

Xerri looks at Lyle again. "I sensed a *feminine* presence."

Right. Lyle finishes his scotch. "Maybe my late wife, Belinda. But you sensed no...demonic presence there?"

"No demons. A peaceful presence." He smiles. "I hope that helps you sell your house."

Sensing this topic is over, Lyle says, "Father, I can't thank you enough for giving me so much of your time and sharing your impressions. You've been very helpful."

Xerri smiles again. "No, it's been my pleasure." He looks at Lyle. "You are the only TV star I have met. This is a strange, fascinating country."

"You mean that TV interview I did?"

"Yes-eh. Monsignor Hannan knew when you were to be broadcast. You and those women. You were right here where we are now. Later Father Wozniak found your broadcast on a website. It had additional material. And my photograph-eh." Xerri pauses and sips more cognac. "This is very good."

"Best in the house!" calls Rooney.

315

He resumes. "I am very sorry you lost your lady friend. I will pray for her."

"Thank you."

"I am also sorry for you…that you seemed so taken with that young television woman. With the hair and the makeup."

Oh no. Lyle begins to recognize the depth and breadth of a stupid TV interview. "You and the Monsignor could see, uh, *that* on TV?"

"Yes-eh. And Father Wozniak and others gathered to watch. The Monsignor is grateful for your work for the parish. And sorry to see you look so forlorn on the TV-eh. We prayed for you."

Ouch. Priests were actually *praying* during his cringe-worthy interview. Lyle's stomach churns. Wow. Georgie was so right.

"I could be wrong-eh," Xerri says, reconsidering. "Maybe you are not in love with that woman. But Monsignor asked us all to pray for you."

Great.

The cognac doing its job, Teo Xerri digresses on his stay in America. Lyle tries to imagine a priest coming here from a stunning vacation destination like Malta and being confronted with the Long Island Expressway, Tanger Outlet Mall, the Pine Barrens, East Hampton and so on. Who got the better end of this deal?

"For me, Long Island is a kind of reward, a sabbatical. I visited last year and was invited back. I love to meet the people of Long Island, and not just Catholics-eh."

"Why?"

"Not unlike the Maltese, you are a melting pot of all kinds on one small island. And you do so many things. Fish-eh, surf, sail, fly planes, drive pick-up trucks, ride motorcycles and dirty-bikes…" Xerri stops as he remembers Lyle is in a wheelchair. "I am sorry-eh."

"It's okay, Father," Lyle smiles, noting that Xerri's gotten pretty loose now. "Remember, I've got a team of medical experts working on me. Please go on."

316

He revs up again. "Well, you make your own beer and wine and then there's your food—corn of the cob, tomatoes, pizza, fried rice, refried beans, hot dogs, ham-burgers, clams-eh, fish tacos, cider doughnuts, both angel's food and devil's food…"

Lyle lets out a little laugh. "We've got it pretty well covered."

"And I love your idioms."

"Really."

The priest smiles. "Yes-eh. I like that one—*Really*. Making a whole sentence from only one word. As with *Dude*-eh. Your idioms are funny but you never laugh at them. *Not for nothing. Get out of my face-eh. The whole shooting match-eh.*" Xerri sips from his snifter. "Lyle-eh, you told me you were a Christian…"

"Yup. Still am. I think. In my own way."

"I see. Your own way-eh." He peers once more into his snifter.

Something's still gnawing at Lyle regarding Xerri's decision to become a priest. A good-looking guy like him. No time like now, given the cognac, to ask.

"Father, I'm curious about something."

"Let's hear it. And please, Lyle-eh, call me Teo. The protocol is friends call a priest by his first name when in an informal setting."

"Okay. Teo, the other night when you spoke of your decision to become a priest…" Teo stiffens. "If you believed the old lady performed the exorcism successfully, why did you 'inoculate' yourself by joining the priesthood?"

Teo lowers his eyes. His head shudders slightly on his neck. Lyle shouldn't have bought him cognac. But a drunk man speaks a sober mind.

"Why did I become a priest?" Teo lifts his eyes to meet Lyle's. "I will tell you, my American friend-eh." Teo exhales heavily. It does not smell good. "Lyle-eh, my mother died in the temple ruins that day when I was a boy—a boy with demons tearing at his insides."

"Your mother? Good Lord! I don't understand…how?"

Teo is fighting back emotion. He speaks in a whisper. "My two friends led my mother into the temple ruins. She found me lying in an ancient chamber, writhing in agony. Foaming at the mouth-eh. My father was fishing. The parish priest was away. The family doctor was not available. So my mother got this old lady from the village. The old lady laid her hands on me. My friends hid and watched. Later they described it to me. My mother laid her hands on me, too. The old one recited incantations—derisive words, mocking the Devil himself. Mother joined in. Suddenly my whole body rocked. My friends said it looked like I was electrocuted. One woman fell violently away from me and collapsed on the tomb's floor in the darkness. My mother. But the old lady stayed with me, repeating her incantations. Soon I was at peace, asleep-eh."

Lyle looks intently at Teo and tries to absorb it all. The Devil does not like to be mocked? That's a new one.

"My friends ran out and stopped a man with a car. The old woman was alone with me. Finally, some men got Mother and me to the hospital. They did not tell me at first that my mother had died. Her heart..."

Lyle shakes his head. "I am so sorry. You were so young."

"The doctor finally came to my bedside. My father returned from fishing. It was not good. Word spread quickly that the old lady had driven out a demon and it entered my mother's soul and took her. That was the story."

"Took her?"

Teo looks at Lyle. "It went back to Hell-eh. But took her soul. So it won-eh."

The two men sit and toy with their drinks for a quiet moment. Neither man drinks.

"How could anyone on earth know such a thing?"

"They could not-eh. But it's easy to believe bad things, as you know. My father believed it. I was destined for the seminary and the priesthood after that. Seminary high school and then the seminary university. A good education. But my father never truly forgave me after that terrible day. He believed I had brought about mother's death. And, perhaps, her eternal damnation. I had

318

disobeyed my parents by sneaking into the ruins—no place for a young boy. Some, like the old lady, believed that unclean spirits waited there in that place of sacrifice…waiting since before Christ to prey upon a weak soul-eh. According to my father, *I* was that weak soul-eh. And I needed the protection of Christ."

You could hear a pin drop in the bar. Lyle realizes Rooney has muted the TV.

Xerri stares at his hands. He seems fairly composed given his tale of horror and guilt visited on a 14-year-old. "So that is why I became a priest, Lyle-eh. I swore to my father I would pray for my mother's soul every day." He lifts his chin and smiles unsteadily. Tears have formed in the corners of his reddened eyes. "Part of my job."

Lyle picks up weird emanations from his priest friend. A deep chasm of sadness and guilt. He reaches for his scotch, but then shifts his hand across the table to Teo's hand. It's quivering. Lyle squeezes it tightly and closes his eyes. Both men bow their heads. Rooney tinkles a couple of beer glasses in the background.

After a moment, a chapped mitt of a hand plops a bar tab down in front of Lyle. There's a gruff throat-clearing. Lyle is still holding the hand of a priest 25 years his junior. He reflexively lets go and looks up.

"Can I help you?"

The chapped hand is connected to a weathered old lobsterman's coat and a big leathery face. One of the patrons from the bar.

"Lyle Hall?"

"Yeah...?" Lyle says warily.

"Well, uh, my friend here," he nods at his weather-beaten beer buddy standing behind him, "wants your autograph, but he's too shy. If it isn't too much trouble...?"

The bar tab is blank. Lyle relaxes and takes out his Mont Blanc.

"If you would, make it out to Lizzie. Amos's daughter."

Lyle does as asked. Teo observes in awe—he's witnessing an actual American celebrity signing an autograph. Something to tell the folks about back home. Lyle hands the man the chit, saying, "Listen. Could you possibly not tell anyone else that I'm here?"

Amos pipes up. "We would, sir, but it's kinda too late. You're all over my daughter's computer. You, that lady Silk. And those people who died last night." He nods at the window. "Surprised your fans haven't found you here already."

The two men thank Lyle, tip their caps to Fr. Xerri and leave.

As the door shuts behind them, Rooney says, "That guy Amos is too shy. Two bricks shy of a load!" He laughs alone, then adds, "And his buddy's brain is too tense. Two tenths the size of a normal brain!"

"I will pray for them," Teo smiles, rising unsteadily from the table.

Rooney still has the TV on mute but something very odd is transpiring onscreen.

Teo shakes Lyle's hand for a long time. "Thank you for this fascinating time," he says sincerely. "I must get back now. I truly wish we could talk more before I return home. Talk about what happened to you in that old house. About the girl you saw. And maybe about the problem you keep locked away. Since we are now friends-eh."

Lyle squeezes his arm. "No, I thank *you*, Teo. Did you get a flight yet?"

"Lyle-eh, I'm sorry, my ticket to Rome is for tonight!" Lyle registers surprise and Teo bends to his ear. Lyle smells cognac. "Lyle-eh...I know about you. You are not such a bad guy. And you have the empathy. *Empatija ta.* You have what I have-eh."

Teo stands up and Lyle flashes on something. "Teo, you said we are dragged both up and down at the same time by hidden forces. I know something about that. You know we have a cliché...an angel on a guy's right shoulder and a devil on the left? Both trying to convince him to go their way? That's how I feel all the time."

"I have not seen that cliché," Teo smiles. "But we are given choices. Angel's food or devil's food." Teo gives a grin and heads for the door.

320

As Teo walks to the exit the TV above the bar is showing breaking "Ghost Hampton" news. The front-loader and other demolition equipment are poised to push down Old Vic. Lettering on one big rig reads ASPLUNDH. But the workers are standing around in their DayGlo vests drinking coffee. One of News12's blond reporters is jabbering away silently. Rooney intercepts Teo and makes a show of shaking his hand while he looks into the priest's eyes.

"You good to drive, Father?"

"Yes-eh. Thanks to you, I am good. But I must go now."

Rooney releases the priest's hand and grins. "When you gotta go, you gotta go."

He watches out the window as Teo pulls Vitalis Wozniak's car out onto Montauk Highway. "So that's a Maltese priest, huh? Young enough to be my son."

Lyle blinks at the weird scene silently unfolding on TV and rolls closer.

"Oh *shit*," he whispers.

~~~~~~

65. News12

NewsChannel 12 offers yet another blond reporter in a live interview segment outside Old Vic. But this one hits Lyle hard. Noah Craig—*Noah*—is onscreen standing next to Becky Tuttle. Lyle and Rooney watch the reporter hold a News12 mic for Becky as she blabs her expert opinion. It's stopped raining. Becky's wrists are crossed primly at her waist. She's wearing her gray sweater set. As before, it's tight. Beneath her talking head a graphic reads: **REBECCA TUTTLE**, *Save-a-Barn*. Noah, who's a smart guy, looks like a total idiot nodding his ascent to whatever she's saying and turning to glance at Old Vic's even older barn.

Rooney ups the volume as the camera turns to the reporter.

"And that's how Southampton Judge Gerald Sloane left it today: Old Vic comes down but the barn remains standing, now the responsibility of the local Save-a-Barn organization. But some were not pleased with the ruling. This afternoon Bridgehampton saw its own Tiananmen Square reenactment as straggling demonstrators calling themselves the Believers put a stop, at least for now, to Southampton's demolition of this abandoned house widely believed to be haunted.

"Earlier today most of the demonstrators, who'd camped out here the past two days in hopes of preserving the derelict house they say is inhabited by the ghost of a young girl, were persuaded by Southampton Police to go home. But one resolute bunch remained in a show of support for their elderly organizer, Glen Stanley, who died last night of a stroke on the porch of local attorney Lyle Hall. With him was Flo Hendricks, a professional clairvoyant, who subsequently suffered a fatal heart attack at the scene. The medical examiner's office is expected to rule natural causes in both deaths. Strangely, Lyle Hall is the man who claimed he'd seen a ghost at Old Vic."

Now News12 cuts to footage of excavation equipment approaching Old Vic, led by a lumbering front-loader truck with a large bucket attachment. The reporter continues.

"This afternoon, after Judge Sloane gave the go-ahead, heavy demolition equipment that had been parked here on Poplar started to roll. But this action only reinvigorated the remaining Believers, and law enforcement officials intervened."

Lyle is stunned by video of Old Sideburns in his hunting jacket planting himself, hands on his hips in the rain, in the path of the oncoming front-loader. Its operator, seated in a protective cab and wearing a hardhat and dust mask, halts the truck, removes the mask and looks around for orders.

The reporter narrates, "Police and town officials seemed uncertain how to deal with one antagonistic demonstrator, given his advanced years. Emboldened by the elderly man's defiance, more demonstrators joined him, taking up their now familiar chant, and tensions quickly escalated."

Video footage shows a water bottle, and then a beer can, bouncing off the front-loader's windshield. Police move in on the demonstrators. Some are wearing the new shirts imprinted with crazy-Lyle's photo and "Lyle Is Fine." The old man won't budge.

The reporter reappears live on camera. "Lyle Hall sparked an uproar earlier this week with his motion in court to save this decrepit house, claiming a ghostly girl named Jewel inhabits it and wants him to preserve it. The ensuing media frenzy took an unexpected turn today when Hall rescinded his motion in court. Meanwhile, the faithful set up a shrine in honor of Flo Hendricks on Hall's front lawn. And, Brent, the resolve demonstrated by that elderly man facing down multi-ton demolition equipment says it all about the esteem for Glen Stanley. This is Daphne Pratt, News Twelve, in Bridgehampton."

Lyle exhales deeply—Noah? Really?—as Rooney places a fresh scotch before him. Now News12 cuts to the anchor desk. Brent Mellon is promoting a special later this evening: *Haunted? The Truth Behind the 'Ghost Hampton' Phenomenon with Brent Mellon*. As Mellon describes the in-depth investigation for which

Lyle Hall did not grant an interview, a sickening series of "Ghost Hampton" images plays over his shoulder, finally resolving to a creepy Photoshopped collage of Old Vic, Jewel and crazy-looking Lyle.

His stomach turns. Noah has turned against him, publicly, for all to see. And Mose Allen's effing photo is all over TV. Lyle gone wild. His hair all crazy-Einstein, his unkempt beard weirdly powdered white, his expression one of murderous fury and insanity, red scratches across his cheeks. Worst of all were his eyes. Like Silk's video whiz, the TV news people did something to intensify Lyle's angry eyes, giving them an unnatural glow. Who knows where that damn photo will turn up next.

News12 downplayed Silk, their big competition, Lyle muses, swigging his scotch.

Rooney, making a new "CLOSED" sign on a place mat, says, "Gotta get one of those Ghost Hampton T-shirts! Lyle is fine!"

"Why? You don't wear T-shirts."

"To hang up behind the bar, Mister Hall." Rooney peers at Lyle. "You know what? You're my most famous customer now, not counting the Rolling Stones!"

Lyle suddenly grows very tired. *I'm an effing T-shirt now, too. With effing Mose Allen's effing photo of my face on it. Idiots are cavorting for the cameras wearing my face. Somebody is very adept at jumping on a fad.*

"Hey Mister Rooney, can you turn that stuff off?"

Rooney half complies by muting the sound. "And to think I served alcohol to Lyle Hall," he muses. "Hey, *that rhymes.*"

"Something to tell your grandkids."

Both men now hear loud sounds outside in the parking area; the grinding, complaining-dinosaur noises big tractor-trailers make when they position themselves.

Rooney looks out the window. "I'll be damned. They must've booked the whole motel. Never thought I'd see this!"

"See what?"

"This big rig's pulled up with a satellite dish on the trailer. They're blocking access to the parking lot. Like they don't want to let the competition in." Rooney turns to Lyle. "Or let anybody out." Rooney opens the door and tapes up his CLOSED sign.

Speaking of *out*, Lyle needs to decide if he's going to contend with Silk face to face or go hide in his motel room and text her. She and her putz cameraman will lean on him about the stupid contract he signed but, Lyle figures, *sue me*. He swore to Georgie that he was done with this. He did go to court and rescind his motion, after all. But breaking with Silk and FEARcom is central to Lyle's oath.

Then the door opens and in strides Silk. Josh and Chad follow her with two new guys. She looks incredible.

Devil's food.

~~~~~~

66. Those Lips

As Silk's video crew gets busy, Lyle remains by Rooney's bar, concealing the fact that he's now half in the bag. His mission is to honor his oath to Georgie and extricate himself from his damn TV interview commitment and Silk's clutches. But Silk's clutches somehow seem even more alluring now that she has good reason to hate him.

He swills some scotch and considers the wording of his resignation as Chad sets up her portable makeup table with lighted mirror. Josh interacts with some new guys from the satellite trailer. They have additional TV gear. Now Chad departs on an errand.

Let's see. How's "I quit"? Maybe "I cannot continue in light of recent tragic events." Or, "My daughter is being harassed by her fellow cops." How about "Sue me." No, no...

Silk sits and gets to work on her face, more essential than acknowledging Lyle. It's not the scotch, Lyle realizes, this girl really does look better every day—and more ready for prime time. For this shoot, Silk again wears a tight black skirt and heels but a different black leather jacket, cut like a blazer. A white doily protects her lapels from makeup. She meets Lyle's gaze through her mirror and finally gives him a curt nod. Lyle got her dagger-eyes this morning outside court, but now there's no overt sign of displeasure. Even though acting on his own and scuttling his "save Old Vic" motion subverts Silk's ownership of the story. She needs him on camera now to reassert her ownership. If he quits now...

Lyle watches her lean closer to her mirror, perfecting the cat-eye effect on her upper lids with eyeliner. Then her eyelash curler creates an upswept effect. Then she separates each eyelash individually with a mascara brush. Then she pouts as she applies a plum-colored lip gloss. Lyle wants to bite those lips. But it's time to roll over to her and lower the boom. Right in the presence of that shit Josh and these strange new men. How will she react? Screech? Rooney at least will understand. They'll toast Lyle's bold rebelliousness later.

Speaking mostly in incomprehensible acronyms, the crew sets up gear and runs cables. Silk discards the doily, takes her seat in the interview area and opens her iPad. Crossing her legs, her calf pops. Still parked by the bar with his rocks glass, Lyle memorizes her legs' smooth contours. This is the last time he'll see them. It's unnerving how not-pissed-off Silk seems. She doesn't get mad, he muses, she gets even. With a cat-who-ate-the-canary curl of her lip, Silk slides something from her briefcase.

She draws a bead on Lyle. "Look what *I* found..." she says in a sultry singsong.

Silk holds up a photo of Lyle at age 40. An image he claimed did not exist. He's shown outside the courthouse wearing his lawyer power suit, talking to reporters. Clean shaven and healthy looking, his hair thick and dark, he's standing tall.

Lyle rolls into the set area. It's now or never. "Ugh. Where'd you get that?"

"What do you mean, 'ugh'? A handsome young lawyer like this would be quite a catch." This comment sends Lyle to half-drunk-fantasy heaven but Silk switches gears. "The librarian lent it to me. Nice old lady. She knows you."

"Not that well..." His fantasy evaporates. Sure she does. Lyle defeated Sheila's husband in a lawsuit years ago. He later died without life insurance. Sheila now has to work well beyond retirement age.

Silk announces that Gregg, her FEARcom boss, is driving down from Connecticut via the ferry to oversee the live shoot. And meet Lyle. This prospect creates a knot in his stomach as he envisions a pushy young media executive who surely has designs on and influence over Silk. But he will have quit before this new joker shows up.

Then Silk describes Flo's replacement. Iko—just *Iko*—is a Haitian woman taking the train out from Brooklyn. Chad is picking her up at the Montauk station.

Lyle rolls closer to Silk. She is bathed in Josh's glowing light.

"Silk, this new woman from Haiti...what does she know about this case? It's pretty involved."

Silk taps away at her iPhone. "Iko will be up to speed."

"What about Flo? Are you doing anything to...recognize her?"

"Flo? Of course I am." She looks up. "I'll lead with a commemoration. Josh has cut a montage of her work with you and footage of the shrine in front of your house. He's also putting together a longer piece, which I will host. Fox News, the Travel Channel, E! and *Entertainment Tonight* are bidding. You'll appear in that, too. As will our photo of young Lyle. But first the live shoot." Back to her iPhone, she adds, "Live, we'll clean up the mess you made in court this morning."

Lyle is stunned by how professional and unemotional Silk sounds in the face of her colleague's death. It's actually despicable. Also, Lyle admits, it's coldly sexy. And why would the Travel Channel want pictures of a dead lady's shrine, anyway?

"The show must go on," he says, trying to be sardonic, and takes a swig.

"Exactly," Silk says, noting what Lyle is drinking.

Now is the time. But Lyle feels jittery. He decides to first demonstrate how he has the upper hand in his grasp of the case. "You know, Silk, I hired people," he fibs—he's not paying Noah—"to research the history of Old Vic. They got nothing on the house itself, but learned that a previous house on the property was owned by a sea captain known for returning runaway slaves to the South for bounty. They'd capture freemen too. And the captain did some other terrible things..."

"We know." Her blasé response deflates Lyle. She continues texting. Finally she looks up. "We do research too. We are a television network, remember?" She adds condescendingly, "We got ours for free."

Noah Craig? Had to be. Lyle is steamed. Boiling. Enough of this. He grits his teeth and puts his chair in gear. Time to lower the boom. Then there's a gust of air as the barroom door opens. Lyle rotates and sees Chad hold the door for their guest from Brooklyn. What fresh hell is this, he wonders.

~~~~~~

67. Iko

Striding in, Iko sweeps past Lyle, sizes up Josh's set and zeros in on Silk. Lyle is struck by many impressions at once. Iko is very good looking, tall, strong-looking, not overweight. Probably north of 30, Lyle surmises, but Iko's age is tough to gauge, with her high cheekbones and smooth cocoa complexion. She moves in a graceful, self-assured way, poised and obviously not a shy person. Wearing a traditional Haitian head wrap and satiny dress, both a teal color, Iko looks like she stepped out of some lush Caribbean photo shoot. And that, Silk would say, makes for good television. This is Iko's big debut on a national stage and she seems ready for it. Lyle searches her black eyes; they're gorgeous, only lightly made-up. He examines her generous mouth. The way Iko's scarf is wrapped atop her head, she looks like a Caribbean Nefertiti. The word *haughty* comes to his mind again as he flashes on engaging in various consensual acts.

Iko bears a dazzling smile as Silk rises to greet her.

Iko's smile fades to a pout as she turns to face Lyle Hall. His mind floods with free-associating fantasies of a married life with Iko. The exotic music, food and relatives. Voodoo. Arduous erotic demands. Culture clash. The utter failure of it. He feels Iko's deep black eyes take his measure. He senses her distrust. Can she read his mind?

"Dis de man?" Iko says to Silk, who is texting. Lyle reflexively extends his hand. Iko considers it. Her eyes pierce his own. They seem to penetrate his soul. He feels like a small boy helpless in the thrall of some ancient spiritual power.

Then the feeling vanishes and the mood shifts.

"Well dis de only wheelchair so you must be LyleHall!" A throaty laugh bursts out as Iko takes his hand. Maybe she doesn't watch much TV.

She searches his eyes again. "LyleHall. LyleHall. Yes...a lot goin' on in dere."

"If you only knew." Lyle feels a sudden shock—maybe she does know.

Wanting to warm him up, Silk says, "Lyle, let's huddle briefly and go over where your story is now. Iko will join in and we'll...*talk*. Okay with that?"

Lyle is not okay with that. He's done with all that. He swore to Georgie. Went to court. Ended it all. He's also drunk, sleep deprived and fighting off depression. And full of lobster salad. But when he looks at the two women together, fantasy overwhelms him: a strenuous *ménage a trois* in a Caribbean seaside hut. That's immediately squelched by a realistic premonition: Silk and Iko excoriating him on national TV soon if he's not on hand to defend himself.

"*Lyle...?*" Silk's condescending tone. Lyle thinks of facing Georgie. At least he accomplished one major task today. He can't be expected to do *everything*. An old saw occurs to him: *It's easier to ask for forgiveness than permission.*

Silk points her chin at Lyle's rocks glass and Chad approaches him, lifts the rocks glass, splashes its contents into a styro cup and nestles that in his cup holder. Silk nods at Lyle. "This needs to play in Peoria." Her new blazer is a bit more conservative, too.

She checks her phone. "Gregg will be late—missed his ferry."

Chad moves the makeup table away. Iko has no need for it.

Josh, busy with a camera, half-sings, "*A three-hour tour...*"

Iko seats herself in Flo's former seat. The set has a low coffee table stocked with bottled water and legal pads. Silk faces Iko and Lyle. Oddly, there's a fourth chair on set.

"Lyle," Silk says, "Iko is very interested in your story. We've provided her with relevant background." She darkens. "And your going rogue in court today. *Bad man.*"

Shit. Lyle feels like he's rolled into quicksand. He feels triangulated.

Iko's eyes remind him of Diana Ross's. Dark and intelligent. Framed by dramatic eyebrows. They fall on Lyle's styro cup.

"You feelin' de pressure, huh, LyleHall?" She nods knowingly.

Lyle likes the lilt of Iko's throaty patois, her deep round vowels. He reaches for his scotch and feels the styro cup. Chad clipping a mic to his collar barely registers.

"This is all new to me," Lyle says, taking a sip. "I never believed in ghosts. Or the spirit world. But after the past week...and after last night...it had to end."

"You became a believer," Iko flashes a brilliant smile. Then her lips relax to a position that allows just a glint of white teeth. Lyle wants her to bite him. And she will.

"Well, there were two tragic deaths last night. I knew both people and feel terribly responsible for them. It would never have happened if I'd just left it all alone."

"You feel guilty for de lady's death."

Lyle feels seduced by Iko's voice. Exotic, knowing. "I do. And now I'm getting calls from Flo's family. I can't use my phone. My voice mailbox is always full."

"Dat's a problem, huh...a friend dies and your voicemail is full."

"That came out wrong, Iko."

"Of course it did." She regards Lyle. "When did you first start to feel contact with de spirit world?"

"Oh, a little over the summer maybe. More in September. A lot more this month."

"All dat contact came after your car accident?"

"About ten months after. I started to hear unusual sounds..."

"Why you tryin' to contact de dead?"

"I wasn't *trying* to."

"Den dey's tryin' to contact *you*, man. The question is *why?* You had a near-death experience when you crash your car?"

"Yes. They first thought I was dead when they got to the scene. Then, apparently, the EMTs hesitated to give me CPR because my jaw and ribs were broken. But I don't remember seeing a white light or my life pass before my eyes."

Iko nods at Lyle's styro cup of scotch. "Maybe 'cause of de alcohol."

"I wasn't drinking, but everyone assumes I was."

"Someone whose car takes an old lady's life hadda be doin' somethin' wrong."

Suddenly Lyle sees Josh circling with his camera. The bastard's been taping their awkward exchange. *Shit.* The interview Lyle swore he wouldn't do is in progress!

Silk leans forward. "Iko, Lyle's a changed man after his near-death experience."

Iko glances again at Lyle's cup. "Different man, same alcohol. LyleHall, I want to know why de spirit world would contact you after you killed dat lady with your car."

Josh swings toward Silk. "Don't budge!" she says to the lens. "We'll be right back with more 'Ghost Hampton'!" And the segment ends.

Steaming, Lyle knows he's been had. *Killed dat lady* indeed. Silk makes only the briefest eye contact with her prey as she goes over technical stuff with Josh. Lyle's been suckered into defending himself on national TV, the Internet, the world. But he can talk his way out of whatever these two floozies have cooked up. He's Lyle Hall, after all, and they're not. Georgie will totally understand he was hoodwinked. He can't just storm out. This is his chance to redeem himself—and he's being handed a national stage.

~~~~~~

68. Good Television

During their break, Josh tapes Silk delivering an intro: some convincing, heartfelt words venerating Flo Hendricks. Iko consults her iPad, ignoring Lyle. He rolls over to Rooney's bar, like a boxer after the bell, and accepts a fresh pour in his cup. Sipping, he watches Josh caress Silk with his camera. It makes him even more uneasy. But this is an opportunity. Restore honor to the Hall name. Make Georgie proud. Lemonade from lemons.

Now Josh brusquely summonses Lyle back to the set but he stays put. Then Silk beckons him. Look at her. Her new blazer is in fact sexier—thank you, Peoria. Lyle realizes he's got a devil on both shoulders. He finally rolls over.

Chad has that fourth chair set up. Mystery guest? Cables run through a window out to the big satellite truck devoted to switching video feeds, mixing audio and placing graphics onscreen for live broadcast. The technical director and an audio guy are working in the truck and talking to the crew inside over headsets. From there, the live feed goes to the satellite dish on the trailer and to the world.

One of the new techies calls for quiet. He's a heavyset guy wearing a T-shirt from FOX News that reads "On the Record with Greta Van Susteren." The Fox anchor in New York delivers his intro for the live "Ghost Hampton" feed. The techie says, "Five...four...three..." His fingers count down the rest silently and he points to Silk.

Shit. Live, national TV. Lyle thinks he's going to vomit on it.

Silk starts anew with a recap of last night's "tragic events." She says tonight's coverage is devoted to their late colleague, Flo Hendricks. Then she promotes a new "Ghost Hampton" special. Then Josh pulls back to a two-shot including Iko. Silk describes Iko and her career—she is a "seer" and a "Haitian Vodou healer." *Vodou*, not voodoo. Iko lives in a Haitian community in

334

Brooklyn and sends money home to family in Haiti who survived the recent devastating earthquakes. She sounds like a Haitian Mother Teresa.

Then Silk introduces Lyle with a brisk rundown of his recent tribulations—Old Vic, apparitions of a young girl, his motion to buy the house from the Township, campers setting up a tent city, intense media coverage, two tragic deaths, a tumultuous court appearance, Old Sideburns and his Tiananmen Square stunt. She then describes vividly the paranormal crisis in the barn last night, her words following what viewers at home see: Josh's chaotic video montage of that drama, including the "last video" footage of Flo. Then Silk pauses. Josh's camera closes in. Silk gravely details the loss of life at Lyle Hall's house—especially that of Flo Hendricks. FEARcom's own clairvoyant died of heart failure in Lyle's arms. The monitor resolves to a composite still of Flo and her poignant shrine in the rain.

Silk asks Lyle to describe Flo's shocking death. Josh's lens swings his way. This is it. It's one thing being filmed unwittingly. This is live TV. Georgie will freak.

But Lyle does a pretty good job of holding it together as he delicately describes Flo's last moments. He speaks of poor Glen Stanley and the rabid possum on his porch. He mentions Flo's collapse to a kneeling position, how he embraced her as she breathed her last. He omits her strange last words. Otherwise, he gives them what they want.

"Lyle," Silk says, "how close were you and Flo Hendricks?"

Close? Lyle shifts in his chair. He flashes on how priests must be watching.

"Well, it was a short time, but we got to know each other as friends. I liked Flo and I respected her approach to the, uh, unapproachable."

"You mean the supernatural."

"I guess. You see, I don't believe in ghosts..."

Silk and Iko make quizzical expressions.

"...That is, I never did before. But now I..."

"Now you're a *believer*," Silk says in a knowing way.

Lyle winces. "Well not like some people. But I can see how there's something else out there. Beyond our daily lives."

"What do you suppose that is, Lyle?"

Lyle thinks. "I imagine it's...energy. Or a memory of energy left behind that has nowhere to go."

"Perhaps as good an answer as any." Silk addresses Iko. "Iko, how do you define energy on the supernatural plane?"

Josh focuses on Iko. She is ready.

"It is energy, ma'am. Dat's a fact. If it can move things...and move people to do things...den it is energy. De question is *what kind?*"

"What kind of energy have you encountered in your dealings with the supernatural?"

Iko forms a world-weary smile. "Oh, both kinds, ma'am! Good and evil energy. De question is why does dis bad energy stay in a certain place, eh? Good energy goes someplace else. It does not stay with de bad."

Iko glances at Lyle. "It's de bad energy, de evil, dat lingers. It *wants* us."

Silk says, "Iko, what about Jewel, the apparition that appeared to Lyle? Surely a young girl can't be *evil.*"

"I've not met dis girl yet, you see? But I know a lady is dead now. And a man." Iko looks at Lyle again. "And dat tells me something."

Lyle's scotch and lobster salad conjure nausea. Silk continues with Iko.

"You say good and bad entities do not occupy the same location?"

"If de good is strong, it will drive out de bad. If de *bad* is stronger..." The set seems eerily quiet as Iko lowers her voice. "Evil, like anything else, wants to grow. To *spread.* Maybe de evil dat took dat lady was waiting in LyleHall's house."

"Waiting?" Silk shifts her weight and shows great interest. "How long?"

Lyle's spirits sink further as Iko laughs bitterly. "Ha! Evil has no clock! No calendar! Watches and clocks—all invented by mankind. Evil is in no hurry, ma'am. It stays where it's comfortable and waits for..." she glances again at Lyle who is now visibly uncomfortable. "...de next opportunity."

"But this Jewel apparition," Silk says. "Apparently she was just a girl."

Iko considers Lyle's story of Jewel for a moment. "Hmmm. Yes. Maybe dat girl is not good and not bad. A captive in dat house. Maybe a *lure*. You ever see a deep sea fish? Way down deep? Dey all teeth! And dey have a little light, like a lantern, attached to de nose. When de innocent dumb fish swims up to de light, de teeth are dere waiting."

Josh moves his camera in on Silk. "Iko, are you saying it's possible Lyle was lured to the old house, one about to be demolished, and the spirit wanted to attach itself? To spread outward into the community?"

"Dat could explain something, ma'am. It wanted to move on to a place with more..." She smiles wickedly "... *potential*."

Lyle shifts uneasily in his chair. Then the scotch in him blurts something out.

"You're saying an evil spirit saw me coming and decided to get its hooks in me?"

Iko smiles. "Well *some-ting* got its hooks in you, man!"

Silk asks, "Iko, if evil can actually have a plan, where does that come from?"

"Originally? Look at Genesis, ma'am. Evil was waiting in de Garden for de first man and first woman, you know. Today, at home in Haiti, I have seen Evil—*capital E!*—hard at work, ma'am."

"What is it about Haiti's many troubles, Iko?"

"Oh, ma'am. When you look at Haitians you look at de descendants of slaves, you know. Slavery is pure Evil. Inhuman. Man subjugating man. Possessing him. Making de slaves work until dey die. You know de Haitian slaves, working sugarcane plantations two-hundred years ago, were not allowed to have families? No children!"

"Why was that?"

"Business! It was cheaper to bring in new slaves to work de plantations when tired old slaves die off—cheaper dan feeding families of slave mothers and children."

Silk is in primetime network mode. She leans into her conversation with Iko and Lyle's exhausted mind focuses intently on Silk; watches her full lips say his name. Why did she say his name? His eyes drift lower to Silk's leather blazer. It forms a "Y" gently pinching tender cleavage. Lyle imagines what it's like in there. He wishes she possessed him. He's not well. Must be love. Lovesick. Or sick love.

In a drunken reverie, Lyle sees himself as some helpless newborn marsupial. Silk kindly allows Lyle-the-marsupial to squirm inside her leather jacket and nestle deep down, snuggling in the soft warmth of her heavenly body. Yeah, sick. Surreal. But better than his reality. If Silk were to see the Lyle of today undressed, she'd scream and run from the room.

"Today," Iko says, "we got de poorest country in de Western World. When disaster strikes, like recently de earthquakes, it makes life unimaginably worse. And again Evil is waiting for de poor people who survived."

"And surely some good," Silk says.

"To be sure. I send money home. But Evil makes de headlines." Iko looks to Lyle who is sipping from his cup. "Makes headlines and attracts crowds, no?"

Josh turns his camera on Lyle, who grows agitated.

"Excuse me? Are you trying to make a case that *I am evil*? That I have something in common with slavery and inhumanity?"

Silk tries to calm Lyle. "Lyle, no. We're on your side. We want to get to the root of this Old Vic mystery—and the nature of Evil."

He looks into Silk's alluring eyes and settles down. He wants to be played by her.

"Lyle, you researched the owner of the house that stood on the property before Old Vic was constructed?"

"Yes," Lyle says, his voice quavering slightly. "There are some records. Some stories. A ship captain lived at that address about two hundred years ago."

"Go on."

"Well he was apparently known for rounding up runaway slaves and returning them...to South Carolina."

Iko nods to Silk. "Dere you are! Dat Evil waiting for someone new to come along." She smiles. "Evil has all de time in de world."

Hearing these words, Lyle flashes on Noah's description of Capt. Milford's slave atrocity. Setting his ship ablaze with human captives aboard. His own home catching fire during an argument with his wife. Hanging himself in the barn. Lyle won't be sharing that with cameras rolling.

Silk says, "Later, in the 1880s, when Old Vic was built, a man turned the place into a house of prostitution."

"Another form of slavery," Iko says, turning toward Lyle. "Men subjugate women. Even young girls. Even today."

Lyle ignores Iko and tries to put Silk on the defensive.

"I'll say it *again*, Silk. I am not the bad actor in this case. If anyone was, it was a long time ago..."

Silk leans toward Lyle. But he does not pick up a sexy vibe this time. Instead it's one of pity. And pity infuriates him.

"Lyle, you've shared privately that you experienced feelings when you saw this girl Jewel late at night at Old Vic." Silk, says, attempting her best Barbara Walters. "Feelings...sensations...in your paralyzed lower body."

Lyle quickly, though drunkenly, makes the connection. He told someone about phantom "sensations." *Flo!* Flo told Silk. Now Silk's telling the world.

Iko chimes in. "Dere's your *lure*."

"Damn it, Silk! I described in confidence an extrasensory experience. A paranormal event! It's not part of my real life. And not for public display!"

"Lyle, it's out in public now. Clear the air. Did you have feelings for this girl?"

"She is only twelve years old, Silk! And how could I have *feelings* for a ghost?"

"Feelings," Iko smiles, "cannot be controlled. Do you know other young girls?"

Rage, drunken rage, builds to a volcanic level that Lyle again directs at Silk.

"Are you people saying I'm *attracted to adolescent girls?*" Lyle's face goes red. "I wanted to somehow help a girl who died a long time ago. That doesn't mean I have feelings for *young girls! Huge difference!*"

"Lyle," Silk purrs, "it's not us saying that. We are trying to address the issue."

Lyle loses it.

"The issue? The *issue??* The *real issue* is..." Lyle trails off. Suddenly he cannot get a grip on any issues. All he knows is these people are not his friends. Never were.

"Damn it, Silk! I'm a *good man!* And I'll sue anyone who tries to defame my good name!" Lyle is hit with the old policemen's truism: a suspect who protests his innocence too loudly is not. His name isn't all that *good* either, but he's still furious.

"That's your right, Lyle. We are just here openly discussing issues of the day."

Iko jumps in. "You know what, LyleHall? I say a *good man*—even a half-a-man—would go to dat place and face whatever spirit is waiting dere. *Face it* once and for all! A bad spirit knows when it's met its match and it will leave. And dat's true."

Suddenly Lyle explodes—not at Iko, at Silk.

"I wanted to buy that house for good reasons! For *good,* damn it! You and your new friend here have no right comparing me to some murdering slave owner! Or some child-whoremonger! Or *half a man!* No right whatsoever! You brought this loony hoodoo woman in to make a case against a retired paraplegic! On television no less!"

Silk leans toward Lyle, trying to calm him. "Lyle, please..."

"Please *nothin'!*" Lyle shouts. "*HALF* a man??"

340

He indignantly throws his chair into reverse and backs away from the table.

Silk rises, cries "Lyle!" and nods to Josh. The interview has lurched into Jerry Springer territory.

Lyle rolls toward the barroom door, Josh follows him with his camera. Lyle's microphone is still live.

"Fuck this shit! Know what? I know a girl! *My daughter! Okay? Age thirty!*"

Rooney doesn't know whether to watch his TV screen or the real Lyle. He tries both and realizes that whatever Lyle does appears on his TV about seven seconds later. As Lyle bursts outside, Josh on his tail, Rooney turns up the TV to hear.

Now in molten rage, Lyle rolls along the sidewalk to his room, cursing vehemently. Josh follows with his camera. Rooney absorbs the action on his TV, noting how swear words are being bleeped out left and right. As Lyle reaches his room, he sees a man approaching Rooney's bar. A dumpy man in a rumpled suit. Carrying a bright blue fabric rolled up like a tube. The color of the Lyle Hall T-shirts.

"And fuck you too, *Mose!!*"

Opening the door to his room, Lyle remembers his remote mic, rips it off and flings it at Josh who's right there, capturing Lyle at his worst—his newest worst. Josh actually catches the mic with his free hand, preserving it for future use.

Inside the TV remote truck, the technical director at his console opts for a split screen: Mose joining Silk and Iko on set as Lyle rants in his doorway. The TD gets word from the network and shares it with the production crew—they go direct to commercial.

Silk now has two minutes to get it together. She quickly introduces Mose Allen to Iko. With a smirk, Mose unfurls a blue T-shirt.

"These are fifteen dollars; but this one's for you, Silk. Makes a good nightie."

Chad takes the T-shirt and clips a remote mic on Mose's lapel. Mose takes his seat—the extra chair. Chad drapes the blue

T-shirt on a barstool so Josh can shoot it. Cheaply made, it features a high-contrast silkscreen of Mose's awful photo of Lyle Hall. Centered beneath it, a slogan.

Lyle is FINE

Josh returns with his camera and positions himself before the three subjects.

Thirty seconds to live air.

~~~~~~

69. To Heat and Serve

During her ongoing overnight assignment, Georgie has been grabbing a nap in the afternoon. Then running personal errands. An hour at the Southampton Gym on Sunrise Highway. Pick up her dry cleaning. Pick up some dinner. Sometimes she'd also get meals for Lyle from Citarella, but not this time. Maybe never again, after the tragedies and betrayals he's involved himself in.

Georgie's using her unmarked Southampton Police cruiser prior to her shift. This way she won't have to go back to the stationhouse and deal with Swanson or whatever bullshit prank may be waiting for her. The desk sergeant doesn't mind checking the car out for long periods; it gives him a feeling of abetting and conspiring with the young blond detective. With all the shit her father's gotten himself into and, worst of all, two deaths at his house, her girlhood home, she has no time for Swan Song. And Frank's Internal Affairs friend snooping around the stationhouse tonight should scare the shit out of the putz.

Back at her condo, she lugs her purchases into the kitchen and slots the prepared meals into freezer shelves. Georgie's heat-and-serve dinners remind her of a scene from *Bullitt*, the 1968 flick with Steve McQueen. In it, the San Francisco detective patronizes his local grocer, hitting the frozen food case for a week's worth of TV dinners. Georgie saw the film as a teenager. Her dad made her watch it with him one night. He dozed off while she fell secretly in love with Steve McQueen. She was jealous of Jacqueline Bisset and yearned to cook dinner for the unfulfilled detective. She never forgot how he didn't read the labels on the frozen dinners—just stacked them up and paid for them. Didn't waste time. She also fell in love with the idea of being a detective.

Heat up one meal—spinach lasagna—in the oven while taking a shower. Georgie had worn shorts, sneakers, T-shirt and a sweatshirt to the gym and on her errands, her hair in a ponytail.

While the shower heats up, she slips out of her sweaty things and experiences her usual vision when she's at her most vulnerable—how many suspense movies have some perv attack the young woman when she's home alone, bathing? And how many of those women survive? Georgie routinely places her service revolver on the toilet top next to the shower.

The TV is on in her kitchen. Georgie's shower saves her from seeing Lyle Hall appear in a nationally televised toxic interview with that cheap tart TV reporter. Tonight's would be the second interview. The one Lyle swore he would not do. The one going wildly viral now as the world devours it on YouTube.

Toweling off, Georgie's cell rings. It's Swanson. Georgie feels a need to take the call—but to first put on her terry robe.

"Sergeant."

"Detective Hall?"

"What."

"Did you see it?"

"See what."

"Then you didn't see it. Your dad? On TV? With that Catwoman reporter?"

Georgie can envision what Swanson is talking about. Lyle broke his oath to her. A wave of rage wells up in her heart but she remains calm while on the phone with this guy.

"Sergeant, the reason for this call is?"

"Yeah. Well, you know, you should know if you don't already know, right?"

Georgie sighs audibly. "Know *what*."

"Well he, you know, cursed a lot. On TV. He actually wheeled off the set and left the interview. Live on TV, cursing. It was really something. People are talking."

Great, Georgie thinks. *Just great*. That means Queeley.

Swanson continues, "It was kinda cool. A camera follows him outside and he curses out the cameraman too. They bleeped out the curse words on TV but I could tell what he was saying."

"Good for you, Sergeant." Georgie is fuming over this new betrayal but unwilling to give Swanson any satisfaction.

"So, I thought you should know, you know?" Swanson pauses. "And Chief Queeley? You know he really wants all this haunted house stuff to stop. Really wanted you to talk to your dad about it, you know?"

"I'm surprised that you know, Sergeant."

"Yeah, well, I heard from Chief. Not too happy, you know. Anyway, thought I'd let you know."

Georgie wants to scream at this guy that he's a brain-damaged useless pus bag but now is not the time. Now she needs to scream at her father. She disconnects with Swanson and goes to the kitchen to retrieve her lasagna from the oven. It's burnt. Fuck it.

News12 is on, already playing an excerpt of her dad's "interview." A text crawl runs below it:

...BRIDGEHAMPTON HAUNTED HOUSE LAWYER ABRUPTLY EXITS INTERVIEW WITH PROFANITY LADEN DIATRIBE...

Georgie mutters some profanity herself and heads to the bedroom to dress for the night's work. Looking at her cell again, she notes a call came in while she was in the shower. Big Frank.

Georgie is too upset to call Frank back. She speed-dials her father while she's got a head of steam. It rings.

"Georgie?" To her shock, he actually picks up.

Without preamble, Georgie lays into her father. She delivers her own diatribe, building in stone-cold intensity and emotion with each thrust.

"What the fuck, Dad? What. The. *FUCK!!*"

"Georgie, I—"

"*You?* You *suck* as a person and as a father. Shuddup and listen to me for once. You gave me *your word*, Dad! Last night, remember? Or were you too drunk? In case I was wondering what your word might be worth, now we know. It's worth shit! You don't grasp the damage you've been causing with your stupid 'haunted house' charade? People are dying. *Dying!* At the house I grew up in! And your drunken foolishness on TV, mooning over that Goth-slut who's younger than me...younger

345

than ME, Dad! And when things get rough, you can only be trusted to do what *you* want to do. What *you* want. I know your history. I lived it. I was a teenager when Mom got cancer and you acted like some holy fucking hero. But I knew you were planning ahead. While Mom had a nurse in our house, you actually had a package delivered from 'Naughty Nurse Costumes'! How do you think that affected your *teenage daughter!!* And look how that turned out! I thank God I went off to college before that woman moved into the house *I grew up in!* I lost my mother, Dad! She was all I had! I had *one* parent! You were no help. Ever. You're better off drunk, aren't you? With your drunk friends and your bartenders and all that never-grow-up bullshit! Well FUCK YOU! You understand me? Once more, since you're drunk—*fuck you, Lyle Hall.*"

Lyle finally interjects. His voice is drained of any strength or resolve, unrecognizable as the onetime heavyweight lawyer. "Georgie...Georgie..." He stammers. "Please. I need you to be careful. I'm serious. *More careful. Please. More...*"

Georgie takes dead aim. As if her words were fists, each word meeting Lyle's face with frozen rage.

"There is no *more*. No more '*Dad.*' No more *you*. That's it. NO. MORE."

She slams down her phone. Even though it's a cell phone. That felt good. And there was nothing to lose, really. She never had Lyle Hall to lose anyway.

Sitting in his Memory Motel room, Lyle could not hear his daughter hang up. Instead, there's a sudden startling boom. The jerk-next-door's thrash-metal racket explodes through the wall again. Over the noise Lyle makes a feeble plea into his cell phone.

"Georgie! I mean it. I'm terrified something's going to happen to you! Soon!"

Then he sees he's been cut off.

~~~~~~

Tonight, Georgie Hall once again drives her white cruiser to
South Fork Transportation Services in Hampton Bays. She wears
her freshly cleaned gray pants suit, the jacket concealing her
holster. She's had no dinner, but isn't hungry. She's got a 7-11
coffee and a granola bar. She's forgotten about the inflated ghost
condom shriveled up on the backseat. And she's going to forget
her "father." What a relief it is. Just work.

The livery cab service is located about a quarter-mile north of
the Hampton Bays train station, situated in a sparse forest of
scrub pines on a deserted stretch of Squiretown Road. The place
has been a cab business as long as there have been cabs. The
structure itself is low, basically a row of three garage bays with a
shabby attached office. A gravel parking lot in the back
accommodates various livery cars and employee vehicles. The
nicer limos are housed in the garage bays. Off to the right stands
a beat up old radio tower, long out of use. Two terra cotta
planters displaying very dead plants flank the office door. A
vintage gasoline pump, rusted solid, stands out front.

Over the past few nights, Georgie's had time to study the old
garage from her vantage point across the road. In a way the depot
reminded her of early days—back home in Bridgehampton, when
she had parents. When life seemed innocent, simple, good.
Dunbar Automotive, the garage around the corner, had an old-
style gas pump twenty-five years ago. It worked. Before a road
trip, Mom would take her down the block to the Candy Kitchen
soda fountain while Dad got gas. One October Saturday they
stopped at a roadside stand for grilled corn-on-the cob and cider
doughnuts. Mom was so sweet to her.

These days Georgie's job is to note who comes and goes
from the dispatch office and when. Her main person of interest is
codenamed "Escobar," a young guy who apparently took over
after Henrique Pena, a slime ball known as "Sabado,"
disappeared a few years ago. Pena is suspected of pimping,
pandering, drug dealing, human trafficking and immigration
fraud. His replacement is probably no bargain either.

Georgie is determined to focus intently on this, her first
assignment of any note, no matter how boring it gets. She's put

the harassment bullshit at the stationhouse out of her mind. She's put Lyle Hall, that drunken old fool in the wheelchair, out of her mind. It's the only way to be a professional.

Tonight, as she pulls to a stop in her usual position across from the garage office, something strange startles her. It flaps against her windshield—weird, alive—maybe a bat? Hard to see, Georgie activates her wipers and the ugly thing gets caught up on a wiper arm which drags it back and forth. Oddly, the wiper seems to yank on a sprig from an overhead branch as it swipes. Georgie kills the motor and the wipers, leaving on the lights. Spooked, she shines her flashlight on the thing from behind her steering wheel. It's trapped against the windshield. It's not alive. It's manmade. A stuffed sock. No, a rough burlap figure shaped like a person. Buttons for eyes. It's a *doll*.

Looking closely, she sees the doll has fishing line around its neck. Her flashlight beam follows the line upward. It's strung from a branch directly above where she parks. Georgie focuses on the doll's head. There is stitching where its mouth should be as if it were sewn shut.

It can't stay there tangled in her windshield wiper but a doll cannot cause her to abandon her post. This means getting out of the car and turning her back to the garage while she disentangles the fishing line. Which makes her vulnerable. Which could be someone's plan. So? Call for backup because of a doll?

Georgie steps out of her car and plays her flashlight across the facade of the limo office. South Fork Transportation Services. Right. It's dark inside, except for the flickering glow of a TV. Georgie can tell when she's being watched. She opens her dinky keychain penknife and reaches across her windshield to free the doll. Could be evidence. Something sharp protruding from the doll pricks her finger. "Shit!" She yelps and withdraws, instinctively sticking her finger in her mouth.

Now a second flashlight beam moves across Georgie and her white cruiser.

"Can I help you?" The accent is vaguely Latino. She hears crunchy footsteps. Still holding her penknife, Georgie turns and shines her light on a man.

"Is there a problem, Miss?" Berto, pumping with a mixture of adrenaline, cocaine and Patron tequila, is fairly jumping out of his skin but can hide his nerves for now.

"Southampton Police." Georgie pockets her keychain and, taking out her badge holder, sees the man flinch. The man the cops call "Escobar" shines his light on her badge while she holds her flashlight on him. He's wearing a black suit and he's sweating.

She nods at the garage. "Do you work here?"

"Yes..." He's a little hesitant. "I'm the manager," he adds as Georgie examines his face and notes the nervous signs of cocaine use. "Is there a problem?"

"Possibly. Reported criminal activity in the area. I'm parked here in case there's a call or any trouble." She looks at Escobar intently. "Have you seen or heard of any suspicious behavior around here recently?"

Berto turns on the charm. He plays his light on the car windshield and the doll. "Oh, like that?" he chuckles. "Kids! Halloween is coming."

"Kids, huh? They're capable of anything these days."

Berto steps toward the car for a better look. "What the heck *is* that?"

It's obviously a doll and Georgie doesn't answer. Berto looks back at her. Tall. If she dressed sexy and did something with her hair she'd look pretty good. A *gringa* could make him some good money. He smiles. "An old doll. Let me cut it free for you."

Berto already has an expensive-looking knife in his right hand, blade exposed. It's gold. Georgie tenses; she doesn't respond. Instead she trains her light on the doll and watches him deftly cut away the tangled line with fidgety motions. As he cuts, the branch wags overhead. Closing his knife with jittery hands, it disappears silently into a jacket pocket. He offers the burlap doll to the cop, holding it by the foot.

Georgie takes it by the other foot and tosses it through her open window onto the backseat. Evidence. Maybe. As if they could snag prints from burlap.

"Thanks." She turns and smiles. "Oh. I didn't get your name..."

Berto hesitates. "Oh, yes. Humberto. Pena. My uncle owns this business."

"Oh, yes. Henrique Pena. Where is he now?"

Berto steels himself. Chantale had fake ID made for him. He is Sabado's nephew if anybody asks. "Uh, yeah, my uncle went back to Colombia to visit family and left me in charge here. For a while."

"Oh. How's it going?"

Berto fights his cocaine fidgets and attempts his disarming smile. "A little slow once the summer ends. A little slow." He adds, "But I'm catching up on paperwork."

Georgie takes in this Humberto Pena. About five-foot-eight, thick black hair, goatee. Not bad looking. Late twenties. Black suit looks tailored, nice pointy shoes. Glint of a gold necklace under his open collar. The outfit's too nice for a limo garage.

"Going someplace tonight?"

He shrugs. "Well, I'm supposed to take my wife out to dinner, but had to work."

"Paperwork will get you every time." Georgie notes he wears no wedding ring. She opens her car door without turning her back on him. "Please keep an eye out for us, will you, Mister Pena? Anything suspicious." She takes her card from a pocket and offers it to Berto. "Please give me a call if you see or hear anything unusual."

This strikes Berto as weird, even sexy. He takes the card and their fingertips touch. He sees the back of the card has absorbed a droplet of Georgie's blood.

"Will do, uh, uh..."

"Detective Hall." She slides into her seat. "I'll be here a few hours," she adds casually, as if that should be a comfort to this guy.

Looking down into Georgie's cruiser, Berto, high as he is, is rocked by a bizarre sight. There, right there next to the doll on the backseat, lays an obscene-looking, white...*condom!* It's stretched-out, wrinkly. So it's *used!* And it has a *face* drawn on the end! Incredible! Maybe he should try to hire her.

Georgie notes his weird demeanor, his eyes wide and jaw working, during this awkward pause. Her diagnosis is he's high or psychotic. Or both.

"Good luck with that paperwork."

Berto's phone rings in his pocket. He generates a fake smile for the policewoman. "That's my girl!" He waves to Georgie and turns back toward the garage.

Georgie briefly shines her flashlight on his back and notes the outline of a shoulder holster under his suit jacket. Things must be slow indeed. He disappears into an open garage bay, passing a parked limo. But no lights go on in the office, no indication of paperwork being done. Maybe he is leaving for a dinner date.

Typing notes into her iPad, Georgie sorts out this strange young man:

> "Humberto Pena" walks softly.
> Sweaty forehead on a cool night.
> Jittery hands, shifty eyes.
> Maybe 27.
> Nice looking, but not a nice man, overly slick.
> Hesitation in giving his name.
> Five-eight, but shoes have lifts, visible from behind.
> New Italian-style suit. Too well dressed for the job.
> Shoulder holster visible under jacket.
> Claims going out with wife, no wedding ring.
> Well spoken, light Latino accent.
> Has a golden switchblade knife. Handles it very deftly.
> Business is "slow" but he has to do paperwork.
> Lights are off in office.
> The crudely made doll. Is it evidence?
> And, again...that knife.

~~~~~

70. Bonus Tail Light

One cool new thing about Georgie's overnight shift is the infrared night-vision binoculars she's been issued. Powering them up, she notes that the battery is charged. Swan Song's been in her car.

She knows her new friend Humberto is somewhere inside the limo office. She knows he parks his SUV behind the garage. Each night she's observed two men, presumably his employees, coming and going, usually together. So far tonight actual livery traffic has been nonexistent. But now there's activity in an open garage bay—the one nearest the office. A remote makes one limo chirp. A dim light glows; Georgie realizes it comes from the open trunk of the limo. She peers through her binoculars.

It's Humberto's two men. The limo is facing out. Georgie sees the guy who opened its trunk, the bald one, get behind the wheel. Mister Clean. At the same time, Trini Lopez, with the pompadour, places a package about the size of a shoe box in the trunk and slams it shut. He takes the passenger seat. These two guys have made it a point to give her the stink eye the past few nights when they've driven past her parked car. Now the limo comes alive and lurches out of the garage, lights off, making straight for Georgie. She lowers her binoculars but does not flinch. Just before impact Mr. Clean swerves left and decelerates enough for her to momentarily make out a sneering Trini Lopez. He even pokes his tongue inside his cheek to simulate fellatio. The limo accelerates and fishtails on the road as its headlights come on. It heads north, doing just over the posted speed limit.

At least this oddly threatening encounter gave her a positive make on the two.

Then, a hundred yards up the road, Georgie sees the limo decelerate briefly at a stop sign. It's a gift. Driver-side brake light is out. She gets on her car radio.

"This is Observer at the taxi stand, copy?"

Georgie hears Sgt. Swanson's pathetic five-note whistle of "Georgie Girl" come over the radio. All the cops hear it.

Letting some annoyance sound in her voice, she says, "I know you're monitoring, Sergeant. This is Observer reporting movement, copy?" A couple of cops in squad cars respond.

"Go ahead, Observer," says one.

"Just had movement at taxi stand. One limo, black. Partial plate reads two-niner-two. Heading north toward Sunrise Highway. Mister Clean driving Trini Lopez, copy?"

"Copy that, Observer."

"Subjects observed placing box in trunk before leaving garage. Limo's driver-side break light is out."

"Copy that."

"Escobar is inside the depot office," Georgie radios. "Will report any activity."

She signs off as the various cruisers near Sunrise Highway in the Hampton Bays area head out in search of the limo, partial plate 292, with one break light out.

Georgie's cell phone rings. Swan Song.

"Detective Hall?"

"What, Swanson."

"Good dispatch." Georgie doesn't respond. "Now all they have to do is step on the brakes and we got em!" Swanson seems to find his comment amusing.

Resisting the urge to say, *What's this "we" shit?* she sighs, "I'm busy here."

"Are you at the whorehouse, Detective?"

"Swanson, you know what? If this is not official business you are out of line."

"Sorry, Detective, just asking if you're still at the location."

"I'm where I just said I was. It's a livery cab dispatch garage."

"Right." Georgie can almost hear Swanson thinking. "So we should monitor their radio dispatches."

"That's the plan, Sergeant. Once we get evidence and the prosecutor gets the judge to sign off."

"Meanwhile..."

"Meanwhile I'm busy, Sergeant, with police work. You should be, too."

"Yes ma'am."

Georgie hangs up and refocuses on the depot. She waits, hoping her radio comes to life once a squad car pulls over the two goons in the limo. They're likely speeding on Sunrise Highway; everybody speeds. But in which direction? She scans the depot's windows with her night-vision binoculars. He's definitely in there, there's the blue glow of a television, and she can make out intermittent motion. She reaches for the burlap doll and examines it through her infrared glasses. Weirdly primitive stitching, but it's not old. Somebody sewed this together recently and she thinks this Humberto creep knows who. Then the embedded needle pricks her finger again, drawing a bead of blood. She tosses the doll onto the backseat with the shriveled condom.

Her fingertip in her mouth, she gazes out at Berto's office. No radio reports. One thing about watching a building, Georgie thinks, the building can be watching you.

~~~~~~~

71. Mundo and Ruben

Mundo swings the limo onto Sunrise Highway heading west and Ruben pictures the box in the trunk sliding sideways.

He asks, "Where we taking the package?"

"Upper West Side. Guy's cool. Berto knows him."

"Is he a pro?"

"No, he wants to dabble. Berto's enabling him."

The two continue west. One police cruiser approaches Sunrise just after the limo has passed. This policeman and others are alert but the limo has a head start and it rarely stops to reveal its brake-light problem. Within minutes, Manorville Road provides a way north from Sunrise to the Long Island Expressway and a straight shot into New York City. As they motor west on the expressway, more law enforcement agencies are made aware of the limo, but the further west the car moves, the more black limos there are. Mundo holds their speed at 65 in a 55. Not too fast, not too slow.

Ruben wants to talk about the drop. "Okay. So we have only one transaction, but it's a big one. We need to count a lot of cash, and quickly."

"And we will. Again, this gringo's supposed to be cool."

"Where was I when Berto told you how cool he is?"

"Probably on one of your porn sites."

"You got a gun?"

Mundo frowns. "No. If anything happens I'd rather not be carrying."

"What about that macho bullshit Berto says about defending the business with our lives if we are real men?"

"It's not *my* business. And I don't need him deciding if I'm a man. If we get ripped off, I want to still be a man, not a corpse." Mundo glances at Ruben. "So what do you think's going on with Berto?"

"He's crazy. I think he got crazier quicker than Sabado did—much quicker—and he definitely scoops shit off the top. That's how he pays himself when it's slow. You saw the 'Andes'?"

"I've seen the mountain ranges. From a full baggie. You know how he's obsessed with the movie *Scarface*? His favorite movie, you know? Pacino?"

Ruben stares ahead. "I know. 'Say hello to my little friend.' Pacino had all the cocaine in the world but it did not end well for him."

"Berto is not so violent but, doing all that coke, he could end up like Rain Man."

"Who the fuck is rain man?"

"Dustin Hoffman."

Ruben tsks. "Too many gringo movies, my friend. Try Lou Diamond Phillips, Benicio Del Toro."

"Advice from an Erik Estrada fan."

Ruben looks at Mundo's profile. "Speaking of the Andes, you think Chantale knows he's doing all that blow?"

"She's got to. She's not stupid. You mention guns—you got a gun on you?"

"Under my seat. My 9mm *pistola*. *My* little friend." Ruben stares ahead at the Long Island Expressway. "So what do you think of Chantale?"

Mundo thinks about this. He chooses his words carefully. "I think she is a lot of woman." He glances at Ruben. "Makes me wonder if she's got a lot of man."

Ruben smirks. "Sometimes I think, if any woman is tired of bullshit men, it's Chantale."

The exit numbers descend and the traffic increases as they draw nearer to New York City.

~~~~~~

72. The Pill

Chantale drives up to the garage, her BMW's convertible top up, and turns behind the office so that woman in the white cop car out front can't get a good look. She parks next to Berto's black Escalade and enters through a screen door. There's Berto, staring out the window at the white car. His 17-inch wall-mounted television is playing a commercial about scrap metal. Chantale's heels click across the cement floor. He's got a baggie open in one hand and his elongated fingernail delivers a bump up his nostril. He places the baggie on his desk and turns to her. She looks terrific—she's got the whole look going: black cocktail dress, bouncy hair, makeup. He likes the little leopard-skin jacket. And how high her hemline is. Stiletto heels. She may even be taller than him.

As the coke courses through him he thinks, Fuck the fancy restaurants. Fuck 'em if they don't like how my woman dresses. *I* like it. A lot.

"Berto. What are you doing? Watching that cop car? It's getting late!"

Berto encircles her waist in his arms. "It's not too late for us! It's the Hamptons!"

He gives her a kiss that turns into a nibble of her upper lip. She ends it, but keeps her hips pressed to his.

"Berto, it's no good to spend so much time with that cop car."

Berto smiles. "Look what I got." He produces his Southampton Police business card. It has a woman's name on the front and a red spot on the back.

"See? From the doll." he says proudly. "First blood!" He kisses Chantale deeply.

She breaks it off again. "Here's what I think, Berto. We take what we have—*cash*—and just leave. Start *new*. Florida. Or

Haiti. Dollars go a long way there." She looks into his dilated pupils, her hips sway against his. "No winter. No cops."

Berto calculates this thought. *Just leave.* He wouldn't have to buy Chantale a fine house at these prices. He wouldn't have to defend himself against whatever the fucking police have on him. Cash is king. Ruben and Mundo are bringing lots more cash soon.

Chantale adjusts the golden amulet that hangs from his neck. Her scent seems to penetrate him. "Berto," she murmurs, "I want you to know...I stopped taking the pill."

The swaying stops. "Which pill?" He frowns. "You mean contraception?"

"It's not good to keep putting it off."

The coke, the tequila, the police stakeout, the lack of steady income, the pressures of trying to be the local drug lord and satisfy this exotic woman—all kinds of demons well up together in his gut. Then they come out. He abruptly pulls away from her.

"Fuck that, Chantale! Are you *kidding me?*" Chantale half stumbles backward. "*Bitch!* How dare you do that to me! And *now* of all times? *Now?*"

Chantale glares back at him with a fire in her eyes he's never before seen.

"Do that to *you?!* It's *my body!* You think I can wait forever for you to get your shit together? I know what you're doing, Berto! You think I like watching you snort our future up your nose? Like a fucking addict?"

Berto thinks about this. His temples are pulsing. He trembles as sweat beads on his forehead.

Chantale isn't done. "You think I like living in a cheap rental house in the sticks for years? Where's the new house, Berto? Where's the wedding? Huh?"

He softens. "Baby, you know I'm working hard to get my...our business going."

She steps forward. "Yeah? You're a businessman, huh?" She points at the baggie on the desk and looks at Berto. "Then sell *that!*"

No way Berto's going to sell that baggie. His lifeline. He looks from it to her and back at it. Chantale steps away from him, wagging her head as if scolding a schoolboy.

"You can't do it, can you?"

His eyes fix on his baggie of white powder.

"*Can* you?" she repeats.

Berto hears an ominous incantation. Like what Chantale intoned over the policewoman's voodoo doll earlier as she stuck a pin into it. Then she says bitterly, "Maybe I gave Sabado's amulet to the wrong man!"

Chantale turns and stalks away, her butt swaying high above her heels. The rickety screen door swats shut behind her. Shit, Berto thinks. Was that a threat? Her BMW roars to life and churns out of the gravel parking lot. She's gone.

Berto blinks. He dips into the baggie and snorts from his fingernail. He fondles his golden djab amulet and recalls how Chantale gave it to him at the end of that awful, bloody night. How she made love to him. Bitches, he thinks. But what if she's right? I'm the wrong man? No. Surely she meant that incantation for the bitch cop. Not me.

Across the street, Detective Hall observes the BMW through her night-vision binoculars as it peals out from behind the garage and bounds onto Squiretown Road. Definitely speeding. An exotic-looking woman at the wheel has a head of hair like exploding coils. Looks pissed. No dinner date tonight. She radios the car and driver description to all cars and adds the woman to her list of subjects.

Then Georgie settles in and focuses on that limo office window.

Inside the office, Berto's focusing too. Getting busy.

~~~~~~

73. Cell Phones

It's getting late. Lyle is alone in his miserable motel room with the remainder of the Dewar's bottle from Rooney's bar. An exorbitant cash tip persuaded Rooney to bring it by. Lyle is impressed with the dent he's put in it so far. The fucker next door is not in. News12 is in late-night-rerun mode. The big TV trucks in the parking lot have moved out. Silk's crew went off somewhere, maybe a late dinner. A few calls have come from Silk's number and bounced away. A strange Connecticut number's been ringing—maybe that guy Gregg? And someone knocked on his door earlier. Fuck 'em all.

The quiet leaves Lyle alone with his tortured thoughts. If he thinks about Georgie, he doesn't have to think about poor Jewel, which means he doesn't have to think about Silk. But he can't think about Georgie. She's disowned him as a father, thanks to Silk. Or is Jewel the culprit? Why did Jewel show him Georgie's name on her mom's tombstone, anyway? Was that a bona fide premonition? Or bullshit? What if Georgie truly is in mortal danger and Lyle knew about it and did nothing? What if he calls her and tells her about this deathly premonition but she's not in danger? She'll disown him *and* have him put away. She's in no mood for his shit. Maybe text her...

Then, as if she'd cast a spell on him, Silk slips back into his head. He drinks his scotch and imagines making up with Silk. Getting busy with Silk. Finally unzipping her motorcycle jacket. Lyle Hall, famous lawyer, preservationist and friend to ghosts, rising to the occasion. He should douse the lights when it's his turn to disrobe, though—the scars would be a real turnoff.

Wait. Every fucking word in that drunken reverie is wrong.

Lyle thinks about Silk's smoky voice. With her looks and that voice and her smarts, she's going places. What was that movie—*Network*—where the beautiful, scheming young woman,

Faye Dunaway, had a thing for the aging but craggily handsome TV executive, uh, Bill Holden! Yeah. That was doomed. Lyle wonders if Silk is scheming. Yeah, she's scheming. He wonders what she's wearing right now. If anything.

Maybe he should return her call. Lyle owes her an apology for cursing on her live TV show. And leaving the set. But it probably made good television. Like on one of those reality shows where fat ladies have violent outbursts on camera. It's now an inalienable right for Americans to go ballistic on live TV. But Lyle should apologize. Silk's number is right here in his phone. Young. Gorgeous. Famous. Who knows, maybe that was Silk knocking on his door earlier. He should have let her in. They could have made up right here in this dreary motel room.

So return her call already. He can't.

Lyle drinks some more scotch and checks his phone. It's overflowing with voice mail and texts. He scrolls through some but he can't take it—piles of strange numbers, Georgie, Noah, Newton Properties. Dr. Susan Wayne again.

Lyle is drunker now than he's ever been in his life. He surprises himself by suddenly punching Silk's number. With each annoying digital ringtone, he grows increasingly anxious. It's too late. She'll be asleep. You'll wake her. You left badly earlier, to say the least. What if she's looking at his "Lyle" caller-ID right now and laughing? Or cursing? Someone picks up. Lyle feels a sharp thrill. Oh, God...

"Hello?"

It's a dusky female voice. Silk. Sounds cozy, like she's snuggled in bed. All warm and naked. All Lyle's fantasies about her flood through him at once. Her perfect skin, her...but they instantly turn to embarrassment. Lyle has nothing really to say. He can't actually tell a TV reporter that he wants to be her paraplegic William Holden. Lyle is yesterday's news—he's over. Worse than over. A total loser. Just say you're sorry, Lyle, and make your escape. C'mon.

"*Lyle?*"

"Silk. I'm sorry. I just called to..."

Then a cold shockwave—another voice. It's close. Male.

"Is that the cripple? Silk, hang up. Fuck *him*."

Josh. The ironic cameraman. There's a rustling sound and the line goes dead.

~~~~~~

The Dewar's is evaporating. Lyle tries to think. Silk. Silk. What was he *thinking?* He has a sudden epiphany. That shit Josh actually did him a favor. Opened his eyes—how right Flo was about Silk and Lyle, a loser stuck in a wheelchair. His obsession with her, growing daily amid all the drama he's caused, has now evaporated. Poof. Thanks, Josh.

Out of all this shit I've stirred up, he thinks, there must be something I can do to turn things around. That Iko—what if she was right? Maybe I really do need to go back to Old Vic and face that...that evil presence. I could feel it trying to get under my skin. Own me. It could be way more real than my fantasies of Silk. And older, for sure.

Okay. Lyle needs to make one "last call." Matteo Xerri. No way he's calling his daughter. That would be too pathetic and might damage her psyche or something. He'll leave her a brief, moving note. Teo would be good. He's leaving for Malta. Lyle dials.

"Hello?" Fr. Wozniak has repossessed his phone.

"Is Father Xerri there?" Lyle feels reeling drunk, his voice slurry at this late hour, but this cell phone number is all he's got. Fr. Wozniak can see who's calling.

"I'm sorry, he's left for the airport. Are you all right, Mister Hall?"

"Lyle is fine."

A pause. "This is Father Wozniak. Father Xerri should be at JFK by now."

"Right. Any way I can reach him?"

"Well the driver has a cell phone. He's a parishioner. I'll call him and maybe you can have a word with Father Xerri if he's still in the car."

Fat chance, Lyle thinks, but he thanks Wozniak and disconnects. He looks at his Dewar's bottle. Near empty. He is now at a new level, beyond drunk.

~~~~~

74. Gozo

At times they went very, very fast but, as they got closer to JFK International Airport, named for a U.S. President shot to death by a U.S. citizen, they moved very slowly, if at all. A kindly man from the parish, Mr. Szymanski, was driving Fr. Xerri to meet his Al Italia flight. They've been driving over two hours. Now, with the effect the rainstorm had on traffic approaching the airport, there would be very little time to check in for an international flight. But Teo hopes his priestly black suit and shirt with white collarino will ease his way through security.

Sheets of rain and worsening traffic force Mr. Szymanski's car to a crawl on the Belt Parkway. Teo looks at his watch and feels tension build in his heart.

He thinks of Lyle Hall's strange predicament. And he thinks of home.

Gozo is Malta's picturesque sister island—its sunbathed Mediterranean coastline, fresh seafood, dramatic rock formations and pagan ruins make it an offbeat tourism destination. The island is tranquil—while Malta's population tops 400,000, Gozo's is barely 30,000. Gozo's small towns are dominated by elaborate baroque churches; its countryside dotted with quaint chapels. Malta and Gozo have been solidly Roman Catholic for most of the past 2,000 years. But rocky Gozo's legendary temple ruins predate Christianity by over 3,000 years. One legend holds that the mythological enchantress Calypso made her home in the fantastic caves overlooking the red-sand beach known today as Ramla Bay.

Matteo knew the prehistoric ruins to be the home of something else. The *Ġgantija* Temples, located in young Teo's hometown of Xagħra on Gozo, attracted certain local adolescent boys in addition to the tourists and archaeologists. If an old "haunted" house on Long Island can draw trespassing kids, Teo reasons, then he and his friends can be forgiven for their fascination with the megalithic ruins perched dramatically over Gozo's central plain. And the boys' homes were right down the road. The brooding pagan temples, built by determined architects and local laborers some 5,600 years ago, beckoned to boys with little else to do that summer. To them, the huge limestone blocks, some as big as trucks, promised fun and mystery.

Fourteen-year-old Teo and his best friends, Silvio and Marco, loved to play their risky hybrid of hide-and-seek in the ruins. They would sneak in at the end of the day. The best hiding places were also the scariest. To be the best at hiding—and Teo Xerri was the best—you also had to be the bravest. The oldest temple housed a deep, dark chamber, behind an apse, where human bones were rumored to have been found by archaeologists. No one Teo's age had the nerve to sneak back there.

Therefore, if Silvio and Marco could not find Teo on this warm evening in June, it was possible he was hiding in the place they were too fearful to enter. But as the sun dipped toward the Mediterranean, dinnertime was coming. And if the boys were not at their respective dinner tables there'd be trouble. They resolved to creep to the entrance to the old apse and at least call for Teo. You didn't win the game without tagging Teo, but it was best to get home and play again another day.

Slowly, the two boys approached the entrance. Here, it's even darker and much cooler. It smells like moist limestone and, they imagine, the dried blood and bones of ancient human sacrifice.

"Teo? Are you there?" Silvio cries, "TE-O!"

No answer.

Marco takes a step into the inky entrance. There's a light shuffling noise.

"Shhh, Marco!" Silvio whispers. "Quiet!"

"What?" Marco whispers. "I did not make a sound."

Something else did. It's more distinct now, this strange shuffling sound. A body being dragged across gravel? How far away is it? What exactly is doing the dragging?

"TEO!" cries Silvio in a harsh whisper. "Marco, don't you have your lighter?"

Marco extracts his Bic lighter from a pocket. He flicks it—it doesn't light.

"Shit," says Silvio. "We need to see what's making that sound. What if some animal has Teo?"

"What if his family has Teo and he's right now back home at dinner?"

"Then he wins again."

The sounds seem painful—a rustling as if some heavy animals or creatures were struggling on the gravel floor. Then something new startles the boys—a guttural grunt! Either it's human or...something else.

If that's Teo in there, something's wrong and we need to help him," says Silvio.

Marco flicks his Bic a few more times. Silvio grabs his arm. "Come. We need to know."

"But it could be a trick!" says Marco.

"Good. I'm glad in that case."

Silvio inches into the darkness, leading Marco along a limestone wall. Now there's a distinctive throaty sound just ahead of them. A throaty groan. Is it human?

"Marco," Silvio whispers, "Try raising the flame on the lighter."

Silvio reaches down in the direction of the shuffling sounds. What if it's a rabid dog? Or worse, a demon? Marco tries to get the Bic to light.

"Oh GOD!!" Silvio screams, recoiling and holding up his hand. "It bit me! It fucking BIT ME!" Silvio instinctively backs toward the entrance clasping his hand.

Just then Marco gets a tall flame to light. He holds up the Bic.

Both boys scream.

There. On the floor. Teo is having an epileptic seizure. His eyes are white, rolled back in his head. His back arched frighteningly, wrists cocked at 90-degree angles, he's squirming helplessly in the gravel and foaming at the mouth.

"Get out of here!" cries Marco.

Both boys flee for open air as Marco's lighter goes out for the last time.

Teo knows that old story well. Looking past Mr. Szymanski's windshield wipers at rain pelting JFK traffic, he cannot stop replaying it. He knows his friends returned to the ruins quickly with Maria, his mother, and, wrapped in a rough cloak despite the warm night, Old Yasmine, a neighbor lady rumored to be a witch. No father—he was on a fishing trip. No doctor. No priest. Mother brought a witch.

Later Teo's friends would describe what they'd witnessed. He never forgot it.

The two women hurried into the ruins, following the boys to the darkest chamber. It was sundown. Maria had a flashlight. She played the beam into the chamber, and sure enough, her son was lying on his back on the stone floor writhing and shuddering. Teo's white eyes were terrifying; that and the stomach-turning froth that gurgled from his mouth. But even worse was the injury Teo had self-inflicted—blood was pooling in the gravel as he helplessly banged his head, again and again, into the floor.

Silvio and Marco cowered behind a hulking limestone block they believed was a sacrificial altar. Sobbing, Maria fell to her knees at Teo's side, the flashlight clunking onto the floor, and prayed to God for help. Then Yasmine knelt, positioning the light so it illuminated the stricken boy. The beam threw exaggerated shadows onto the Neolithic stone blocks surrounding Teo. Old Yasmine's back was turned to the boys; they could not view her actions. They could see that both women put their hands on Teo. Then they heard strange incantations. It was Yasmine. She shouted out Greek phrases Silvio dimly recognized– σκατά τρώγων! χοίρος εραστής! and μαλάκα σπήλαιο κάτοικος! She was reviling the demons she found gripping the boy's soul. Then, louder and louder, she repeatedly shouted, "πάμε πίσω στην κόλαση! πάμε πίσω στην κόλαση!"

In addition to violently cracking his scull on the floor and arching his back, poor Teo's feet were shaking uncontrollably. The women bent over his chest.

Suddenly one woman shot upright with explosive force. She spun backwards and collapsed like a sack onto the stone floor. Silvio and Marco gasped. They could see part of her face in the flashlight's beam. Teo's mother. Her eyes staring blindly.

Old Yasmine was doing nothing for Maria.

"Maybe she can only heal one person at a time," Silvio whispered.

"Let's get out of here!" cried Marco.

The two stumbled their way outside and gulped the fresh currents of air that follow the sunset. Then they ran from Ġgantija. They ran down a cobbled street and stopped at a corner by the village's al fresco cafe. The shaken boys faced each other, catching their breaths. Were they in trouble? The question was how much trouble. Things would never be the same; that they knew.

"Silvio," Marco panted. "What was that old witch saying? She was shouting something over and over!"

"It was Greek," said Silvio, catching his breath.

"It was so frightening…what did it mean?"

Silvio looked his young friend in the eye.

"Go back to Hell."

Then Silvio spotted an uncle driving by slowly in an old car. He ran alongside the window begging him to help the people in the ruins.

When Teo awoke in the hospital room, he had no mother. Just his stern father, Mikele Xerri, who'd returned from his fishing trip a widower. His son, who'd been forbidden so many times, had snuck into that bad place again. He learned that his son suffered an epileptic fit and nearly died in a godforsaken chamber of primitive stone. That his frantic mother, with her weak heart, did everything she could under the circumstances. Mikele did not understand that there had been no time. That Maria had to beg the old crone next door to accompany her to the temple ruins. The woman who everyone says was some kind of witch. How his Maria spent her last tragic moments before her heart gave out— kneeling with a pagan witch over her convulsing son. The

368

solution for the boy would be priesthood. Starting now. Seminary high school; seminary university; ordination. The Church would protect Teo. Protect Mikele too. Teo would need to pray for his mother's soul every day. Best that it came from a priest.

But protect them from what? Teo's father could not have known.

As that summer wore on and they were not allowed to see their friend, Silvio and Marco grew restless. One evening they dared each other to sneak into the ruins without Teo for old time's sake. The sun set as the boys ventured deep into a deserted chamber. There, as the light failed, Marco lost his footing while scrambling over two giant stone slabs. He slid between the slabs and, as he struggled, became wedged between them up to his chest. Marco tried to scream but he could barely inhale. Silvio tried frantically but could not free the boy by himself. Frustration turned to real fear. Silvio had to go for help. Marco was slipping deeper into the crack and the stones were forcing his lungs shut. He was gasping and crying. Leaving his friend, Silvio urged Marco to pray.

Silvio soon returned with some men, including his father, Marco's father and Teo's father, Mikele. They had been playing cards outside the local café. Back inside the stone temple, all was silent. The men made Silvio turn away from what they found between the slabs. But Silvio peeked. His friend Marco was unrecognizable—he'd turned a purple-blue color, his eyes bugging from their sockets, his ribs crushed. His hands held up pathetically in prayer. Rigor mortis had set in. Silvio closed his eyes as the dead boy's father began to wail. The temple had become a tomb.

Silvio, smart, verbal, athletic and fourteen years old, never spoke again after that night. He never returned to school. He would rock in his chair, stare out his window and pick at the blanket covering his legs. Eventually his parents consigned him to Mount Carmel Psychiatric Hospital on Malta. Over the years a young priest would occasionally stop in and visit him.

Fr. Xerri snaps out of it. Mr. Szymanski's car is finally moving forward through the downpour toward JFK's International Departures terminal. Life has been good as a priest. Teo knew it. The decision his father made 16 years ago, abrupt and final though it was, seemed wise in hindsight. There was a problem and Mikele had the answer. Teo was on the right team. And now he's journeying home.

From nowhere, Lyle Hall's riddle occurs to him—that phrase Flo Hendricks whispered as she died. *Sustain low*. It's Greek. And it's chilling.

~~~~~~

75. The Boy Next Door

The room next to Lyle's is quiet for now. So Lyle can think. Thinking leads directly to morbid depression. He's so drunk, he doesn't want to drink anymore. Bad sign. And something terrible, ancient and full of hatred, has its hooks in him. It wants its hooks in Georgie too. And it will move elsewhere once 111 Poplar comes down. Move where there are more souls to take. Just dragging a hateful guy like Lyle Hall to Hell is no great shakes. This entity, Lyle now believes, craves God-fearing folks. Like Georgie. And kids. Jewel was a kid once. What if Becky actually turns that barn into an effing museum?

I can't stand the thought of any kids being possessed by demons, Lyle thinks. Like Teo as a boy. I can hardly believe demons are fucking real. But Teo says they are. Lyle opens his nightstand drawer. Behind the motel's Gideon Bible is his gun.

The Glock is cold and heavy on his lap. Over two pounds of metal.

But Lyle is only imagining he can feel the weight of his semi-automatic pistol. His legs are dead. He'll never move them. He'll never get Silk. Never make up with Georgie. Never see Jewel. Lyle picks up the gun. It's the M9 design. Loaded. Luger 9mm cartridges. He vaguely remembers the day he bought the gun and ammo. If Lyle Hall wanted to defend his home and Dar from intruders, he damn well had the right.

But now he'll never go back to his fucking house. Yeah, using the f-word feels good. Why not? The house has been overrun—dead people on the porch; poltergeist in the kitchen; devils in the basement and dirtbags camped outside. Fucking toilet paper hanging from the trees. And Belinda's moldy furniture's still down in the basement with a demon possum or whatever lurking. What the fuck.

Lyle handles the gun.

Fuck it, he drunk-thinks, I could go see this fucking demon at Old Vic right now and fuck it up good. Just like Iko said I should, if I were half a man. I'd make the damn thing sorry it ever got its hooks in me. Probably be the only one sorry. Georgie sorry? Why? A crippled old problem-dad is just a burden. She has a badge and a future. Lyle tries to think. I can't shoot something that's already dead. Iko was right. Half a man.

Lyle examines the Glock. He recalls it can fire a burst of three rounds. Meaning he can't miss. What do these miserable losers do? They stick the damn muzzle in their mouths and pull the trigger. Then it's all over. All over but the demons. Fuck them.

Lyle tries it out in his mouth. The metal is cold and bitter. He sees his pathetic reflection in the bureau mirror. How does that look, his drunk self wonders, to die with this thing in your mouth? And look at that shitty, old-man beard. Lyle removes the muzzle and fingers his unkempt whiskers. What if he shaved? Georgie begged him to. Would that set some kind of record for weirdest last act?

"Ghost Hampton" Lawyer Dead in Montauk Motel

Controversial local man shaves face prior to blowing it away

By MOSE ALLEN for the *Southampton Press*

Absurd. But that's what life is. So why not death, too?

The mirror starts to pulsate. Lyle dimly realizes that Harley, his name for the fucker next door, is back and turned on his MTV or whatever. A fitting end. The "music" is so loud it's unrecognizable. Well the son-of-a-bitch's cranky old crippled neighbor is about to ruin Harley's night.

Lyle grabs his Dewar's bottle and takes a swig from it, then another. Why the fuck not. He raises his pistol, this time to his temple. The shitty music is literally pounding through his head. This is probably what they play in Hell.

End it. Now.

The ring of Lyle's cell phone is very subtle against the racket pounding his wall.

Almost too subtle. But for many years Lyle's life and career revolved around that ring. His stupid love life too. Lyle notices the thing jittering on his dresser. He picks it up and looks at the caller ID. Hmm. Hamptons area code. The bodybuilding Montauk bartender lady? No way. Who the fuck is it?

Lyle finally pushes the green button before the voicemail overflow kills the call. He can barely hear the caller's voice. What? Day-old Sherry?

Drunks try hard to sound not-so-drunk when they have to talk. Drunks about to blow their own head off try harder.

"Teo? You're at the airport?"

"Yes, Lyle-eh, my flight is soon. Father Wozniak told me you called."

Lyle can hardly hear his new friend over the pounding in the next room.

"Lyle-eh, is that your radio?"

"Listen, I'm sorry it's the fucker next door..." Lyle realizes his slip.

"A trucker next door? Lyle-eh, I'm having trouble hearing you."

"Of course. I'm sorry. I only called because..."

There's a pause. Only infernal thumping and screaming can be heard.

"There is trouble," Teo says. "You have trouble."

"Well, yes. I wanted to talk to you, but you're getting on a plane."

"I have a few minutes but I cannot hear you well."

Lyle thinks about this. Drunk think.

"Listen, Father. Can you call me back in two minutes?"

Teo agrees and they disconnect. Lyle rolls out his wheelchair-accessible doorway onto the pavement. The thrash-metal is roaring loud outside too. Look at his bike. It's not a Harley after all. It's a Kawasaki. Lyle stops at the crazy neighbor's door. He knocks. Nothing. Then Lyle raps the Glock's handle loudly on the door, interspersing it between fanatical drumbeats. Nothing.

Inside the motel room, the "music" is really blasting. Lyle's tormentor, a meth dealer, is trying to dial his cell phone. His girlfriend is curled up on the bed. He wears a black wife-beater T-shirt emblazoned with an illegible graffito threat. His shaved head is sprouting a five-o'clock shadow. His long arms are festooned with tattoos, many depicting religious themes. There's even a likeness of Jesus on one deltoid.

Suddenly a tremendous explosive boom rocks his door sending a shockwave through his heart and digestive tract. *What the fuck was that*? His heart pounding, he kills his boom box, cutting off "Highway to Hell." Sudden quiet. The girlfriend sleeps on. He creeps to his door's peephole. His phone call connects.

"Yeah. Dude. Lissin-me. Some muthahfuckah just set off a bomb outside my fuckin' door! Fuckin' believe that shit? No shit! Now I look out the peephole and nobody's there! Fuckin' believe this shit? Maybe it was kids and they ran away. No, not cops. Cops come right in. Look. I gotta check this out. I'll swing by later, okay? Yeah. No, it's not cops. No, I don't have fuckin' *enemies*. Probably some shit-ass kids. It's almost Halloween, okay? Later."

There's nothing outside his door. His heart starts to calm but the tension persists. His eye on the peephole, the door suddenly reacts to violent hammering. He jumps back, then looks out again. Nothing. *What the fuck?*

The dealer gets up the nerve to open his door a crack, its chain holding firm. Through the crack he sees something he's never beheld in his life. An old guy in a wheelchair is pointing a fucking gun right at him.

Their eyes meet and Lyle receives a flood of impressions: surprise, ignorance, fear, aggression, addiction and, oddly, amusement. This dirtbag finds Lyle comical.

"Dude!"

"Listen to me," says Lyle Hall, plenty drunk enough to put on a good, menacing show. "Turn that *fucking music off* and *keep it off*. Understand me?"

The dealer cracks a nervous, incomplete smile.

"Dude, you pointin' a fuckin' *gun* at me, man??"

Lyle narrows his eyes and directs the Glock at the dealer's chest. The muzzle shakes slightly as Lyle's cell phone starts to ring. It's Teo.

"I need to take this call, dammit! Keep that fucking music *off*, you understand?"

The man stares out at Lyle in disbelief. "You gotta be fuckin' kiddin' me, man!"

"I am so *not* fucking kidding you, man."

Lyle's phone continues to ring. Teo should be boarding—it's a red eye flight. Lyle had better answer it. He places his handgun on his lap, crooks the phone to his ear and backs his chair toward his own open doorway. Harley Kawasaki can hear him.

"Father? Yes, thank you for getting back to me. Got a minute?"

His door ajar, the dealer watches Lyle roll away in reverse.

"A *priest?* Gotta be fuckin' kiddin' me..." he says in a hushed voice. His own cell phone rings and he shuts and deadbolts his door.

~~~~~~~

76. Supersaver to Rome

Phone tight to his ear, Lyle rolls into his room and closes his door. It's mercifully quiet.

"Lyle-eh, I am sorry but it is an awkward time," Teo says. "The man who drove me here lent me his phone but the police say he must vacate the area."

"I'll make this quick." But Lyle hesitates. Quick? What can he say *quick* to this well-meaning man? That he's about to blow his own head off?

"Lyle-eh? Are you all right?"

Lyle is very drunk. "Teo, you were *right*. I been hiding something from you. Gotta tell you—Jewel, the girl, showed me a terrible vision. Made me sick. My wife's headstone with my *daughter's name* on it. Her date of death is *tomorrow!*" He cuts off.

Honking horns at the airport drown Lyle out but Teo could hear a sob. "You have my prayers, Lyle-eh. I am so sorry you've been subjected to this." He continues, "Lyle-eh, I was thinking about *sustain low*, your friend's last words. I realized that it's Greek. It might be important." A lump forms in Teo's throat. "Lyle, it means…*I want you.*"

Lyle chews on that briefly as a new, even more hopeless drunk-plan dawns. "Oh, *really?* Well it's gonna *get me*, Teo! In that barn. It's in that *damn effing barn!*"

"Lyle-eh, no, we need to pray. And you need to stay away from that place!"

"You know Becky Tuttle thinks she's gonna *preserve* the goddamn barn? Believe that? She wants to bring *school kids* into that barn. There's something evil in there, Teo! I felt it! Nobody'll believe me. And she's gonna bring *children* in there! Well I'm not gonna let that happen."

"Lyle-eh!" Teo sees his driver, Mr. Szymanski, having words with a transit cop.

"After my meltdown on TV today Georgie will never speak to me again. I swore to her I'd put a stop to all this. And I will!" His mind swirling, Lyle gags. "Teo, I'm so afraid I'll never see my daughter alive again!"

With that Lyle breaks down into drunken sobs. Teo wants to console him, but now there's a new challenge—Mr. Szymanski's car is about to be towed.

Lyle can hear a heated exchange on Teo's end. He closes his eyes and exhales.

"Mister Hall? Hello?" It's Mr. Szymanski, the parishioner from Southampton—a short, balding man in a camouflage hunting coat standing by his illegally parked Ford Taurus. He's attracted a JFK transit cop and a second guy in a DayGlo yellow vest. The Taurus's trunk is open; Teo is removing his black travel bag. Due to congestion in the drop-off lane, Mr. Szymanski had positioned the Taurus at an odd angle. He's now in an airport hell of honking vehicles. An NYPD cruiser is bleating its rapid-fire siren at him, the cop behind the wheel barking, "Move your vehicle now," on his mic as a tow truck approaches.

"Hall here." The full weight of exhaustion and depression crushes down on him.

"Yeah, Mister Hall, Father Cherry here was using my phone but I gotta get outta here. Cops are gonna tow me. And Father has to make his plane, okay?" He pauses. "He wants to say goodbye, but I gotta go! Here..."

"Lyle-eh! I am sorry, everything happening at once. I must say, it is good you told me your deepest fears. I can only imagine the torment you feel for your daughter."

Mr. Szymanski is crying out to Fr. Xerri. Horns are honking. Somehow Lyle can hear Teo speak clearly through it all.

"Lyle-eh, listen carefully. Do not go back to Old Vic. When we went inside I am now sure something evil entered you. That was all *my fault*. My friend, promise me you will stay away. I will pray to God to watch over you. I will call you as soon as I land."

But Lyle has already devised a new drunk-plan. "Yeah, thanks, Teo. I have no problem with the *house* per se." He pauses. "Hey, know what? My only friend is a priest! Nice, huh?"

Szymanski returns. "Father! I gotta go!"

Lyle hears rustling sounds. Men yelling, horns, a siren bleep. The phone disconnects. Teo's gone. And Lyle's made up his drunk mind.

~~~~~~

77. Sixty, Not Sixty-five

Berto looks into his quart-size plastic baggie. Its contents are sadly depleted now. So what if there's less shit in the package he sent to his gringo Manhattan client? Berto does not like this surveillance, this blond lady cop. He's going to do something about it. Tonight. Chantale will be impressed. Things will be good again.

He just has to steady his nerves. Two abrupt bumps. One up each nostril. White powder sprinkles into his black goatee.

He has to load his semiautomatic rifle. His head buzzing and crazed by Chantale's rebuke, Berto managed to formulate a bold plan: make it look like the girl cop entered his property and he fired on her as an intruder. It will work.

Berto's cell phone rings. Not Chantale. Ruben.

"Berto?"

"What."

"We made the delivery."

"Got the sixty-five?" Berto is counting on sixty-five-thousand dollars.

"Well, we need to talk about that."

"No, we *don't*." Berto sounds frigid cold. "You either got it or you did not."

Ruben was afraid of this. "Berto, the customer was cool, like you said. Very cool." He pauses. "But he had a scale and he weighed it. Weighed it twice."

Berto says nothing. He grinds his molars instead.

"He said we were short and paid us sixty thousand. He was only a gringo amateur, you know, but…"

Berto sounds deadly over the cell connection. "You are on your way back with sixty thousand."

"Yes." Ruben looks at an etching of Grover Cleveland. "Thousand-dollar bills."

Berto pauses an uncomfortable moment. He looks at his five-thousand-dollar plastic baggie. Thousand-dollar bills are way too large, but they are money. "Come directly here. And do not speed."

"On our way." They disconnect and Mundo meets Ruben's gaze. Ruben slips a fat white envelope into his jacket pocket. Its top edge is visible. He pats it.

"Gotta be a better way to earn a living, Mundo."

An autumn squall has blown in from the West. Hitting Manhattan, then moving on to Queens and Long Island, it pelts the limo as Mundo drives back to Hampton Bays.

Pacing around his office, Berto looks out the window at the white cop car. He picks up his semiautomatic rifle, checks it. The magazine is fully loaded. He stands it by the door to the garage bays. He takes a bump of coke off his fingernail, then opens a cabinet and grabs more ammunition: a box of 5.56x45 NATO shells and an empty Magpul 30-round magazine. He holds a brassy cartridge in his fingers. The bullet itself is pointed. Including the shell casing, it's longer than a double-A battery and resembles a rocket ship. Berto feeds 30 shells into the magazine and slips it into his jacket's breast pocket. The same pocket that holds his knife. Including the shoulder holster, his tight Italian-style suit jacket is getting restrictive. Berto unholsters his pistol. It's a pea-shooter compared to his AR-15, but it may come in handy. Looking out the window again, he takes a bump of coke. His sinuses are clogged now with blood. It happens. His hands are shaky but his plan is solid—just gotta get her to come over here. He knows she'd love to snoop around his office.

So, Berto tells himself, *invite her in.*

~~~~~~~

78. To Hell for Good

Sitting in his dreary motel room, Lyle is thankful that at least the dirtbag next door is gone. No thrash-metal, no TV news channel to distract him, Lyle's settled on what he has to do. And Fred is the man of the hour. The really late hour. Fred keeps his MediCab in his driveway and he's on his way. Lyle's call woke him up, but Mr. Hall is his biggest tipper and late night is double fare. Destination 111 Poplar.

After being disowned by his daughter who may not live through tomorrow; after the torment of discovering Silk in bed with that wiseass; after Teo flying off to Rome; after that haughty Haitian calling him a pedophile on national television; and Becky taking over a barn possessed by demons; and after polishing off a bottle of scotch; Lyle finally sees how this will go down. Drunk man, sober mind.

Iko was right. Lyle must go back to that property and face whatever is in that barn once and for all. Tonight. There's no time to dillydally. Maybe confronting that hateful thing will distract it from whatever it wants to do with Georgie. But what if she *isn't* in mortal danger? What if this is all a bunch of paranormal bullshit? Lyle's head pounds as irreconcilable thoughts crash around. This is why people drink.

He holds up his Glock and studies it. It's loaded. He fired a round outside. It works. It even smells dangerous. Now let's reason this out: Old Vic will be torn down. But the evil barn will remain standing—thank you, Becky. And the demonic presence that killed two nice people and tried to take hold of Lyle's house—it's surely still lurking in that barn where something terrible happened. And it will be waiting there to get its claws into the souls of more youngsters who come to see Becky's restored barn or play on the playground. So Lyle will go there soon, thank you Fred, with his gun. Suicide sends you directly to Hell for good, right? All God-fearing people know that, even

Lyle. This demon wants Lyle to serve as its next human vessel. Well, it's in for a surprise.

It wants Lyle, and it's gonna get Lyle.

Fred rings that he's outside now for the trip back to Bridgehampton. This is the last call Lyle will take. No more phones. He needs the gun to work. Not the phone.

With Lyle's chair secured inside the MediCab, Fred offers to recharge its low battery during the trip. He notes weirdness in Lyle's expression as he responds that he won't need to. Once they're underway Lyle asks Fred to stop at a Hess station coming up on Montauk Highway.

"I have gas, Mister Hall."

"I don't." Lyle empties the dregs of the Dewar's down his throat. "Please stop?"

At the gas station it hits Fred how drunk his passenger is. Crazy, too. He convinces Lyle that, if he really needs some gasoline in his Dewar's bottle, he can siphon a little from the MediCab's tank. Fred has a siphon tube for an emergency. During this conversation Fred receives another twenty and promises to put out his cigarette.

Fred pulls away from the gas pumps and positions the MediCab so the night attendant cannot see this suspicious act— siphoning gasoline into a Dewar's bottle. Fred tightens its twist-off cap and hands it inside to Lyle. It reeks.

"Mister Hall, you know you have to be very careful with this."

"Just don't light up till I get out, okay, Fred?"

Fred has driven many a drunk in his career, but never a drunk in a wheelchair with a liquor bottle full of gasoline. He's never seen Lyle like this. Something's up.

Speeding west to Bridgehampton, Lyle, coddling his bottle, is struck by the many places he's frequented in his career, all closed for now, as they flash by his window. There are funky joints— Cyril's Fish House, the Clam Bar, the Stephen Talkhouse. Tonier places like the Maidstone and Bobby Van's. In each case his drinking, combined with his real estate exploits, had made him persona non grata. Which was why he'd backed himself out to the Montauk bars in the end. Now some mom-and-pop places, closed at this hour, resonate on a deeper level as they whip past—an ice cream stand, the Candy Kitchen, a roadside pumpkin-and-corn-maze operation that sells apples and makes cider doughnuts. Lyle had been to these homey stops with his wife and little girl a lifetime ago. Now, his face reflected in the window, he looks finished.

Entering deserted Bridgehampton, Fred slows to turn off the highway and avoid the village's war memorial. Up ahead, its traffic light is green. But Lyle has an urge.

"Fred, just go straight through tonight, please." At this point, why not.

"Go straight, Mister Hall?" Another unusual factor.

"Yeah…and slow. Please." Fred slows to a crawl. Way unusual.

Lyle grips his armrests tight. Nothing. Then he sees it. The intersection has been "micro-paved" a tarry black recently. It's painted with bright lane stripes demarking where you can turn safely, directing you away from potential danger, such as Lyle Hall and his Hummer. He couldn't have noticed it the other day, convulsing in the FEARcom van. The local "traffic calming committee" finally came up with this, after a year. The fresh paint job is what diverted traffic onto Poplar the afternoon Fred picked him up at the train. When they detoured past Old Vic.

As Fred slows, Lyle has a moment of dreamlike clarity. Only Lyle sees this—the old guy walking his dog. He's not really there. But he was, a year ago. Now Lyle sees who the man was. Augie Dunbar. Walking Augie's Doggie, that crazy black dog behind the gate at Dunbar Automotive. The dog lunges, straining on its leash, as the MediCab passes. This dog made Elsie swerve into Lyle's Hummer last year. Augie knew. Only Augie. This realization sinks into Lyle's heart, deeper than his drunk consciousness. Elsie's was a natural reaction. A dog, plus blinding sunset, equals physics.

Holy shit. Blame it on the drunk, the greedy lawyer.

But the lawyer lived.

"Okay, Fred, let's get out of here." Fred gives it gas and they get out of there.

A moment later all that is behind him. Lyle is taking decisive action. He looks at his cell phone and its annoying low battery icon. Better do one very important thing before it's too late. Text Georgie. Let's see... Don't do a pathetic suicide note. Don't be lugubrious. She likes matter-of-fact, give her that. Pray she lives to read it. Wait. You don't pray where Lyle Hall's going. Whatever. His thumbs start fumbling.

> Dear Georgie. Pleas be careful in everything you do. Your life is precious. Jus crossing a street is danger. If you do one thing in life, should start a family. Yul do it right. You no how not to do it by watching me. You make a good parent. Wound be sorry. Sorry like I am for evthing. Sorry I'm even wasting good air. I realize now how much I love you. Which also makes me sorry...

Nah, this text sucks. Kill it. But Fred's hasty turn onto Poplar makes Lyle press Send instead. Georgie will see it. Whatever. Drunk man speaks a sober mind.

Poplar Street looks deserted now. Sgt. Frank and his boys in blue did a good job cleaning up the riffraff. Fred pulls onto the back street behind Old Vic and stops by last night's back driveway. The shadowy outline of Old Vic's cupola looms in the darkness beyond. Fred feels he must get out of the van and see off his best customer. It's quiet out here. A few die hard crickets. Lyle seems to have conflicting emotions even Fred can see.

Lyle insists Fred take a twenty for his Bic lighter. Fred hesitates; it's too weird, but Lyle always gets his way. Fred notes how the Dewar's bottle is tucked in his basket along with a soiled white sock. He cannot see Lyle's gun zipped inside his canvas pouch.

384

Lyle tells Fred not to wait. Fred asks if he plans to roll back to his own house, despite the chair's low batteries. Lyle waves off that idea saying, "Goin' where I belong," and tucks a thick wad in Fred's shirt pocket. He winks at Fred, then turns and rolls quietly up the driveway, disappearing into shadows.

Fred drives off, his shirt pocket bulging with twenties. Lyle didn't even count them, just emptied his fanny pack. A few blocks away, Fred pulls over. He takes a card from his wallet and dials a number.

"Sergeant Barsotti."

"This is Fred Merkel, Lyle Hall's MediCab driver? You gave me your card?"

"What's up, Fred." Big Frank is at the stationhouse in Southampton.

Fred describes delivering Lyle to the driveway behind Old Vic. How drunk Lyle seemed. The low batteries, the huge tip. Fred omits the bottle of gasoline since that could implicate him.

"He definitely went onto the property?"

"Yeah. You said if anything unusual..." Fred realizes the line is dead.

Big Frank is busy at the stationhouse with his friend from Internal Affairs. But now he has some calls to make. And there may not be enough time.

~~~~~~

79. Two-man Job

Mundo, Ruben seated beside him, is stopped at a red light at the intersection of Route 24 and Montauk Highway in Hampton Bays, directly across from the Hampton Bays Diner, when blue and red lights create a dazzling display around them. It's after 3 AM. Ruben fears he's going to soil his pants right there in the car.

"Oh, shit! Mundo! What the fuck we gonna do?"

Mundo makes it a point to stop strangling the steering wheel. There are two cop cars, one behind and now one ahead of the limo. He shuts off the engine. Mundo does not go for his wallet. He doesn't want the cops to think he's reaching for a weapon.

"Ruben, don't do anything to make them suspicious. We've done nothing wrong. There is no evidence."

"The fucking gringo spilled some shit in the trunk when he weighed the package."

"There's no reason to open the trunk."

A cop approaches the limo from the rear. Now at Mundo's window, he mimes the international sign for roll down the fucking window. Mundo complies.

"Is there a problem, Officer?" Mundo squints into a flashlight beam.

"Can I see your license and registration please?" It's Officer Petry.

Mundo takes out his wallet and hands Petry the cards. With the "Ghost Hampton" bullshit seemingly over, he's back in a cruiser.

"You know you have a tail light out?"

"I'm sorry, Officer, I didn't know."

The young cop takes Mundo's cards back to his car. The license says the driver is one Reymundo Alvarez. Meanwhile the cop from the second car appears at Mundo's window and shines his flashlight in on both men. Sure enough, there's Mr. Clean at

386

the wheel and Trini Lopez in the passenger seat as described four hours ago by Detective Hall. This cop is Mackey, the older black man with sergeant stripes. He notes that Trini Lopez is visibly tense. He winces into the light briefly, but is distracted by a text on his cell phone. His leather bomber jacket is open. The edge of a thick business-size envelope protrudes from the inside pocket, packed tight with something shaped like bills. Carrying cash is not a crime. But extreme nervousness—he is sweating— combined with a wad of cash interests Sgt. Mackey. Now Trini starts texting like crazy.

Ruben types furiously with his thumbs and gets almost instantaneous responses:

> *Berto, cops stop us at Hampton Diner. But its cool.*
> *WTF U DO???* Berto replies, in full caps mode.
> *Tail lite out. All cool.*
> *DONT FKK THIS UP!!!*

Ruben looks up at the blinding white light. Red and blue swirls around him.

"Everything okay tonight, sir?" says the sergeant.

"Yessir." Ruben tries to sound affirmative and...innocent. "Everything's good." But it's so hard. He can feel his unregistered handgun radiating under his seat. The flashlight illumines his white envelope. Ruben adjusts his jacket and it slips out of sight.

Ruben's phone pings and the sergeant observes how it draws his attention.

> *WTF U AT DINER? GET BACK HERE!!*
> *Not at diner. At traffk lite.* Ruben quickly retorts.

The two policemen confer outside Petry's cruiser while they wait for computers somewhere to run Mr. Clean's ID.

"They fit Detective Hall's description," says Petry, who's logged a lot of hours watching Lyle Hall's house the past few days.

"Trini Lopez is a nervous man," says the sergeant. With many years on the job he sports a fully realized beer belly that strains against his dark-blue uniform shirt. "I'd like to know why," he adds.

Sitting in the limo, Ruben looks down at his cell phone and a repeating phrase.

WTF?? WTF?? WTF??

~~~~~~

Soon the cops receive Mundo's driver's record—nothing of note—and they return to his open window. The cops' heavy belts are laden with disconcerting gear: holstered service revolvers, handcuffs, crackling radios and various pouches. Mundo, both hands on the wheel, seems calm. Ruben quietly texts while shitting a cinder block. Petry ran a check indicating that Mr. Clean was born in the U.S. Not so sure about Trini Lopez.

Both cops are itching to find a reason to get these men out of the car and search them but an envelope and perceived nervousness will not stand up in court.

Petry hands Mundo back his documentation along with a citation.

"That's for the tail light, Mister Alvarez."

"I'll make sure it's fixed tomorrow, Officer."

Sgt. Mackey bends down to the window. "You both work for South Fork Transportation?"

"Yeah," they say in unison.

"How come you have two employees in this car?"

"We had to drop off...a car," Ruben improvises. "In the city."

Mundo glances over at Ruben.

Petry asks, "Did you two leave town earlier in this car?"

"We did," says Mundo, praying they won't get caught in this lie. "We had to pick up a car up-the-island and drop it off for a customer in the city."

Petry sees there's very little to go on. Mackey gives him a "wasting our time" look. Trini Lopez's cell phone pings with more incoming texts.

"Okay, gentlemen," the sergeant says. "Take this car directly back to the shop. Fix the tail light and you can make the ticket go away in traffic court."

Both cops step back from the limo and Mundo starts up the engine.

"Thank you," he says through his open window.

"Be safe," says Mackey, still observing them.

Ruben gives a two-finger wave as Mundo maneuvers the limo around the cruiser in front of him. The light is green; he pulls onto Montauk Highway, turning east.

"Shit. Shit. Fucking SHIT!" says Ruben. "Berto is going fucking ballistic, man!"

Mackey moves to his cruiser as he watches the limo drive off.

Petry gets on his radio. "Yeah, we're at Twenty-four and Twenty-seven-A. Hampton Diner intersection. Two subjects in limo with one dark tail light. Should be heading to the taxi stand. Will follow."

Georgie Hall hears the call. She's still sitting across from Berto's office. It's been quiet since the woman sped off in her Beemer. But for the past few minutes a shadow has been moving agitatedly past the office window.

~~~~~~

Ken McGorry

80. Try Me

Lyle is trundling over the scrubby yard when his phone rings. Not now. Without looking to see the caller he chucks the near-dead thing into some weeds behind Old Vic. He pulls up to the barn door. It's still ajar from last night. He unscrews his fifth of gasoline and stuffs his white Gurney's sock into the bottle's throat. The other sock remains on his foot. He cannot feel the incongruity of wearing only one sock. He looks up at the bleak structure before him. It's a tinder box. Old, see-through and rickety, but still tall and imposing, especially from a wheelchair. He rolls forward, crossing the warped threshold. Into the dark.

As if on cue the chair poops out and stops in the middle of the barn floor. It was not the most expensive chair, Lyle had no intention of relying on it permanently, but it was useful. And "transportable," once you remove the two 29-pound batteries, as Lyle's helpers know. That's no longer an issue.

It feels different inside the barn tonight. Thin slits between wallboards allow dim moonlight to slice here and there. The musty place almost seems to breathe—as if it's alive. With all the dirty bats hanging overhead and maybe a rabid possum crawling around in the dark and that hairy spider crouched in its web on the wall, the place kind of is breathing. And aware of him. Alone. In a dead wheelchair. The back of his neck tingles.

It's quiet enough to hear the hateful bats rustling above. His wheels rest on bat shit. Shouldn't they be flying off somewhere, biting the throats of virgins in their sleep? Speaking of virgins sleeping, Lyle has one last thought of Jewel. His awful yearning to help her. Why? Why all this trouble? Those beautiful sad eyes? It hits him that maybe he was obsessed with Jewel's predicament because he was so poor at fathering his own daughter when she was 12. What did Flo say—"Everything is Freudian"? Belinda had become too ill and too weak to cajole the VIP Lyle Hall, Esq., into being a very important person in

390

Georgie's life. What the hell. Georgie's got a good start in her career of choice. Thanks to Dad. Tonight, Dad plans to make her headstone a lie.

Taking in the forlorn barn, he thinks, If Teo calls Old Vic "unclean," what would he call this godforsaken place? A sudden shock smacks Lyle in the chest. A horrific image recurs—a jagged vision of a knife attack floods his mind. He tries to blink it away.

Blood splattering. A stabbing knife. Long ago.

The savagery fades with the echo of an unearthly hiss. His heart skips. It came from that bad corner of the barn. He admits to himself he's terrified to be here alone.

But he's here on a mission. "That all you got?" Lyle growls. "C'mon, you fucker. Crawl up my dead legs, into my black soul. *Try me*, motherfucker!"

That's when the hissing intensifies. It's nauseating. A pale form takes shape in some dead grass, like dry old hay, collected in the corner. Lyle ignites Fred's lighter and sees its grin. It's real. The fucking oversize possum. Harbinger of death. Beady black eyes set deep in its dirty white face. Its horrid pointy teeth. Lyle hit it with a rocks glass last night. Fuck him. Or her.

"You're going bye-bye, you goddamn piece of shit!"

Lyle holds the lighter to the sock dangling from his fifth of gasoline and it flares. He flings the burning thing at the corner, at that hateful animal, at the memory of evil and carnage—and the bottle shatters, splashing gasoline. But the possum is unaffected. It just turns and skulks away, fat ass, naked tail, disappearing through a hole.

But the white sock from Gurney's did not stay lit.

Shit. No matter. Lyle unzips his canvas pouch. There's his gun. He didn't come here for a fucking marsupial.

"C'mon, motherfucker! *Try me!!*" he screams.

Something heard him.

Very faint muscular tremors creep up through his lifeless legs. His heart's desire. Shit. He suddenly can feel he's wearing just one sock. Then the tremors intensify severely—like a charley horse in both legs. Good. As planned. Now pain floods up into his ruined abdomen and chest. It's grimly satisfying—it's time. But then this cruel laughter swirls up from the dirty floor. Hateful voices. Are the demons real? What can they possibly do with Lyle Hall?

Inflict worse pain. It spikes to gut-wrenching proportions but he welcomes it, even as it ravages his wasted internal organs, even as it spreads upward reviving his broken jaw and teeth. Then the breath is knocked out of him and he doubles over. Shit. Where is Jewel now? This is not a visit from a sweet, sad girl. It's that thing, that evil remnant of past horror. It wants new children. And it wanted Lyle all along.

His whole body throbbing with excruciating pain now, the derisive voices intensify. Savage screams envelop him in his chair, stalled in the middle of the barn. Cold fear grips him—*This is going out of control.* His blood pressure is surely spiking. *Is blood oozing from my ears?* He senses a sharp blade swinging violently overhead. Or is it the bats? *Force yourself to sit upright, Lyle. Don't die ducking bats.*

Now he relives his near death on the operating table. Looking down on himself from above, his abdomen is entirely cut open. Some organs are outside his body, available to surgeons. But there are no surgeons tonight. No anesthetic. And he's conscious. How can anyone conscious possibly endure surgery? The crazy, evil laughter wells up again.

C'mon, get the Glock out of the pouch. You need to sense the precise moment to use it. When the demon enters your soul. That's when to take it—and yourself—down. Soon. Breathe, dammit. Raise the Glock. Shit, it's heavy. Here it comes. The hateful thing is here in the barn. The agony can't get worse. Now is the time.

Lyle closes his eyes and brings the revolver shakily to his lips. Somehow he recalls the Glock's slogan. *Ideal for versatile use.*

He hears women scream. A man's hateful voice curses viciously.

Through a tight squint he sees a flash of light. Strange. But the time is *now*. The pain is so excruciating. Can't breathe. The Glock's blunt barrel slides into Lyle's mouth. It tastes like what it is; cold, bitter metal. But it's relief. And it's efficient.

The Glock has no safety. It's ready to fire. It rattles Lyle's teeth.

Shut your eyes for the last time. God will understand. He doesn't need Lyle Hall. Embrace the pain, the endless misery.

Screams and derisive laughter reach a high-pitched crescendo.

They can all go back to Hell!

A heavy hand lands on Lyle's shoulder. Its dead weight feels like fate itself. The demon has come. There's a chill breeze. The pistol is so heavy. Lyle's hands shake. The tip of his tongue finds the hollow muzzle. *To Hell with you all...*

"Lyle-eh!"

Fuck. Amid the screams, one voice mocks Teo Xerri. The good priest. Lyle's only holy friend. Squeeze the trigger, shithead! Time to go.

"Lyle-eh! *Please!*"

Eyes tight shut, his finger curls around the trigger.

An unseen force lunges at the Glock.

"Oh, God!" Lyle screams. He squeezes the trigger, there's a sharp *BANG* as the pistol recoils. The sound detonates through the barn. Dark things flap in the air.

Then there's quiet.

~~~~~~

81. Irritata

Afraid to look. This is what it's like to be dead. On the highway to Hell.

But Lyle unsquints as a huge black figure forcibly flings away his Glock. It lands hard in the corner near the broken bottle and skids under the old hay, moist with gasoline. The air is bitter with burnt gunpowder.

"Lyle-eh! What were you *thinking?*"

Lyle hears the Great Liar imitating the saintly Teo Xerri. He tries to focus on it.

"Lyle-eh, we must get out of here! This place is unclean!"

"Good God! *Teo?*" Lyle is shocked by recognition. "How are you *here?*"

"I lied-eh. I told Mister Szymanski I missed my flight. He was *irritata*, but he drove me here." Teo squeezes Lyle's shoulder. "I had to find you. Now we'll go!"

Lyle is unnerved as he feels his severest pains drain quickly out of his body. His eyesight clears. The numbness returning to his legs is welcome relief. But he knows what this means—Teo's hand is on his shoulder. "Teo, you mustn't touch me! There's something in this place, something terrible, and it wants me. Me! *Not you!*"

"I know," Teo whispers. He withdraws his hand and all Lyle's pains go with it. His legs go completely dead. But Lyle's relief turns to dread. A new terror rears up—what if Flo's *attachment* story is not paranormal bullshit? "Teo, don't touch me!"

The priest ignores that and tries to push Lyle's chair toward the doorway and safety. But it won't budge. And now a familiar, sickening weakness overcomes him.

"Lyle-eh, please! We *must go.*"

"Teo. I *can't go!* You don't know what's happening here!"

But Teo does. His muscles start to twinge involuntarily, his breath becomes labored. A horrific childhood memory returns and fear floods through him. Teo knows there is very little time. He has a penlight. He illumines the corner where he threw the pistol. Why does it reek of gasoline? A faint puff of smoke wafts upward.

"I know, Lyle-eh, this structure must come down. Before anyone else is hurt here. Including you-eh!" Teo, shaky now, plays his penlight along the rafters supporting the barn's high A-frame roof. He lights the row of fidgety bats hanging from the crossbeam directly above, their eyes radiate red. Ignoring them, he focuses on the upper rafters of the old post-and-beam structure. "English tying-joint rafters," he mutters. "Very old-eh."

Lyle's body pains have subsided but not his delirium. "What are you doing, Teo? You have to get out of here now!" he insists.

The priest directs his penlight to the sidewall and spots a huge old mallet hung from pegs long ago. The old wooden farm tool is camouflaged behind the gauzy web tended by the fist-size hairy spider from Lyle's previous visit to the barn.

"Let me try this one thing-eh. Very quickly. Then we leave together."

"Teo! What the *hell?*" Lyle is beyond drunk, beyond scared.

His muscles seizing, Teo moves stiffly to the wall. He shines his jittery penlight on the spider web. Unlike the web in the kitchen, this one's a silky tunnel, large and deep enough to lose your arm in. On cue, its resident emerges, partially at first. Teo detests spiders as much as Lyle Hall does and this thing is the size of his hand. He reaches for the old mallet. It's surprisingly heavy. As he tries to dislodge it, the spider suddenly skitters out of the web and jumps onto Teo's hand.

"*Teo!*"

The priest slaps the thing away, dropping his penlight. With two hands now he frees the big mallet from its pegs. Teo recognizes it as a "commander," used long ago in timber framing—whacking big wood into position. It's three feet long. Spider webbing trails from its business end, its thick mallet head easily weighs eight pounds. The spider makes a run for his pant leg and Teo's mallet catches it on the floor with a disgusting crunch.

The priest turns to Lyle, mallet in his hands, his face illuminated faintly now by an orange flicker from the barn's corner. White spittle is visible at the corners of his mouth. There's an ugly bite mark on his right hand. Lyle's eyes begin to sting. There's smoke.

"Teo! I'm telling you, get the hell out of here!"

But he raises the mallet menacingly. "No. I must end this!"

Lyle looks up at his friend. Frothing at the mouth, wild-eyed now and wielding a huge mallet. Lyle did this to Teo. The priest should be over the Atlantic right now sipping a cognac. Lyle slaps his chair arms. "I'm not going anywhere without you!"

Lyle is shocked by the black intensity in this man's eyes, almost bugging out of his head. The white froth means only one thing. The priest rotates suddenly and swings the old mallet upward with terrible force. Lyle shuts his eyes and ducks as the mallet head whips though smoky air. It thunks into its target and the whole barn shudders.

Lyle opens his eyes.

Teo's ferocious swing struck the main post supporting the barn's roof. His back to Lyle, Teo musters a last bit of strength. His arms shaky, his head cocked at an angle, he takes another big swing at the post. It's old and dried out, Teo knows. He grunts as the mallet strikes low and hard. The base of the post cracks loudly and dislodges from a position it's held since the Revolutionary War. There's a terrible groan as the roof buckles. Ancient dust showers down on the men. Bats flutter wildly through the smoky space. The big old post now leans at a dangerous angle.

Satisfied, Teo drops the mallet and turns to face Lyle. His features, constricted in pain, gleam with sweat set off by flickering firelight. The priest stumbles to his knees. He steadies himself against Lyle's lifeless legs and looks into his eyes. Teo's black pupils jitter frighteningly. "The roof will cave in. Soon. I had the strength to do that...or save you-eh. Not both..." Teo struggles for breath. "I am sorry I am so weak."

"No, Teo, please...just get yourself out of here now!"

"No. I came back because I am not good," Teo wheezes, a vein pulsing in his neck. "And you were desperate," he pants. "You know I caused my own mother's death." He starts to sputter. "And now I've caused yours! I am not good."

"Teo!" As Lyle grabs the priest's shoulders there's a loud groan above them. Suddenly the central crossbeam, the bats' perch, gives way and plummets the 16 feet to the floor, crashing directly behind Teo. Lyle realizes it's the beam old Milford hung himself from long ago. The bats flit in blind circles above the men.

"Okay, Teo, let's get out of here together! Don't give in to this!"

But Teo has given in—to an epileptic seizure. Staring blindly into Lyle's eyes, he topples to the filthy barn floor, bat shit everywhere. Lyle reaches down to cradle his twisted face. Dust, lit by an orangey flicker, sprinkles down. He's horrified Teo might swallow his tongue. How do you stop that? Something about a wooden spoon, right?

The unsupported roof groans again, now sending down splinters and wooden slats trailing more dust. Suddenly an awful CRASH—a section of roof clatters to the floor near the men. A jagged, gaping hole results and bats swarm through it into the night air. The cold half-moon briefly peeks inside for the first time in 250 years. Then it's occluded by storm clouds moving in. The barn's dust cloud mingles with rising smoke.

Lyle grabs Teo's arm. With his free arm, he struggles to move his chair manually. Now the remaining roof creaks; deep moans mix with high-pitched squeals of old wood; more rafters giving up the ghost. Lyle can barely budge his chair without power even when it only bears his weight. Teo's entire body is shuddering now, like he's being electrocuted. His wrists contort, setting his crooked hands at odd angles. Terror and self-reproach course through Lyle Hall. All his fault.

But then Teo's convulsions calm. Good. His fingertips reach up and grip Lyle's knees firmly. The priest's trembling head rises between Lyle's knees, but his eyes are closed, his face still constricted with pain. Lyle senses something new. Hatred. A guttural voice gurgles out of Teo's throat. The terrifying thing about it is, Lyle's heard it before.

"Sus...tain...low."

~~~~~

82. Intruder

"Sustain low."

It rocks Lyle's heart to hear that spew through the froth in Teo's distorted mouth. It's not Teo speaking, and that's not good. Got to be a relapse of his boyhood epilepsy attack. And it's Lyle's fault. Teo faces down at the dirty floor, head jerking like he's disagreeing with something. Before Lyle can think what to do, Teo growls at him.

"What are you doing in my barn?"

It's sickening to hear. Lyle cries, "Teo!"

"Little Teo's not here." Dirty, guttural laughter follows this.

Then Lyle's own words sound in Teo's throat. The priest's shuddering head rises to face him. Eyes rolled back, only the bloodshot whites show. Teo claws Lyle's dead knees. Lyle's heart breaks for his young friend.

"C'mon, motherfucker! Try me!"

Old lady voices rise from the floor and swirl around his wheelchair.

"Oh, Lyle! Oh, Lyle!"

Not Lyle's mother. So not Teo. The voices dissolve into derisive laughter.

Lyle screeches, "Where's Teo??" right in his face. "I want to talk to the priest!"

"Ohhhh...the lost boy. His phone doesn't work here. Talk when you both burn together!"

Could Teo really be possessed by a demon? Lyle wonders, is this the very demon he wanted to enter him? Lyle is sobering up fast. And an odd detail from Teo's crisis in the Gozo ruins hits him. The old shaman lady ridiculed the demon. Try it.

"Shut the fuck up, you perverted piece of shit! I want to talk to Matteo. Now!"

Teo's mouth forms a distorted leer. He repeats ominously, *"Sustain low."*

"You pathetic loser!" Lyle shouts, "Come out of him! NOW, dumb fuck!"

Teo looks uncertain for a beat and Lyle yells at him, "Go back to Hell, fucking asshole!" He hauls off and smacks his friend hard across the face.

Teo recoils, then digs his claws deeper into Lyle's knees. Lyle thinks he can actually feel it. Head cocked, Teo leans to Lyle's face. His breath stinks. His frothing mouth cracks a sick smile. The weird laughter returns, mocking mixed with moans.

Lyle can see Fr. Xerri clearly now, he's lit by firelight. The corner of the barn is in flame—what Lyle thought he wanted. His first and only Molotov cocktail, and his sock didn't absorb enough gasoline. A spark must have caught in the gas-soaked hay and rubbish. The corner where Lyle heard bloodcurdling screams last night is now being licked by crackling flames. And they're spreading. Bitter smoke catches in his throat as more wooden slats clatter down from the unsupported roof. There must be a way out of this but, looking at Teo, fear shoots through Lyle's gut. He seems held up by jerky puppet strings, steadying himself against Lyle's knees. All Lyle's fault. His alcoholic phone call brought Teo back here. He could be near death; his body writhing and trembling, obviously in great pain. Then his twitchy mouth rasps.

"Arson! Burning flesh is exquisite agony. Come to us now. Your cries will mix with your endless tears."

"Pathetic," Lyle responds. "The best you could do was a crippled small town lawyer."

"You are 'quite a catch.'" The disembodied laughter returns. Teo's leer is disgusting. *"And you make it so easy. Sustain low..."*

Suddenly Teo grabs Lyle's groin with shocking force. *"...means 'I want you'!"*

Then an evil grin. *"You can feel! Progress! 'Progress is our friend'!"*

Oh, shit. Incredibly, Lyle can feel the claw squeezing his groin, but he won't admit it, not to this thing. He shouts, "Teo!" and pushes the priest's shoulders backward violently. But his grip holds. Is Teo truly possessed? And *shit*, the damn fire he started is spreading, coming closer.

The voice taunts him. *"Now pray to your God. It amuses us."*

"I don't pray, you stupid shit." He's really hurting Lyle. "Let me talk to Teo!"

"He cannot hear you. But your many whores can hear you plea as your organs roast in endless fire. Dear Mother. Poor Belinda. Elsie. Becky. Flo. The whore Dar..." Teo laughs bitterly in Lyle's face. *"And the whore Silk! They'll all ridicule you. Soon. Forever. There is no such thing as time where you are going."*

Okay, Teo from Malta couldn't possibly know all these women. This is not good. A sickening *hiss* arises, circling Lyle like writhing snakes—taunting voices repeating *"Silk...Silk..."* Then they dissolve into a chorus of morose laughter.

Lyle's heart's desire, the return of feeling and strength, has turned into agony—a miracle in reverse. He tries to conjure any way to save his friend, but acrid smoke chokes the air as flames reach up to the rafters above. The whole barn is going up. Lyle digs his thumbnails into Teo's wrist to loosen his grip, but it's like a vise. Lyle blurts out an involuntary "Oh, God!" and the thing inside Teo grins sardonically inches from his face. Why do we say *Oh, God* at the worst times? Fiery embers start to plummet randomly from above. Lyle needs a solution fast. He needs Matteo to get out of here. But he can't leave. Lyle's heart starts to flutter like a bird in a cage. More miserable laughter…

"Your little whore 'Jewel' wants you, too. You always wanted a pretty girl!"

"Bullshit! None, *not one* of these women is in Hell, you lying shit!"

"Fools always argue before they suffer. Soon, lawyer. And forever."

Now another shattering CRASH shocks Lyle's struggling heart. A big flaming rafter, loosened by Teo's mallet, swings down from above, just missing them both. Teo smiles blindly as the timber thuds hard to the floor nearby, burning furiously. The heat is unbearable. Harsh smoke sears Lyle's throat. A banshee wail comes through the open roof. His mind, his body cannot generate even one more attempt to escape.

Teo's white collar has popped open. Tears run from his sightless white eyes. The advancing flames illuminate his glistening face and pulsing neck tendons. His breath is nauseating. A good man imprisoned in his own body. He sneers…

"Imagine there's no Heaven! Your 'god' lies to you. But he serves us well. He makes you, we burn you! We enjoy it. Terribly. Now beg to your god. Make us laugh!"

Miserable laughter wells up from the dirt floor, swirling around Lyle's chair. More burning shingles clatter down around them. One strikes Teo's shoulder and his suit jacket begins to smolder. The remaining rafters creak and moan. It's hot as blazes. Lyle is about to pass out here, even though he's sobered up.

"Okay, fucker. Take me, but I'm all you're gonna get!"
Voices laugh derisively. Pure evil. And time's up.

"Too late, crippled small town lawyer! We have your whore daughter now!"

A smoke cloud parts, revealing Belinda's grim headstone. Lyle gasps, inhaling only smoke. There's more hateful laughter as words etched in stone deliver a gut punch:

GEORGIA HALL
Loving Daughter
June 4, 1980 – October 16, 2010

Lyle squints at this too real horror, trying to will it to disappear. Georgie's date with death is tomorrow. *No—it's after midnight! It's October 16 now!* His heart condition worsens, fluttering like a hummingbird. Not getting enough blood pumping. Not enough air. Gasp for air…

"NO!!"

"No? The lawyer wants to negotiate?" More laughter.

"Here's an indecent proposal. Pray to ME. Beg ME to spare the whore's short, pathetic life."

More derisive laughter. *Could this be real? Make a deal with the Devil?* Smoke from Teo's smoldering shoulder wafts upward.

"Beg me. Now, pitiful cripple."

The claw twists Lyle's gonads even harder. Lyle must silence the voices. He's losing his friend; losing his daughter. His heart, his body pains are throbbing. This thing wants him to die here.

"Beg like a dog and I may spare that whore."

Lyle can't think. His breath is a feeble wheeze. But he heard the demonic words.

His right hand hardens into a rock-hard fist. His left grips the armrest. And then Lyle Hall does something he's never even contemplated before now.

Through stinging eyes, Lyle sees the priest's sickly grin flinch just as his knuckles, galvanized by rage, rocket across Teo's mouth. It feels great. A spew of froth and a bloody tooth fly out as Teo's head jolts backward.

"Go back to Hell, asshole!" Lyle spits.

The priest wobbles. He finally releases Lyle's groin.

Lyle's workouts worked. Teo's eyelids close. He goes down.

And stays down. Another burning ember lands on Teo's suit jacket.

Lyle hears the plaintive banshee wail outside. Now he's really done it.

~~~~~~

83. Convergence

The October squall that followed Mundo and Ruben from Manhattan has reached the East End. Cold drops are making Berto's oily garage apron shine as he creeps into the darkened garage bay. His AR-15 is loaded. His men are very close now with the cash from what will be his last deal. He's called Chantale and instructed her to pack for warm weather. Bring the passports. And the "luggage" with their savings. Enough of this.

His delivery men will be out of a job. Fuck 'em. But they must not come here and see this bitch still sitting outside his office. He'd look weak. Like she scared him off.

Chantale has coolly accepted Berto's fevered plan. He'll pay off Mundo and Fuckhead and collect that cash. Then he and Chantale will drive to Jersey; ditch the Escalade at Newark Airport; get the first flight to Miami; then Port-au-Prince.

Before they run, his men will see the policewoman's body and know the caliber of man who employed them. And the police will understand who they were dealing with, too. She's not likely to come in for coffee. But she would come to make a drug bust. Berto intends to light up the garage bay, stand in the doorway with his baggie and snort blow in full view. In the garage bay now, Berto positions his rifle just out of sight, ready to blow away an intruder. The next events will require precise timing. And with each passing second, Berto's temples seem to pulsate harder. This is his big moment.

He flips on the garage lights.

Using her night-vision binoculars, Georgie Hall had been observing Berto/Escobar making some kind of preparations in the darkened garage. She puts them down as the fluorescent lights flicker on. Strange. Berto steps into the open doorway, backlit by ugly garage lights. His hips undulate to some unheard rhythm. He's holding a quart-size plastic baggie half-full of white powder. Careful to stay sheltered from the rain, Berto shovels a fingernailful up his nose and laughs maniacally. It's time.

"Hey! Lady! Georgia Hall! C'mon girl! Cops like to party too, right? It's Friday night! I had a fight with my girl! Let's you and me par-tay!"

He takes another ostentatious snort, laughs loudly. "Ohhhh! The *best!* You want some, girl?" He sways his hips, but a bloody sinus eruption makes him step out of view.

"All cars: this is Hall at taxi stand. Subject 'Escobar' has been quiet but is now out in plain sight, snorting white powder from a baggie. Disturbing the peace, making menacing statements and gestures, behaving erratically. Requesting backup. Requesting backup."

The radio comes alive with chatter. Many respond they're on their way to the taxi stand. Then Georgie's cell rings. It's Frank again—no time now, but she picks up.

"Frank. I'm a little busy," she spits.

"I gathered." Frank's tone gives her a cold shock. "It's about your father."

"What about him?"

"There's a four-alarm fire in Bridgehampton. At the haunted house."

"What??"

"Not the house, the barn. It's fully involved. EMS is on the scene. There's someone inside the barn." Frank takes a breath. "A man in a wheelchair."

Another pause.

"Oh my God."

"I'm at the stationhouse now. I'll check back when I know more. Good luck."

Frank disconnects. Georgie's heart sinks and her head pounds. *That fucking old man, right in the middle of the first bust of my career!* Then her heart starts to flutter—is it fear, stress, excitement? She's got to do something. But what? Georgie starts her engine, throws on her lights and wipers. Backup is on the way. It would be okay to leave the scene. Lyle has become a major shit but she can't let her father die alone in a burning barn. Queeley wouldn't hold it against her. *Would* he...

Now flashing red-and-blue lights flicker between the scraggly trees. Two squad cars are flying down Squiretown Road. Georgie is facing north like every night so far. Uncertain and torn, she puts her car in gear and slowly rolls forward one car length.

Then she stops. Without warning Berto is back. He was watching Georgie while blowing bloody mucus into a paper towel. Now he clutches his crotch with his right hand.

"Hey Girl! C'mon! Get off the phone, bitch! You *know* you want some! Come and GET IT!!" His voice reaches a pitch that makes him sound certifiably insane. He laughs harshly.

Taking in the spectacle from her driver-side window Georgie tries to focus, weigh a plan, but things are getting scrambled. The squad cars are almost here—lights on, sirens off. *Wait.* She must not leave the scene after calling for backup at a developing situation with an active suspect. Even Lyle would understand. She throws the gear selector into park and studies crazy Berto and his shitty garage from this new angle. She feels the reassuring pressure of her holster against her breast.

Something's gotta give.

Berto screams, "Where you goin' girl?? You know you WANT some of this!"

Just then one squad car, lights flashing, skids to a fishtail halt between Georgie and Berto. She recognizes the black veteran sergeant at the wheel. Georgie unholsters her service revolver as a second squad car screeches to a halt just past the sergeant.

Shit. Where the fuck did the perp go? Suspects sometimes disappear at the most critical moment. But now "Escobar" steps back into view. Armed.

In an instant a fusillade of gunfire rips through the falling rain. Berto's assault rifle riddles the sergeant's squad car on the passenger side. All three cops instinctively duck down. Georgie peeks up—Berto's shooting from the hip, barely able to control his gunfire. He's screaming some crazy bullshit, one arm waving free, gesturing wildly at the cops. The sergeant's car is in roughly the same position Georgie's white car had been all week. Suddenly his windshield explodes as Berto fires a new spurt of rounds. The sarge's passenger-side window spider-webs, then blows inward. His squad car rocks, absorbing another burst of rifle fire at close range. Georgie ducks down; her car's exposed front end bucks as it also takes fire—*pang-pang-pang*—as AR-15 shells strike metal.

Then a pause. Raindrops spatter the sergeant through the open windshield.

Georgie cannot see the sergeant. But she can see Berto take something from his jacket pocket. Not what he wants, he drops it. Now he fishes out a fresh ammo clip.

It takes the coke head three seconds to reload. At the same moment, telling herself this is no different than the firing range, Georgie steadies her revolver in her open window. Berto senses this and their eyes meet as he swings his weapon in her direction. Georgie gets off one shot; then ducks again as the AR-15 erupts, puncturing metal with a long burst—*pang-pang-pang-pang-pang*.

Continuing fire from the assault rifle is so loud it's disorienting. *Where is the fucker now?* She envisions this creep approaching and firing through her open window. Georgie raises her head slightly, her revolver ready, and peeks. The sergeant's car is shivering, bouncing in place like a low rider. His passenger door takes many more thunking rounds; the front tire blows; the front end sags down. The shooter is aiming low.

Then eerie silence. Only raindrops.

~~~~~~~

84. Blazes

It's hot. Very hot. And fire is surprisingly loud. Teo Xerri, here to save Lyle Hall, lies on his side on the dirt floor. He's not convulsing. His eyes are closed: good? His black suit jacket is smoldering: bad. Only thing is to drag him outside somehow and get help. Sure as hell can't stay here. The barn door is maybe 30 feet away. Despite his pounding heart, Lyle puts the chair in neutral, bends and hooks his left hand under the priest's shoulder. Right hand on the chair's right wheel. Maybe it will roll.

Searing pain!

Lyle's knuckles are throbbing; his right hand must be broken after socking Teo so hard in the jaw. He needs a plan as fire consumes the walls to his right and dance overhead along the remaining rafters. Sizzling orange flames produce a low cloud of gray smoke; it billows over the men, choking Lyle. He tries to think: do these batteries have any reserve power? He throws his chair into reverse. Forget the broken hand—he grabs Teo's shoulder with his good hand and uses his injured hand to gun the accelerator. Good God—the chair budges! Teo's body drags a few inches across the bat-shit floor. Lyle can see he must do this dozens of times to make it to the door before the rest of the place collapses in flame on them. Shit. If only he still had his old Mr. Potter wheelchair now.

Hitting the chair's accelerator again, Lyle manages to yank Teo backward some more, making a little progress. Too little. His right hand, as good as dead, throbs with pain. Lyle's every pore is sweating freely, releasing alcohol; his heart is fluttering; he gasps for air and gets a lungful of blistering smoke.

The fire he started wants more dry wood and it spreads hungrily upward engulfing the remaining roof, crackling as the structure groans. There's a terrifying creak like an ancient scream and more roof comes down. Crashes sound everywhere around them as a large roof section, fully aflame, plummets to the barn floor, heavy rafters and all. Planks spear the floor like flaming arrows. It's raining burning wood and shingles. Lyle covers his head but has no way to protect Teo.

One fiery shingle lands on Teo's pants and the unconscious man does not react. Lyle panics, trying to roll forward to reach the burning shingle. But his chair is now dead for good.

Now a high-pitched shriek pierces the smoke. Incredibly, it's coming *from* the fire—the corner where all the trouble was. Lyle is sure he's hallucinating as a large ball of fire rolls toward him, actually dodging the fallen roof beams. It's big, it's on fire. And it's alive. It's running toward him on all fours.

Giving a bloodcurdling screech, the possum, fully engulfed in flame, leaps onto Teo's body. It's burning alive. It smells like hell. Yet Lyle imagines that it's smiling.

"Oh, God!" he cries. Lyle makes to kick the damned thing but his leg won't obey. The creature gives one final hiss and rolls onto the barn floor in a ball of flame. Lyle realizes he's succumbing to smoke inhalation. He can do no more.

Harsh voices cry out. Beams of light zigzag frantically through smoke clouds.

Weird. His eyes tearing from acrid smoke, Lyle senses Teo's body sliding involuntarily across the floor. Not using his legs or arms. He's been possessed. Taken.

From somewhere very close by, a louder banshee cry slices through the smoke, rising into the night along with the scorching orange flames. A light hits Lyle in the face. A monstrous figure suddenly emerges from the smoke, angry and looming large.

Some superhuman strength grips the handles of Lyle's chair. This is it. Demonic power propelling him into the inferno—death and damnation, as planned. He can feel the heat broil his face and hands. It will burn perpetually. That's how this works. He's lost Teo. Lost Georgie. At least he burned up an old barn. And a possum.

Oddly, now that it's time, Lyle feels a stab of regret. Maybe he didn't truly want this. Too late now. He asked for it. Blazing heat and choking smoke. His last thought is the name for his

heart condition: *supraventricular tachycardia*. Then he passes
out.

Unseen strength pushes the chair forward. Hard. Once again it
barely budges. It's dead.

"Gotta pick him up!" a muffled voice shouts. "One, two,
three!" More fiery planks clatter down. Banshees wail as Lyle's
eyes squint open. He's being manhandled. The wall to his right
collapses, sending a burst of flame in his direction. He sees a
huge roof beam above him burning furiously. He's too far gone
to react as it dislodges with a squeal and swings down toward
him, spearing the floor nearby with a deep thud. Right where
Teo's body had lain a moment ago. The heat from it is blistering.
But Lyle is floating out of the barn. He looks back at his
wheelchair as it goes up in flame.

Then he's outside. Coughing.

The air is fresh and cool. Fat raindrops meet flames raging
into the heavens.

~~~~~~

85. Swiss Cheese

Laughter breaks the quiet outside the limo depot. High pitched, strange at first. It's the laughter of relief. The shooter is down.

Service revolver drawn, Officer Allan Petry exits his mostly intact car and cautiously approaches the downed shooter from the left. Out of her car now, Detective Hall is moving on the assailant from the right, holding her target—Berto's head—at gunpoint. The two cops triangulate on the perp, who's on his back. But there's no movement. And, Georgie can see from her angle, there won't be. Berto's head lies in a spreading pool of his own blood. She eyes Petry and nods at Berto's rifle, still clutched in his right hand. Petry approaches Berto on that side but pauses for a second. With his free hand, he takes a cellphone picture of the body as it lies, still armed. Then he quickly kicks the AR-15 away. The assault rifle is hot and it steams as raindrops pepper it.

Now Petry stoops and frisks the perp's body.

There's movement to Georgie's left. She flinches briefly, then relaxes.

"WooHOO! Will you look at THAT!" Sgt. Mackey has worked his way out of his bullet-riddled car and approaches the body. Everyone calls Sgt. Arthur Mackey "Mack." One of the better liked cops on the Southampton Police force, he was the source of the laughter a moment ago. His perforated, sizzling cruiser is now a large hunk of Swiss cheese. He takes in the scene around them.

The shell casings, at least 60, are strewn everywhere. Taking in the surrounding mayhem, he makes a hushed whistle. Then he stifles himself—he's the ranking officer on the scene and Detective Hall likely just saved his life with one bullet.

The rainfall stops. Mack and Hall watch Petry take more cellphone photos of the shooter as he fell. Berto's body, legs flailed in crazy directions, lies on slimy concrete, unseeing eyes fixed on the garage bay's sputtering fluorescent light. There's a clean hole above the left eyebrow. The left hand grips a golden charm hung around his neck. A gold switchblade lies nearby, sprung open. A dark pool of blood spreads from the back of the head, mingling with the grease on the floor. It reaches the knife.

Georgie's first shooting. It strikes her now that Berto's fumbling with the knife in his jacket pocket when trying to reload bought her extra seconds to take aim.

Petry checks Berto's pulse, a formality, and looks up at Mack and Georgie. "He's still dead."

Mack wipes his forehead and exhales deeply. Then he looks at Georgie Hall and smiles. "Nice shot, Detective. Where'd you learn to shoot like that?"

"It helps if you already dislike the shooter intensely."

Mack snorts. "I have to keep that in mind."

Humberto Duvan, man of many aliases and nicknames, went down shooting. His assault rifle continued to discharge as he lay dying on the garage floor, puncturing Mack's cruiser with rounds.

Georgie is startled to see Mack's forehead is smeared with blood. His hands, pricked by a hundred glass shards, are bloody mitts he's barely aware of.

"Mack..." she begins.

Petry steps over. "Way to take fire, Sergeant. You need first aid for those hands."

Mack shrugs. He's just glad Hall took out the shooter.

Georgie thanks the two cops for responding so quickly. Then she explains about her father, the fire in Bridgehampton and his dire straits.

"You need to go see to that man, Detective," Mack says. "We can handle this. You only have one dad, right?"

Georgie hesitates. "Mack, you know all those bullets were meant for me."

Mack smiles broadly at her. "Well, he wasn't much of a shot."

The night air fills with wailing sirens. Cop cars in pursuit nearby, lights on, sirens on. Petry gets on his radio to report shooter down at the taxi stand.

Detective Hall is uneasy about leaving a crime scene where she was actively involved. But, despite all the rounds fired and the dead shooter, hers is an extreme situation. She knows Sgt. Mackey, as the ranking officer on the scene, will stick up for her when the time comes. And it will come—once Swan Song wakes up Chief Queeley.

Mack can tell how shaken she is. He wishes her luck and extends his hand to shake hers, then chuckles at his own bloody paw. "Just a flesh wound."

That's when all three cops hear one solitary shot fired. About a quarter mile north. Georgie hops into her car. The Crown Vic's lights are mounted behind the grille as well as inside the windshield above the sun visors. Georgie gets them all flashing and speeds silently north on Squiretown Road toward Sunrise Highway and the sound of the gunshot.

Her radio is alive with chatter. Mr. Clean's limo is stopped. Trini Lopez has fled on foot. Georgie opens her mic and adds a new detail. "All cars. Note a late-model BMW sports car, black, driver is non-white female. Female is involved with shooter."

As she approaches Sunrise Highway, there's police activity ahead. She slows and sees that three squad cars, lights flashing, have boxed in Mr. Clean's limo, stopped in mid-U-turn. Mr. Clean sits in the back of one car. Two cops are shining their big flashlights into the scrub oak woods that stretch west from Squiretown Road to the Hampton Bays Cemetery. Trini Lopez has bolted into the woods.

But Trini Lopez is not Georgie Hall's concern now. She has to get to her father. She feels a chill of dread as she hits the gas and sounds a few bleeps. Hers has become a unique cop car: flashing lights, ventilated front end and, in the backseat, a voodoo doll and a condom with a face. Bridgehampton. In a hurry.

Ruben is in a hurry, too. One of those gringo cops actually fired a fucking warning shot over his head. Now he's got 300 yards of scrub oak to run through—or hide in. More cops could be anywhere in these shitty woods. He pauses, catches his breath.

Trembling, he makes a call. Fuck—no answer. The cemetery is dead ahead. Sunrise Highway is north to his right. Got to decide his best course. Then his phone silently lights up.
CHANTALE BENOIT

~~~~~~

86. Sirens

Out here, you can tell how hot it was in there. And how loud a fire really is—the crackling and burning, the crashing timbers. You see the glowing orange sparks rise skyward, then lose their way in a night sky full of mournful wails. Sirens. And rain. Cool rain. Lyle's heartrate calms considerably. A keyboard riff, a high, repeating synthesizer figure, emerges from his subconscious and flits upwards, rising like the sparks to meet the raindrops. It's from "Love, Reign O'er Me" and he flashes on seeing the Who perform long ago with Noah. He watches those sparks. So graceful. Almost like glowing orbs, they disappear into the heavens.

Harsh, urgent voices. So many men in DayGlo and coats with reflective stripes. Abrasive radios. The horizontal bleats of a rescue truck. Lyle lies on a stretcher, coughing. The barn is a safe distance away. He's in Old Vic's backyard near the kitchen door. The firefighters have hose lines extended. *God, don't let anyone get hurt.* Smooth streams of water douse the inferno he started. More coughing. Do people in Hell cough? His eyes close.

Lyle wakes with a start to the chaos of a fully involved fire. He rubs his crunchy eyelids to see, trying to make sense of his surroundings. He props himself on one elbow. Shit. Where is Teo? There, lying nearby on a stretcher. Lyle gasps. A first responder in a heavy firefighter coat and helmet lit with flickering LEDs hovers over the priest, pumping his chest. He removes his helmet and bends to breathe into Teo's mouth. CPR. But the priest is not responsive. His olive complexion is sickly pale.

Teo! Lyle thinks, this must be when people pray for someone. What do you say to God? Please let my friend live? Then the shock of Georgie's date of death stabs his heart. *Today.* It may be too late! Oh, God. He should pray. Get her help. How do you pray?

"How many people were in there?"

It's another first responder. He also wears a blinking helmet, this one's white, and a heavy coat, boots too. One of the men who carried Lyle out of the burning barn. Like a victim. Or like a perpetrator? The white helmet bends down to Lyle.

"How many people were in there?" he shouts in Lyle's face as if he's some kind of moron. Maybe he is some kind of moron now. More sirens. And horns.

"My daughter!" Lyle coughs. "Gotta save my daughter!" He seems delirious.

"Your daughter is in that barn?" shouts White Helmet.

"No!" Lyle can hardly speak. "Need to call her! Protect her!"

"Alright, Mister, we need to know who else is in that barn! Can you tell me?"

Lyle shakes his head, coughs and points to Teo.

"Just the two of you?" Lyle nods yes. White Helmet yells into a squawking radio. "Yeah, two adult males. Got 'em out. The conscious one confirms there were only two." He kneels in front of Lyle and actually takes his face in his scratchy hands, examining Lyle's eyes.

"Can you tell me your name?" Lyle tells him. White Helmet's grimy face is oddly familiar. "What is the other man's name?"

Lyle coughs it out—"Father Matteo Xerri"—over the sirens and bleating fire truck horns. He adds, "Epileptic!" White Helmet does not react to that.

Through stinging eyes, Lyle can see the barn is a raging inferno. But there's not much left to burn. The fire's heat negates the cold raindrops—its glow must be visible for miles. There's a shattering crash and his heart jumps as another barn wall collapses on itself. Lyle hopes all those firefighters are safe— what if one gets injured? His fault.

Insistent beeping joins the sirens and horns. An ambulance backs up into Old Vic's bumpy yard, lights flashing. A phone's ringing, too. Someone is calling the weeds.

The ambulance's back doors swing open. It's brightly lit inside like a mini emergency room. There's a woman EMT. Working together, the two first responders position Teo's stretcher on the ambulance lift gate. Teo's head lolls to the side, facing Lyle as the lift ascends. The priest's black eyes are open! Lyle is convinced that, at least for the moment, Teo is conscious. Quiet words cut through the din. "*I am...tajba ta.*" Only Lyle hears this. He senses the meaning. It's Maltese.

I am good.

The words rock Lyle to his bones.

A shadowy figure emerges from behind Old Vic, observing the raging barn and all the activity. Orange flames illuminate the heavy man's wet raincoat and comb-over. He raises his camera and clicks as firefighters work to quell the blaze. Once more, he captures Lyle Hall. And a priest on a stretcher.

The EMT helps the first responders roll Teo inside the mobile ER and they secure his stretcher. Lyle sees her go to work on the priest right away—clearing the mouth of obstructions, pumping the chest, strapping on an oxygen mask.

Then both first responders get in Lyle's face.

"There's enough room for him," one of them says.

"Mister Hall!" Says White Helmet. "We're taking you to Southampton Hospital."

Very quickly Lyle is up on the lift. His stretcher secured inside the ambulance, the lift retracts. Drawing closed the ambulance doors, White Helmet notices a cell phone out in the weeds, lit up and ringing. The ambulance isn't quite ready to roll so he hops out, plucks it up and clambers back in. He holds the phone for Lyle to see. Its battery icon is red. Red means dead. As the call evaporates Lyle reads: GEORGIE.

Then he's hit with a new horror. Oh *shit!* What if that's *not* Georgie calling? He winces and coughs. They start to roll over the bumpy yard.

There are more sounds right outside—keening sirens and squawking horns. Voices on radios. The Bridgehampton Fire

Department is outside Old Vic, more trucks can be heard approaching.

"Lyle Hall! You with us?" White Helmet is still holding the iPhone.

Lyle's injured hand gestures to it. "Need to call my daughter," he chokes.

His eyes close as the ambulance jostles onto the rutted driveway.

Two honking pumpers and a huge ladder truck are now at the scene. There's a fire chief's red SUV. More firefighters hustle up the driveway, running hose lines back to the burning barn. The ambulance creeps between them and the front-loader still parked there. Not much barn left to burn; the job now is to prevent the blaze from spreading. They hose down Old Vic, too.

Lyle looks over at Teo. His only thoughts, *What have I done? Where's Georgie?*

Old Vic is getting a soaking. As the EMS truck pulls away, Lyle wonders, is Jewel watching? Could Jewel get wet? Was this disaster what she was asking for? Did *any* of this help? Is it too late to help Georgie? The ambulance moves down Poplar. The man's white helmet is on the floor now. "Chief" is printed on its gold shield. Chief Velcros a blood-pressure gauge tight around Lyle's arm. Who *is* this guy? The face is eerie, more familiar without the helmet.

Reading the gauge, Chief says some numbers aloud. Bad numbers.

The ambulance passes more demolition equipment parked on Poplar.

Groggy, Lyle croaks, "How's my friend?" before a racking cough erupts.

The EMT is busy with Teo. She doesn't answer. Lyle's eyes close again. He can still hear. Or maybe he's dreaming.

"The priest has a broken jaw along with everything else," says the woman.

"A fall?" says Chief.

"It's consistent with a nasty blow to the jaw, like in a bar fight."

Chief calls her attention to Lyle's injured hand. "You believe this?"

She winces and nods at Teo. "And he's a priest no less."

Poplar to Montauk Highway. It's over eight miles to Southampton Hospital, but an ambulance, especially late at night, can cover it in 12 minutes or less.

The ambulance siren sounds as Chief, crouched by Lyle, gets on his phone.

"Sergeant? Yeah, this is Assistant Chief Cronk. You wanted an update. Well we got two men at the scene. Yeah, two. Lyle Hall, like you said, and a young man. Yes. A priest. The barn was fully involved. It's gone."

Jimmy Cronk listens for a moment, then responds. "Mister Hall is in very serious condition. Smoke inhalation. Very high heart rate and blood pressure. Burns." He listens. "Yes. The priest, not good. Possible epileptic seizure."

Big Frank asks Chief Cronk for more on Lyle's condition but Cronk cannot hear him over the bleating siren. Cronk holds his phone so Frank can hear the EMT describe the priest's condition. Frank thinks she's describing Lyle Hall.

"He's critical," she calls out. Frank tries to hear. She adds, "We're doing all we can until we get him to the hospital. Gonna be very close."

Cronk puts the phone to his ear. "Sergeant? Southampton Hospital. Ten minutes." He signs off.

Lyle's eyes open and for the first time he really sees Jimmy Cronk and knows him. A wave of conflicting emotions flood his head and his weak heart.

"Jimmy Cronk," Lyle whispers. "Why would you rescue me?"

Jimmy Cronk narrows his eyes at Lyle as the ambulance flies down the highway.

"So I can sue you," he deadpans.

"Don't bother, Jimmy," Lyle says, slipping away again. "You already won."

The siren makes a long shriek as they speed through rain toward Southampton.

~~~~~~

Sgt. Frank Barsotti is at the Southampton Town Police stationhouse. Disconnecting with Assistant Chief Jimmy Cronk, he calls Detective Hall. He will meet her at Southampton Hospital. Critical condition. They're doing all they can.

Georgie, beyond distraught now, reroutes to the hospital. Her knuckles are white on the steering wheel. This is worse than being shot at—there's nothing she can do about it. At least she can try her best to see her father while there's still time. Maybe disowning him wasn't such a good idea. Her siren goes on.

Things are coming to a head at the stationhouse. Big Frank is now standing a few paces from the imposing desk where suspects are booked by the duty sergeant. Over the past year, the duty sergeant has routinely been Bert Swanson, whose ass is widely thought to form a convex mirror image of his chair seat. The man before him now is Detective Andy Peel, Suffolk County Internal Affairs, an old friend of Frank's. He's speaking quietly with Swanson. Peel has been in the stationhouse for hours performing the unenviable task of inspecting the men's lockers. Now it's Swanson's turn and Peel is offering the short-timer the courtesy of accompanying him on the inspection. He's sweating bullets.

The radio is squawking like crazy between the firefight in Hampton Bays and the four-alarm in Bridgehampton. But Swanson abandons his post. The tubby sergeant gives off an odor as he steps down to the floor. Sixteen-plus hours in the same uniform. Like a cabby after a long shift behind the wheel. Perps give off a smell like that too, Frank thinks, when they're about to cave. Swanson knows his prints were lifted from Georgie's locker. His self-preservation instinct is kicking in. Andy Peel makes eye contact with Big Frank as he walks Swanson back to the locker room.

Frank follows them. He's got a few minutes before heading to the hospital.

~~~~~~~

87. Father Unknown

To the east, spent storm clouds turn orange. Saturdays are quiet and beautiful, once summer ends. The halls of Southampton Hospital's ER are congested after a busy Friday night. Patient Hall is on a gurney with an IV drip, waiting for a room. He sees a big cop lead a tall woman toward him, navigating between patients, gurneys and staff.

"Dad! Dad, are you all right??"

Bleary Lyle focuses on her. His heart leaps. Beautiful Georgie Hall. His girl.

"Georgie!" he whispers. "Are *you* all right?"

Georgie searches her dad's red eyes, pushes back a hank of his dirty hair.

"I'm fine. Dad..." She squeezes his uninjured hand and Lyle can actually feel his daughter's emotions well up. "They were afraid you weren't going to make it!"

"Kind of them not to tell me. I'm just *so glad* to see you! You'll never know!"

Tears form in Georgie's eyes as she bends and hugs her father hard.

"Ow!"

"Sorry, Dad..." She recoils, releasing him.

"Wait. Can we try that again?" He looks into his daughter's eyes. "Please?"

Georgie hugs him again, tenderly. "I'm just so glad you're going to be okay."

"Let's not over-promise."

Georgie breaks into a warm smile. Lyle ponders when he's ever seen her like this. Oh yeah, never. Georgie cradles her dad's sooty face as she fights more tears.

"We gotta clean you up."

"You don't know the half of it." He feels sleep coming on.

Georgie continues to smile at him. But something's on her overwrought mind.

"Dad. When you're up to it, Frank has something to show you."

"The collector's edition first issue of *Playboy*..." His eyes start to close.

"Better than that, Dad."

Lyle resists, but peaceful sleep comes over him. Georgie gently touches his cheek. To herself, she says, "First I need to look up my high school Italian teacher."

~~~~~~~

By lunchtime Lyle had been admitted and sponge-bathed and had napped a few hours. Now Georgie's back. She has her briefcase. She's just come from the home of Mrs. Frances Strangio, retired Bridgehampton High School Italian teacher. She'd been surprised and pleased to see the grown up Georgie Hall at her door.

Lyle is propped up in bed. Georgie notes the peaked-looking items on his tray.

"Hi, Dad. You're looking much better. How was lunch?"

"Yellow. Jell-O."

"Go easy on that stuff, okay?" She turns serious. "So I talked to your nurse. You have, among many issues, *alcohol poisoning?*"

Lyle senses a bout of Stern Georgie coming on. "Fell off the wagon. Long story."

"Well that story is now over. Dad, apparently you even had alcohol poisoning on TV. *Self inflicted*. People all over saw you like that. I just..." Georgie gives in to frustration. "I just wish you returned *one* of my calls!" That comes out a bit loud.

"I'm sorry. Won't happen again. I promise. I did leave a pathetic text."

She looks in her Dad's eyes and takes his left hand in hers. "Yeah, I read it, Dad. I guess that counts." She looks down at his bandaged hand. "I'm sorry for your friend."

Lyle fights a vision of facing Teo in a burning barn. Causing a good man's death.

"How exactly did you break your knuckles?"

"Long story. I'm sorry. Won't happen again. Next?" He makes a show of looking at a monitor mounted above him. "See? You're raising my blood pressure."

"That's not your blood pressure, Dad. Listen. I want to show you something if you're up to it. It's...interesting."

Georgie removes the untouched lunch tray—green tea, broth and Jell-O—and places a bulging manila folder on Lyle's adjustable dining table. Lyle can feel his daughter's pulse quicken as she slides out a photocopy of an old photograph. She watches his expression as he focuses on it.

"Anybody you know, Dad?"

Lyle's jaw drops, his face goes white. A monitor actually does beep faster.

"Georgie...*Omigod!*"

It's Jewel.

The girl in the photo looks very much as she originally appeared to Lyle.

"Can you believe it?" says Georgie with satisfaction.

Lyle is incredulous; he can't swallow. They are looking at a very old crime-scene photo. Sure enough, it's Jewel, photographed the way they found her. She's not floating. She's collapsed, her back against a rustic wall, her face very pale, sad eyes open. Dead.

Georgie says, "Frank found this in an old cabinet in a back room at the stationhouse. Like you suggested. The girl lived at One-eleven Poplar—'Old Vic'—around the turn of the last century. And yes, the place was a house of prostitution operated by one Armand Keller. Late one Saturday night in October 1910, a woman named Gianna Rossi fled the house and ran to the local police station to report a grisly crime."

Lyle seems to go somewhere else. Long ago. If he truly is an empath, now's the time to absorb these events. Georgie takes out a copy of an old document.

"Looking for Jewel, Dad? Here she is."

Odd. It's a birth certificate for one Jewel Rossi, daughter of Carlina Rossi, dated October 16, 1910.

"Jewel died at birth, Dad. A hundred years ago."

Georgie looks into Lyle's staring eyes. All he can say is, "No. That can't be."

She picks up the old photo. "Dad. The face you talked about on TV was this girl's, twelve-year-old Carlina Rossi, the child of Gianna Rossi, father unknown. This picture was taken, photographer unknown, on October 16, 1910. Carlina had died that early morning in Old Vic's barn. Fatally stabbed by this Armand Keller character."

Lyle stares silently at the picture and the birth certificate, signed by some old judge. Then he closes his eyes and listens as his daughter describes that night. He feels like he's there—observing the monstrous events of a century ago.

"Gianna, only thirty-two, was Carlina's mother, baby Jewel's grandmother. She signed this statement, written in her own hand in Italian." Georgie refers to notes she took from Frances Strangio's translation. "She describes how Keller, who'd run his whorehouse since the 1890s, would keep girls unlucky enough to get pregnant in the old barn. There were no nearby neighbors back then. Girls close to term could not make him money, but he derived another revenue stream from them. When a sex worker gave birth, Keller could sell a boy baby. He'd have the mother raise a girl baby. Each mother knew Keller would eventually rent her child to pervert customers who wanted young girls." Georgie adds, "Clients came off whaling ships, sometimes higher-ups from local government—even the old police department. But this murder led to a cover-up and the disappearance of official records."

Lyle opens his eyes and stares at the papers before him.

"Dad. Gianna was an immigrant. Keller would prey on poor girls when they got off the boat in New York. They were often without papers. He promised employment. What they got was enslavement. According to her statement, in 1898, Gianna, at age nineteen, gave birth to Carlina in Keller's barn. Keller freely

426

sampled his own wares and had a self-propagating inventory. When little Carlina turned twelve, she got pregnant too."

"At the age of twelve?"

"Twelve. So Gianna understood what a birth would mean—a third-generation sex slave. After a busy Saturday night, actually early Sunday morning, Gianna got into a bitter argument with Keller in the barn, threatening to expose him. Carlina was coming to term at that point and living in the barn. It had a makeshift kitchen back then. He was strangling Gianna when Carlina intervened. She stuck the sonofabitch with a kitchen knife, a mortal abdominal wound. But Keller disarmed the pregnant girl and stabbed her viciously with the same knife. He then turned on Gianna again, but collapsed. Keller bled out right there on the floor. Carlina...her wound was fatal. She hung in for a little while, but miscarried there in the barn."

Lyle winces with pain for the girl's suffering as Georgie continues.

"Gianna was horrified. She wrapped the stillborn grandchild in a towel and laid it on her daughter's lap. She lied, telling Carlina that her baby was asleep. Carlina's dying wish was that her baby get an official birth certificate. She named her 'Jewel.' And she passed away holding Jewel in her arms."

Lyle raises his eyes and stares out the window. He whispers, "*Help. Jewel.*"

"Dad. You with me?"

He returns his gaze to the picture and the birth certificate, shaking his head. Georgie continues from her notes. "It was the wee hours of October sixteenth. Gianna ran into town to alert the police. She must have been terrified, but she was brave. She told them everything she could in broken English and insisted they wake up the local judge to have him create official birth certificates validating the baby's existence—and Carlina's—as U.S. citizens. Gianna wrote out the ugly events in Italian, kind of a deposition. Missus Strangio translated it for me this morning."

Feeling excited but woozy, Lyle knits his brow. "Missus who?"

"Strangio. My high school Italian teacher. So Dad, police officials were reluctant to act on this strange woman's claims. Most locals had never seen Gianna Rossi around town. She'd spent her years in America mostly confined to Keller's property. She spoke very little English. Given the early Sunday morning hour and Keller's known VIP clientele, the police stalled— possibly wary of repercussions. Gianna was frantic to get back to her daughter. Sensing they would not help, she ran in tears from the police station.

"Sunday morning the official contingent finally arrived at Old Vic—cops, a doctor, a photographer, too. They found sex workers aimlessly wandering the property."

Georgie pauses and looks at Lyle. She continues quietly.

"Dad, once they made it back to the barn they saw the scene. Keller's body on the barn floor in a pool of his own blood. Fatal abdominal wound. Big knife still in his hand."

Georgie slips another photo from her folder. A man, mid-40s, dark hair, bushy mustache. His body is coiled on the floor, his face a rictus of pain and, Lyle senses, pure hatred. Oddly, his face looks wet. The image turns Lyle's empty stomach; more so when he makes out animal footprints. Tiny hands in black blood lead away from Keller's corpse.

Georgie continues, "Propped up against the wall they saw the body of a twelve-year-old girl with a tiny bundle in her arms..."

Georgie trails off, fighting a wave of emotion. Then she adds, "The photographer first shot Carlina with the bundle that was Jewel." She shows that photo to Lyle. It's surreal. Carlina's unseeing eyes stare straight forward at the camera. Georgie slides the other photo of Carlina into view. "You described this to Linder—without the baby."

Lyle stares at it again. The girl's hands lie open on her lap, as if imploring, missing something precious. There's a large dark gash below her ribcage.

"Dad, I don't know how, but your description was uncannily accurate." She almost loses her composure. "Maybe something good will come from all this."

Lyle shrugs off the paranormal compliment. "Where did her mother go?"

"Gianna was there, Dad. Despairing that the authorities would help, she returned to the barn and wrote another note." Georgie tries to keep calm. "A suicide note. She hanged herself from a rafter." Georgie's last photo includes Gianna's body, hanging over Keller, her daughter slumped in the background with her baby. Three generations, dead.

Lyle looks up at Georgie. That rafter. That godforsaken barn.

"When police arrived that morning, they found Gianna, her feet swaying over Keller's dead body. He was soaked in urine."

"Good God," Lyle says softly. "Georgie, how did you get hold of all this?"

"Someone long ago stashed this stuff in an old police file cabinet which was eventually moved to Southampton Police headquarters. The file included Gianna's suicide note which gave additional details. It also held depositions from some of the other women, looks like six, who Keller held. All immigrants. They describe quite an operation. Some said they were forced to give up their babies, born in that barn, to Keller. One woman wrote that Keller lit a lantern in the cupola on Old Vic's roof to alert clients when new, young inventory was available. Keller had a way with the women he kept. They say he'd tell each one she was 'special' and he'd let her return to her family once she earned enough money. They were too fearful to run because they knew he could make problem girls 'disappear.' He also had a way with his customers. Keller was quite the host—liquor was free, the girls were expensive."

Georgie takes a breath. "After the events of October 1910, someone expunged the property's deed and any records of the atrocity—from the library, the town's records, the police files and even the local paper, which later went out of business."

"But Georgie, where did you find this file?"

She gives a little smile. "That little shit desk sergeant who was giving me a hard time? He had the file tucked in his locker."

"But why?"

"He was reciprocating to his boss. Chief Queeley was giving the sergeant lots of overtime to beef up his retirement package. He repaid the favor."

"But why is hiding this old file a favor?"

Georgie narrows her eyes. "The old file was simply labeled 'Q.'" She takes a copy of an old deed from her folder. "This is Old Vic's original owner. Keller had a silent partner by the name of Owen Queeley."

"*Queeley?*" Lyle gets new energy and adjusts his bed higher.

"Yeah. Old Owen Queeley purchased the place in the 1880s as a hotel, but it failed. He found a partner, but Armand Keller was the worst kind. Queeley had relatives on the local police force, including his young son, Regis."

"Regis?"

"An Irish thing. So the old local paper suggested that Owen Queeley could be involved in Keller's pimping and human trafficking. The Queeleys responded by suppressing any and all such reports, as well as the public records. Years later Regis Queeley went on to join the greater Southampton Police and brought his file cabinet with him. His son would grow up to be the family's first Chief of Police."

"Aiden senior?" Lyle's eyes have grown wide.

"Right. Junior is your pal, my boss. He did not want any of this to get out."

"Georgie! Let me see everything! Good God, I need to call Noah Craig!"

More monitors start beeping and a nurse finally bustles into the room.

~~~~~~~

88. Blank Slate

Georgie is gone somewhere. With no one around, exhaustion overcomes Lyle. And then he sees something strange. Belinda Hall's tombstone. But it's bare, no inscription yet. The earth is dug up. Astroturf carpet surrounds the dirt hole on this dreary day in 1995. A small backhoe sits about 40 yards away. People converging on the gravesite are wearing black. The mourners are teary-eyed but resigned—this is the way of all flesh. There's a minister with a black book. The Zacherle-lookalike undertaker distributes roses and chrysanthemums and the mourners place them on Belinda's casket. Everyone is sad, particularly Old Man Cheswick, Belinda's pinch-faced dad. Belinda's mom, Bea, is inconsolable saying goodbye to her girl. And there is Georgie. Good Lord, she's a beautiful 15-year-old. Dressed appropriately in black, she is composed, save her streaked mascara. And she won the fight to bring her lap dog, an excitable white Bichon Frisé, to say goodbye to her mom. Proving Lyle "so wrong," Cosette is not yappy at the interment. Everyone feels for the teenager who endured her mom's long decline. And everyone suspects Lyle Hall of fooling around with a strapping younger legal assistant. Why do they think the worst? Why don't they see the high-quality casket Lyle selected—solid-poplar hardwood with light-pink French-fold crepe interior, high-gloss finish and polished-brass hardware—as emblematic of Lyle's devotion? He didn't even dicker with Zacherle over price.

Lyle gave Georgie only one cursory hug during the dismal service; his body language indicating that her little dog's presence kept him at arm's length. Lyle told himself that Georgie brought Cosette along to keep him away. Looking back at this tableau, Lyle's failure to comfort his only child is shocking. Belinda's dowdy sister had to fill that role.

Despite it all, Lyle now experiences a wave of Belinda's gentleness; it ripples through his nervous system. Her sweetness—he knows he doesn't deserve it.

He sees the mourners take their leave. A grump in a wheelchair—Lyle's father was alive—with his law partner Edgar Lowell, Esq. Fraser and his wife. Josie Philips. A few golf buddies. And an unexpected face.

Lyle never knew Noah Craig, his opponent, attended Belinda's interment.

~~~~~~~

89. Noah

Ensconced in the library sublevel, Noah answers his cell phone against regulations.

"Lyle?"

"Noah."

"You called me back. Finally."

"From my hospital bed. And I have a broken hand." Lyle sounds exhausted.

"Did a pretty candy-striper dial for you?"

"No, I'm using a system of ropes and pulleys. Look, I only have a minute."

"To live?"

"They're replacing all the blood in my body with fresh blood."

"Maybe you can sell vials of the old black stuff along with your T-shirt."

"I had *nothing to do* with that damn T-shirt, Noah."

"Right. So. Lyle. What the fuck happened to you? You get me doing all this research; I even put my assistant on it; then you don't call; you don't write; then you're all over the Internet with your ghost girl; then you're on TV drooling over that botoxy reporter; then your likeness appears on a T-shirt of all things; then people actually *die* on your property; the next night you run amok and pull a Jerry Springer stunt live on national TV; then you go into a burning barn—in a *wheelchair*—WTF, Lyle?"

"Thanks for the recap, Noah. Listen, they're trying to keep my blood pressure down here, so let's take it easy."

"I'm coming over."

"No. Not in my delicate condition."

"Soon, then. So what's the word on your priest friend? With the foreign name?"

Lyle closes his eyes and pauses. "Noah, he died. Matteo Xerri was his name."

Quiet pause on Noah's end. That hasn't been reported on TV yet.

"I'm sorry."

"I made three new friends and they all died. Four if you count Jewel."

"Making friends with you must be unhealthy."

"I'm sorry about not returning your calls, Noah. The reason for this call is regarding the ownership of that house. I have an answer for you."

"From the spirit world?"

"From the police world. Noah, Old Vic was owned by a *Queeley*. Even back when it was a brothel. Owen Queeley. Chief Queeley's great-grandfather."

Noah processes this for a moment.

"You're *shitting me!*"

"Not shitting you. Georgie showed me documents, including a deed. And a hundred-year-old newspaper clipping." Lyle pauses. "And an old photograph of Jewel."

Noah works this over in his mind.

"A photograph of *Jewel?* For real? Omigod, Lyle! I'm coming over!"

"No. Too soon. There's too much to tell you."

"Tell me about Jewel now!"

"Noah, it's complicated. Jewel wasn't Jewel. She was...maybe a memory of something that happened, and almost happened to me. In a way."

"That is complicated. Okay, tell me about Queeley! That's so good I could wet my pants!"

"Don't let me stop you."

Noah boils over with excitement. "Lyle! Remember the time we rode our bikes to Old Vic to throw rocks and Junior Queeley came with us?"

"A million years ago."

"He threw my homework through the window! We tricked him and left him stuck in the window cursing his red head off! Hey, was my binder really still there?"

"I was yanking your chain when I said that. Sorry."

Regardless, Noah is overjoyed. "I can't believe it was a *Queeley*'s house!"

"Believe it. I've seen the deed."

"I can't stand it!" Then Noah turns quiet. "Lyle, I'm sorry I sort of sided with Becky Tuttle in that News Twelve interview the other day. They asked us what should be done with those shitty old buildings. I was unhappy with you for blowing me off. And for taking your priest friend, not me, inside Old Vic. You'll recall that was one of my two provisos to do your research. And I got caught in Becky's gravitational pull."

"Understandable. Must be hard to resist a piñata when the cameras are rolling."

"Well I'm sincerely glad that barn burned down. It would have sucked as a museum and kids would not have appreciated it. And that's coming from a historian. It's almost like Becky wanted to save the barn just to bust your balls."

"And succeeded. Noah, I'm tired."

"Understood. Well, I won't plan on getting inside Old Vic now. They're knocking it down today. Even though Saturday means huge overtime."

That's news to Lyle. But no surprise. Old Vic is coming down. Hard to care now.

"Who said Saturday was not a news day?" Lyle sighs.

Noah can feel Lyle's energy ebb over the phone. "I don't know. Lyle, thanks for the call. And I'm truly sorry about your friend. Let's talk tomorrow."

"Maybe." Lyle sounds very weak. "Thank you, Noah."

"For what?"

"For being on the short list of people who put up with me."

Disconnecting, Noah is startled by a tall figure looming behind him at the big oaken table where he works, at no charge, in the library sublevel.

Arms crossed, two fingers drumming in the crook of her elbow, she wears a gray sweater set with a cameo pin at the collar. A wiry gray coif. Wrinkles. Her pursed lips show an attempt was made earlier with lipstick. She harbors deep-seated animosity for Lyle Hall. And anyone who would help him. And use a forbidden cellphone.

Noah wonders how long Sheila Dowd has been standing there.

~~~~~~

90. In and Out

Lyle is going in and out of consciousness. There's definitely something potent in that IV bag overhead. He's having a dream. It's weird. Weirdly realistic.

At Gurney's, seated for lunch at his usual table. A brilliant afternoon, bright sunlight glints off everything. There are two glasses of golden white wine. And across the table sits Becky Tuttle in a nice sweater. But wait—she's not Becky, is she? She morphs into someone else. Someone dead. And smiling.

"Knew I'd get your attention this way," the woman says.

Lyle says nothing. He's seated in a regular chair, no wheelchair. He could get up and walk away, but wants to hear what she has to say. She's so pleasant and relaxed.

Flo Hendricks.

"Yours was my most interesting case, you know," she smiles. She raises her wine glass, holding it properly, by its stem. Lyle clinks and both sip. It's the best white wine ever. Flo really can smile. Especially without her eyeglasses.

"Want to know what I think? Thanks to your accident, you truly became attuned to other people's suffering. A gift. You might never have asked for it, but good things can come from bad."

She grows solemn. "And I believe the girl who lived in that house long ago sensed your new empathy. That you could somehow help her, her mother and her little baby. So she got your attention. But a monstrous evil discovered her attempt to contact you. Many women and girls suffered in that house, forced to do depraved things. I think past evil still lingered there. I hope it did not retaliate against her. I sense that entity targeted you too, toying with you, tormenting you."

It's like Flo has been watching Lyle's ordeal from some safe place. He remains silent and listens.

"I don't think your *Jewel* cared about the old buildings where that depravity took place. She wanted you to eradicate the evil that caused it. And set them all free."

Flo Hendricks smiles again at Lyle. She is actually quite pleasant to look at.

"Lyle, showing you Georgie's shocking headstone was her gift to you. She lost something precious and you stood to lose something precious, too."

That headstone still hurts. He blurts out, "How could Jewel see the future?"

"Lyle, the concept of 'future' is only for the living. Man invented calendars."

He tries to process this as Flo adds, "Your gift in return was to punch that damned thing in the face so hard it left your friend, Teo. And went down in flames." Flo nods at his bandaged hand. "I'm nonviolent, but you did the only reasonable thing. Impressively."

Flo raises her glass once more. They sip. "Good, huh?" The waiter approaches with the check. "Lyle, I gotta run. And so do you." Again her smile. "One more thought? Becky Tuttle is not your true friend, you know. Someone else is."

"Who?" Lyle asks.

Flo winks. "I must be going!" She rises gracefully.

"To where?" he whispers.

"Malta," she whispers back. Then she's gone.

Lyle looks at the check. It says only "N/C."

He closes his eyes and hears a repeating moan. Familiar.

~~~~~

91. Fraser Weighs In

Lyle's lids part slightly. He forgot to disable his cellphone's humming ring. He picks up.

"Please hold for Fraser Newton."

"Hi Josie."

"Hi Lyle. Are you okay?"

"Could be a lot worse."

"*GLAD* to hear it!" Fraser booms. Josie remains on the line. "So! When are they sending you home?"

"Never, I hope. For obvious reasons. Georgie has a couple of places she wants me to look at when I'm up to it."

"Assisted living?"

"Fraser...."

"You should get one of those 'fallen and can't get up' medical alert devices."

"Don't make me hate you."

"You also might consider using a *nom de voyage*. Rescuers would be more inclined to rescue you if they don't know it's you. For example, when appropriate, I go as 'Rhodes Reason.'"

"I'm sorry that one's already taken."

"Surprise your friends and confuse your enemies, I say. Now Lyle, your daughter didn't ask me, but I know a cozy place you'd love. A fixer-upper with *loads* of character. Lots of people interested in it. Needs updating. Walk to train..."

"Can you stop?"

"It won't last. Actually, it won't last past today."

"I heard. Is that why you called?"

"Actually, I thought you'd like an opportunity to thank me."

"For what, Fraser?"

"Ly-yull. I cawlled *Dawr Haw-wull!*"

"Oh. Yeah. You left a voicemail that succeeded in pissing her off."

"Success is what I do."

"Goodbye, Fraser, I'm not well, in case you haven't heard."

"Are you having visitors?"

"Not if they're you, given my delicate condition."

"I didn't mean *me*. I'm okay with 'visit the naked,' but the infirm make me squeamish."

A wave of deep exhaustion smothers Lyle. He murmurs, "Gotta run," hangs up and tries to disable the ringer.

Later, it's quiet. Some monitor is beeping somewhere. Lyle opens crusty eyelids and peeks at his phone. It's been "off."

A Fraser voice message somehow got through. An urge for guilty pleasure moves Lyle to click on it.

> Dude. Just saw this on TV news. People are actually attending Halloween costume parties AS LYLE HALL. *Believe it?* Big uptick in wheelchair rentals for the weekend. They had a medical-supplies guy on, said he knew you. The reporter gal says guys only need a Lyle Hall T-shirt, a dirty white beard and a fright wig. So they showed this guy done up as you, with a big Styrofoam cup. Pretty good, in a *Saturday Night Live* kind of way. And get this, pushing his chair is his date, in a Victorian dress! Wig, black stuff around the eyes. Get it? Lyle, this puts you up there with Frankenstein. Freddy Krueger. Not sure how you capitalize on this, but get a lawyer! Boy, am I glad you're no longer my partner. Gotta run. Call me!

~~~~~~~

92. Dredge

The bay near the Big Duck is known as Reeves Bay. It opens to Flanders Bay which in turn opens to Great Peconic Bay, the deep body of water that separates Long Island's North and South Forks.

Blue tape, sagging now, is still staked along the length of the scrub forest behind the Big Duck. It denotes ownership. The scraggly oaks have been pushed aside in places by heavy equipment leaving muddy ruts. A contractor's trailer sits on site.

A few years ago, a speculative real-estate firm had purchased this tract for the expressed purpose of building a deep-water marina with sunset-facing condo complex, fine dining and designer shopping experience. Detailed plans were drawn up. The purchaser, doing business as Newton-Hall LLC, was not a construction company. Their scheme was to flip the site, dubbed "Peconic Yacht Club," to a developer who would then go through the hassle of getting the permits, hiring the construction company and spending years and untold millions turning the architect's miniature model into reality. Salespeople could then begin the job of selling condos and boat slips at special "early bird" pricing. But first a specialized marine construction company would need to dredge the swamp.

After two martinis Fraser Newton still calls Flanders Bay "the crotch of the Hamptons." But a few years ago, before the real-estate bubble burst, Newton-Hall sold the nonexistent Peconic Yacht Club for serious dollars and four million in profit. Today Fraser refers to the development of swampy Reeves Bay as "delousing the crotch."

And today, the new owner finally has its ducks in a row. The subcontractor, Sustainable Marine Construction Partners, is ready to dredge before it gets too cold. Their dredge of choice—a Moray with hydraulic pump, weed-cutter head and extra-wide suction mouthpiece—was in position the Saturday Old Vic came down. And about to discover a sunken Escalade.

~~~~~~

93. Helium

Later Saturday afternoon, Georgie is back in her father's room watching him sleep. She hears a muffled cell phone thrumming somewhere under his blankets and tries to locate it before it wakes him. In her hand, it's louder. She sees its battery is almost expired. And she sees who's calling. Silk. Lyle's eyes open. Georgie offers him the phone.

"Want it?"

He holds up his hands, making a cross-shape with his fingers. The call bounces out of Lyle's overflowing voicemail and sprinkles into the vastness of digital space.

"Georgie."

"Dad."

"Georgie, tell me how work's been going. Besides the harassment issues. I mean police work. Surveillance. Last night I was very afraid for you." Lyle doesn't know how best to broach this topic but hopes he can elicit some kind of informative response.

Georgie's eyes are a wall of cold blue steel. Then she relents.

"Last night, Dad? Uh, well we got our man. He's out of business. My first real bust. I'll tell you about it sometime when you get your strength back."

"I'm glad. I was so worried for you." He frowns. "Was it a gang?"

Before Georgie's professional code of silence kicks back in, she says, "It was a loosely organized operation. The hope is, cut off the head and the body dies." Surprising herself, Georgie adds, "Dad, thank you for helping me get my promotion. It was very important to me."

Before Lyle can respond Sgt. Frank Barsotti gives a quiet knock and steps tentatively into the room. He's in uniform. Georgie grips Frank's arm and pulls him to Lyle's bedside.

"How you feeling, Mister Hall?"

"I feel like I'm in the end of *The Wizard of Oz*. Where's Auntie Em?"

Big Frank smiles.

Lyle adds, "It's good to see you, Frank. Good to see anybody at this point."

"Dad, it was Frank who figured out there was a lost file and where it was."

"Used the alphabet," Frank says. "There was no 'Q' file in an old cabinet."

Georgie adjusts Lyle's pillow and he winces. "The alphabet is our friend."

Frank looks down at Lyle's taped up right hand.

"I'm sorry about your priest friend, Mister Hall."

Lyle stares off to a faraway place. His sore eyes have ointment around them. Tears form silently on his red lower lids. Georgie squeezes Lyle's left hand and they stay quiet for a moment.

A TV extends above his bed on a boom. It's playing News12 Long Island with the sound off. Lyle looks up as video footage stamped "Earlier Today" shows the town's demolition equipment making short work of Old Vic. Lyle becomes engrossed by the scene and Georgie and Frank watch as the rickety old place collapses safely into a pile of kindling. Except for the cupola—it comes to rest at an angle atop the shattered lumber. The oval oculus looks like a demon's egg in a splintered nest of old timber. The man operating the front-loader raises the bucket attachment, brings it down hard, and crushes it. With Old Vic down, the charred shell of the old barn is visible. Saturday was a news day after all.

News12 is running the demolition in tandem with coverage of last night's fire. The news feature cuts from video of firefighters soaking the blazing barn to a series of still photos. In quick succession, they rerun Mose Allen's shot of crazy Lyle, followed by the still of Lyle giving Mose the finger (blurred digitally) outside the courthouse. They show Matteo Xerri giving

Lyle CPR. Then there's Lyle outside the courthouse a few days later, surrounded by reporters. Nothing new, really.

Then Lyle gasps—they put up a still of Teo on a stretcher, being loaded into the ambulance, looking as good as dead. It's credited to that rectum Mose Allen. It's a huge invasion of privacy. Is that what news is today? The screen dissolves to Mose's photo of Teo looking heroic and strong, holding Lyle that night outside Old Vic. Lyle can only imagine the bullshit being spewed to describe the young man who saved his life.

The photo series ends with something extraordinary—a vivid still of the barn burning, flames roaring into the night sky. Hard to believe anyone could have been in that and come out alive, Lyle thinks. Those first responders are miracle workers. In the center of the photo stands the dislodged roof beam, the last one that speared the barn floor and stood upright. Its English tying-joint gives it arms protruding left and right. Like what Teo called "Roman carpentry." Long ago it gave Gianna Rossi a place to hang a rope.

Cut to video of the T-shaped beam smoldering as firefighters drench it. The accompanying onscreen graphic attempts to associate this scene with something spiritual. Then the program cuts to live-in-the-studio and Lyle sees something so *not* spiritual. The anchor, square-headed Brent Mellon, has a guest— the intrepid journalist who took those pictures. The man who scooped the "Ghost Hampton" story. That damn fool Mose Allen.

Georgie sees Lyle wince at Mose Allen, his comb-over and his bad suit, eyeglasses off for the camera. She takes the remote, kills the picture and Lyle relaxes visibly.

"Next those news trucks will be outside waiting for me," he sighs.

"Oh, they've been outside for hours, Dad."

Lyle blinks and looks at Georgie and Frank. "What are they saying about the fire?" he asks, starting to sound tired and dreamy again.

Frank responds. "Well nobody was hurt." He corrects himself. "I mean no firefighters or first responders." He adds, "That barn was a tinderbox."

Lyle nods.

Something else is on Frank's mind. "Fire marshal noted the use of gasoline as an accelerant." Lyle meets Big Frank's gaze but says nothing. "Police report says Father Xerri confessed to Chief Cronk that he threw a bottle of gasoline inside the barn and it ignited."

Lyle's jaw drops as his thoughts of last night run wild. Georgie grips his hand as he makes an effort to speak.

"*Teo* said that? There's no way! He swallowed his tongue. He was incapable..."

"Mister Hall, the report has first responders and EMS saying you punched him in an attempt to stop him. Broke his jaw. And a tooth. And fractured your knuckles." Frank's gaze shifts from Lyle to Georgie and back. "So the case is closed."

Lyle opens his mouth again but Georgie squeezes his fingers harder.

"Ow! That's my good hand!"

"Monsignor Hannan is arranging for Father Xerri's remains to be returned to Malta," Frank says, looking pointedly at Lyle. "The page of the report describing use of accelerant will not accompany the body." He shifts his weight. "Maybe you want to contact his dad at some point." Frank pauses. "He's the only family."

Big Frank awkwardly makes to leave. "So I hope you have a good convalescence, Mister Hall. We'll see you all later."

He turns for the door and almost mows down a delivery guy. After a brief dance Frank exits and the delivery guy begins to work his way backwards into Lyle's room. There's a sudden loud POP! out in the hallway. Lyle's heart jumps—gunshot? But some nurses and orderlies outside start laughing; one even applauds.

Cautiously, the delivery guy ushers twenty-three intact Mylar balloons into Lyle's room. The clasp binding their ribbon streamers has come undone and it's like herding cats. The balloons are tight, full of helium and uncontrollable. They float to the ceiling and bob alongside the fluorescent light fixture, displaying their get-well-soon sentiments. Ribbons dangle everywhere as Georgie signs for the balloons, noting that the sender is one Josie Philips of Newton Properties. She gives the delivery guy a five as an orderly pokes his head in the room, smiling.

"Mister Hall! This must be some kind of a record!"

The balloon that popped droops on Lyle's bed. It bears a shriveled cartoon image of a pink unicorn. And it all comes back to Lyle. His hospital room a year ago. The dumb balloons from Josie. How he thought he was going to die. Josie surely knew he was at death's door. How hard it is not to die.

Georgie closes the door and moves back to his bedside.

"Dad, maybe you'll tell me what you were trying to accomplish in that barn some time? And maybe convince me that you will never get involved in anything remotely..."

"I'll stick to my knitting, Georgie."

Georgie seats herself by the bed, reaches for Lyle's hand again and smiles. "You can knit those broken knuckles."

Her dad is struck by how very rare this is. She adds, "Thanks for being good with Frank just then."

Lyle nods at an intravenous bag hanging above him. "The narcotics are bringing out my human side."

"So, are you finally going to start taking care of yourself?"

"Myself and others." He looks into Georgie's eyes. There is no need to read her. "Georgie, what's going on with your college loans?"

"You mean the crushing debt that keeps me in a Corolla that will qualify for the antique car show next year?"

"I want to make it go away."

"My Corolla?"

Lyle winces a little. He's tired. "Yes. And your debts. Please include any relevant bank documents next time in the bag with my meals-ready-to-heat from Citarella."

Still holding Lyle's hand, Georgie rises and kisses her dad warmly on the forehead. There's really nothing to say.

"Owch."

She settles back in her seat. Tears well up in her eyes. She purses her lips.

Composing herself after a moment, Georgie says, "Dad, I should do more for you than drop off meals."

"If you only knew how to cook."

"I can microwave."

"Right. But let's not get crazy. Maybe once a week."

"Deal."

Lyle gets a faraway look in his eyes. Something comes back to him. "Georgie, can you ask Mrs. Strangio something for me?"

"What."

"Uh, *tee eye you toe*. What's that mean?"

"That's easy. I remember from her class. That's *I help you*."

Lyle nods and looks at his daughter. Years speed by in his mind. He sees her metamorphose from cute-as-a-button little girlhood to the accomplished grownup before him now. His heart sinks when he realizes there's such a big scoop missing from the middle of that life. When he was busy drinking. She rises now, ready to leave.

"Maybe bring that man with you for dinner sometime," he offers.

"That man?"

"We'll set an extra place." His voice grows quiet. "I like cops who save my life."

"Really. Frank saved your life?"

Lyle blinks. "Him and a few others. It takes a village."

Georgie smiles, gives his hand a nursing-home pat.

Time to go.

Alone now, Lyle reflects on Jewel's words that night outside Old Vic. In English. *Help us* and *I help you*. Was that just four days ago? Or a quid pro quo from a hundred years ago?

Doesn't matter. He starts to doze off. And sleep.

~~~~~~~

EPILOGUE

MAY

Lyle Hall sits outside on a sunny spring morning, observing a gaggle of preschoolers romping on a playground. They are closely watched by moms, grandparents and nannies.

The watchers are also watching Lyle warily. Old guy in a self-propelled wheelchair. A MediCab parked at the curb on Poplar Street.

The playground is spanking new. It's been expertly landscaped on a half-acre, fresh green sod everywhere, some skinny young trees. Near the sidewalk squats a wide tree stump with a rotten center; once a huge white pine. At the far end of the property is a relic—a rickety old gate that leads to the driveway of a summer home. The playground features a space-age jungle gym complete with slides and swings. Kids run rampant.

Lyle's cell phone rings. It's Georgie, calling from Southampton Town Police headquarters.

"Dad? What are you *doing?* I just got a call—are you menacing small children at the park?"

"Snot running down my nose? No Georgie, I'm looking for something."

"Like *what?* A grandmother, who's probably glaring at you right now, just reported a suspicious stranger in a wheelchair..."

"I can't refute that."

"Dad, we don't need trouble. Can you please stop doing whatever you're doing?"

"I wanted to see if I picked up any...sensations from the area where the old barn used to stand."

"Great. I trust you were sensation-free. What else are you doing?"

His eyes scan the small park. "There! I see it! They finally installed it!"

"Installed what, Dad?"

"The plaque! I'm so excited!"

"About a plaque? Please be cool, okay, Dad? Promise me? Look, I'll see you later. I'm stopping by your condo with some meals."

"Thanking you in advance. Listen, gotta run. I'll send you a picture!"

Lyle waves to Fred and he approaches with two forearm crutches. Using the routine his physical-therapy gal taught him, Lyle arises from his Mr. Potter chair and achieves a standing position leaning on the crutches. With effort and determination he progresses up the path on the crutches. Little ones play noisily and pay him no mind as he passes the fancy monkey bar set with its rubber-padded safety floor. Lyle stops in front of a wooden plaque, recently bolted to two posts. Its wording is carved in artful gilt lettering. He balances on one crutch, holds up his phone and snaps:

JEWEL PARK

====

Dedicated to Glen and Maeve Stanley
Donated by the Hall Foundation

~~~~~~~

Midday is warmer and sunnier still. Gazing out the kitchen window of his new condo, Lyle answers his phone.

"Dad? What are you doing?"

"Going out to lunch."

"Why."

"It's lunchtime. And it's a beautiful spring day."

"Josie told me you're meeting with that woman. Where?"

"*That woman!* You make her sound so notorious! It's just lunch, girl! What could be more innocent?"

"Does she wear as much eye makeup during daylight hours?"

"I hope so."

"Dad. Miranda Silkwood is thirteen years younger than the man I'm dating."

"She can't help that. And I'll have Josie along to protect me."

"Is Josie why you shaved off your beard?"

"She asked me to try it. Turns out I don't look like a pirate."

"I like Josie. What does she see in you?"

"Money."

"Are you paying off her college loans, too?"

"It's times like these a man is glad to have only one child."

"So where exactly are you going? Josie's driving you?"

"Is this a quiz? We're meeting Silk in Sag Harbor. Wonderful seafood place."

"And...?"

"And...well, there's this old boarded-up hotel on the edge of town."

"Oh? How did Elvira find out about this?"

Lyle hesitates. "I give. I texted her. She's interested."

"Old and boarded-up being your specialty."

"Georgie, it's nothing. Silk just wants to check it out."

"Really. So it's a handicap-accessible abandoned hotel?"

"I can deal. Josie takes good care of me. There's her horn. Gotta run."

They disconnect and Lyle makes his way to the kitchen door, passing the butcher-block table with its three china place settings and gleaming silverware. He leans heavily on his new crutches. He calls them his "FDR's" and insists they're temporary.

He swings open the door to sunshine and a warm breeze full of birdsong. A gentle ramp leads to the driveway. A bee buzzes by. Arms folded, Josie is leaning against her new SUV positioned at the foot of the ramp. She's not supposed to help. Working his way down to her, their eyes meet. She's wearing a floral dress and a smile.

END OF BOOK ONE

ACKNOWLEDGEMENTS

Ghost Hampton's fictional story unfolds in the real world. Below are some of the very important people who helped integrate the real world into this novel. They have my sincere thanks.

John Chirico, Detective, Dobbs Ferry, NY Police (ret.)

Brian Dwyer, former Senior Safety Officer and Chaplain, Westhampton Beach Fire Department

George N. Longworth, Commissioner of the Westchester County Department of Public Safety

Stephen J. Lynch, Judge of the Court of Claims, State of New York

Yvonne Burke Malone, Licensed Clinical Social Worker

David McKeon, Chief of Staff, the New York Stem Cell Foundation

Gregory Meade, eagle-eyed nitpicker and brother from another mother

ABOUT THE AUTHOR

Ken McGorry's fiction features surprising comic relief amid often tense dramatic scenes, as readers of his novels *Smashed* and *Ghost Hampton* know. Ken's novels unfold in the here-and-now present tense; their cinematic point of view owes a lot to his years toiling at scriptwriting. Readers praise *Ghost Hampton*'s energy level, realism and its balance of action and paranormal suspense. They enjoy its characters, their humanity and how they interact.

Ken is also known for his 20-plus years as an editor of the professional film-and-TV-production monthly *Post*. While he loves the many real characters he got to know in that industry, Ken got hooked on creating his own a few years ago. Television production comes to the fore in *Ghost Hampton* in a climactic scene Ken calls "a *Jerry Springer* event."

Ken lives with his wife and dogs on Long Island. They have two strapping sons. And they have a little summer place in Westhampton Beach. It's not far from an old house rumored to have been a brothel long ago …and haunted today.

For more on *Ghost Hampton*, including Book Club talking points, visit
www.ghosthampton.com
www.facebook.com/ghosthampton.

For Ken's short humor pieces, such as *Babies on a Plane* and *Killing Santa*, visit
www.kenmcgorry.com.

Hear Ken's original songs, recorded with The Achievements, by visiting
https://soundcloud.com/ken-mcgorry.